Safe? _____
yards from _____ _____ _____ _1
body reas _____ _____ _____
wouldn't let her. Isabella didn't know how she knew
that—but she did.

"I'm going to sit up," he said slowly, his gaze on
hers. "And you're going to loosen your grip on me
just a little bit."

She swallowed hard and shook her head. "I don't
think I can let you go," she said, her teeth chattering.
But slowly, she loosened her hold.

The steady rain had stopped, a slice of moonlight breaking through the clouds, and she took a
better look at her rescuer. As her gaze traveled back
to his face, goose bumps ran down her arm. Even in
the shadows, she knew this face. She'd seen it in her
dreams.

"It's you," she muttered in amazement.

He gave her an uncertain look. "Have we met?"

How could she tell him she'd dreamed about a
man she'd never met? "You saved my life," she said
instead.

"I was in the right place at the right time. Luck
was on your side."

She nodded, but she didn't think that luck had
had anything to do with their meeting.

*Turn the page for praise of bestselling author
Barbara Freethy's wonderful Angel's Bay series.*

ON SHADOW BEACH

"A lovely contemporary romance. . . . You can never get enough of Freethy's excellent characters. She's a master at creating whole relationships in just a few short paragraphs."

—*Romantic Times*

"*On Shadow Beach* teems with action, drama and compelling situations. . . . A fast-paced page-turner that unravels small-town scandals and secrets."

—*BookPage*

"*On Shadow Beach* has a fascinating touch of magic plus an abundance of genuinely heartfelt emotions, where everything is wrapped around an intriguing mystery."

—Single Titles

"This compelling story is fast-paced, filled with renewed acquaintances, complicated relationships and plenty of mystery. You will love the story and be surprised on several accounts by the ending."

—Fresh Fiction

"An excellent, easy-to-read novel. It flows beautifully with intriguing and appealing characters. It will grab you within the first few pages and just keeps getting better."

—Romance Reviews Today

SUDDENLY ONE SUMMER

"*Suddenly One Summer* delivers a double whammy to the heart. Ms. Freethy cuts to the core with her depiction of a woman in jeopardy and a man who no longer believes that life has anything to offer. . . . A story that will keep you spellbound."

—*Winter Haven News Chief* (FL)

ALSO BY BARBARA FREETHY

In Shelter Cove
On Shadow Beach
Suddenly One Summer

Now Available from Pocket Star

BARBARA FREETHY

At Hidden Falls

POCKET STAR BOOKS

New York London Toronto Sydney

Pocket Star Books
A Division of Simon & Schuster, Inc.
1230 Avenue of the Americas
New York, NY 10020

This book is a work of fiction. Names, characters, places, and incidents either are products of the author's imagination or are used fictitiously. Any resemblance to actual events or locales or persons, living or dead, is entirely coincidental.

First Pocket Star Books paperback edition February 2011

POCKET STAR BOOKS and colophon are registered trademarks of Simon & Schuster, Inc.

For information about special discounts for bulk purchases, please contact Simon & Schuster Special Sales at 1-866-506-1949 or business@simonandschuster.com.

The Simon & Schuster Speakers Bureau can bring authors to your live event. For more information or to book an event contact the Simon & Schuster Speakers Bureau at 1-866-248-3049 or visit our website at www.simonspeakers.com.

Designed by Jill Putorti
Cover illustration by Tom Hallman

Manufactured in the United States of America

10 9 8 7 6 5 4 3 2 1

ISBN 978-1-4391-7649-8
ISBN 978-1-4391-7650-4 (ebook)

To my friends at the Peninsula Tennis Club—thanks for the friendship, support, and the exercise!

ACKNOWLEDGMENTS

Writing friends are so important. They share the journey of creating something from nothing. They understand that every book has its moments of despair as well as pure joy. And they're always there to offer up a plot twist, a glass of wine, or a box of chocolates because sometimes the muse needs a little help. I have some wonderful writing friends. Thanks to Diana Dempsey, Kate Moore, Lynn Hanna, Barbara McMahon, Carol Grace, and Candice Hern, some of whom have been there since the beginning! Thanks also to Bella Andre, Anne Mallory, Veronica Wolf, Tracy Grant, Jami Alden, Penny Williamson, and Monica McCarty. You all helped bring Angel's Bay to life, and I am forever grateful for your friendship.

ONE

Dark clouds blotted out the glow of the sun setting over the ocean, and the threatening storm sent a chill down Isabella Silveira's spine. Her hands tightened on the steering wheel as the Pacific Coast Highway took another terrifying twist along a steep cliff that dropped abruptly into the wild, crashing waves below. She'd always been a spontaneous person, but this trip was giving her plenty of second thoughts.

She was exhausted, haunted by a series of tormenting dreams for the last two weeks. They'd begun shortly after she'd received a birthday present from her brother Joe, an antique turquoise and gold pendant that he'd found in the house he'd inherited from their uncle Carlos in Angel's Bay. He'd told her that the turquoise reminded him of her unusual eyes. All of her other siblings had brown eyes, but somehow in the Irish-Hispanic mix of her parents, she'd ended up with dark hair, olive skin, and deep blue eyes.

Her eyes were part of her special gift, her grandmother Elena had told her—the gift of insight im-
parted by their Mayan ancestors and shared by only
a few women in the family. Her teasing siblings had
told her that her "gift" was a story their grandmother
had made up to make her feel special. But that didn't
explain why touching certain items belonging to
people she cared about triggered dreams and visions
of the future. Unfortunately, those flashes of insight
were rarely helpful. Even when she tried to warn
someone, she often wound up getting somewhere
just in time to pick up the pieces.

After several troubling incidents, she'd learned to
shy away from deeply emotional relationships, because they often brought on the disturbing flashes.
It was easier to skate along the surface, never settling
too long in one place or with one person. She could
have fun, have friends, have sex—but love was another thing entirely. Love could make her crazy.

For months her brain had been quiet, until she'd
put on the necklace. That night, she'd dreamed of
Angel's Bay.

She'd never been to the town where Joe had
taken over as police chief almost a year earlier. But
the images haunting her had included this highway
and the Angel's Bay sign she'd passed three miles
back, as well as shadows and silhouettes swirling
around landmarks and people that seemed meaning-
ful in some unfathomable way. Just when she came
to the brink of discovery, she woke up sweating and

shaking, with a certainty that she was supposed to do something, save someone—but she didn't know what to do or whom to save.

She'd taken to exercise, running, spinning, kick-boxing, anything that would leave her too exhausted to dream. She'd lost five pounds, but the dreams had continued to come. Finally, she'd stopped fighting. The pendant had come from Joe. What if he was in trouble and she did nothing? She'd never forgive herself.

Fortunately, she was between movie projects. She worked as a freelance costume designer, and the start date of her next film had been pushed back until January, leaving her at loose ends for the next two months. While she normally helped out at her sister's clothing boutique between design jobs, she'd decided to go to Angel's Bay instead. Even if she couldn't figure out her dreams, at least she'd get to see Joe. And she was more than a little curious about Angel's Bay. Joe seemed to be in love with the town—so much so that he'd agreed to divorce his wife rather than move back to L.A.

As raindrops splashed across her windshield, she turned on her wipers and her headlights. The road had widened, the hills on her right side falling back to vast open meadows, closed-up fruit stands on the edge of farmland, and an occasional rural road heading inland toward the mountains. There weren't many cars and very few lights. She felt isolated, alone, and inexplicably tense.

A crack of thunder jolted her. She'd heard that sound in her dreams. But she wasn't dreaming, she reminded herself as goose bumps ran along her arms. This was reality.

She hit the defrost button as her window began to fog, telling herself everything was fine. A few more miles, and she'd be in Angel's Bay.

As she drove around another turn, a flash of light blinded her, high beams from an oncoming car that wove recklessly across the highway. She hit the brakes as the car suddenly turned in front of her, skidding onto a dirt road heading toward the mountains.

Her brakes couldn't grip the rain-soaked highway, and her car began to skid. She hung on to the wheel, fighting for control, but she was heading straight toward the cliff on the ocean side of the road. She jammed the brakes to the floor, but there was no way to stop.

Her car ripped through the guard rail, plunging down the rocky hillside in a wild, jolting ride. The front of the car hit something, and the windshield shattered. She threw up her hands as her airbag deployed and stars exploded before her eyes.

Minutes or hours later, she heard someone yelling, tugging the car door open. Rain hit her face, and she blinked in bewilderment. The front window had splintered, and smoke was coming off the hood of her car.

"Are you all right?" a man demanded.

She stared at him in confusion. His clothes were drenched, his hair soaked, his eyes dark and worried.

"You've been in an accident," he said. "Are you hurt?"

She put a hand to her forehead and winced as she saw the blood on her fingers.

"The cut on your head doesn't look too bad," he told her. "Can you move? I want to get you out of here. There's no telling how long the rocks will hold."

He'd barely finished speaking when the car slid a few inches forward. Isabella grabbed his arm in panic. "Don't let me go."

His jaw tightened in determination. "I won't. I'm getting you out of here right now."

His voice held so much confidence, she felt marginally reassured, but the car was pitched at a precariously steep angle. The man reached across to undo her seatbelt, and she tried to get out, but her left foot was pinned where the side of her car had smashed against the rocks. "My foot is stuck!" A wave of terror ran through her as she tried to pull her leg free.

"Hold on. Let me see if I can figure out what's pinning you down."

He squatted next to the car, his hand running down her leg. She could feel his fingers against her ankle as he pushed down on the metal. He grimaced with the effort, but she was finally able to yank her foot out, sending the car sliding forward another few inches. The wall of rocks holding the car back from the sea began to break apart.

The man grabbed her arm and pulled her out of the car just as the vehicle lurched forward. He

rolled on top of her, digging his feet into the soil as
the vehicle slid down the mountain. She watched
in shocked horror as it plummeted over the edge of
the bluff in a shower of rocks, the roar of the waves
swallowing its splash.

She'd almost been inside. She'd almost died.

Her breath stalled in her chest. She tightened
her arms around the man who had her pinned to the
ground, terrified that they would slide down the hill
just as the car had done.

"You're okay," he told her soothingly. "You're
safe."

Safe? She was lying on a slippery hillside, yards
away from the edge of a cliff, but the weight of his
body reassured her. She wasn't going to fall. He
wouldn't let her. She didn't know how she knew
that—but she did.

"I'm going to sit up," he said slowly, his gaze on
hers. "And you're going to loosen your grip on me
just a little bit."

She swallowed hard and shook her head. "I don't
think I can let you go."

"You're not letting go. We're just going to move
toward those rocks, where the ground is more stable." He gave her a small smile as if what he was asking her to do was no big deal. "It will be fine."

Something about the certainty in his eyes made
her trust him. Slowly, she loosened her hold on him,
digging her hands and feet into the dirt as he moved
off of her. He didn't let go of her entirely, keeping a

strong hand on her arm. Sitting up, he scooted backward, pulling her with him, until they reached flatter ground and another outcropping of rocks.

Letting out a breath, she was finally able to sit up without feeling as if she was going to slide down the hill.

The steady rain had stopped, a slice of moonlight breaking through the clouds, and she took a better look at her rescuer. He was wearing a suit and tie, not exactly superhero attire. How had he made it down the cliff in leather shoes? As her gaze traveled back to his face, a shock of awareness ran through her. She'd seen his face in her dreams.

"It's you," she muttered in amazement.

He gave her an uncertain look. "Have we met?"

"I dreamed about you." The words came out before she could stop them. "I just didn't know it was you."

By the frown on his face, he had no idea what she was talking about, and she wasn't completely sure herself. While his face was familiar, her dreams had never put her on the side of a cliff in the middle of a rainstorm.

"All right, take it easy. Help is on the way," he said.

She lifted her head at the distant sound of sirens.

"I called nine-one-one as soon as I saw your car go off the road," he said. "What happened?"

"A car turned right in front of me onto a side road. I braked, but the road was too wet, and I had no traction. I turned the wheel, but the car skidded toward the side." She shivered and pulled her knees to her chest, wrapping her arms around them as a horrified chill ran through her.

"I didn't see the other car, just your taillights disappearing off the side of the road. A minute later, I wouldn't have seen a thing. I don't know if I would have even noticed the broken guard rail in the rain. I was concentrating on getting home." He stopped abruptly, frowning. "You're freezing." He stripped off his coat and wrapped it around her shoulders. "Better?"

She nodded, her teeth chattering from the cold. Her head throbbed, and everything seemed surreal, as if she were in a dream. But there was blood and mud on her clothes, and her wet hair was plastered against her head, all signs of reality. She glanced at her rescuer again. "What's your name?"

"Nick Hartley. And you?"

"Isabella," she murmured, looking into his dark eyes. She extended her hand, and as his fingers gripped hers, a burst of color, almost like flames, flashed in her head. She wanted to let him go, but she couldn't. Was it because he'd saved her life? Or because he was part of whatever had put her on this highway in the first place?

Nick Hartley pulled his hand from hers and stood up, looking toward the road high above, where a fire engine's strobe lights bounced off the hillside.

"They should be able to get you out of here in a few minutes," he said.

"How did you ever get down here?" she asked in wonder. The hillside was steep and rocky and hard to see in the dark. Yet he had rushed down it without a thought.

"I don't remember exactly. I had some adrenaline going. Getting back up won't be as easy, but we'll make it."

"You saved my life. I don't know how to thank you."

"You don't have to thank me. I was just in the right place at the right time. Luck was on your side tonight."

She nodded. But as another shiver ran through her, she didn't think that luck had had anything to do with their meeting.

Thirty minutes later, Nick stood on the edge of the highway, watching the ambulance take off toward Angel's Bay. He let out a relieved breath. He hadn't had a chance to think, only to act, but now the reality of what he'd just been through washed over him. He was soaked from the rain, and his clothes were filthy, but at least the woman was alive. She was damn fortunate.

A shudder ran through him as he flashed back to the moment when he'd pulled her free of the car, crushed her body against the hillside, and prayed the ground would hold. She'd been terrified, her eyes wide and shocked. She'd clung to him as if he were the only thing that stood between life and death for her. And he had been.

He could still feel the force of the car plunging toward the sea, threatening to take them with it. It had taken all his strength to pull her free. Thank God he'd been successful.

The way she'd looked at him had rattled him, her fingers wrapped around his as if she'd never let go. For a second, he'd felt a ripping fear that he might not want to let her go, either. Which was crazy, because where women were concerned, he always let go first. The only time he hadn't had ended in painful disaster.

Getting into his car, he started the engine and turned on the heater. Isabella still had his suit jacket. He'd check in at the hospital later to see how she was, but first he had to get home. He had another, much younger female to worry about: his daughter, Megan.

He pulled out his cell phone. There were no missed calls, which was disturbing. He'd been trying to get in touch with Megan since three o'clock, when she was supposed to get home from school. He'd tried to set down some rules since her arrival, but so far, he was the only one following them. He punched in her number again, but it went immediately to voice-mail.

He tossed the phone onto his console and pulled onto the highway. He probably should have thought about Megan before he'd charged down that slippery hillside, but he wasn't used to worrying about anyone but himself. His fifteen-year-old daughter had been out of his life for the past twelve years, returning under duress only three weeks ago. She didn't want to live with him, didn't want to stay in Angel's Bay, didn't want anything to do with the father she believed had abandoned her.

He'd been only twenty-one when her mother had taken off with her and gone to Europe. He'd had no money, no job, and no way to fight for Megan. By the time he had the means, years had passed, and he'd thought she was happy with her mother and her stepfather, that it was too late for him to be a dad.

He'd never imagined that his ex-wife, Kendra, would suddenly ship Megan back to him, claiming that it was his turn to take care of her. He knew Megan was hurt and furious at both of them; he just didn't know how to make it better. Nor did he know how to be a father. Megan wasn't the sweet, loving three-year-old he remembered. She'd dyed her blond hair black with shades of purple, had a nose ring and an attitude that was bigger than she was. He had no idea how to handle her.

The ring of his phone gave him a small moment of hope. But it was his mother's number that flashed across the screen.

"What happened?" Pamela Hartley asked worriedly. "I got a call from Phyllis, who heard from her son that you were in an accident."

"That was fast. I wasn't in the accident. I just got the woman out of the car to safety."

"Is she all right?"

"I think so. She has some minor injuries."

"And you?"

"Wet, cold, and dirty but otherwise fine. I'm on my way home. I'm more concerned about Megan. Did you check on her after school?"

"Was I supposed to?" his mother asked.

"I called you this morning on the way to my meeting," he reminded her.

"Oh, that's right, you did. I got so caught up in work that I completely forgot. I'm sure she's fine."

That was his mother, completely offhand and reluctant to focus on anything or anyone who wasn't involved in her world of the theater. Why was he even surprised? His mother had often forgotten to pick him up from school when he was a kid. He should have asked his sister, Tory, to check on Megan.

"Well, I'm *not* sure Megan is fine," he said. "She isn't answering her phone."

"Probably to annoy you. She's been uprooted, and she's angry. You need to give her some time. Her whole world changed in a second, and she hasn't caught up yet."

"I feel exactly the same way. I never imagined Kendra would suddenly bail on Megan."

"You should have seen it coming. Kendra was always selfish. I never knew what you saw in that girl."

He'd seen long legs, big breasts, and a sexy mouth—but then, he'd been eighteen when they'd met during a summer production at his family's theater. They'd had a passionate romance that ended with an unexpected pregnancy. They'd married, thinking it was the right thing to do and that their love would last—but it hadn't. Kendra had gotten a better offer and taken off.

"I don't know what I'm going to do with Megan," he said, not expecting his mother to have an answer but needing to talk to someone.

"You're going to be her father."

"It's a little late for that. Megan hates me." It hurt to say the words out loud. "She thinks I deserted her, and in a way, I did."

"She doesn't know the whole story. She'll come around eventually. She likes being with us at the theater. And why not? It's in her blood. She gets along with Tory, too. It's all going to work out, Nick."

"I hope so." His extended family was the reason he'd brought Megan to Angel's Bay. While they often drove him crazy with their quirky, eccentric personalities, he needed reinforcements, and everyone was in town to put on the Winter Workshop. So instead of taking Megan to the one-bedroom condo he owned in L.A., he'd brought her to the two-bedroom fixer-upper in Angel's Bay he'd purchased a few years earlier.

"We started auditions today," his mother continued, "and some of the locals came in. Kara Lynch was much better than I expected. Of course, we still have a lot of people to see. And there's so much to do to get the theater ready. I can't believe this is the last production we'll have in this old building, but I also can't wait to see your designs for restoring the theater to its original glory."

Nick's mind drifted as his mother rambled on

about preproduction planning. The theater was her life, as it was for everyone else in his family. The Hartleys had been running the Angel's Bay Regional Theater for six decades; he was one of the few who'd broken away.

"Mom, I'm pulling into the driveway," he said, interrupting her ramble. "I'll talk to you later." As he turned off the engine, he noted the dark house. One thing he'd learned about his daughter was that if she was home, every light in the place was on.

He entered through the kitchen door, snapping on the overhead light. He called for Megan and checked her bedroom, but there was no sign of her.

Returning to the kitchen, he debated his options. Megan had been testing her boundaries ever since she arrived, and he doubted she was lost or anywhere she didn't want to be. Maybe he should be glad she'd found somewhere to go, making friends, getting out of the house. On the other hand, she could be in trouble, and he couldn't just do nothing. Perhaps his sister would have an idea. He was about to call Tory when the kitchen door flew open and Megan ran in.

Her face was flushed, her hair damp, as if she'd been out in the rain. Her brown eyes were bright and a little guilty. She'd been up to something. He was sure of that.

"Where have you been?" he asked.

She stared back at him, her eyes as stormy as the weather. "I could ask you the same question. What did you do, fall into a hole?"

He glanced down at his mud-caked clothes.

"Something like that. Don't change the subject. You were supposed to stay home after school, and you were supposed to answer your phone."

"And you were supposed to be my father. But you disappeared for twelve years. So what if I took off for an hour or two? That doesn't come close to making us even." She ran down the hall and slammed her bedroom door.

Nick drew in a deep breath and let it out. It had been a long day and it was getting even longer. He walked down the hall, knocked on her door, and then turned the knob. Fortunately, there was no lock, so she couldn't keep him out even if she wanted to.

Megan was sitting cross-legged on her bed in front of her laptop. She gave him a scowl. "Aren't you going to take a shower?"

"In a minute. Where were you?"

"Out with friends."

"I thought you said you didn't have any friends."

"Well, I do. Isn't that what you wanted?" she challenged.

What he wanted was for them to have a conversation without a wall of anger and pain between them, but that wasn't happening tonight.

She picked up her headphones and slipped them on, clearly dismissing him.

He needed to find a way to connect with her. She was his daughter, and he loved her. No matter how unhappy she was now, he didn't intend to let her go again.

Two

Joe Silveira strode through the emergency room entrance at the Redwood Medical Center, his heart pounding against his chest. He'd been headed home from the police station when the 911 call had come in about a car accident on the highway south of town. He'd left it to his officers to handle, never dreaming that the driver was his youngest sister. He still couldn't quite believe it was true, but when the receptionist waved him inside, he found Isabella sitting on the examining table, a man's jacket around her shoulders, her long dark hair curling from the rain and caked with mud, her forehead swollen, and tiny cuts spattered across her pale face.

Her blue eyes widened when she saw him, and her lips began to tremble. It reminded him of the time she'd flown over the handlebars of her bike when she was six. She'd limped all the way home as brave as could be, then burst into tears when she'd seen him. He'd been eighteen, and he'd felt as helpless then as he did now. Isabella was the baby of the family, the one they were all supposed to look out for.

"Hey, Joe," she said, her voice shaky as she fought for a smile.

"Izzy? Are you hurt?"

"Some bruises and maybe a sprained or broken wrist." She held up her swollen left arm. "But other than that, I'm fine. I'm alive." Then the tears came like a flash flood, streaming down her cheeks.

He quickly moved forward, putting his arms around her as she cried against his chest. "It's okay. You're going to be all right," he said, trying to soothe her, but he'd never been good with tears. Not that he hadn't had practice. He had four sisters, after all, but he usually let them take care of one another. What he wouldn't give right now to have one of them there.

Fortunately, Isabella regained her composure fairly quickly, pulling away from him with a sniff. "Sorry about that. I guess I've been holding that in for a while."

He reached for the box of tissues on the counter and handed them to her. "From what I hear, you've been through a lot. It's a miracle you made it." He shuddered at the alternative. "Do you want to tell me what happened?"

"I came around a turn. A car was weaving across the highway straight at me. Then it turned onto one of those side roads. I hit the brakes, but the road was too wet, and I skidded off the side." She drew in a tremulous breath. "A man, Nick Hartley, saw my car go through the guard rail, and he came down the hill and managed to pull me free before . . . before the car went into the ocean."

His pulse leaped at the reminder that she'd come very close to dying. "What the hell were you even doing on that road? Why are you here?" he snapped, fear finding its way out in a burst of anger.

"I wanted to see you, Joe."

"So you just hopped into the car and drove three hours north on a whim?"

"Why not? You're my brother."

He frowned as she averted her eyes. She wasn't telling him the whole story. "What about your job?"

"I'm between projects."

He wasn't surprised. Isabella never stayed too long in any one place.

"I thought you could use some family support," she added. "You and Rachel were together a long time. We're all worried about you."

He couldn't lie and say he was happy about the divorce. Rachel had been a huge part of his life, but the last couple of years had been rough. He didn't like to fail, and it wasn't his nature to quit, but he'd had to accept that his marriage was over.

Seeing Isabella's gaze on his face, he hastened to reassure her. "I'm all right. You didn't need to come up here. You could have just called."

"I have called. And so has everyone else in the family. You always brush our questions aside."

"It is my business, Izzy," he reminded her.

"Yes, but you're always there for us; we want to be there for you."

"So you were elected to come?" He didn't like the idea of his siblings feeling sorry for him.

"I volunteered. I didn't just want to see you; I wanted to see Angel's Bay. Rachel said this town has stolen your heart." She paused, giving him an apologetic look. "I didn't intend for my arrival to be quite so dramatic."

He shook his head, still shaken by her close call. "Can you tell me anything about the car that ran you off the road?"

She thought for a moment. "It happened so fast. I remember the lights, and then I was sliding across the road." She shivered and crossed her arms in front of her.

He hated making her relive the fear, but he wanted to find the person who'd nearly killed her. "I don't want to make this more difficult, but if you can remember anything—the kind of vehicle, the color, how many people were in the car . . ."

"There were two people— I think. Right now, it's a blur. My head is pounding."

"I shouldn't be pressing you; it's too soon."

"I lost everything, Joe. My suitcase, my cell phone, my purse—everything was in the car, and now it's in the ocean."

"But you're alive. That's all that matters."

"Because of Nick Hartley," she said. "He was amazing. He risked his life coming down that cliff after me. A lot of people would have waited at the top until help came, and by then it would have been too late."

"I'm very grateful that he was there for you." He shifted his weight impatiently. "Where's the doctor?"

"He's been in. He wants me to get an X-ray on my wrist. He said someone would be in to take me there."

"What did he say about your head?"

"Just a bump." She gave him a small smile. "I'm okay, Joe. What I really need is to soak in a hot bath."

"As soon as you're done here, I'll take you home. But first, I want a friend of mine to take a look at you. She's also a doctor here. I've already called her to come down and check you out."

"The other physician seemed very capable."

"Maybe so, but you're my little sister, and I trust Charlotte." He cleared his throat, seeing the thoughtful look in her eyes. He'd forgotten what it was like to be around family, to have someone looking at him who knew him as more than the chief of police. He'd kept most people in Angel's Bay at a distance, with Charlotte the one exception, but even their flirtatious friendship had never gone very deep. He'd been too married for that, at least until lately.

A knock came at the door, and Charlotte stepped into the room. Every time he saw her, his gut tightened, and today was no exception. She wore a white coat over black slacks and a silky blouse. Her blond hair was pulled back from her face, and her blue eyes were curious as she glanced from him to Isabella.

"Thanks for coming," he said. "This is my youngest sister, Isabella."

Surprise flashed in Charlotte's eyes, then she turned to Izzy. "It's very nice to meet you. I'm Charlotte Adams. You look like you've had a rough night."

"I had a little accident on my way into town. I usually make a better first impression," Isabella said lightly.

He had to give Isabella credit. She was very good at bouncing back from disaster.

"I spoke to Dr. Sawyer, who gave me the update on your condition," Charlotte continued. "Maybe we could speak alone for a few minutes? Do you mind, Joe?"

"Sure, no problem," he said, happy to leave Isabella in Charlotte's capable hands.

"Joe is being overprotective," Isabella told Charlotte as soon as the door closed behind him. "I've been completely checked out."

"I know," Charlotte said, a twinkle in her eyes. "But why don't I do a quick exam, just so we can ease your brother's mind?"

"Have at it. I'm waiting to go to X-ray, anyway."

"Can you lie back for me?" Charlotte asked. "I'm an ob/gyn, by the way, but I handle a lot of women's health issues."

"Well, I'm not pregnant, so no issues there."

Charlotte smiled. "Where do you fall in the Silveira family lineup?"

"I'm the baby. There's twelve years between me and Joe."

"And you have a couple of sisters as well, don't you?"

"Three. Two of them are married with kids. The other one is engaged."

As Charlotte examined her, Isabella couldn't help thinking that Charlotte was the exact opposite of Rachel in looks, with her golden blond hair, blue eyes, and light tan. She moved with athletic grace and had a warm smile and a reassuring bedside manner. Rachel was model skinny, with jet-black hair, dark eyes, and pale skin. Although why she was comparing them, she couldn't say. There was just something about the way Joe had looked at Charlotte.

"I don't see any signs of internal injuries," Charlotte said. "I would suggest taking it easy for a few days."

"Thanks," Isabella said as she sat up. "Are you and my brother close friends?"

"I don't know about close, but we're friends. Angel's Bay is a small town. Everyone knows one another."

"Joe seems to love it here."

"He's an excellent chief of police. And usually very calm. When he called me tonight, there was pure panic in his voice. I've never heard him so upset."

"He's always been protective of family." She paused, then said, "We've been a little worried about

Joe since he and his wife decided to divorce. Did you know Rachel?"

"We met a couple of times," Charlotte said, her voice neutral. "I was sorry it didn't work out for them."

"I can't remember a time when Joe and Rachel weren't together. She was like another sister to me. Not that I needed any more," she said dryly. "I still have hope that they'll work things out."

Charlotte nodded. "I hate to see any marriage break up. I'll tell Joe he can come back in, and then I'll find someone to take you to X-ray. I'm sure you'd love to get out of here."

"I really would." She'd barely finished speaking when a nurse entered with a wheelchair. "It looks like my ride has arrived. Thanks, Dr. Adams."

"Please call me Charlotte." She helped Isabella off the table and into the wheelchair.

Joe was waiting outside the door when they left the room. "I'll be here when you get back," he said.

As the nurse wheeled her away, Isabella saw Joe put his hand on Charlotte's arm in a manner that suggested far more than friendliness. Maybe it wasn't Angel's Bay that Joe didn't want to leave. Maybe it was Charlotte.

"How is she?" Joe asked, letting his hand rest on Charlotte's arm for a moment. He felt more unsettled than he had in a long time, and he didn't like it. He'd always been in control of his life, especially since he'd come to Angel's Bay, where he only had himself to worry about. Now Isabella had dropped into his life, almost dying in the process. He couldn't imagine having to make that call to his parents.

"She's going to be fine," Charlotte said with a reassuring smile. "I'm more worried about you."

"Isabella could have died. If Nick Hartley hadn't seen her go over the side of the road, she—"

"Don't even go there," Charlotte interrupted. "Don't think about it."

"I can't think of anything else. Isabella is the baby of the family. I'm used to taking care of her—or least knowing that someone else is taking care of her."

"She's all grown up now, Joe, and she seems very resilient."

"She's never been short on courage."

"She has amazing eyes, doesn't she? Where does that blue come from?"

"Our Mayan ancestors, according to my grandmother."

"She's beautiful."

"I guess." He paused, noting the dark shadows under Charlotte's eyes, her weary posture. "Thanks for coming down. I owe you."

She waved a hand. "Not a problem."

"You look tired."

"It's been a busy couple of days," she admitted. "I'm still recovering from Annie's long labor and delivery. I'm usually not so personally involved in the process. Annie has become like a little sister to me, and I wanted everything to go perfectly for her."

"And it did," he said with a smile. Annie had gone into labor in the middle of Kara Lynch's Halloween party on Sunday night. "For a few minutes there, I was afraid she'd have the baby in my car."

Charlotte grinned. "It wouldn't be the first time I've delivered a baby in a car. It's hell on the upholstery."

He winced. "Too much information."

"Anyway, I've had two other babies come into the world since then, and it's only Tuesday night. Fortunately, I don't have anyone else near delivery for another couple of weeks."

"How's Annie doing?"

"She came home yesterday. Physically, she's fine; mentally and emotionally, she's a mess. She's driving herself crazy about whether she should give up her baby for adoption. The adoptive couples she's spoken to are all desperate for her to make up her mind, and I can't blame them, but this isn't anywhere close to an ideal situation. Annie has already held her son in her arms. How will she be able to give him up now? Maybe if she'd done it right away, the second he was born, but he came ten days early, and she wasn't ready to say good-bye. She's still torn between wanting to keep him and wanting to give him a better life with a stable family. I don't know what she'll do."

"It's a big decision. Will she stay with you and your mother until she decides?"

Charlotte and her mother, Monica, had taken Annie in six months earlier. The eighteen-year-old had no living relatives except a mentally ill father,

and she'd desperately needed support. Charlotte
had stepped up; she couldn't stand by and do nothing when she saw someone in pain. It was one of the
things Joe liked most about her. But he wondered
if she and her mother were really prepared to help
Annie raise her baby over the long term.

"She'll stay for now. We'll see how it goes.
There's still the unresolved issue of paternity, but one
thing at a time." She glanced down at her watch. "I
should get home. My mother has been with Annie
and the baby all day, and none of us got much sleep
last night. That seven-pound bundle of joy can really cry. Annie is afraid to breastfeed, thinking she'll
get even more attached, so we all took turns with the
bottle. Her baby is picking up on her indecision."

"Sounds like you have your hands full."

"As do you," she said with a smile. "It's nice to
meet someone from your family. Maybe I can get
Isabella to tell me some of your secrets."

And maybe he'd made a mistake putting the two
of them together, but it was too late now. "I've already told you my secrets," he said lightly.

"I've barely scratched the surface. But I'm not
done trying," she teased.

It was the perfect opportunity to ask her out. But
while that question had been hovering on his lips for
the past few days, he'd held it back. He wasn't officially divorced yet. Nor was he quite ready to get
involved with another woman, and Charlotte wasn't
just any woman. She was already someone he cared

about. He wasn't ready to dive into something deep and intense, but with her, he didn't think it could be any other way.

Or maybe he was a coward. Because if he did ask her out, he really didn't want her to say no, and he wasn't completely convinced that he'd get a yes. She might be willing to flirt, but he wasn't so sure about her taking a bigger step forward.

Charlotte's cell phone began to vibrate. "This is my mother. Hang on a sec, will you?" She moved a few steps down the hall into a quiet alcove.

He didn't want to intrude on her call, but when she said, "What do you mean she's gone?" he walked down the hall to join her.

"I've got to get home," Charlotte said, ending the call.

"Something wrong?"

"Annie went out for a walk hours ago and never came back. The baby was napping, and my mother had a friend over, so she didn't realize until just now that Annie hadn't returned. I can't imagine where she could be." Charlotte glanced down at her watch. "It's after eight."

"Maybe she's talking to the father," he suggested. The identity of the baby's father was still a mystery to everyone but Annie. "She needs to get his release to give the baby up."

"I suppose, but she's had nine months to talk to him. You're probably right, though. She doesn't really have any other friends, so he seems the likely choice.

But still, to stay away so long when she just got out of the hospital and had a baby . . . I don't have a good feeling about this."

He didn't, either. "There's another scenario to consider."

"I don't want to believe she's run away," Charlotte said quickly, shaking her head.

"She's been under a lot of pressure. It might have gotten to her."

"She wouldn't leave her baby behind. She loves him."

"She's also exhausted and confused."

"And her hormones are running rampant," Charlotte added. "I hope you're wrong."

"Call me when you find out more. I'll help any way I can."

"You have a dog," Isabella said in amazement as she stepped into Joe's living room, and a large golden retriever jumped up and smothered her with kisses. "And he's *really* friendly."

Joe grabbed his collar. "Sorry about that. Down, Rufus."

The dog gave an eager bark in reply.

"He belonged to Uncle Carlos," Joe explained. "The neighbors took him for a while, but once I moved in, he dug his way back into the yard and hasn't left since. He'll settle down in a second. He always gets excited when I come home. Don't you, boy?" he added as he scratched behind the dog's ears.

"I feel better knowing you're not coming home to a quiet, lonely house," she said.

"Rufus is good company. Man's best friend," he said with a smile.

She smiled back. "And you always wanted a dog. But Teresa had allergies, so we couldn't have one at home, and Rachel didn't like dogs. I guess you can finally do what you want."

"The silver lining to divorce," he said, his smile slipping away. As she shivered, he moved toward the thermostat on the wall, and said, "It will be warm soon. This place doesn't take long to heat up."

Isabella looked around the small house her brother had inherited from their uncle almost a year ago. The rooms were sparsely decorated: a brown futon and a recliner in front of a big-screen TV, some chairs and a table in the dining room, none of which she recognized. These pieces had not come from the house Joe had shared with Rachel. He'd left his L.A. life behind in every way.

"The house needs a remodel," Joe said, following her gaze. "Uncle Carlos let things go. The roof leaked with the last rain, but the view from the deck is spectacular. Do you want to take a look?"

She shook her head. The dark night and the sound of the ocean would only remind her of those terrifying moments on the cliff. "Later." She picked up a photo from the mantel. "Is this Uncle Carlos? I don't remember him."

"That's him. He only came to L.A. a few times. Dad used to bring me up here to fish when I was about ten or twelve. Carlos was actually Dad's uncle, our great-uncle. He was quite a character, and he could tell a story like no one else. You would have liked him."

"I probably would have. I did like the pendant you sent me." She pulled it out from under her blouse. "It was a good thing I had it on, or I would have lost it, too."

"It looks good on you. The blue reminded me of your eyes. I found it in a wooden box in the basement with some other costume jewelry. There are a lot of boxes I still haven't gone through yet. And anything I found that looked like it might have sentimental value for someone in the family I stuck down there as well."

"Maybe I can help you sort through it while I'm here," she offered. "Who knows what might be down there waiting to be discovered? I'm surprised you've left it this long. Where's your sense of adventure?"

"I get enough excitement on the job."

"In Angel's Bay?" she asked dubiously.

"There's enough to keep me busy and on my toes," he said, stiffening a little.

"I wasn't criticizing. I'm the last one to judge someone for making a change in their life." She paused, fingering the pendant. "It's funny that Uncle Carlos would have this necklace when he never married. I wonder who it belonged to."

"I have no idea." His gaze narrowed thoughtfully. "You're awfully curious about Uncle Carlos all of a sudden. Is something going on?"

"I don't know what you mean."

"I don't think you've told me the real reason you're here."

"I wanted to see you, Joe. I've been worried about you."

"There's not more? Maybe something to do with that pendant?"

She'd forgotten how perceptive he could be. "Can we talk later? I really want to take a bath."

"Sure. Sorry. You're freezing, and I'm interrogating you." He waved his hand toward the hall. "The bathroom is the first door on your left. I'll find you some sweats and a T-shirt. And while you're cleaning up, I'll make us some dinner. You must be starving."

"I am—but you're going to cook?" she asked doubtfully.

"I can make a few things," he said dryly. "It won't be Dad's tamales or Mom's Irish stew, but I can scramble up some eggs and put in some toast."

"I'll take it. But don't start them yet. I plan to be in that tub for a while."

"Take all the time you need. And Izzy, I'm glad you're all right."

"Me, too." She headed into the bathroom and glanced into the mirror. Big mistake! No wonder Joe had been so freaked when he saw her, she looked like a ghost. There was no color in her face, making the raised cuts appear worse. Her hair was a muddy mess, and her eyes were huge, still reflecting the horror of seeing her death come so close.

Glancing away, she started the bath and undressed,

wincing when she had to use her left hand. There was no fracture, thank goodness, just a sprain. When the tub was full, she sank into the warmth with a grateful sigh. Resting her head on the back of the tub, she closed her eyes and let herself breathe. She needed her heart to slow down, her body to relax. She tried to remember the mantras from her yoga classes. Yoga was about living in the moment, which was her preference. Seeing the future never seemed to make anyone happy, least of all her.

But her mind seemed to have other ideas. As she tried to find that peaceful place, Nick Hartley's face flashed through her brain.

He was telling her something, but she couldn't hear him. There was a roaring in her ears. Was it the wind? Or was it her own heart pounding?

She'd hoped that her earlier visions had been foreshadowing the car crash, in which case they should have stopped. But she couldn't shake the feeling that this was just the beginning.

THREE

An hour later, dressed in Joe's oversized sweats and T-shirt, Isabella sat down at the dining-room table and dug into a plateful of scrambled eggs. "These aren't half bad," she said in surprise. Joe had mixed in veggies and had also fried up some bacon. She was impressed with the effort. As her stomach filled, her tension eased. She was clean, warm, and alive, and for now, that was enough.

"How can you tell how good they are?" Joe asked dryly. "You smothered them in salsa."

"Everything tastes better with hot sauce," she said with a grin, repeating their father's favorite phrase. "And I love breakfast for dinner."

"Then you won't starve around here."

She smiled. "It *is* nice to see you, Joe."

"Likewise."

"Really? You haven't exactly sent any invitations to the family to come and visit."

He shrugged. "I've been getting settled in. But

you know you're always welcome. What's going on with your work?"

"My next movie project got postponed until after Christmas, so I have some time to kill."

"What about that guy you were seeing? He won't miss you?"

"Jarrod and I were over six months ago," she said with a dismissive wave.

"I'm sorry to hear that. It's hard to keep up with your love life."

"Why do I feel a big-brother lecture coming on? I haven't met the right guy, Joe. I know you and everyone else in the family think I need to settle down and pick something—a guy, a nine-to-five job, a permanent address—but I'll know when I've found where I belong and who I belong with. And then I'll stick."

"I wasn't going to lecture," he said with a smile. "I actually admire your adventurous spirit and your unwillingness to settle. More people should be like you."

Isabella felt surprised and pleased. She'd taken a lot of heat from her parents and her sisters about her multitude of jobs and boyfriends. She'd been out of step with her family for most of her life.

As Joe lifted his beer for a swig, his face grew pensive, and she had a feeling he was thinking not about her love life anymore but about his own.

"So what happened with you and Rachel?" she asked. "I didn't think you two would ever split up. It shocked all of us."

"We grew apart," he said shortly.

When it didn't appear that he intended to elaborate, she said, "That's it? That's all I get?"

"What do you want me to say?"

"When I saw Rachel a few weeks ago, she was really thin, and she looked tired. I asked her how she was doing, and she almost started to cry. I don't think she's happy about the divorce."

Joe's jaw tightened. "It was her idea."

"If you didn't want it, why did you sign the papers?" she countered.

"I don't want to get into this, Isabella."

"I know you're not used to confiding in me. There are too many years between us. But I am your sister, and I'm not a kid anymore. I'll listen if you want to talk."

"There's nothing to talk about. Rachel and I don't want the same things. I was burned out on L.A. I was turning into someone I didn't recognize and didn't like very much. When I came here, everything changed. I hoped that Rachel would like Angel's Bay, but she didn't. So she left."

Isabella shook her head. "It's not that simple, Joe."

"No, it's not," he admitted. "Rachel and I had a lot of problems that had nothing to do with Angel's Bay."

"I want to help you fix it."

"I know—because that's what you do. You're our fix-it girl," he said with a soft smile. "It must come with your gift for sewing: your desire to repair things, to make them right."

That was true. There was nothing more satisfying to her than fixing something that seemed beyond repair and giving it new life.

"Let's get back to you," Joe said. "I know I'm your favorite brother—"

"My *only* brother," she corrected.

"And that you care about Rachel and me, but did you have another reason for making this trip? Are you in some kind of trouble? Do you need my help?"

How much did she want to tell him? "After you sent me the pendant, I started having bad dreams. I'd see a sign for Angel's Bay, the winding highway and the shadow of a man who seemed to be in danger."

"And I'm the man?"

"I thought you might be, but I'm not sure anymore." She didn't want to get into the idea that she might have been dreaming about Nick Hartley, which seemed ridiculous. Her visions had always come from an emotional connection to someone she cared about.

"These dreams—they're like the ones you've had before?" he asked, keeping his voice carefully neutral.

"Yes." Like most of her family, Joe was practical and logical, and her visions had always been pretty much a family joke. "It's okay, and you don't have to believe me."

"These visions always seem to get you into trouble."

"Grandmother says that's because I haven't yet embraced my gift, and that's why nothing is clear to me. I'm fighting my inner nature. I need to be still, to let the wisdom flow."

"That sounds like Grandmother," he said dryly.

She nodded. Their Grandmother Elena was a tiny Mexican woman with a fierce, loving spirit who believed in the legends of their ancestors, the power of the universe. Of all of the Silveira siblings, Isabella had spent the most time with her grandmother after their mother went back to work full-time. It was from Elena she had learned to sew, from Elena she had learned to dream, and from Elena she had come to believe that she was blessed with a psychic gift. "Grandmother would like this town," she said. "Don't you have angels here?"

"I haven't personally seen any, but others claim to have had that experience."

"Maybe this town will turn you into a believer." Although she doubted that. Joe was as pragmatic as they came.

"So you came to save me and almost got yourself killed in the process. There's something wrong with that equation, Isabella."

"It is what it is."

"Well, I'm fine, as you can see." He grabbed his phone off the table as it began to vibrate and glanced down at the number. "I need to get this."

"Go ahead." She cleared the table while he took the call. He was doing more listening than talking, but she could tell by the tension flowing from him and the rigid posture of his back that he had gone into his chief-of-police mode.

She'd always admired Joe's willingness to run straight into trouble; he had more courage than anyone she knew. As a teenager, though, that confidence had gotten him into some risky situations. Her older sister had told her that for a while, they weren't sure which side of the law Joe would end up on.

"Police business?" she asked as he ended the call.

"A teenage girl has gone missing; there's a chance she's run away."

"How old is she?"

"Eighteen," he said as he stood up. "Annie had a baby a few days ago. She doesn't have family, so she's been staying with Charlotte Adams and her mother the past few months."

"That was Charlotte on the phone?"

"Yes. I won't be gone long. Will you be okay here alone?"

"I'll be fine, Joe. Do what you have to do." She paused. "You and Charlotte are pretty close, aren't you?"

"We're friends," he said with a warning gleam in his eyes. "Don't make assumptions, Izzy. You don't know anything about my life. And whatever Rachel told you isn't the whole story."

A dozen reasons to explain why Annie hadn't returned home ran around Charlotte's head. She couldn't believe that Annie would run away, nor could she imagine a darker alternative. She needed

Joe to help her make sense of things and, more important, to find Annie.

As the baby cried louder, Charlotte paced around the living room, trying to find a rhythm to soothe his frustrated screams. He'd been fed, changed, and examined for any sign of a physical ailment. He was just very unhappy, and she had no idea why. She was used to delivering babies, not taking care of them. This was completely new territory.

"I'll take him," Monica Adams said, weary lines in her face, as she came into the room. "I can't stand it a second more. I know what to do."

Charlotte heard the unspoken *you don't,* but this wasn't the time for an argument. They were both tired and worried. She handed the baby to her mother and sat down on the couch with a sigh.

"I wish we had a name to call him," Monica said as she put the baby on her shoulder and patted his back.

"Annie thought it would be too difficult to give him up if she gave him a name."

Her mother's lips tightened, and there was a fire in her eyes when she said, "Annie is being completely irresponsible. I didn't expect this from her. She knows how lucky she is to have us, and she's always been appreciative and thankful. How could she do this to us?"

It was the first time her mother had criticized Annie in the six months they'd all been living together. The two of them had gotten along so well it had made Charlotte wonder why Annie could get along better with her mother than she could. But then, Annie had never tested her mother's authority until now. Charlotte had spent most of her life butting up against her mother's opinions and rules. And the real break in their mother-daughter tie had come a long time ago . . . with another baby and another teenager.

She'd been seventeen and a senior in high school when she'd had to tell her mother that she was pregnant. There had been disappointment and anger in her eyes, cruelty in her mother's words and in her actions. Charlotte had shamed the family. Her father was a minister. He preached abstinence and responsibility, and she had fallen short on both. But it wasn't her father with whom she'd shared the secret, and her relationship with her mother had never recovered. There were still secrets and lies between them. They hadn't talked about that horrible time in more than fifteen years, but it was always there in the background, making any hope of a closer relationship impossible.

"It's okay; you're fine. Sleep now," Monica murmured, her voice soft and tender when she spoke to the baby.

Her mother had lost weight. Not that she'd ever been heavy; she was far too controlling to overeat or overindulge in anything. But she seemed more fragile now, more vulnerable, which seemed unthinkable. Monica Adams had always been a force of nature, powerful, opinionated, and invincible in Charlotte's mind. Her mother had played the role of minister's wife to perfection, tending to the physical and emotional needs of the congregation while her father addressed their spiritual needs.

When her father died, her mother had been left without a role to play. She'd gone from being very, very important to being very, very alone. Her father's death was the reason Charlotte had come back to Angel's Bay. Her sister and brother didn't think her mother should be alone, and they both had other responsibilities, so Charlotte was elected.

She'd never planned on staying this long. But she'd found herself settling into her hometown, accepting a job at the Redwood Medical Center, reconnecting with old friends, and helping her mother move into a new house. She'd become even more entrenched in Angel's Bay when she'd offered Annie a place to stay for the duration of her pregnancy. After that, she couldn't leave. And to be honest, she didn't really want to go—at least, not yet.

The baby's cries began to diminish with a hiccup, a final sob, and then quiet—blessed quiet. Charlotte drew in a breath of relief.

"That's better," Monica said with approval, pleased with her success. "I'm going to put him down in his crib."

Charlotte followed her mother into Annie's bedroom. Monica carefully set the baby down in the crib next to the bed. He squirmed for a second, then dozed off again. All of that crying had exhausted him. Her gaze moved to the unmade bed. Annie's bathrobe was tossed over the back of a desk chair.

The room was unusually messy. Annie had been almost obsessively neat, as if afraid she'd be asked to leave if she made one wrong move. The turmoil in the room now seemed to be a direct reflection of Annie's emotional distress. Charlotte wished she'd offered more comfort or reassurance, something to ease the pressure Annie was feeling. But she'd never anticipated that Annie would take off. And she couldn't imagine how the girl could make it on her own with no money, no car, and no real skills of any sort. She hoped this was a temporary flight, that Annie had just needed some space to think.

Her mother turned on the baby monitor and motioned her into the hall. They'd just returned to the living room when the doorbell rang. Charlotte rushed to open it, greeting Joe with a relieved smile. "Thanks for coming. We're not sure what to do."

"No problem. I'm happy to help," he said with a calm, reassuring smile. He then turned to her mother. "Mrs. Adams, how are you?"

"Not particularly well. Can I get you some coffee or tea?"

"No, I'm fine, thanks," he replied as they walked into the living room and settled on the couches. "When did you last see Annie?"

"Around three o'clock," her mother replied. "The baby was asleep. Annie said she was going to walk down to the Oak Grove Market to pick up some formula. I had friends in the kitchen. We were making plans for the church bake sale. I assumed Annie had come home while we were talking, and it wasn't until the baby woke up around six that I realized she was still gone."

Joe checked his watch. "It's almost ten now. Does she have a cell phone?"

"It's in her room," Charlotte interjected.

"Is anything missing? Clothes? A suitcase? Did she have cash?"

"She had some money," Monica said. "A few families in town sent her cards with checks and cash. There might be some clothing missing; I'm not sure."

"What do you think, Joe?" Charlotte asked, unable to read anything in his neutral expression.

"I don't know yet. How was Annie acting before she left?" he inquired, directing his question to her mother.

"She's been stressed out ever since she gave birth," Monica replied. "Today was just the same. She was quiet, a little teary, exhausted, not moving very fast. I was surprised she actually wanted to walk to the store."

"Did she get any calls? Talk to anyone that you know of?"

Her mother shook her head. "I don't think so. As far as I know, Annie doesn't have many friends. There's a young woman at church who's also pregnant, and Annie has spoken to her a few times after service. Her name is Kim Swanson. I called over there, but no one was home."

"I'll follow up with her," Joe said with a nod. "Anyone else?"

"There is the baby's father," Charlotte said.

Joe's gaze turned to her. "But you don't know who he is, do you?"

She hesitated, and when she didn't reply right away, her mother cut in sharply, "Charlotte, is there something you haven't told me?"

She debated breaking the promise she'd made to Annie several weeks ago. She didn't have a choice; Annie had been gone too long. "I know that he's one of five men," she said finally.

Her mother's jaw dropped in astonishment. "What are you talking about, Charlotte?"

She winced at the storm brewing in her mother's eyes. She would pay for this secret, even though it wasn't her own. "Annie told me that the father is one of the men who's trying to adopt the baby. He doesn't want his wife to know he had an affair, and his solution is for Annie to give the baby to him without saying anything."

Her mother tightened her lips. "Why didn't you tell me? I had a right to know. I let Annie live in my house. I could have helped her figure out what to do."

"She made me promise. She wanted to make her own decisions. I had to respect that."

"I can't believe she didn't confide in me! I thought we were close," her mother muttered with an irritated shake of her head.

"I'll need a list of the men," Joe said.

She was happy not to see any judgment in his

eyes. But then, he turned on a switch when he was on duty. She supposed she did the same when she was with her patients, and she was happy for his objectivity now. "I have the information. I got it out of Annie's room earlier." She retrieved the files from the desk, then spread them out on the coffee table.

Attached to the front of each folder was a photo. There was Dan McCarthy, a fireman, married to Erin, who worked at the quilt store. Steve Baker, a dentist, married to Victoria Hartley Baker, who ran the community theater with her parents. Adam Goldman, a lawyer, married to Louise Jennings Goldman, a nurse at the medical center. Mitch Lowell, a contractor, married to Corinne Lowell, a bank teller, formerly of Angel's Bay but currently residing in Montgomery. And Kevin Holt, a fisherman, married to Donna Holt, a florist.

"It could be any one of these guys," Charlotte said, lifting her gaze to meet Joe's. "I know several of them, none of whom I would suspect of being unfaithful to his wife. What do we do, just start talking to them?"

Before Joe could answer, the doorbell rang again. Her mother got up to answer it. When she returned to the room, Andrew Schilling was with her, an expression of concern on his face.

Andrew was an attractive man with golden blond hair and light blue eyes. He'd been Charlotte's most serious high school boyfriend, but their teenage relationship had ended in disaster, and they hadn't seen each other for more than a decade until Andrew had returned to town several months earlier—ironically, as the minister hired to replace her father.

Since Andrew's return, they'd been dancing around the possibility of dating. Andrew had broken her heart once, and she wasn't sure she wanted to go down that path again. But Andrew was trying to persuade her to give him another chance. It was quite the turnaround: she'd been the one after him when they were in high school, and it gave her some pleasure to have him doing the pursuing now.

But right now, the main concern was Annie. Andrew had been acting as a liaison between Annie and the prospective adoptive parents, and while Charlotte was happy to have his help, Andrew and Joe seemed to rub each other the wrong way whenever they were in a room together, especially if she was present.

"How can I help, Charlie?" he asked as he moved toward her.

She got to her feet, accepting his concerned embrace. "I'm not sure. We were just talking about what to do." She stepped back, feeling a little awkward under Joe's watchful eyes.

"Apparently, Annie had a secret only Charlotte knew about," her mother cut in.

"What was that?" Andrew asked.

Before she could reply, her mother jumped in. "One of the men asking to adopt the baby is the biological father."

Andrew's eyes widened in shock. "Are you serious? Why didn't you tell me, Charlie?"

"It wasn't my secret to tell," she said again, seeing the same glint of anger in his expression as she'd seen on her mother's face. "Annie is an adult. She has a right to privacy, a right to make her own decisions."

"Legally, she might be an adult, but emotionally, she's a child," Monica said sharply. "She needed you to be a counselor, not a co-conspirator, Charlotte."

"I told her that she needed to tell the truth," Charlotte replied. "But Annie was torn. If she wasn't going to raise the child, then she thought he might be better off with his biological father. She wasn't sure she could give the baby to anyone else. But she was also uncomfortable going along with the lie."

"If you'd told me, I might have been able to help her make a good decision," Andrew said quietly. "I am a trained counselor, Charlotte."

She saw the disappointment in his eyes, but she couldn't feel guilty for keeping Annie's confidence. Annie had been her patient as well as her friend.

"What we need to do," Joe said, cutting through the tension, "is retrace Annie's steps and come up with a timeline of her activities the last few days. Right now, there's no evidence of foul play. Everything points to her leaving of her own accord. At the moment, we'll consider her a missing person, and I'll put out an advisory to that effect. In the meantime, we'll check with the market, see if she ever made it there, and I'll have some of my officers speak to the neighbors, the shop owners, anyone who might have seen her on her walk. I'll also contact the prospective parents. Maybe she'll come back on her own. As for the baby—"

"We'll take good care of him," Charlotte said quickly.

"That's fine for tonight. But if Annie isn't home by tomorrow, I'll need to contact Child Protective Services."

"I'm a licensed foster parent," Monica said. "My husband and I took in a couple of children a few years back."

"I didn't know that," Charlotte said in surprise.

"If you'd called or come home more often, you would have known," her mother returned.

"That should make things easier," Joe said. "But let's take this one step at a time." He rose to his feet. "I'll be in touch."

"I'll walk you out," Charlotte offered. She followed him out to the porch, shivering in the cool night air. "Thanks for coming so late, Joe. I know you'd probably rather have one of your officers handle this."

"I'm happy to take care of it. I owed you one."

"No, you didn't. How was Isabella feeling when she got home?"

"Tired and bruised but all right. She was on her way to bed when I left."

"That reminds me—I packed up some clothes for her, so she'll have something to wear. She said she lost her suitcase and everything else she'd brought with her." Charlotte stepped back into the house to retrieve the canvas bag she'd placed on the hall table. "It's just a few things. I wasn't sure if Rachel left any clothes at your house."

"No, she didn't." He took the bag from her hand. "I really appreciate this. You're very generous. You never stop thinking of other people, even when you've got your own problems."

She sighed, wishing she were as unselfish as that. "Not true. Right now, I'm thinking about myself and how much I don't want to go back into that living room. Andrew and my mother are not happy with the fact that I kept Annie's secret."

"You did what you had to do."

"Do you think so?" she couldn't help asking. "I want to believe that, but then again, Annie is missing, and her baby doesn't have his mother. I hope I didn't make a mistake."

"We'll find Annie. In the meantime, it looks like you're the babysitter."

"Me and my mother. Not exactly the dream team."

"I think Andrew wants to be on your team, as well."

She saw the question in his eyes. "I'm sure Andrew feels partly to blame for Annie's turmoil. He put a lot of pressure on her to consider adoption. I don't really know why."

"Maybe because it gave him a reason to be close to you," Joe suggested.

His words surprised her. "I'm sure that had nothing to do with it."

"Are you?" He tipped his head and walked down the front steps.

Charlotte was still trying to come up with an answer when he got into his truck and drove away.

The headlights blinded her. Isabella squinted against the brightness. The car was coming straight toward her. She could see two people in the front. They were arguing or struggling or something . . .

She hit the brakes, clinging to the wheel, praying the skid would stop, but she was flying . . . and then he was there, yelling at her. She couldn't hear the words; she could just see the fear in his eyes.

She tried to move, but something was holding her down—the airbag?

But she wasn't on the cliff anymore. And he was in the shadows. He was turning away from her, going in another direction, but he didn't know what was coming. She had to get him before—

Isabella woke up with a start, sweating and shaking.

The past, the present, and the future were all mixing together now.

Why?

Because of Nick Hartley?

Was he really the man in her dreams? Or had she put his face on that shadowy figure because he'd rescued her? When he'd first appeared in the rain, she'd been dazed and confused. Had her mind played tricks on her?

Turning on her side, she stared at the digital clock. It was seven A.M. She'd actually managed to sleep a few hours, though every muscle in her body ached. She sat up and stretched, swinging her legs over the side of the bed. The swelling in her wrist had gone down, but it was still tender to the touch. Getting out of bed, she walked to the window, shivering in the cool morning air. She pulled the curtain to the side and was amazed by the view.

Beyond the back deck, there was nothing but ocean and a clear blue sky—no trace of yesterday's storm. She could see a few boats out on the water, but otherwise the horizon was wide open. No wonder Joe loved this place. It was a far cry from the L.A. streets where they'd grown up.

The smell of coffee drew her out of her room. Joe was already up, leaning against the counter and reading the newspaper while he sipped from a mug.

"I thought you'd sleep in," he said, concern in his eyes.

"I don't sleep very well these days," she said as she grabbed a mug and filled it with coffee.

"How's the head?"

"Achy, along with all the muscles in my body. But when I think of the alternative—"

"Don't." He nodded toward a bag on the counter. "Charlotte sent you some clothes."

She was surprised and touched. "That was nice of her. Now I'll have something to wear when I go shopping today." She sat on a stool and sipped her coffee. "So what was the drama last night?"

"The teenager I was telling you about has disappeared, leaving her baby behind. It looks like she ran away. Hopefully, she'll change her mind and come back."

"Charlotte is taking care of the baby?"

"Along with her mother. They took Annie in several months ago, supporting her through the pregnancy. Now they've been left with her baby. I'm sure they didn't see that coming."

"Charlotte seems like a very generous person." She gave him a thoughtful look. "You like her, don't you?"

He visibly tensed. "If you think I cheated on Rachel—"

"No, of course not. I would never think that," she said quickly. "I didn't mean it that way, Joe."

"Good, because Charlotte wasn't part of my breakup." He cleared his throat. "Sorry I jumped on you. I don't know what Rachel has been telling people."

"She hasn't been saying much of anything beyond the fact that you were willing to let her go rather than move back to L.A."

"Our divorce was not just the result of geography. We wanted different things. And we were struggling to hang on to something that wasn't there anymore."

"I understand that, but you were together a long time, and I can't quite believe neither one of you was willing to move to make things work."

"It wasn't a decision made lightly. The last thing I wanted was to get a divorce. I just couldn't live in L.A. anymore."

"Why not?"

"I don't have time to get into it. I need to get to work."

"Okay, I'll drop it—for now," Isabella added. "For what it's worth, I'm on your side—whatever and wherever that is. We're blood. It's that simple."

He smiled. "Thanks. I'm also going to follow up on your accident today. Is there anything else you remember?"

She thought for a moment. The glare of the headlights seemed to blur everything else in her mind, although . . . "There were two people in the car," she said slowly.

"Anything else? Color, make, size, anything?"

"No, sorry. I'm sure that's not very helpful."

"Well, it's something. Maybe over time, more details will come back to you."

"Isn't it too late? I won't be able to prove anything. Even if we found the driver, it would be my word against his."

"I'd still like to talk to him. There's a gas station on the edge of town, and the old guy who works there keeps an eye on who's coming and going. Maybe he saw something." Joe set down his coffee mug. "If you want to drop me off at work, you can take my truck, and I'll use one of the police cars today."

"That would make things easier—thanks."

"Do you feel up to driving? You must be a little shell-shocked. I'm going to see if we can get your car out of the ocean."

"I don't want to see it. It will only remind me of

how close I came to dying. It's shocking how fast things change. One minute I was looking forward to getting to town, and the next I was fighting for my life. It was crazy."

"It was criminal. And I *will* find out who was responsible for your accident, Isabella. It happened in my town, on my watch. I want answers."

FOUR

Isabella dropped Joe off at the station, then stopped by the dry cleaner's to have Nick Hartley's coat cleaned. After that, she strolled through the downtown area, pleasantly surprised to find a number of clothing boutiques, antiques stores, art galleries, cozy cafés and restaurants. The mix of upscale sophistication and small-town charm was very appealing.

With the mountains behind her and the sea in front of her, everywhere she looked was a picture-postcard view. People smiled when they passed her on the street, and she felt more relaxed than she had in a long time. Even before the dreams had started, she'd been feeling restless and unsettled. While she loved designing clothes, working for the film industry wasn't quite the dream job she'd expected it to be. Her last project, for a ruthless, egotistical director, had been one big headache and made her question her career path.

But that was a decision for another day. All

she had to do now was shop. She stepped into the Morning Glory Boutique with a surge of excitement. The business side of fashion might be taking its toll on her, but she still loved clothes—the feel of the fabrics, the color palettes, the shapes and silhouettes. Her grandmother had taught her to sew before she'd learned to read, and she'd begun designing clothes for her dolls by the time she was in the third grade.

While she'd made a lot of her own clothes over the years, she also loved to buy from other designers, especially those who weren't afraid to use color. She liked prints, bold patterns, mixing and matching pieces that might not always go together. But since she had a closet full of clothes in L.A., today she just needed enough pants, sweaters, and lingerie to get her through a few weeks.

At the last shop, she put on a pair of jeans, black boots, and a red sweater over a camisole top, then asked the salesperson to cut off the tags so she could wear them home. While the clerk was ringing up her purchases, she picked up a flyer off the counter.

The Angel's Bay Regional Theater was putting out a call for local talent to assist with the Winter Workshop production of *Les Liaisons*. Besides actors, they were looking for backstage helpers, dressers, stitchers, painters, and construction workers. A tingle ran down her spine. Designing for the stage was quite different from designing for film. It was more immediate, more real. The actors were living and breathing in their clothes in front of a packed audience. She hadn't done theater in many, many years, but she'd never forgotten how much fun it was.

"Are you going to try out?" the woman behind her in line asked. She had dark red hair and friendly brown eyes and was gently pushing a stroller back and forth, probably hoping to keep her baby asleep.

"I don't know. I just got into town last night."

The woman's eyes widened. "Last night? You're not Joe Silveira's sister, are you?"

"Yes, I'm Isabella Silveira," she said, surprised. "How did you guess?"

"Everyone at Dina's Café this morning was buzzing about the accident on the outskirts of town, and you said you just arrived." She put out her hand. "I'm Kara Lynch. My husband, Colin, is a police officer, so we're well acquainted with your brother. Joe is a great guy and a wonderful chief of police."

Isabella nodded as she shook Kara's hand. "Yes, he is. I've been trying to live up to his reputation for years."

"I know what that's like. I have some overachieving siblings myself," Kara said with another warm smile. "So how are you? The accident sounded horrific."

"It was bad," she admitted. "Everything happened so fast. It feels a little surreal now."

"I can imagine. I'm so glad you're all right."

"Me, too. I lost all my clothes, though, so I'm restocking," she added, waving her hand toward the busy clerk. "Sorry to keep you waiting."

"It's fine. Faith is asleep, so no worries."

"Your baby is beautiful."

Kara's eyes brightened. "She is, isn't she? I have a hard time not spending most of my day just staring at her. Will you be in town for a while, Isabella?"

"I hope so."

"I'd love to have you and Joe over for dinner. From what I saw at the last chili cook-off, your brother isn't much of a cook, and I wouldn't want you to go hungry."

"Joe made chili?"

"Not very well," Kara returned with a grin.

Isabella grinned back. "I didn't think so."

"Talk to Joe and see when he's free. Then we'll pick a date. Our phone number is in the book, and Joe has it, as well. If you'll be in town for a while, you should try out for the play. The bigger parts will be played by actors from a visiting Los Angeles theater company, but they always have smaller parts for locals, and they need lots of backstage help. The Winter Workshop is an annual tradition around here."

"I'm actually a costume designer. I've been working on films the last couple of years."

"What perfect timing! I'm sure they could use your help. If you want to, that is. Perhaps you came here to get away from work."

"No, I came to spend time with my brother and check out Angel's Bay. But I haven't worked on a stage production in a long time, and it sounds like fun. Plus, Joe will probably be happier if I keep myself busy and out of his business. He's not big on meddling sisters."

"He has that in common with my brothers," Kara said. "I have three of them and a sister, and lots of extended family, as well. Since you're a sewer, you should check out the Angel's Heart Quilt Shop. My family runs it. My grandmother, Fiona Murray, is the queen of the quilters, and if you're looking for fabric, it's the place to go. We have a lot of events, and it's a great place to meet people."

"Good to know." As the clerk finished ringing up her purchases, Isabella handed over the cash Joe had taken out of the ATM for her until she could get replacement bank and credit cards. "It was nice to meet you," she said, gathering her bags together.

"Joe has been really good to me." Kara added more seriously. "My husband was shot a few months back while he was on duty, and he was in a coma for a long time. Joe was tremendously supportive. I've been trying to get him over for a thank-you dinner for a long time. If you'd persuade him to come, I'd appreciate it."

"I'm sorry about your husband," Isabella said. Her family had lived with the fear of Joe getting hurt ever since he'd gone to the police academy. It was bad enough having a brother for a cop; she couldn't imagine being married to one.

"Colin is almost fully recovered now, so it's all good. If you need anything, feel free to ask. I grew up in Angel's Bay, so I know just about everything and everyone."

"I do have a question. Do you know Nick Hartley and, if so, where I might be able to find him?"

"Sure, I know Nick. He grew up here. He has
an office on the corner of Grand and Lark. It's just
around the corner. He's not always there, but I'm
sure you can leave him a message." Her gaze turned
curious. "He's the one who pulled you from the
wreck, right?"

"Yes, he did."

"Nick is an interesting guy," Kara commented. "A
little on the wild side when we were young, but he
grew up, just like the rest of us."

"Thanks." Isabella smiled and headed out the
door.

As she walked toward the harbor, the sun shining on her face, the dreams that had haunted her
for weeks seemed very far away. It didn't seem possible that something bad was lurking in the shadows
of this beautiful town. But even as she tried to talk
herself into believing that her visions meant nothing,
a voice inside told her not to be a fool. She'd been
down this road before, and whenever she tried to
fight her instincts or wish them away, it only made
things worse.

She put her bags into Joe's truck, locked the
doors, and turned down the opposite street. The
two-story brick building on the corner showed a
listing for Hartley Architecture on the second floor.
Maybe seeing Nick in the light of day would take
him out of her head, make him seem more real, less
a part of her dreams.

She took the elevator to the second floor. In the reception area, a middle-aged woman finished a phone call, then smiled and said, "Can I help you?"

"I'd like to see Mr. Hartley, if he's free."

"He's on the phone. If you want to wait a few minutes . . ."

"That's fine."

"You've got the look of someone I know," the woman said thoughtfully. "But I can't think who."

"That would probably be my brother, Joe Silveira."

"You're the chief's sister?" she echoed, surprise in her eyes. "The girl who was in the accident last night? The one Nick saved?"

"That's me. Isabella Silveira." She'd had no idea her arrival in Angel's Bay would set the town talking.

"I'm Colleen Lawrence, Nick's second cousin," the woman said as she stood and extended her hand. "You were all the talk at Dina's Café this morning. And here you are."

"It's nice to meet you," Isabella said, giving her hand a shake. "I haven't been to Dina's Café yet. Is it good?"

"They have the best blueberry waffles you've ever tasted. Believe me, I've had more than a few," she said with a laugh, putting her hands on her plump hips. "But so has my husband, so we're keeping up with each other." She tilted her head again. "I don't think it's the chief you remind me of, though. He doesn't have your striking blue eyes. I'm sure it will come to me, I'm pretty good with faces. Speaking of which, you look a little beaten up. Are you feeling all right? Can I get you some water?"

"I'm fine, thanks to your cousin. He saved my life."

"That's what I hear—not that he'll tell me anything about it. He didn't used to be so shy when it came to bragging." Colleen had barely finished speaking when the office door opened.

Isabella straightened, a tingle of anticipation running through her as Nick stepped through the doorway.

"Colleen, do you have—" Nick's voice broke off when he saw her. His dark eyes turned surprised, then a little wary.

Without the blur of her dreams or the foggy shadows of the accident, she saw that he was even more attractive than she'd realized. He'd traded in his business suit for jeans and a dark sweater, the sleeves pushed up on his forearms. His dark, wavy hair touched the edges of his shoulders, and he had a strong jaw, a long nose, and a full, sensuous mouth. He was tall, too, well over six feet, with a strong, lean build.

She needed to say something. The silence between them was going on for too long. But he was returning her gaze with the same scrutiny. She wondered what he saw, now that she wasn't wet and muddy and frozen with fear.

Colleen finally cleared her throat. "Miss Silveira wants to speak to you," she said.

"Yes," Isabella said, finally finding her voice. "I do want to speak to you."

"Why don't you come in?" Nick stepped back and waved her into his office, closing the door behind her.

The room was large and airy, with windows on two sides bringing in lots of light and offering a great view of the boats in the harbor. A large oak desk sat in front of one window, a conference table ran along the wall, and on the opposite side of the room were two drafting tables. What a wonderful place in which to create. She'd love to design in a studio like this.

"This is a beautiful room," she said. "You must feel inspired here." She turned back to face him.

"On occasion," he said, digging his hands into his pockets.

She tried to tamp down the nervous flutter in her stomach. She wasn't a shy person by nature; she liked people. But this man made her feel tongue-tied. There was something between them that she didn't understand and couldn't explain, but it was there, so palpable she wondered if he could feel it, too.

"I took your coat to the cleaner's," she said finally. "A guy named Otto said they'd have it done by tomorrow. I can pick it up for you and bring it here."

"That's not necessary. I'll take care of it."

"You saved my life last night. I wouldn't have made it out of the car without your help. And I'm not sure I said thank you."

"You said it—several times."

"Words don't seem like enough."

"I'm just glad I was there," he said, sounding uncomfortable with her gratitude. "How are you feeling today?"

"Like I drove off a cliff."

A light sparked in his eyes, a smile crossing his lips. "Nice that you didn't lose your sense of humor."

"Just everything in my car. But I know how lucky I am."

"I spoke to your brother on the phone a few minutes ago," Nick said. "I told him I didn't see the other car. I wish I could have been more helpful."

"At this point, I don't know what difference it makes, but Joe won't let any crime go unpunished if he has something to say about it." She should leave and let Nick get back to work, but she wasn't at all ready to say good-bye. Who knew when she'd have another chance to talk to him? She needed to find out more about him so she could figure out why they were connected. "So, do you design buildings or homes?"

"I've been concentrating on commercial projects the last few years, mostly in Los Angeles. There's not a lot of skyscraper work in Angel's Bay."

"I wouldn't think so."

She glanced around the room, noting a building model on the conference table. She moved closer to take a better look. "What's this?"

"It's a new city hall in Montgomery."

"The detail is amazing. I love the curve of the

windows and the majesty of the columns. You've merged the past with the future in this design. I'm impressed."

"Thank you," he said. "They break ground next week."

"You must love seeing your buildings come to life."

"It's a great feeling," he admitted. He gave her a close look. "Was there something else you wanted, Isabella?"

She liked the way her name rolled off his tongue, as if he were savoring every letter. There was something deliberate about him now, the way he spoke, the way he moved, the way he watched her. On the cliff last night, he'd been moving at the speed of light. "You risked your life coming after me."

"I probably should have stopped to consider the options. It was the first time in a long time that I didn't do that," he added, as if he were talking to himself. Then he shook whatever thought he'd had out of his head. "I'm afraid I have a meeting to get to, so . . ."

"I should get out of your hair." She wished she could share her visions with him, but past experience had taught her that wasn't a good idea. Instead, she asked, "Do you think we've met before?"

He looked curious. "Definitely not. If we had, I'd remember. Because you, Isabella, are not at all . . . forgettable." His gaze dropped to her mouth, and she swallowed hard.

A knock at the door made them both jump, then

Colleen stuck her head in. "Tory called, Nick, and I told her you were on your way. Was I wrong?" she asked, raising a quizzical eyebrow.

"No," he said abruptly. "I'm leaving." As Colleen stepped out, he said, "I'm sorry, Isabella. I have to go."

"Sure." She moved forward and extended her hand. "Thanks again, Nick."

He hesitated before putting his hand in hers. Just like the night before, she felt a rush of heat as his fingers curled around hers. And just like last night, he yanked his hand away before she was ready to let go.

He shook his head, a look of bemusement in his eyes. "There's something about you . . ."

"About us," she said, meeting his gaze. "I feel it, too."

He shook his head at her bold words. "You're a beautiful woman, Isabella, but I'm not looking to get involved with anyone. Another time, another place, maybe, but not now."

"Usually, people get to know me before they blow me off," she said lightly, wondering why she was absurdly disappointed by his words. It was probably a good thing. They'd shared an intense experience, and they needed to come down off that high.

"My life is complicated." He ran a hand through his hair. "I have a kid. I've neglected her for most of her life. She has to be my priority now."

Her heart skipped a beat. "You're married?"

"Divorced. A long time."

She wondered why he'd felt the need to add that.

Did he want her to know that he wasn't hung up on his ex-wife?

She wasn't in the habit of throwing herself at men who weren't interested, but Nick was clearly interested. She could see it in his eyes, hear it in his voice, feel it in his touch. He just didn't want to be attracted to her. And she didn't want to be attracted to him, either. She'd come to Angel's Bay to drive the visions out of her head and find some peace. Getting involved with the man in her dreams was not part of the plan. An emotional connection would only make things worse.

"Good-bye, Isabella," he said firmly.

She heard the finality in his voice, but she knew they weren't over—even if he didn't. "I'll see you around."

Nick blew out a relieved breath as Isabella left. Last night, he'd chalked up his reaction to her as too much adrenaline, but what was his excuse today? He hadn't been this unsettled by a woman in a long time. And he didn't like it. He didn't have time for a powerful distraction like Isabella.

But God, she was gorgeous, with her long, thick black hair, striking turquoise-blue eyes, clear tanned skin, and soft, full lips that seemed to smile so easily. When he'd touched her, the strangest feeling had run through his head, as if it was important for him to hold on to her—so important that he'd forced himself to let go.

Damn. He sucked in more air, because, for some reason, he was still having trouble breathing.

Colleen came back into the office. "So that was the woman you saved last night. She's really pretty. And don't even try to tell me you didn't notice, because I haven't see you this rattled since you asked Beth Haldeman to the prom."

This is what he got for hiring his cousin to work in his office. "I noticed. It doesn't mean I'm going to do anything about it."

"Why not? You're single. Maybe she is, too," Colleen said hopefully. Happily married to her high school sweetheart, Colleen had been trying to set him up for years.

"Stop trying to matchmake. I have my hands full with Megan. Besides, Isabella is just visiting."

"She's from L.A. Last I heard, you had an apartment there, too."

"Right now, my base is Angel's Bay. Megan needs the whole family, because at the moment, she wants nothing to do with me."

Colleen frowned. "Things aren't going better?"

"They're not going at all. We're sharing a house, and that's it. She barely speaks to me."

"You have to keep trying."

"I am, but I'm not getting anywhere."

"I don't want to add to your worries, Nick, but Cord told me Megan is hanging out with the skateboard crowd, and he's worried about her."

Since Colleen's oldest son, sixteen-year-old Cord, was a straight-A student and an all-around good kid, that wasn't the best of news. "I don't know what to do. I can't pick her friends, can I?"

"No, you can't," she said with an understanding look. "We'll talk later. Right now, Tory and the rest of the family are waiting for you."

"I should have my head examined for agreeing to talk about theater renovations with them."

"How could you not? They need your help."

Ironic, since his parents hadn't been available when he'd needed their help. But that was in the past, and his parents had short memories when it came to their own failings.

After saying good-bye to Colleen, he headed down the stairs and drove across town to the theater, his thoughts going back and forth between Isabella and Megan. It irritated him that Isabella was in his head at all. He'd spent half the night tossing and turning, trying to forget her image. When he'd pulled her from the car, she'd clung to him, pleading with him not to let her go. Of course, he hadn't then, but he needed to let her go now.

He needed to forget that jolt of attraction that had caught him by surprise a few minutes ago. He hadn't felt that gut clench in a long while. Maybe seeing death come so close had bonded them in some way. They'd shared a highly charged, emotional experience, but it was over.

He didn't do emotionally intense relationships anymore. After his disastrous marriage, he'd put his heart away and kept his relationships casual and short-term. He didn't need to change that now.

He also didn't need to get involved with his family's plans, he thought as he turned into the parking lot of the Angel's Bay Regional Theater. He'd managed to stay out of their business for a long time, but since he'd brought Megan back to the bay, they'd been after him to come up with plans for restoring the eighty-year-old theater to its former glory and bringing it up to new earthquake standards. While a part of him wouldn't have minded seeing the theater shut down for good, he knew he couldn't walk away from the work that generations of Hartleys had devoted their lives to without at least taking a look.

Victoria was sitting on the steps in front of the courtyard that led into the theater. Two years younger than he, Tory was a slender dynamo with short, light brown hair and green eyes. She always seemed to be handling a dozen things at once. She had more patience than he did, more tact, and more compassion. She was also usually the calmest person in a family of drama queens and kings, but judging by her worried expression, something had thrown her off her game.

"I'm not that late, am I?" he asked, stopping in front of her.

She shook her head as she looked up at him. "It's not you. Annie Dupont has disappeared. The teenager whose baby we were hoping to adopt," she reminded him.

"What are you talking about?" He sat down on the step next to her.

"No one has seen Annie since yesterday. I just

got off the phone with Joe Silveira. He wants to talk to Steve and me this evening. He's meeting with all of the prospective parents, hoping that Annie might have said something to one of us."

"Did she?"

"The only thing she told me was that she thought I'd make a great mother." Her voice caught on the last word, and she drew in a shaky breath, obviously barely hanging on to her composure.

Tory's struggles with fertility had been going on for more than seven years, and she'd only recently come to terms with the idea of adopting. "I'm sorry. I know your hopes were high," he said.

"You'd think I would have learned by now not to get my hopes up. It was a long shot. Annie was talking to other parents, but I still let myself imagine holding that baby in my arms." She shook her head. "What a fool I was."

"You said no one has seen Annie, but what about the baby?"

"She left him behind with Charlotte and her mother. It looks like the pressure of trying to decide what to do became too much for her, and she ran away. I don't know what will happen now. Maybe the chief will know more when we meet later." She paused. "All that aside, I'm worried about Annie. She's young, scared, and alone. I'm sure she's emotionally fragile, and I don't want her to hurt herself in any way."

"Is there any chance of that?"

"Well, Charlotte met Annie after she jumped

off the pier into the bay when she was a few months pregnant."

"So she's not very stable."

"She had a rough childhood. Her father is a war veteran and crazy, from what I understand. Her mother died a few years ago. But Annie has been thriving with Charlotte and her mother. I want her to come back, even if she chooses not to give her child away, because her baby needs a mother."

Nick put his arm around Tory's shoulders and gave her a hug. She had always had a soft heart. "I know how much you care about both of them. Maybe this is a temporary thing. Annie got scared and took off to clear her head. She'll come back and make the right decision."

"I hope you're right. But since when are you the optimist in the family?" she added dryly.

He smiled. "Don't get used to it."

She got to her feet. "We should go inside. Mom and Dad have been driving me crazy, asking when you're coming. They want to get you started on plans as soon as possible."

"I haven't agreed to anything yet," he reminded her as he stood up. "I said I'd take a look."

"Oh, please. Once you set foot in that building, there will be no turning back. Besides the fact that everyone in the family will hound you relentlessly, you'll get caught up in the excitement, in the magic—you know you will. Deep down inside, you're a Hartley, and theater blood runs in your veins."

He wanted to deny her words, but he couldn't quite do that. And as he looked at the tall building that held so many of his family's dreams, he couldn't help but be inspired by the architecture, a mixture of Spanish revival and colonial. Designed in the 1920s by a renowned California architect, the theater had been constructed with a sense of importance. For almost a hundred years, this building was where people came to escape the dull reality of their lives. Despite the somewhat isolated location on the central coast, the winter and summer productions were always well attended, drawing audiences from all over the country, the professional performances packing the house for each and every show.

As he followed his sister under the archway and through the courtyard, he imagined the scene on performance days—summer nights when the fountain statues would flow, and audience members would sit at small tables and sip cocktails during intermission. Without the benefit of the lights, tables, and people, the courtyard looked old and worn, much like the rest of the theater.

Stepping through the front doors, he noticed how the ornate lobby also showed signs of age, from the chipped paint in the wall murals to the cracks in the ceiling. The carpeting on the stairs leading up to the balcony was threadbare in places.

"There's a lot that needs to be done," Nick said. "And that's just what I can see on the surface."

"I know, but we have to find a way to make it happen."

"It will take an enormous amount of money. Mom and Dad need to be realistic."

"No one in this family is big on reality," she said with a smile. "You should know that by now."

He knew all too well. There had been a time when he'd chased his own dreams and been just as caught up in a world of illusion.

"Ready?" Tory asked, reaching for the door leading into the auditorium. "This might be your last chance to back out."

"I'm not committing to anything until I've done my research."

She shook her head. "I never thought you would grow up to be so restrained. You used to be a lot more spontaneous, Nick. Sometimes I barely recognize you."

Sometimes he barely recognized himself, but spontaneity had turned him into a father at the age of nineteen. These days, he looked before he leaped.

As he followed Tory into the auditorium, he realized it had been at least a decade since he'd been inside. He'd always managed to avoid the building on his visits to Angel's Bay.

The inside of the theater was just as ornate as the exterior. The side boxes on the mezzanine levels were beautifully carved and separated by thick velvet curtains and ropes. The ceiling high overhead had been painted with twinkling stars to make the audience feel as if they were watching an outdoor performance.

As he took in the details, a surprising sense of

anticipation ran down his spine. This theater was where he'd first fallen in love with designing and construction. His uncle Richard had taught him how to build sets as soon as he was old enough to pick up a hammer. He'd been amazed to see worlds created within days, and he'd been hooked.

Professionally speaking, this architectural project could be spectacular, but he had a lot of personal reservations. He kept his feet grounded in reality, and this old theater had a way of making people believe in the impossible, which usually led to a painful let-down.

Today there was a lot of action going on inside. Seats were being pulled out to be reupholstered, two men were putting up a frame along the back wall of the stage, and various members of his family were standing around a long table at the front of the stage As usual, they all seemed to be talking at one time. Where there were actors, there were egos, and demanding needs for attention.

He drew in a deep breath as he climbed the stairs. He loved his parents, his grandparents, his aunts, uncles, cousins . . . but they were all devoted to their theater world, and since his relationship with Kendra, he'd found it difficult to be a part of that.

His mother looked up and saw him, giving him a welcoming wave. Pamela Strathmore Hartley had met his father, Paul, during a production of *Phantom of the Opera* in New York. She'd played the ingenue, and his father had fallen in love with his mother's spectacular voice and beautiful face. Her hair was shorter now, with a dark red tint, but she still had a smile that could light up a stage. His father was a true leading man, with dark, handsome looks that always brought droves of women to the backstage door.

His grandfather, Harrison Hartley, was also on-stage. At six foot three, Harrison had an unmistakable presence and a deep, booming voice that carried to the last row of the theater. He'd played a lot of villains in his time, parlaying a sinister, menacing quality to his strong features into a successful career. His grandmother, Alice, was a foot shorter than her husband, and while the others had all been leading-role material, Alice was a character actress who always played the best friend or the sister or the nanny. She had a round face, pale blond hair, and a nervous manner. She could also cry on cue, her most marketable talent. His uncle Richard filled out the group, a boyishly charming man with a big personality and an even bigger smile.

"You're late, Nick," his grandfather barked as he made his way onto the stage.

"My fault, Grandpa," Tory interjected. "I stopped him on the way in."

Despite being younger, Tory always tried to protect him. She'd sensed early on that someone needed to be a bridge or a translator between him and the rest of the family.

"Are you ready to do some sketches for us, put together a plan?" his father asked.

"I can get you started, but I'm not sure how

involved I can be. I have some other projects going on and Megan to worry about. Frankly, you still need to figure out if you can even raise enough money to do the restoration."

"We've been working on some fundraising ideas," his mother cut in. "Seat sponsors, endowments, that kind of thing. We have to find a way, Nick, because if we can't bring the theater up to the new earthquake codes, then we'll have to shut down. That can't happen."

He couldn't imagine what his parents and grandparents would do without the theater. But that might be a reality they would have to face.

"Richard sketched out a few ideas for the renovation," his father continued. "We want to keep as much of the history as we can."

Nick stepped over to the table, taking a look at his uncle's rough drawings.

"They're not what you can do," Richard said. "But I wanted to give you a jump start."

"I can see where you're going."

"And we need you to help us get all the way there," Richard said with a smile. "I know it's a big job, but you're up to it, right? I was down in Morro Bay the other day. I saw the work you did for their library. You've come a long way from the days when you used to hammer your nails in sideways."

"I was always better with concept than execution," Nick admitted. His early construction days had helped him be a better architect. "Can I take these with me?"

"Absolutely."

"We really need your help, Nick," his mother added pleadingly. "I can't imagine anyone in this family surviving without this theater. It's our livelihood."

"There's always another theater, another town," he pointed out. He'd spent half his childhood on the road, trading one backstage playground for another as his parents took roles in other productions during the off season.

"We're getting too old to traipse around like we used to," Pamela said.

"We know you want to refuse this job," his father put in. "But we won't make that easy for you. You're good at what you do, and we need the best."

Nick felt an unexpected surge of pleasure at his father's proud words. He'd never really known what his parents thought of his career. Although . . . as he studied the earnest faces surrounding him, he couldn't help wondering if he wasn't being played. This cast of characters could persuade anyone to do anything.

"You also need the cheapest," he said pragmatically. "Let's be real."

His uncle grinned. "That's true. And speaking of reality, I've got to run down to the hardware store and pick up some supplies. Paul, are you coming?"

"Yes." Paul turned to Harrison. "Dad, do you have that list of supplies?"

"It's in the office," Harrison said. "I'll walk out with you."

"Nick, we'll talk soon," his father said.

"Sure." Nick rolled up the rough sketches as they left.

"We're really glad you're going to be in town for a while, Nick. We've missed you and Melanie," his grandmother, Alice, said, giving him her sweet smile. He loved her, but she'd been flighty and forgetful even before she could blame old age as an excuse. "It's Megan," he reminded her. "My daughter's name is Megan."

"What did I say?"

"Melanie."

"Oh, well, it's close," she replied as she wandered off.

"Is she all right?" he asked his mother.

Pamela shrugged. "It's difficult to say. She loves to act, even when we're not performing."

"Like the rest of you," he said dryly.

His mother rolled her eyes. "We're not that bad."

"You all live in dreamland. Renovating this theater is another example of your complete lack of reality."

"Or perhaps an example of our faith and commitment to keeping this place going. Angel's Bay needs this theater, and so does our family. Where there's a will, there's a way."

"Don't try to talk her out of it," Tory warned. "You'll only be wasting your breath."

"I want us to have a family dinner," his mother interjected. "We haven't sat down together, all of us, since Megan arrived. We'll do it this weekend."

He nodded, but he wouldn't be surprised it didn't happen, since she'd made the suggestion three times already without following through.

"Hello? Excuse me?"

Nick whirled around, shocked to see Isabella coming up the steps. What was she doing here?

"Can I help you?" Tory asked.

"I saw this flyer and thought I'd offer my services," Isabella said, holding out a yellow piece of paper. "I'm Isabella Silveira." She gave Nick a cautious look. "Hi. I didn't realize your meeting was here."

"You're Joe's sister," Tory said. "And that means . . ." Her gaze darted between Isabella and Nick. "You're the one Nick rescued last night."

"You're the woman?" his mother echoed, curiosity in her eyes. "I'm Pamela, Nick's mother."

"And I'm Tory, Nick's sister."

"It's nice to meet all of you," Isabella said. "Anyway, I'm a costume designer, and I normally work in L.A., but I'll be in town for a while, so I thought I'd see if you needed any help with costumes. I'd be happy to volunteer to do whatever."

Great, Nick thought with a sigh. Not only was Isabella spectacularly pretty, with a body that a man would happily die for and a touch that had made him feel as if he was going to spontaneously combust, she was also a theater person. No wonder alarm bells had gone off in his brain.

"We can always use help with the costumes," Tory said, "especially experienced help."

"Particularly this year," his mother added. "Our designer, Mariah Olin, has been having health problems, and I didn't know what we were going to do. We have some ladies who can sew but no designers—no one to help us create a new look to go with the new production. You're like an angel sent from costume heaven." She smiled at Nick. "And you were the one to save her. How perfect is that?"

"Just perfect," he drawled. "I need to get back to my office."

"I'm sorry if I interrupted," Isabella said quickly.

"You didn't at all," Tory said, waving off her apology. "I'll take you down to the costume shop, so you can see what you're getting into. We're still trying to figure out what costumes we can reuse and what we need to create."

As they turned to leave, they ran into his grandfather. Harrison stopped abruptly, his gaze catching on Isabella. His face paled, and he drew in a quick breath as he put a hand to his chest.

"Grandpa, are you all right?" Tory asked.

He made it up the last two steps, his gaze still fixed on Isabella. "Your eyes," he murmured, and shook his head in disbelief. "It can't be you. It's not possible."

As his grandfather began to sway, Nick rushed to his side. His sister grabbed a nearby chair, and they helped him into it.

"Should I call nine-one-one?" Tory asked with concern.

"No. I'm okay," Harrison said quickly, putting

up a hand as Tory reached for her cell phone. "I just need—water."

"I'll get some," Nick's mother said, running down the stairs.

"Is it your heart?" Tory asked, putting a hand on his shoulder.

"I'm fine," Harrison said, his voice stronger now. He patted her hand. "It's all right. I didn't mean to scare you. I just need to sit for a minute. I didn't eat anything today." His gaze darted back to Isabella.

Nick glanced at Isabella, who returned his look with a silent question that he had no idea how to answer. It was obvious that his grandfather was unsettled by her appearance. "Why don't you take Isabella to the costume shop?" he suggested to Tory. "I'll stay with Grandpa until Mom gets back with the water."

"All right," Tory said, still a bit hesitant. "Grandpa?"

"It's okay. Go." He waved her off.

As Tory led Isabella down the steps, Nick pulled up another chair and sat down across from his grandfather.

His grandfather gave him a scowl. "I'm fine. I don't need a damn babysitter."

"Well, I need an explanation. What happened? You looked at Isabella as if she were a ghost. I thought you were going to pass out."

"She reminded me of someone for a second, that's all. What did you say her name was?"

"Isabella Silveira. Her brother is the chief of police. Is that who she reminded you of?"

"I don't think she should work on the production," Harrison said abruptly, a faraway look in his eyes.

"Why do you say that?"

"You need to get rid of her, Nick. She's not for you."

A shiver ran down his spine at his grandfather's words. "I never thought she *was* for me."

His grandfather's gaze met his. "She'll take you in, and she won't let go. She'll cast a spell over you. And all your plans, your goals, will get pushed aside. You need to make her go away before it's too late."

Harrison Hartley was the king of drama, but there was a fear in his words that Nick had never heard before.

"Find a way," his grandfather added as he stood up.

"If you want her gone, then *you* need to do something," Nick replied. "I don't have any say over what goes on in the theater. If Isabella wants to work on the costumes, I can't stop her."

"She didn't come here to make costumes. She came here for you."

"We barely know each other." But as he finished speaking, he flashed back to when Isabella had looked into his eyes and said, "It's you," as if she'd recognized him, as if she'd known all along that he would be the one to save her.

Was she crazy? Was he? Or was he letting his grandfather's imagination fuel his own?

His cell phone rang, and the name of the high school appeared on the screen. *Damn.* This could not be good. "I've got to go, Grandpa."

He punched in the school's number as he jogged out of the theater.

FIVE

Isabella didn't know why she was surprised to see Nick in the theater. Ever since she'd started on this trip, she'd felt as if she were dancing to someone else's tune. She'd been meant to have that accident and meet him, meant to find the flyer, meant to go to the theater. She didn't know why, but she would eventually. When it came to her visions, trying to rush to a conclusion never worked. She wouldn't know until it was time to know.

"I hope your grandfather is all right," she told Tory as they walked down the stairs and into an adjacent building housing props and costumes. The older man's reaction to her had been unsettling. He'd looked at her as if she were someone else, as if he knew her.

"I hope so, too. He has such a strong voice, I sometimes forget that he's eighty-three years old." Tory paused, giving her a thoughtful look. "I probably should have asked you if you wanted to do this now. You must still be feeling the aftereffects of your accident."

"I'm a little sore, but I'm okay. And I'd love to see the costume shop."

"Here it is." Tori pushed open the door and waved Isabella inside.

As soon she stepped through the doors, Isabella felt a rush of excitement. She stopped to drink in the atmosphere, the racks of clothes and shoes, bolts of material, shelves laden with hats, buttons, belt buckles, zippers, and other accessories that would be used to transform ordinary people into extraordinary characters. A trio of sewing machines lined one wall. Large work tables were in the center of the room, surrounded by empty dress forms. This was her world, and she loved it.

"We've accumulated quite a bit over the years," Tory said. "For this particular production, we'll need both alterations and new pieces. We open just four weeks from this Friday, and saying that makes my heart race! It always feels like a rush, but somehow we get it done."

"I'm happy to help. It's been a long time since I've worked on a stage production, and it will be a nice change." Isabella paused. "I'm not sure your brother is too excited about me working here, though. I went to his office earlier to say thanks for saving my life, and I got the impression he barely wanted to talk with me."

Tory gave a dismissive wave. "That's just Nick. He keeps most people at arm's length these days; I wouldn't take it personally. He's a little distracted right now with his teenage daughter, Megan. She is trouble with a capital T."

"Most teenagers are."

"True, but Megan is carrying around a lot of extra emotional baggage. Her mother took her away from Nick when she was three years old. She's only recently come back." Tory took a breath and smiled. "And Nick would kill me for gossiping. Anyway, I hope they can find a way to make things work. They both really need each other, even if they don't know how to admit it. Nick's ex-wife is Kendra Livingston—maybe you've heard of her."

"Oh, wow," Isabella murmured. Kendra Livingston was an accomplished stage and film actress and had won several awards for her work. She was also gorgeous, a leggy Marilyn Monroe look-alike.

"Wow is right. She's a piece of work. Anyway." Tory paused, glancing around the room. "I know Mariah left a list of things that need to get done first. Let me see if I can find it, to give you an idea of what we're working on."

While Tory searched for the work list, Isabella wandered around the room. One wall was lined with photographs of actors and actresses from various productions over the years. A lot of famous people had played in this theater. It would be a shame if they couldn't find a way to keep it going.

"We actually did this play once before," Tory said as she riffled through the papers on a nearby counter. "The run ended early because of a fire. We lost almost all of the costumes, except those few over there." She tipped her head toward a sparsely filled rack of costumes near the door.

Isabella moved closer to take a look. As her fingers curled around the material of one dress, her nerves began to tingle, and a wave of heat ran through her. Tory's voice faded away.

A woman called for help as the flames drew closer and the smoke grew thicker. She could feel the heat, a burning sensation in her chest, terror pounding through her veins.

"Isabella?"

Tory's voice brought her back to the present.

She let go of the dress and drew in a deep breath, trying to calm her jangled nerves.

"Everything okay?" Tory queried as she walked over with a sketchbook in her hands.

Isabella tucked her hair behind one ear, needing some movement to expel the sudden rush of adrenaline. "I guess I'm more tired than I thought."

"Well, you can come back tomorrow or even the next day. You should probably be home resting."

"Did anyone die in the fire?" she asked, still feeling shaken by the brief vision, the emotional connection to someone in the past. She'd never had a costume trigger a flashback or a vision. The clothes were part of a pretend world, worn by characters, not by real people, and they'd never had any effect on her before. So why now?

Tory gave her an odd look. "Yes, my grandfather's sister, Caitlyn, died in the fire. She was sixteen.

My grandparents don't like to talk about it. Some people think putting on this revival is a big mistake, that the show is cursed, because it was the one and only production that never finished its run. But theater people tend to be superstitious. I hope that doesn't scare you off."

A chill ran through Isabella's body, in direct contrast to the heat she'd felt moments before. "Not at all," she said. But she had a feeling that the fire was another clue to deciphering her dreams.

Nick strode through the door of Angel's Bay High School, feeling a mix of emotions. He'd been a terrible student himself, more interested in music and girls than in academics. His parents had moved around so much that he'd always felt behind whenever he was actually in school, so he'd skipped class as often as possible.

He'd also spent quite a bit of time in the principal's office back in the day. Apparently, his daughter was following in his footsteps.

Megan sat in a straight-backed chair in the outer office. Next to her, a boy slouched in his seat, his hair down to his shoulders, an earring in one ear, and a cocky smile on his face. Megan didn't look nearly as confident as her friend—at least, not until she saw Nick. Then she stiffened and put on her usual I-don't-give-a-fuck-what-you-think-of-me expression.

"Are you all right?" he asked.

"I'm awesome," she said sarcastically, a slight

British lilt to her words. She'd lived all over the world with her mother, and he wasn't really sure where she considered home to be—except not with him.

"Who's your pal?"

"No one."

Nick glanced at the kid, who didn't seem at all concerned about his fate. Yeah, he knew this attitude. He'd shown it off a few times himself in this very office.

"Mr. Hartley?" The secretary motioned him toward the principal's office. "You can go in."

When Nick took the seat in front of his desk, Mr. Donohue gave him the usual grim expression of a school official about to deliver bad news.

"Megan was caught with alcohol on school grounds," he said, getting right to the point. "That's an automatic two-day suspension. She'll also need to undergo an online alcohol education class." He pulled out a piece of paper and handed it to Nick. "Here's the information."

"Megan is new here," Nick said, pleading his daughter's case. "She's struggling to find her place, to make friends. Obviously, she made a bad choice, but can't you give her a warning?"

"No, I can't."

"Were there other students involved?" Nick asked. "Are you sure Megan was the one drinking?"

"She was with two boys, J. R. Reming and Will Harlan, not the best influences for your daughter. They were caught in the woods on the outskirts of campus during lunch with two bottles of beer. It's possible that she didn't actually drink, but we have no way of determining that, and everyone receives the same punishment. It's school policy."

"When can she come back?"

"Monday. In the meantime, I hope you can talk to her about the choices she's making."

"Of course," Nick said, but he had a feeling that the conversation wouldn't go much better than any of the others they'd had. "She's had a rough transition, but she's a good kid. Don't let the purple in her hair fool you."

"I've been a public school principal for twenty years, Mr. Hartley, and I've seen all kinds of hair colors. I have no doubt that your daughter is trying to find her way in a new school, but she has to follow the rules. I can't make exceptions. I've notified her teachers, and they'll put together some schoolwork for her to do at home. You'll be sent an e-mail with the information later today, and a copy will go to Megan. Any questions?"

"No," Nick said, seeing the steel in the principal's eyes. There was no battle he could fight here, but Megan was another matter.

He left the office, gave a brisk nod and said, "Let's go."

Megan got up, throwing her backpack over one shoulder and giving the boy a quick look. Nick didn't have a good feeling about whatever passed between them.

She didn't speak on the way home, and Nick was

still trying to figure out how best to talk to her when they walked into the house.

Megan dropped her backpack onto the kitchen table, then opened the refrigerator door, giving the contents a long stare before shutting it again.

"Are you hungry?" he asked.

She shook her head.

"Are you drunk?"

A spark flashed in her eyes, and her lips tightened, but she just gave him another shake of her head.

"Come on, Megan. Tell me what happened. Were you drinking?"

"No, I was just talking to Will."

"He was the one who was drinking?"

"What do you care?" She walked out of the kitchen, down the hall, and into her bedroom, slamming the door behind her.

He hesitated for a moment, then walked down the hall and knocked on her door. He gave her a minute, knocked again, and said, "I'm coming in." When he entered the room, she was sitting in the middle of her bed, a defiant expression on her face. "It's not going down like this, Megan. I've let you walk away from me too many times. We're talking now."

"You let me go twelve years ago. It's a little late to be interested in my life."

He met her challenging gaze, knowing she could see his guilt in his eyes, which only made her feel as if she was justified in her attitude.

Sitting on the corner of her bed, he said, "If you want to start at the beginning, that's what we'll do."

Megan's eyes widened in surprise, but she quickly covered up her reaction with a shrug. "Whatever."

Nick drew in a breath. Would Megan judge him even more harshly when she'd heard the whole story? Or had she already heard it? He had no idea what her mother had told her about their separation and, later, their divorce, but he couldn't keep sidestepping the subject.

"I was eighteen when you were born, three years older than you are right now. When your mom got pregnant, I married her. I thought we'd stay together."

"Yeah, right," she muttered, chipping at the purple polish on her fingernails.

"I moved with Kendra to New York, because she wanted to work on the stage. We lived in a studio apartment that wasn't much bigger than a closet, and you slept in a dresser drawer for the first six months of your life. But we were a family. I don't know if you remember anything from those years—"

"I don't," she said quickly, cutting him off.

"You and I were close." A knot grew in his throat. While Kendra was at the theater, he'd been the one to rock Megan to sleep, to give her her bottle, to read her bedtime stories, to hold her when she cried. Those days seemed like a million years ago. How could he expect Megan to remember them?

"We used to go to the zoo together," he continued. "You loved the giraffes and the monkeys, but you thought the elephants smelled bad." Megan wasn't looking at him, but she appeared to be listening. "One day, I came home from work to find your mom packing. She had an offer to play on the London stage. I asked her not to go, but she said it was her career and too big of an opportunity to pass up. It was only going to be a few months. What was a couple of months in a lifetime, she asked me.

"I didn't have enough money to buy a plane ticket to London. I was working two part-time jobs that barely paid anything. Even if I could have gotten myself there, I didn't have any way of bringing in money or supporting you. So I told her I'd be waiting for you both when the play was over.

But the run didn't end. It went on and on. And then there was another play, another opportunity. Your mom kept telling me next spring, next summer, next Christmas. I never imagined that she wouldn't come back at all. That she'd meet someone else, divorce me, remarry, get divorced again . . ."

"You should have come to get me," Megan said, raising her gaze to his. The pain in her eyes made his heart hurt. For the first time, she didn't look like a rebellious teenager but like a sad little girl—*his* little girl.

His heart ached with longing for what he'd lost so long ago.

"Why didn't you come?" she demanded, her lips trembling. "How could you just let me go?"

"I did come, Megan, but it took me a couple of years to get my act together. I went to college, working on the side, saving my money so I'd have something to offer you and your mother. But it was three years before I saw you again."

"No." She gave an emphatic shake of her head. "You didn't come at all. You didn't see me."

"I did. You were six by then, almost seven. And you were happy. I went to your school. I saw you run into the arms of your mother's fiancé. You smiled up at him the way you used to smile at me. And then your mom got out of the car, and the three of you were together—a family."

"Why didn't you talk to me?"

"I came by the house later. Your mother confirmed what I already knew—that I was too late. You were happy, and I couldn't disrupt your life. She convinced me that a custody battle wouldn't be good for anyone, and I couldn't compete with the lifestyle she had to offer. But more important, Kendra said that seeing you would only confuse you. That if I truly wanted to be a good father, I should let you be."

"That's so fucked up!" Megan's eyes blazed with anger. "You want me to believe you're some kind of hero now? That you let me have this great life from nobility? That's bullshit."

"That's *not* what I'm saying. I made a huge mistake, Megan. I should have stayed and fought for you."

"But you didn't. You saw a way out, and you took it. You never wanted me. I was an accident—admit it."

"You were unplanned, but I wanted you from

the first second I saw your heart beating on the ultrasound," he said forcefully, needing her to believe him. "If I could go back and change things, I would. But I can't. All I can do is move forward. And you're here now."

"Not because you want me to be." She hugged a pillow tightly, her eyes defiant and still hurt. "It's only because Mom dumped me on you."

He couldn't deny that's exactly what Kendra had done. That would only be insulting, Megan was a smart kid. She needed the truth from him.

"What about all the other years?" Megan demanded. "You came one time, and that's it?"

"I sent you letters, presents for your birthday and Christmas. I gave your mom money toward your support. I didn't know what else to do. I really thought it was too late, Megan." He paused. "You never wrote me back, other than a few polite little cards, thank you for the present. That was it."

"Why would I say anything else?" she challenged. "A lot of strangers gave me things. It was no big deal."

The stranger crack hurt, as she'd intended. He'd never loved anyone as much as he'd loved Megan. He hadn't shown her that, but he had a second chance now.

"Being together is a big change for both of us," he said. "But we have a wonderful chance to get to know each other again. What do you say—will you give it a try?"

"Do I have a choice?"

"If you meet me halfway, it might make things easier."

"If I say yes, will you take me out driving?"

He smiled at the determined glint in her eyes. She wasn't giving in without a negotiation. The first thing she'd done upon arriving in California was to get her learner's permit, and he was excited to teach her how to drive. It would be one of the few father-daughter milestones that he hadn't already missed.

"Fine, but you have to promise to drive on the right side of the road," he teased.

She made a face at him. "Very funny. Can we go now?"

He had work to do, calls to return, plans to draw up, but the expectant look on Megan's face shifted his priorities. She'd been waiting years for his attention. "All right. Did you have lunch?"

"Not really."

"Then I guess you'll have to drive us to Rusty's so we can get some pizza." He took the keys out of his pocket and dangled them in front of her.

She grabbed them with an eagerness that was completely out of character and scrambled off the bed. "Let's go."

He followed her out to the car. It felt very odd to get into the passenger seat and see his daughter buckling up behind the wheel. She adjusted the mirror, then turned the key in the ignition.

"Okay," he said. "Let's go over a few things. You're going to put it in reverse and back out very, very slowly."

She rolled her eyes. "I've driven before."

"I didn't know that. When?"

"Outside London. Mom's boyfriend took me one day. He was trying to impress Mom. He didn't really care about me."

Nick hated how cynical she was, but he was partly to blame, so he said nothing.

Megan backed out of the driveway and they weaved down the street, making a head-jerking stop at the street sign. Nick was about to say something, but when he saw the smile on her face, he just told her to take a right and prayed they'd make it to Rusty's in one piece.

"So who are these boys you were with at lunch?" Nick asked, over sodas and pizza. He hoped Megan's good mood would make her more talkative.

"J.R. and Will," she said shortly, taking a big bite of pizza. "They're cool."

"They drink, though, right?"

"Everyone drinks in high school," she said with a roll of her eyes.

"Do you?"

She shrugged. "I have, and I would again if I wanted to."

"What if I said I didn't want you to?"

She looked him straight in the eye. "I could lie, and you'd never know what I was really doing. Mom didn't. Not that she cared."

Nick considered her words. "You didn't get along well with your mother?"

"She wasn't around much. I spent more time with the nannies than with her. I don't know why she even took me with her—I guess I was a good photo op for a while. She used to make me wear the most hideous dresses and do up my hair in curls whenever reporters came to the house. I was like her pet dog."

"I had no idea. Kendra was a good mother when we were together. She was a little self-absorbed, but I know she loved you and wanted you with her. Maybe she got caught up in her career, but you're still important to her, Megan."

"Why are you defending her? You don't know her any better than you know me," Megan told him with a wisdom beyond her years. "She's a really good actress."

He nodded. "I know what it's like to grow up with parents who can act. Sometimes it was difficult to tell when they were being real or playing a part. I remember hearing them fight once, and they actually fell into a scripted argument from a play they'd been in years earlier. It was almost funny. I don't even know if they realized how blurry the lines were between their work and their reality."

"Did you act, too?"

"I did when I was young and forced to do so, but I was always more interested in music. I played whatever I could get my hands on—the guitar, the piano, the saxophone. I used to live in the orchestra pit while my parents were onstage. That was my favorite place to be."

For the first time, his daughter actually looked interested. "Were you any good as a musician?"

"I used to be in a band. I thought for a while I might be a rock star, but that career path didn't quite work out," he said with a smile.

She didn't smile back. "Because of me. Because you got Mom pregnant," she said flatly.

"Because of a lot of things. You weren't to blame for my not making it in the music business."

She rested her arms on the table. "So what are you going to do if Mom decides that she wants me back? It's not like her marriages last very long."

"Whatever decisions need to be made from here on out, I think we should make them together, don't you?"

"No one has ever asked me what I wanted."

"Well, that's going to change. But Megan, there still have to be some rules, and drinking and getting suspended from school, that's not okay. You don't have to do that kind of thing to get my attention. You already have it."

"Who said it was your attention I wanted?" she countered.

"Do you like one of those boys?" The idea terrified him.

She shrugged. "Maybe. But you don't have to worry."

"Why not?"

"Because I'm not stupid. The last thing I would ever do is get knocked up like my mother did."

Nick hoped she was as smart as she thought she was. He remembered the days when being young, reckless, and stupid seemed to go very well together.

"While you're on suspension," he said, "you'll need to help out at the theater. I have to go back to Montgomery for a few hours tomorrow."

"I can stay home alone."

"I know, but the theater is a family business, and you're part of the family. They could use your help."

"You don't help there."

"I'm actually working on some plans to renovate the theater."

"I thought you hated the place."

"Who told you that?"

"Cord," she said, referring to her cousin. "He said you only came back to Angel's Bay because of me. That you don't get along with anyone in the family."

"That's not true. I have some issues with my parents, but I love them. They're not perfect, but neither am I." He gave her a smile. "And believe it or not, neither are you."

Megan shrugged and reached for another piece of pizza. "Whatever."

When Isabella returned home from the theater, she unloaded the clothes and groceries she'd bought, took Rufus for a short walk around the block, then decided to explore Joe's house. He'd said he'd found her necklace in a box in the basement, so that's where she'd start.

The small basement was crowded with boxes, an old steamer trunk, and a water heater. She opened the trunk first, surprised to find layers and layers of material. She pulled out the fabric, amazed by the bright colors and the silky textures, although some of them had faded with age. Why on earth would her bachelor uncle have kept a trunk filled with fabric? She sat cross-legged on the floor as she dug a little deeper.

She pulled out a dress of deep blue silk that had tiny silver sequins sewn along the plunging neckline. As her hands absorbed the texture of the fabric, Isabella felt herself slipping away.

She worked the tiny needle in and out of the material, her fingers aching from the painstaking detail. She didn't want to sew this dress for the woman he would marry. But it was her job, not her choice. It wasn't fair. It wasn't right.

It also wasn't right for her to want him when he belonged to another woman. Even if he'd been free, he was not for her. She was Hispanic and poor. He was white and rich. They lived in different worlds. He breathed life onto the stage; he was a star. She worked behind the scenes, in the small, stuffy room filled with costumes.

But she loved him.

And he loved her.

He hadn't said it, but she'd felt it when he'd held her by the falls, when he'd kissed her, when he'd forgotten for just a minute that they could never be together.

The door slammed overhead, jolting Isabella back to reality. She dropped the dress back into the trunk, her heart racing, her palms sweaty. She didn't know the woman she was connecting to, but she felt very close to her, as if she were in her head, in her soul. It was the same way she'd felt at the theater. This woman who had worked in the costume shop was trying to tell her something. Why? What did the past have to do with the present?

As Joe appeared at the top of the stairs, she got to her feet, wiping the dust off the seat of her jeans.

"There you are," he said, giving her a curious look. "What are you doing?"

"Just looking around," she said, moving up the stairs. "I was curious about the pendant you sent me. Uncle Carlos wasn't married, so I wonder who it belonged to."

"Maybe a girlfriend," he suggested. "Or a relative. I'm sure that over the years, someone from his side of the family came to visit."

"Probably," she agreed, deciding to leave it at that. While Joe was the least judgmental of her siblings when it came to her special gifts, he was still a pragmatic cop.

"I picked up some Chinese food earlier," she said. "Are you hungry?"

"I could eat. So what did you do today?" he asked as they headed into the kitchen.

"I did a little shopping."

"Of course," he said with a smile.

"Hey, my clothes are in the ocean."

"That's the first time I've heard one of my sisters make that excuse," he teased.

She made a face at him, then pulled plates out of the cupboard and set them on the counter. "I ran into a very friendly woman named Kara. She said her husband is a cop, and she wants me to get you to come to dinner one night. Apparently, you're a hard man to say thank you to."

Joe shrugged. "Kara has nothing to thank me for," he said as he spooned rice and vegetables onto a plate.

"That's not what she says."

"Her husband got shot in the line of duty. We all did what we could for her and Colin." He opened the refrigerator. "What do you want to drink?"

"I'm just going to have water," she replied as she fixed a plate for herself, then followed him out to the dining table. "Kara told me the local theater is look-ing for backstage volunteers. I thought it would be fun, so I went by the theater and offered to help with the costumes."

"And here I thought you might spend the day resting."

"I'm not one for sitting around."

"No, you're not. You've always had an amazing amount of energy, and you make friends faster than anyone I know." He gave her a smile. "While I've grown used to living alone, it's kind of nice to have you in the house."

"Rufus isn't much of a conversationalist, huh?"

she asked with a grin as Joe slipped a piece of beef under the table to the dog, who had his head on Joe's knee.

Joe laughed. "He's a good listener, though. He doesn't talk back to me or tell me I'm wrong."

"Man's best friend."

His smile broadened. "Exactly. So you're going to work at the theater. The Hartleys are an interesting family, lots of colorful characters."

"It seems that way. I wonder if Uncle Carlos had anything to do with the theater," she mused.

"Why would you wonder that?"

"Because there's a trunk filled with fabric, dresses, and jewelry in the basement."

"Maybe he was a cross-dresser," he joked.

"Do you know how Uncle Carlos came to Angel's Bay in the first place? Were there other family members here? Did he inherit the house from someone?"

"I've been told that there was a Silveira on a ship that went down in the 1850s," Joe said. "Fiona Murray keeps trying to tell me the story, but I've managed to avoid hearing it."

"Why? Don't you want to know about our ancestors?"

"Not particularly."

"Really? I love history and bloodlines and all that." How could she not, when the visions in her head showed how connected the past and the present really were?

"Then you should talk to Fiona. She runs the quilt shop. I think we might even have a square on the old quilt they keep remaking."

"I will definitely talk to her," Isabella said, excited at the prospect. She touched her fingers to the pendant, which was warm against her skin. She felt sure the necklace was part of her family history, too. It had called her back to Angel's Bay for a reason. She just had to figure out what it was.

SIX

The next morning, Isabella woke up after a surprisingly dreamless sleep, threw on running gear, put Rufus in the truck, and drove to a trail Joe had told her about. The path wound through the hills, which was perfect, since the nightmarish accident had made her want to avoid the sea. They'd found her car crushed and filled with seawater at the bottom of a cliff, with no sign of her suitcase or her purse— probably washed away by the tide. She'd had no interest in seeing her car and being reminded of how narrowly she'd escaped death.

She started up the trail at a brisk walk to warm up her muscles. While her bruises and strains were fading, they weren't completely gone. The morning air was cold, with a foggy mist trying to burn its way off, but the scenery was gorgeous, the trail winding under thick canopies of redwood trees, opening up now and then to a spectacular vista.

She passed a few people along the way, each one offering her a friendly greeting. Angel's Bay was nothing like L.A., where people either averted their eyes or were too busy texting or talking on their cell phones to say hello to a stranger.

It took almost a half hour to reach the summit, offering a spectacular view of the ocean and the harbor, the downtown area, central square, and the bluffs that ran along the coastline. She took a sip from her water bottle as Rufus flopped on the ground, happy to take a break. It had been an uphill climb the last mile, but it had felt good to exercise, and she'd always been a big fan of mornings, when reality chased away the dreams.

The sound of footsteps drew her head around as another runner came up the hill at a brisk pace. The man wore a navy-blue windbreaker over dark sweats, and she knew it was Nick Hartley even before he looked up. A little tingle ran down her spine.

As he drew closer, she could hear his ragged breathing; he'd pushed the hill harder than she had. His hair was damp from the mist, his cheeks red, his eyes bright and a little wary as they met hers.

"We meet again," she said.

"Yes, we do. You must be feeling back to normal, since you made it up the hill."

"I took it slower than I normally would." She swept her hand toward the horizon. "The view was worth the effort."

"It's not bad." He bent down to give Rufus a

scratch as the dog started to sniff him. "How you doing, buddy? Does this guy belong to you or your brother?"

"To Joe. His name is Rufus. He actually belonged to my uncle Carlos, but Joe inherited him along with the house." She gave Nick a thoughtful look. "Did you know my uncle?"

Nick straightened, giving a nod. "I knew him, but not well. One of my buddies, Shane Murray, used to go fishing with him when we were in high school."

"Did he participate in any of the theater productions?"

"I don't know. Why?"

"I'm trying to find out more about him. Joe said that our family tree might go back to the shipwreck, and I'm intrigued," she said with a smile.

"Well, I'm sure you'll find plenty of people in town who will be happy to answer your questions. Shipwreck descendants usually find themselves to be popular, especially with the older generation intent on keeping the legends alive."

"Does your family go back that far?"

"No. My great-grandparents came to Angel's Bay and built the theater in the nineteen-twenties."

"If your great-grandparents built the theater, I can see why your family wants you to do the renovation. Tory told me about their plans," she added.

"Yes, they do want me involved but the theater is probably the last building in the world I'd want to save. It offers up a world of illusion, of make-believe, an homage to pretense. People get lost in that world. They forget it isn't real."

She gave him a curious look. "Is that what happened to you, Nick? Did you get lost?"

He started, as if he suddenly realized how much he'd revealed. After a moment's hesitation, he said, "Yes. I got swept away by the magic of a summer production fling, and I married an actress who didn't show me who she really was until it was too late. I should have known better: I'd spent my entire life surrounded by actors, and they were all damn good at playing parts."

"I'm sorry."

He shrugged. "It was over a long time ago, but being around the theater reminds me of that time in my life."

"Will you turn down the job?"

"I'd like to," he said with a sigh. "But I can't picture my family without the theater. They're too old to be gypsies. My grandparents are in their eighties. My dad has had some health issues. They need to stay in one place and have that theater functioning for the next decade, at least. But whether or not I'm willing to handle the design issue, they're going to need to raise a lot of money for the renovation. And dealing with reality has never been their strong suit."

"But it is yours."

"It is now. So you've signed on to work backstage?"

"Yes, it sounds like fun." She cleared her throat,

his intense gaze sending a flutter through her stomach. "I've been working in film, and this will be a nice change of pace."

"My grandfather told me to watch out for you," Nick said.

"Why?" she asked in surprise.

"I have no idea, but you certainly rattled him." He tilted his head as he studied her face. "You have incredible eyes—not quite the blue of the sea or the sky. I can't figure it out. It's an unusual color."

"According to my grandmother, only a few women in our family have had this eye color." She hesitated a moment. "Legend says that all of them are blessed with the gift of insight, passed down by a Mayan priestess."

He raised an eyebrow. "Really? That's quite a story."

"According to my sisters, that's all it is—a lovely story created to make me feel special. And being the youngest of five kids who all excelled at whatever they were doing, it was nice to have some reason to stand out."

"I can't imagine that you didn't always stand out." His gaze clung to hers, and she felt a tension building between them. "You're beautiful, Isabella."

Her heart caught in her throat.

"I should go," he said, but he didn't make any effort to move. "This is not . . ." His voice drifted away.

"How you want to feel," she finished, meeting his gaze head on. "You're attracted to me, and you're not happy about it."

He sucked in a quick breath. "You cut right to the chase, don't you?"

She had no choice. She needed to get close enough to Nick to find out why she was dreaming about him. "I feel the same pull to you."

He cleared his throat, his eyes darkening. "Look, Isabella, I'd have to be dead not to be attracted to you, but that doesn't mean I'm going to do anything about it."

"Then maybe I will," she said impulsively.

She stepped forward, put her hands on his shoulders, and kissed him. The coolness of his lips turned to heat the second they touched. She lingered there for a moment, then pulled away, not wanting to push her luck.

Nick's gaze burned with an intensity that shocked her. Then his hands were on her hips, and his mouth was coming down on hers. The quick kiss she'd stolen turned into a full-blown, tongue-tangling, heart-stopping, breath-stealing inferno.

Nick couldn't seem to get enough of her, pulling her against his hard groin, her body pressed against his from head to toes. She couldn't think, couldn't breathe; she could only feel. It was too much, yet it wasn't nearly enough. She slipped her hands under his shirt, feeling the sleek, sweaty heat of his abs. He was a strong, physical man, and her body wanted to get a whole lot closer.

Nick groaned into her mouth, his hungry hands running through her hair, down her back, cupping her ass.

Rufus's barking finally broke the spell. The dog barreled past her, the leash whipping her legs as he took off into the woods.

Isabella pulled away from Nick in shock. She had no idea what had set Rufus off. She couldn't believe the old dog was even moving that fast.

Dazed, she glanced up at Nick. "I—I have to get him." She took off after Rufus, trying to catch up with him before he got too deep into the woods.

Off the trail, the brush was thick, the tall trees throwing shadows in her path. When she came through a thicket, she stopped abruptly, shocked to see a beautiful waterfall that splashed into a large pool of clear, sparkling water.

Rufus was on the other side of that pool, barking at something in a tree. She knew she should grab his leash before he took off again, but the waterfall was mesmerizing.

She had the odd feeling that she'd been here before. As she stared at the falls, her body began to tingle the way it did when she touched something that triggered a vision. She wasn't touching anything now, but she felt as if someone was touching her.

He pulled her into his arms with rough, needy hands. "You're late," he said, a hint of desperation in his voice. "I thought you weren't coming."

"Alice wanted more alterations. She suspects something."

"No, she doesn't."

"Even so, I shouldn't have come. This is wrong. In my dreams I see disaster coming. There is nothing but pain."

"You have such an imagination," he said with a conciliatory smile.

"Sometimes they come true." She wanted to make him believe her, but it was beyond him. He was too logical, and she didn't want to drive him away or waste the little time they had arguing. Still, the worry gnawed at her. "I'm concerned about your sister. Caitlyn is getting into trouble with that boy—"

He put a finger over her mouth. "Shh. I don't want to talk about my sister or anyone else." He gazed into her eyes. "We might not have forever, but we have right now."

She wanted more than just now, but she loved him too much to ask for what he couldn't give. "Yes. Right now," she whispered as he pulled her into the dark alcove behind the falls.

"Isabella?"

Nick's voice snapped her out of her reverie. He gave her a questioning look, then moved across the clearing to grab Rufus's leash. The dog was pawing at the trunk of a large tree, barking at the cat just out of reach.

She walked over to join them. Joe had warned her that Rufus loved to chase cats, but she hadn't expected to come across any in the woods. The cat leaped onto another branch and then sped away. Rufus barked in dismay and sank to the ground as the cat disappeared.

"Thanks," she said, taking the leash from Nick's hands. "I didn't know Rufus could move that fast."

"Apparently, he can when he wants something. Kind of like you."

She wasn't sure what to say, so she changed the subject. "I had no idea there was a beautiful waterfall just off the trail."

"That's why they call it Hidden Falls. We used to come up here in high school. It was a good place to drink, make out, and tell ghost stories."

"I can imagine."

"Are you all right?" Nick asked, his eyes curious.

"Of course."

His eyes narrowed. "About what happened before . . . it was a mistake."

"It didn't feel like a mistake," she said, meeting his gaze. "It felt amazing."

"Yeah," he murmured, his voice husky. "But it's over."

"Is it?"

"Yes. I'm trying to figure out how to be a father to a daughter I barely know, I've got my crazy family to worry about, and it's all I can handle."

He was trying very hard to convince himself, but she could feel the swirling heat of his mixed emotions. As he turned to leave, she put a hand on his arm.

The flash almost blinded her.

Nick looked at her with desperation, his fingers biting into her skin, his voice raging with fear as he said, "Help me."

She let go of his arm with a shaky breath, her heart thumping against her chest, her blood rushing through her veins.

"What's wrong?" Nick asked.

A dozen memories ran through her mind, other people looking at her with the same concern, the same question—other moments when she'd made the wrong choice, when she'd put her heart and her soul on the line.

"Nothing," she said finally.

She could see the relief in his eyes when he said, "All right. Well, I need to go to work. I'll get you back to the trail." He took off at a brisk pace, giving her no choice but to follow. When they reached the trail, he asked. "You'll be okay from here?"

"Yes."

Nick sprinted down the path, kicking up a cloud of dust in his wake.

Rufus barked and gave her a questioning look, as if to ask her why she wasn't following. "Don't worry," she told the dog. "He won't get away. No matter how fast he runs." Their story wasn't finished yet, however much he wanted it to be.

Charlotte felt as if she was losing her mind. The baby's screams hammered the ache in her head. Would he never stop? She juggled him in her arms, trying to soothe him with rocking, bouncing, and calming words. But nothing seemed to work. He'd been crying off and on all night. He'd slept two hours at the most, and she'd probably slept one, because between crying bouts, she'd stayed awake, listening to every breath he took.

"I don't know what's wrong," she told him. "I've

fed you. I've changed you. I've burped you." His bottom lip jutted out as he grabbed more air to cry with. "No, please, stop. Please, please, please." Exhausted tears gathered behind her eyes as she sat down in the rocking chair.

She kept a steady rhythm, stroking his head with her fingers. An old song came to mind, and she began to sing, the words coming from some long-ago memory. It worked. After a few moments, his sobs turned to hiccups, then his eyes drifted shut, and he slept.

She let out a breath, afraid to move. But it seemed he'd finally worn himself out.

"I didn't know you remembered that song." Her mother stood in the doorway, an odd look in her eyes.

"I didn't know I did, either, but the words just came back."

"I used to sing you that song before you went to sleep."

"Really? I don't remember you singing to me." The idea seemed rather extraordinary.

"I used to sing at the church, too. But then I got busy with you and your brother and sister and all your dad's needs." She sighed. "Those days seem like a million years ago." Her soft, wistful gaze sharpened. "You should put him down. He'll get used to you holding him, and he won't be able to sleep on his own."

"So far, he doesn't seem able to sleep much at all." But some obedient-daughter gene made her get up and put the baby in his crib. He squirmed for a moment, then went back to sleep.

As she moved across the room, she became very aware of her wrinkled pajama bottoms and her camisole's odor of baby spit-up. She hadn't brushed her teeth or her hair, and thank goodness she'd had her office reschedule her patients for the next few days. Because she would definitely not inspire anyone's confidence.

Her mother, on the other hand, looked positively glowing. She had on a skirt and a silk blouse with high heels and panty hose. There was eyeshadow on her lids and gloss on her lips.

"Where are you going?" Charlotte asked as they walked into the hall.

Her mother flushed. "I have some things to do."

"Like what?" she asked curiously. There was an almost guilty look in her mother's eyes.

"I'm meeting Peter at Kellum's Antiques. He needs my help picking out some furniture."

Peter Lawson? No wonder her mother was blushing. The good-looking older man had been around quite a bit lately. Charlotte wasn't sure how she felt about it. It was less than a year since her father had died, and her parents had been married for forty-plus years. It was difficult to imagine her mother with another man—any man.

"He seems to need your help a lot," she commented as they entered the kitchen. She poured herself a cup of coffee, desperately in need of caffeine.

"He isn't very skilled when it comes to decorating," Monica answered. "You know how men are."

Charlotte sipped her coffee and leaned against the counter, keeping her thoughts to herself.

Her mother cleared her throat. "We need to discuss what we're going to do if Annie doesn't come back."

"Let's not go there yet," Charlotte said, cutting her off. "I don't want to consider that possibility."

"You can't stick your head in the sand."

Charlotte smiled at her mother's choice of words.

"What's so amusing?" Monica asked sharply, raising an annoyed eyebrow.

"The irony of what you just said. You're the queen of not seeing what you don't want to see." She regretted the statement when she saw thunderclouds in her mother's eyes. Monica Adams could dish it out, but she definitely couldn't take it—especially from her middle and always-disappointing daughter.

"You're the one who pretended she wasn't pregnant for two months. Who was avoiding the truth then?" her mother challenged.

There it was—the elephant in the room they'd managed to avoid for so many years.

"And you're the one who made me wait another month to go to the doctor, because you wanted to take me to someone out of town who didn't know us, who wouldn't spread my shameful behavior around," she replied.

Her mother's lips tightened. "You blame me for

your miscarriage. But some things just aren't meant to be. You were lucky."

"Lucky?" Charlotte echoed in shock and anger.

"Do you think you were ready to raise a baby at seventeen? Do you think you would have become a doctor—that your life would be anything like it is now—if you'd had that child? Because it wouldn't have been. I know that for a certainty."

"You can rationalize all you want, but you can't diminish the pain I felt. I was carrying a child, and I lost it, because I was young and stupid and I let you talk me into keeping it a secret. I wasn't feeling well. I needed to see a doctor. I never should have told you or let you make me wait. I should have gone on my own."

"That wouldn't have made any difference, and you know it. For heaven's sake, Charlotte, you're a doctor. Miscarriages happen all the time."

Logically, she knew that, but her heart and her head had never been in agreement when it came to that tragedy. Because no matter how terrified she'd been of having a baby, she'd still grieved for the life she'd lost. She'd still felt responsible, because she'd done so many things wrong, made so many mistakes, not all of which she could blame on her mother. Worst, she'd gone through it all alone, because her mother had convinced her that no good could come of talking about it after the fact. It was better if she stayed silent. Maybe it had been better—for everyone else. But for her, the pain had eaten away a part of her heart that she could never get back.

It had been many years since she'd relived that pain. Taking care of Annie's baby had brought back a lot of memories—apparently for both of them.

"Charlotte," her mother said uncertainly. "We shouldn't have started this now. You're tired, and I'm on my way out."

"This conversation has been a long time coming." She paused. "I know that the miscarriage was probably inevitable, but you were wrong to keep me from going to the doctor."

Her mother's face paled, her eyes dark beads of anger. "I did what I thought was best for all of us. And it was only a couple of weeks. You were a strong, healthy girl. I never thought you'd lose the baby."

"But you were happy that I did."

Her mother stared back at her. "What do you want me to say? I didn't want that life for you, a single mother at seventeen. I wanted you to have more. And in the end, you got more. Things worked out the way they were supposed to."

"The lie split us apart. And keeping it a secret from Dad hurt my relationship with him, too."

"He would have been devastated if he'd known."

"Is that what you honestly believe?"

"He was a man of God."

"He was a man who understood that people sometimes make mistakes."

Her mother crossed her arms in front of her chest. "Was it a mistake, Charlotte? Or was it deliberate?" she challenged. "Another act of rebellion?"

"You think I got pregnant to spite you?" She was amazed by the thought. "You never knew me at all."

"You hated living under our rules. You were always challenging me. You could never just go along, to trust that I knew what was best for you."

"You didn't always know."

"Yes, I did. I was your mother. I did for you what you're doing for Annie's baby. I stayed up all night while you cried. I held you and rocked you and fed you, and I loved you every second of your life, from your very first breath." Her mother's voice shook with emotion. "I wanted you to have everything, Charlotte. The world would be yours. You would be happy. You would be successful. But you wouldn't listen to me. You fought me at every turn. And as you got older, you looked at my life and decided you didn't want anything to do with it." Her gaze burned into hers. "Do you think I didn't feel your judgment?"

"My judgment?" she echoed in astonishment. "You were the one who criticized *me.*"

"And you did the same, every time you defied me. You didn't want the life I wanted to give you." She took a deep breath, then said fiercely, "Whatever I did, I did because I loved you. And I wanted to protect you, so I made rules. I was willing to let you hate me, if it meant you'd have what I wanted you to have. But you couldn't understand that."

Charlotte shook her head in bewilderment. "What I wanted to have was a relationship with my mother."

"That's not true," her mother said in disbelief. "You never wanted to spend time with me."

"When did you ever ask? You were always with Doreen. You got along so well with her. And Jamie was your baby. He couldn't do anything wrong. They were always your first choice."

"My first choice? I couldn't *find* you half the time. Once you hit puberty, you were always sneaking out. And after the miscarriage, you wouldn't even look at me."

"It wasn't just you I couldn't look at it," Charlotte confessed. "It was myself, too. I knew I screwed up."

Monica gazed back at her. "I don't think you've ever said that before."

"And I probably won't say it again," she returned. "But it's been a really long night."

A gleam of compassion softened her mother's eyes. "You're exhausted, aren't you?"

She nodded. "I could fall asleep standing up."

"I'm sorry I'm leaving you on your own."

"It's fine. I'm going to lie down while he's sleeping. I cleared my schedule for the day." As she finished speaking, her cell phone rang. Joe's number.

Clearing her throat, she said, "Hello." Joe's words were concise and to the point, and a wave of fear ran through her. "Are you sure it was Annie's?" she asked, then listened to his reply. "Of course, bring it by. I'll be here."

As she ended the call, she glanced at her mother. "Joe said they found the bag of items Annie bought at the market yesterday. It was tossed behind a fence in a yard about two blocks away. On the sidewalk, they found a broken gold chain with a cross on it."

Monica's lips tightened in dismay. "Annie's?"

"He's bringing it over." She paused, feeling suddenly very afraid and seeing that same fear reflected in her mother's eyes. "He doesn't think Annie ran away anymore."

"It's still possible," her mother said, a desperate note in her voice. "Annie could have thrown the bag away when she decided she wasn't coming back."

For once, she wanted to believe her mother. "That's true. But there was something in Joe's voice."

"He's a police officer. He's used to dealing with the worst-case scenario."

The doorbell rang. "That's Peter," her mother said, casting a hesitant look over her shoulder. "Do you want me to stay, Charlotte?"

"No, do what you need to do. I'll talk to Joe."

"You'll call me if anything comes up."

"Of course."

"I'll be back by one. I can watch the baby this afternoon."

"That would be great."

As the doorbell rang again, Monica turned to leave, but Charlotte couldn't help asking the one question she'd never asked. "Mom . . ."

Her mother stopped, raising one eyebrow at the lengthening pause. "Yes?"

She took a breath and said, "Why didn't you ever ask me who the father of my baby was?"

Her mother paled, but her eyes were steel. "Because I didn't want to know. I still don't."

And that was her mother, always operating on her own terms. But at least they'd finally kicked the biggest elephant out of the room. It was a start.

In ordinary circumstances, Joe would have sent one of his officers over to Charlotte's house. But it was Charlotte. He didn't need any more reason than that.

Talking to the prospective adoptive couples the night before had been depressing and not very illuminating. He'd seen and heard how desperate some of them were to have children but, not surprisingly, no one had stepped forward to claim paternity. A simple DNA test would prove who the father was, and now that he had evidence that Annie hadn't run away, he intended to get those tests.

But who would want to get Annie out of the way at this late date? She'd always had the freedom to reveal the father of her child. So what had changed?

He was still thinking about that when he knocked on Charlotte's door.

She answered a few moments later, a little flushed and breathless. She wore jeans and a clingy knit shirt that showed off her curves. His breath stalled in his chest. She wasn't wearing a speck of makeup, and there were weary shadows under her eyes, but she still had that just-got-out-of-bed look that reminded him of how much he'd like to see her *in* bed.

"Joe, you got here fast," she said with a smile. "Come in. The baby is asleep, but who knows how long that will last? It's amazing how little I can get done while taking care of one small child. I was excited just to take a shower."

He smiled back at her. "I've heard my sisters say that exact same thing."

"Do you want some coffee?" she asked as he stepped through the doorway.

"If it's no trouble."

"No trouble at all. We keep the pot going night and day." She led him into the kitchen, grabbed a mug out of the cupboard, and filled it up.

"Thanks."

She waved him toward a small round kitchen table. "So you brought something to show me?"

He took a plastic bag out of his pocket and set it on the table. A thin gold chain and cross were inside. "It could belong to anyone," he said.

She shook her head, worry in her eyes. "Annie had one just like it. And the fact that it was close to the bag from the market . . . Joe, what does this mean?"

"It means we're stepping up the investigation. I've got Jason canvassing the neighborhood around the market. If anyone saw anything, we'll find them."

She nodded, concern on her face. "But why would someone grab Annie? Do you think it was random?"

"I don't. However, I have nothing to back that up but gut instinct."

"I trust your instincts. If you don't think it was random, then who?"

"That I can't say."

"You spoke to the adoptive couples?"

"Four of them. I have one more this afternoon. No one has stepped up to claim the child." As he finished speaking, a baby's scream came from the monitor. He winced. "That kid has some lungs."

"Tell me about it." She got up from the table and hurried down the hall. Joe followed her, watching from the doorway as she picked up the baby and put him on the changing table. He was screaming and kicking his feet, mad as hell, and Joe had never seen Charlotte so flustered.

"I'm not very good at this," she told him.

"How are you so rattled? You deliver babies all the time."

"I give them to their mothers right away. Still, I thought I was good with babies until this kid. He does *not* like me. Obviously, I wasn't cut out to be a mother."

At her words, he remembered a night a few weeks ago when she'd told him about her teen pregnancy and miscarriage. Suddenly, it was clear where her insecurity was coming from. He crossed the room and put his hand on her shoulder.

She gave him a nervous look. "What?"

He gazed into her eyes, giving her a reassuring smile. "You're the most loving, generous, kind woman I know. From what I can see, you're loaded with motherly instincts."

She swallowed hard, her eyes blurring with tears. "I'm so tired, Joe. You're going to make me cry."

"Well, that's not going to help," he said lightly. "Just trust yourself, Charlotte. You're not that scared pregnant teenage girl anymore, and he's not the baby you lost."

She sniffed and lifted her chin. "You're right. It's the lack of sleep. It makes me a little crazy."

"Why don't you let me take this diaper?" He pushed her gently out of the way.

"Okay, have at it."

The kid tried to spray him when he took off the wet diaper, but Joe was ready for it and soon had him powdered and dry.

"Wow," Charlotte murmured. "If I hadn't seen it with my own eyes, I don't think I would have believed it. The chief of police changing diapers."

"I have seven nieces and nephews. This wasn't my first time." He picked the baby up in his arms and pressed him against his chest, rubbing his back until he quieted down.

"You're good," Charlotte said. "Why don't you have children? Oh, sorry—that was rather personal," she added quickly.

"It never seemed to be the right time," he said quietly. "Rachel and I talked about it a lot, but we couldn't agree on when to do it. And it wasn't always her putting things off. I did as well."

"It's not too late. You're still young."

"I'm pushing forty."

"Well, until you're pushing up daisies, you've got time."

He handed her back the baby, who now snuggled into her soft chest with a satisfied sigh. "See, he does like you."

"Parts of me," she said with a laugh.

"They *are* very nice parts." He grinned back at her.

She shook her head. "I walked right into that one."

"You did." He paused. "I'll call you as soon as I find out anything about Annie."

She gave him a heartfelt smile. "Thanks, Joe—for everything."

"You're more than welcome. I'm going to do more for this kid than change his diaper. I'm going to bring his mother back," he promised.

"I know you will," Charlotte said, trust shining out of her eyes.

He'd be damned if he'd let her down.

SEVEN

After her hike, Isabella showered, changed into jeans, and threw on a bright red sweater over a cream-colored top, adding high-heeled boots to complete the ensemble. She blew her hair dry but left it long and curly rather than wasting time with the straightener. She was eager to get to the theater. Not only was she looking forward to working on the costumes, but she also felt sure that the theater was tied to the dreams that had brought her to Angel's Bay. After her disturbing flash at the waterfall, she was more determined than ever to find some answers.

When she entered the lobby, she found a hum of activity. The ticket office was crowded with volunteers organizing the presales, and a line was forming in the lobby for auditions. She waited for Tory to finish announcing the schedule for the day and then made her way over.

"Isabella, hello," Tory said with a smile. "I was hoping we hadn't scared you off."

"Not a chance. You look busy," she said, noting the pile of scripts in Tory's arms.

"Once we get into preproduction, this place becomes a madhouse."

"It's exciting," Isabella said, feeling the energy in the old building.

"You're going to fit right in," Tory replied with a knowing gleam in her eyes. "You're already feeling the magic."

"I am," she admitted. "I'd forgotten what it's like to be in a playhouse. There's an unbelievable energy."

"We need that energy to get everything done. I'll walk with you; I was on my way to the costume shop to drop off the new scripts. Mariah, our head designer, is out this morning, but Erin can help you get started."

"I'm looking forward to it."

They went down a short staircase and through a hallway to the costume shop. Erin was a skinny, pale brunette who wore jeans and a T-shirt, her hair pulled back in a ponytail. She got up from behind a sewing machine as Tory introduced them. "It's nice to meet you," she said. "We can really use your help around here."

Despite her welcome, there was a strain behind Erin's smile and worry in her eyes. "I don't want to step on anyone's toes," Isabella said quickly, knowing that some designers could be territorial.

"You don't have to worry about that. We have more than enough work." Erin turned to Tory. "I was just about to come and find you. Have you heard the latest rumors about Annie?"

"No," Tory said as she set the scripts down on the worktable. "What's going on?"

"One of the prospective adoptive fathers is the biological father of Annie's baby," Erin said.

"What?" Tory gasped, putting a hand on the table to steady herself. "That's crazy. Who would say that?"

"I don't know, but it's all over town. I called Dan, but he's out on a call and hasn't gotten back to me yet. He's going to be furious."

"Steve will be, too," Tory muttered. "After everything we've been through, now this? It's too much."

Isabella saw the look of commiseration pass between the two women. She was just wondering if she should leave them to their conversation when Tory sent her an apologetic glance.

"Erin and I are both on the list as possible candidates to adopt Annie's baby," Tory explained, "along with three other couples. Annie disappeared before she made her decision. Now we're all in limbo."

"I'm so sorry," Isabella said. "It sounds like an awful situation."

"And getting worse by the minute," Erin said darkly. "I can't believe what some people in this town will say."

"The gossip doesn't matter," Tory said. "What's important is finding Annie. Now, I need to get back to the auditions." She gave Erin a quick hug. "Don't lose faith."

Erin wiped a tear from her eye as Tory left the room. "Sorry," she mumbled to Isabella. "It's been a stressful morning."

"What can I do to help?" Isabella asked, feeling a wave of compassion for Erin. While Tory had lifted her chin and rallied her fighting spirit in the face of the rumors, Erin seemed quite fragile, almost ready to break.

"I need to run an errand and get my head together," Erin said. "Let me get you started before I go." She walked over to a rack and pulled out a dress, then laid it on the worktable. "This beading needs to be repaired. And the director wants to update the neckline and the hem like this." She pulled out a sketch and set it next to the dress. "What do you think?"

"It's a great improvement," Isabella said, studying the sketch. "I'd love to do it. Who is the director, anyway?"

"Blake Hammond. He'll be arriving next week, and he'll probably have additional ideas when he gets here. Here's a list of minor alterations that needed to be handled." She gave a piece of paper to Isabella. "Everything is on that rack over by the door; just make yourself at home."

As Erin left, Isabella blew out a breath and looked around. She was happy to be alone for a few moments. Erin's emotions had cast a thick pall that lingered even now. Or perhaps the emotions she sensed weren't coming from Erin's distress but from a more distant past.

Isabella put a hand to her pendant. It felt heavy
and warm against her skin, reassuring yet also making her feel oddly expectant. She waited for some
flash of insight to come, but there was nothing. Still,
she had the feeling that this costume shop was important in some way.

Picking up the list of alterations, she sat down
to sew. Soon she was lost in the world that had always been her second home. Stitching had been her
therapy all of her life. When she'd felt sad or lonely
or lost in her head, she'd turned to the needle and
the thread, finding joy in repairing a costume to its
former glory or in creating something new and wonderful. When she sewed, she had control over the
outcome. She could fix what needed to be fixed.

Caught up in her stitching, she didn't hear anyone enter until a backpack landed on the table next
to her with a thud.

A teenage girl sank into a nearby chair with a
sullen frown. Despite the black hair streaked with
purple, heavy eyeliner, nose ring, and an abundance
of teenage swagger, the girl's irritated gaze was all
Nick. This had to be his daughter.

"Hello," Isabella said, offering a smile. "I'm
Isabella."

"Megan," she said shortly. "Grandma said you'd
give me something to do." Megan crossed her arms
in front of her chest and gave Isabella the same no-
trespassing sign that had flashed across her father's
face earlier that day.

"Do you know how to sew?" Isabella asked.

"Are you kidding me?"

"I take it that's a no. Do you want to try?"

"I'm sure I'm just supposed to sweep the floor or pick up trash or something."

"Well, there's no garbage at the moment." She lifted a dress off the alteration rack. "I do, however, have to sew about twenty buttons down the back of this dress. I could show you how."

Megan hesitated, then shrugged. "Whatever."

Isabella brought over the box of buttons, then showed Megan how to sew them on. It wasn't a difficult task, but it needed some care and attention to detail. Despite Megan's initial reluctance, she picked it up very quickly.

They worked in silence for almost half an hour, the quiet becoming less tense as the minutes passed.

Isabella finished her beading and paused to take a look at Megan's work. "Very good," she said approvingly. "You're a natural."

"Anyone could do it."

"No, they couldn't. Believe me, I know. One of the last people I worked with stitched her own sleeve to the costume."

"She must have been stupid."

"Just clumsy."

"Where did you learn to sew?" Megan asked as she picked up another button.

"My grandmother. She was an incredibly talented designer, but as she got older, her arthritis made it difficult for her to sew, and she eventually retired. It was lucky timing, because my mother wanted to go back to work and needed someone to watch me. We became very close. And it was nice to have my grandmother all to myself. I was the youngest of five kids, so my parents were tied up with my older siblings most of the time. They tended to forget about me."

"My mother forgot about me all the time," Megan grumbled. "And the nannies didn't care what I was doing, as long as they got paid."

Isabella was happy that Megan was finally talking, but she sensed it wouldn't take much for her to stop, so she didn't reply, hoping that Megan might go on.

"My mom didn't want me," Megan continued. "Neither did my dad. I was a big mistake, and I ruined their lives."

"Ruined seems a little strong," Isabella observed. "Your mother is a successful actress, and your father is an architect. Seems like they're doing okay."

"Well, that's because they both ignored me," Megan snapped, pain flashing through her eyes.

Isabella felt immediately sympathetic. While she'd never doubted her parents' love, she'd never felt quite as wanted as her other siblings.

"Now my dad is stuck with me, because my mom is getting married again, and she doesn't want me around. She's in love," Megan added with a disgusted roll of her eyes. "She wants to have sex all over the house. I'm too old for a nanny, so here I am. Angel's Bay sucks. I hate everyone here."

Isabella suspected that Megan hated everyone

because she was afraid to love them, afraid to set herself up for more rejection, and who could blame her? Why had Nick been absent from his daughter's life for so long? He seemed like such a responsible guy.

"How come you're not in school today?" she asked.

"I got suspended."

"For what?"

"I was just talking to some kids at lunch. They had some beer. I didn't drink, but it didn't matter, they kicked us all out for two days. Like that's a punishment," she added sarcastically.

"I thought you hated everyone in Angel's Bay," Isabella said mildly. "But it sounds like you have a few friends."

Megan didn't reply right away, then said, "There's a guy who's kind of cool."

"What's his name?"

"Why? Are you going to tell my dad?" Megan asked suspiciously.

"No. I was just curious."

"It's Will," Megan said a moment later. "He grew up here, and he can't wait to get away. He's going to leave the second he graduates in June."

"He's a little older than you, then?"

"What does age matter? My mother is marrying a guy who's ten years younger than her. He doesn't know, because she lies about her age and gets plastic surgery. That's another reason she doesn't want me around. I'm too old now; she can't stand the thought of being photographed next to me."

"Maybe it's good that you're here with your dad, then."

Anger burned in Megan's eyes. "Like he wants me. He didn't see me for twelve years. That's how much he cares. I can't wait until I'm eighteen and I can do whatever the hell I want."

Megan tossed down her needle and got to her feet. "I'm bored and hungry. I'm going to get some lunch."

"I could eat," Isabella said, glancing down at her watch. It was after one. "Want some company?"

"What are you, my jailer?"

Isabella laughed. She couldn't help it, Megan was the picture of teenage rebellion. "No, and you can feed your bad mood all alone if you want. I just thought you might know where I could find a good cheese-burger. I've only been in town a couple of days."

Megan gave her a suspicious stare but finally said, "I know a place."

"Great. Do you need to tell someone you're leaving?"

"Do you really think anyone in this theater cares what I'm doing?" Megan countered. "My grandparents and great-grandparents are so caught up in this production they probably wouldn't notice if I walked by with my hair on fire."

Isabella smiled. "Well, I'll let Tory know that we're off to lunch, just in case you're not as invisible as you think."

* * *

Twenty minutes later, Isabella and Megan were ordering chili fries and cheeseburgers. It had been a long time since Isabella had eaten like a fifteen-year-old, and it was sure fun. Jax's Burger Shack was set on a bluff above the beach. Two guys, one of whom appeared to be named Jax, flipped the burgers, french-fried the potatoes, and handed out orders in red baskets. They took their meal to one of the outdoor tables on the patio overlooking the bay. It was after the noon crowd, and school was in session, so there were only a few other customers.

"This burger is delicious," she said to Megan, who was downing her own burger in record time. "You're a girl after my own heart."

"I can't believe you're eating the double-double," Megan said as she reached for her vanilla shake. "My mother would die before putting one bite of a cheeseburger in her mouth."

"Is she a vegetarian?"

"No, she's skinny and an exercise freak, probably bulimic. I've heard her throw up a few times. And she can't walk by a mirror without looking in it. It's disgusting."

Isabella wondered if Megan had changed her appearance so she wouldn't have to compete with her beautiful mother. "What color is your hair normally?" she couldn't help asking.

Megan scowled. "Dirty blond—boring."

"It's not boring now."

"I might change it again. I haven't decided. Nick will probably freak if I dye it red."

"How come you don't call him Dad?" Isabella asked curiously.

"Because he sucks as a father. I don't want to talk about him," she added quickly.

"Okay. Tell me about the boy you got in trouble with."

Megan hesitated, then said, "Will rides a motorcycle. He doesn't care what people think about him. And he's never heard of my mother. The other kids look at me like I'm from Mars, just because my mother is an actress and sleeps with famous men. Most of them are pricks."

For all of her coarse language and worldly ways, Isabella saw a vulnerability in Megan that made her worry. She hoped this Will was a good kid and not playing Megan by telling her what she wanted to hear. "It must be hard to have your mother's reputation hanging over you wherever you go. I can't imagine what that's like. My parents are not extraordinary in any way."

"You're lucky." Megan finished her burger and glanced out at the water, where boats were making their way in and out of the harbor.

"I never thought of it that way, but you might be right. I did grow up in the shadow of very talented siblings, though. My brother is the chief of police here in Angel's Bay. The top cop," she added with a smile.

"So you can't do anything wrong."

"I'm sure he'd prefer that I didn't."

Megan didn't speak for a moment, then said,

"I always wanted to have a brother or a sister, but my mom would never choose to have a child. The only reason she had me was because she was stupid enough to get knocked up." There was a lonely look in her eyes.

Megan had been tossed aside by too many people, Isabella thought. She needed to be loved, to feel secure. It seemed as if Nick wanted to make that happen, but Megan wasn't going to let him in without a fight. And Isabella couldn't blame her. She didn't know why Nick had been absent from his daughter's life, and she couldn't imagine a reason that would make that absence okay. But Nick seemed to want to make things right now. He'd made it clear to her that Megan was a priority. Had he made it clear to Megan?

Megan folded her arms on the table. "Are you going to have kids?"

Isabella was taken aback by the direct question. Not that she hadn't been asked it before; her mother and sisters were always on her to find a man, settle down, and have babies. "I'd like to at some point. But I don't know what life has in store for me."

Megan raised an eyebrow. "What does that mean?"

"I've found that making plans is usually a waste of time. My life seems to turn upside down whenever I least expect it."

Megan nodded in understanding. "I know what you mean. Every time I start to like someone . . ."

She drew in a breath. "Anyway, now I live for today and forget about tomorrow."

It was the same philosophy Isabella had followed the last few years, but hearing it come out of Megan's young, brash mouth, she couldn't help but worry. Megan was looking for trouble—for someone to love her, for someone to give her attention. She wanted to find her place in the world, to stand outside her mother's shadow, which was all fine if she did it in a mature, rational way. But she was fifteen; that wasn't going to happen.

It was one thing to accept fate, another to tempt it.

"Megan, if you ever need someone to talk to, I'm a good listener."

"And how long will you be staying in town?" Megan challenged.

"For a while."

It wasn't a good answer. Megan needed a friend who could commit to being around, but Isabella wasn't in the position to make that promise.

When Nick arrived at the theater at around two o'clock, he was surprised to see his brother-in-law storm out of the building. Steve Baker usually had a charming smile and an easy manner that worked well in his busy dental practice. But there was nothing easy about him today.

"Steve," he said, realizing his brother-in-law was so caught up in his thoughts that he hadn't even seen him. "What's going on?"

Steve stopped in mid-stride, then stared at him in bemusement. "Nick, I didn't see you there."

"You look pissed off. Did you and Tory have a fight?"

"You could say that. All your sister can think about is having a baby, being a mother," he said in frustration. "It's never enough to be just the two of us. I thought adopting Annie's baby would finally make her happy, but now there's just more trouble."

"I heard about the girl's disappearance. What's going to happen to the baby?"

"No one knows yet. Now the police think someone kidnapped Annie."

"That's crazy." Nick couldn't imagine such a thing happening in Angel's Bay.

"This whole thing is a nightmare."

Nick knew his sister was obsessed with having a child, but he hadn't realized the toll it was taking on Steve. "Is there anything I can do to help?"

"When you talk to Tory, remind her that I'm the guy who loves her."

As Steve walked away, Nick wondered why his sister would need reminding. Maybe there were more problems between them than he knew. While he and Tory had gotten closer since he'd moved back to Angel's Bay, they'd spent more time discussing his problems with Megan than anything else.

When he entered the theater, he saw Tory coming out of the box office, looking as stressed out as her husband. "I need to talk to you," he said.

"Can it wait? I'm busy."

"It can't." He led her over to the stairway leading up to the balcony, where they could have a little privacy. "I ran into Steve outside. He was upset."

"Well, I'm upset, too," she snapped, anger in her eyes. "Did he tell you about the rumors?" That one of the prospective adoptive fathers is the biological father of Annie's baby?"

He stared at her in shock. "You're not serious."

"Oh, but I am," she said tightly. "And when I told Steve, he didn't exactly jump up and down declaring his innocence. Instead, he got furious with me for 'even suggesting' that he might have done something wrong. Then he went off on me, wanting to know why I couldn't just be happy with him, why I needed a baby so much." She shook her head. "I know my obsession with motherhood has put a strain on our marriage. But I thought he wanted a family, too. I need him to want that as much as I do."

"I'm sure he does," Nick said. "Tory, you can't buy into gossip. You know your husband better than anyone."

"That's what I've been telling myself. But things haven't been as good between us as they once were."

"Steve loves you, Tory. Focus on that."

"I'm trying. I want my happily ever after, Nick. Is that too much to ask?"

He saw the pleading look in her eyes and wished he could make things right for her. She was his little sister. They'd anchored each other when their parents had cast them adrift on too many occasions to count. But they were adults now, and Tory had problems that he couldn't fix. That perhaps no one could fix.

"You had Megan without even trying," Tory continued. "You don't know what it's like to yearn for a child."

He did know what it was like, but not in the way she meant. And he couldn't argue that losing Megan to Kendra was in any way the same thing, because he'd had choices. He just hadn't made the right ones.

But Tory hadn't done anything wrong. "I hope you will get a chance to be a mother," he said quietly. "Because you'd be fantastic."

Her eyes blurred with tears. "I would be," she said with a shaky smile.

"You'll find a way to make it happen. If not with this baby, then with another."

"I hope so." She paused, tilting her head. "When did you get to be optimistic?"

"I've always been that way where you're concerned."

"And I've been that way for you," she returned. "I want you to have a happy ending, too, Nick."

"I'm working on it. Have you seen Megan?"

"She went to lunch with Isabella."

His gut tightened. He'd spent most of the morning trying to forget their incendiary kiss, which had definitely not been part of his game plan. Although she'd initiated the kiss, he'd taken it to a higher level.

He could still taste her on his lips, and he'd never had such a strong reaction to a woman. It had to be because of the way they'd met, the intensity of the rescue, the nearness of death, connecting them in some deep, elemental way that he didn't understand. They'd skipped all the simple steps of getting to know each other and jumped right into something messy and complicated.

And now Isabella was out with his daughter, invading yet another aspect of his life. "Megan was supposed to say here," he snapped. "She's on suspension, not vacation."

"And she's just having lunch, not taking a cruise." Tory's gaze narrowed. "Oh—I get it."

"You don't get it," he grumbled.

"Isabella is as pretty as her name," his sister said with a knowing smile. "And you saved her life."

"Which does *not* mean I have to spend the rest of my life seeing her every other second—even though that seems to be the case."

"You like her."

"As if I'd ever get involved with another theater person," he scoffed.

"She's a costume designer."

"Just another street in the world of make-believe."

"She's creative and forward-thinking—like you. She designs clothes; you design buildings. You might have more in common than you think."

What they had in common was a rampant desire to tear each other's clothes off, but he didn't intend to share that with his sister. "Tell Megan I'll be back to pick her up."

"Tell her yourself." She tipped her head toward the door. "Looks like your daughter finally found something to smile about. She must like Isabella, too."

His jaw dropped at the sight of his sulky daughter laughing at something Isabella was saying. Megan was completely lit up, as if some of Isabella's warmth had rubbed off on her. He was pleased she'd found something to smile about but disappointed that it wasn't he who had made Megan happy.

As soon as Megan saw him, her smile disappeared. He'd thought he'd gotten a little past her defenses the night before when he'd let her drive to Rusty's, but apparently, that had been wishful thinking.

"Where are you two coming from?" he asked, walking across the lobby to join them.

"Megan took me to the greatest little hamburger shack by the beach," Isabella replied. "We ate way too much."

"Jax's," he said with a nod. "It's the best."

"It was," she agreed.

"I'm going to finish sewing," Megan said, barely giving him a glance.

"Wait," Nick said. "If you want to come home with me now, that's fine. I've finished my meeting."

"I have things to do here. Someone will give me a ride later."

Megan was gone before he could tell her that he wanted to spend time with her. "You should have checked with me before you took Megan to lunch," he told Isabella. "She's on suspension from school. She's not supposed to be wandering around town having fun."

Isabella raised an eyebrow at his tone, and he knew he was being unreasonable. But he was frustrated with his inability to get closer to his daughter, and the fact that Isabella could waltz in and be Megan's best friend in less than an hour was hard to swallow.

"We checked in with Tory before we left," Isabella said calmly.

"I told Megan to call me if she was going to leave the theater."

"She didn't mention that." Isabella gave him a thoughtful look. "Come outside with me."

"Why?"

She didn't answer, just turned and headed through the doors, not speaking until they reached the far end of the patio. Then she said, "I'm sorry if I stepped on your toes by having lunch with your daughter. She was working with me in the costume shop, and we were both hungry. There was nothing more to it than that."

"Did Megan talk to you about me?"

"A little. She said she didn't see you for a long time."

"I'm sure she said more than that."

"No. Your daughter isn't real chatty." She paused. "I know it's not my business, Nick, but why didn't you see her? You don't seem like a man who would turn his back on his child."

"It's a long story."

"Can you give me the highlights?"

Sharing private details would only bring Isabella closer, yet he found himself wanting to tell her. "I was eighteen when Megan was born, twenty-one when my ex-wife took her to London. Kendra had the chance to star in a play, and I didn't have the means to stop her. I didn't think it would be forever. But the months turned into years, and by the time I got my shit together, it was too late. Kendra was marrying someone else, and Megan had a new stepfather. I wish I could go back in time and change it, but I can't."

She gazed back at him with no judgment in her eyes. "Well, Megan is here now."

"And I can barely get her to talk to me. Occasionally, she lets down her guard for a brief moment, then two seconds later, she's freezing me out again. And I can't blame her. She has every right to hate me."

Nick sighed. "I don't think Megan wants to hate you. She wants to love you and to have you love her. She's afraid."

"I thought she was happy with her mother. It's only since she moved here that I realized I bought into Kendra's pretenses. She told me Megan was happy, but Megan paints a completely different picture."

"It sounds like you're not the only one who let Megan down. But you have a chance to make things right. So do it," she urged.

"How? Megan is a fifteen-year-old girl. I didn't

understand teenage girls when I was a teenage boy! And in case you haven't noticed, Megan is not exactly a little angel in pink."

Isabella smiled. "No, she's not. She wants attention. And if she doesn't get yours, she'll go for the next-best thing—a cool guy named Will, who rides a motorcycle and tells her what she wants to hear."

He drew in a sharp breath. "I don't think I've ever been more scared in my life."

"You should be scared. Hormones can be powerful at that age."

"So how do I stop Megan? I'm not the best role model."

"She doesn't need you to be perfect. She just needs you to be there."

Nick was silent for a moment. "You're right." He was impressed and dismayed at how easily Isabella had gotten past his defenses. Outside his family, he'd never talked about Kendra or Megan, never put that part of his life up for judgment or analysis. Until now.

"Maybe I can help," Isabella added.

A warning tingle ran down his spine. "In what way?"

"Well, I was a teenage girl, so I have a little experience in that area."

"Did you color your hair and go after bad boys on motorcycles?"

"I did add some red streaks, once. No motorcycles, but one guy had a sweet Mustang convertible. His name was Tony, and he was so hot, with dark hair and dark eyes. We used to drive out to Santa Monica and park by the pier." A shadow passed across her eyes.

"What happened to him?"

"It's not important."

"And that's not an answer."

"I should get back to work," she said. "Your family is going to think I'm quite the slacker."

"Nick?" His mother's voice interrupted them. "I need your help."

"I'll be right there." He glanced back at Isabella. "I'd say good-bye, but somehow, I feel certain I'll see you later."

As Nick left, Isabella let out a breath of relief. She hadn't meant to bring up Tony or that time of her life. Putting the past back where it belonged, she returned to the costume shop. Inside, she found Megan working diligently on her buttons. The girl didn't even glance up, so Isabella took her cue and sat down, settling into her own work.

Five minutes passed before Megan lifted her head. "How do you know my dad if you just came to town?" she asked suspiciously.

"He saved my life," Isabella replied. "I thought you knew. I was in a car accident on the way into town, and your father pulled me out of my car before it plunged into the ocean. He was amazing."

"That was you?" Megan asked in surprise.

"Yes. Your dad climbed down a very steep and

slippery hillside to rescue me, a complete stranger. Not many people would have done what he did."

"I'm sure it wasn't that dangerous."

"It was," she said, refusing to make light of Nick's efforts.

"Don't try to make me like him," Megan warned, steel in her eyes.

"Don't you want to like him?" Isabella countered.

"Why? So can I feel bad when he ditches me again? And don't try to tell me that won't happen. You don't know him."

"Do you? Why don't you give yourself a chance to find out who he really is?"

"I know who he is. He's the man who let my mother take me away. He's the man who never came to see me. And the only reason I'm with him now is because my mother dumped me on him. That's all I need to know." Megan jerked to her feet so abruptly the chair fell over. "I'm done with this. Just because you like him doesn't mean I have to. He didn't save *my* life. I don't owe him anything."

Isabella let out a breath as Megan left the room. She was one mixed-up, angry, sad kid, but hopefully that would change with time.

A few minutes later, a sound made her look up, and she was surprised to see Nick's grandfather step into the room. Harrison Hartley might be in his eighties, but he was still a tall, intimidating man, and Isabella couldn't help but feel wary after the way he'd reacted to meeting her.

"Mr. Hartley, can I help you?" she asked.

"I never thought you'd come back. Never thought I'd see you again," he said quietly, a faraway look in his eyes. Whoever he was talking to, it wasn't her.

"Why not?" she asked.

He swallowed hard. "Because you left me when I needed you most." Then he shifted his feet, cleared his throat, and gave her an uneasy look, as if he realized he'd drifted away. "You shouldn't be here. No one else can get hurt."

"I'm not here to hurt anyone."

"That's what *she* said."

"Who?" she pressed.

"Leticia." The word slipped through his tight lips. "You look so much like her, it's uncanny. And you're here in this shop where she used to be."

Her heart skipped a beat as another piece of the puzzle fell into place. "Was Leticia a costumer?" she asked.

He gave a slow nod. "She was gifted. When I wore the clothes she made, I became invincible."

"What happened to her?"

"She left a long time ago, more than fifty years now." His gaze came into focus. "Are you her granddaughter? You have to be related. There's such a strong resemblance."

"I'm not her granddaughter but perhaps a relative." She put her hand to her throat and pulled the pendant out from beneath her blouse. "Was this hers?"

Harrison sucked in a quick breath, staring at the necklace in shock. "Where did you get that?" he demanded.

"My uncle's house."

"I gave it to Leticia for her birthday. I thought she'd taken it with her, but apparently, she left it behind," he said in a voice laced with pain.

"You loved her, didn't you?"

"I wasn't supposed to. It was the biggest mistake of my life." He raised his gaze from the necklace to her face. "I won't let Nick make the same one. He's getting his life together. He doesn't need someone like you to shake things up, to get him off track. He can't let himself be seduced by your eyes."

"The way you were by Leticia's eyes?"

"You need to leave here and never come back."

"I can't do that," Isabella said.

"Why not?"

Her gaze held his. "Because Nick needs me for something."

"What?"

"I'm not sure yet."

He shook his head in dismay. "You really *are* like her," He stared at her for a long time, and the silence might have gone on even longer if Tory hadn't popped her head in the door.

"Grandpa," Tory said with relief. "I've been looking all over for you. We need you upstairs. We're doing the male auditions now." She gave Isabella a quizzical look, picking up on the tension in the room. "Everything okay?"

"It's fine." Harrison left abruptly.

Tory lingered behind, curiosity in her eyes. "What's going on with you and my grandfather?"

"Apparently, I remind him of a woman named Leticia. She was a costumer here a long time ago. Have you ever heard the name?"

"No, but she was probably before my time. There's a lot of history in these walls." Tory's gaze went to the necklace that Isabella had been unconsciously stroking. "That's very pretty. The blue matches your eyes."

"Yes. Have your grandparents been married a long time?"

"Fifty-eight years. And my parents have been married for thirty-four. They've loved and lived and worked together every day of their lives." She paused. "I don't know who this Leticia is, but please don't ask my grandmother about her. She's been a little fragile the last year, and if my grandfather had something on the side fifty years ago, she doesn't need to know about it now."

"Don't worry, I wouldn't even know what to say. Your grandfather was fairly cryptic. I don't know what his relationship with Leticia was. But I think she might be an ancestor of mine."

"You should check with Fiona Murray. She's the matriarch of the Murray clan; they're the founding family of Angel's Bay. She runs the Angel's Heart Quilt Shop, and she knows everything that goes on. She's also about the same age as my grandfather, so she might have known this Leticia."

"I will, thanks."

As Tory left, Isabella's hand tightened on the pendant. Had she started dreaming about Nick because the necklace was given to Leticia by Nick's grandfather? Was that where the connection had come from? There was no doubt that their families were intertwined. She would talk to Fiona Murray, but first, she'd call her grandmother. She pulled out her cell phone but didn't get any reception, so she headed outside to the patio.

Elena answered on the third ring. *"Hola."* She'd left her native Mexico when she was ten years old, but she'd never lost the Spanish lilt to her English.

"It's me, Isabella."

"Are you all right?" Elena said worriedly. "Your mother told me you'd been in an accident. Why didn't you call me?"

She'd played down the accident to almost nothing when she'd spoken to her parents. But her grandmother had always been able to see past her white lies, which was why she hadn't called her.

"I'm fine now. I even have a job at the Angel's Bay theater. They're putting on a winter production, and they need costumers. It seemed like a lovely coincidence, until I discovered that a woman who apparently had eyes similar to mine worked here some fifty years ago. And the pendant belonged to her. Her name was Leticia." She waited for her grandmother to respond, but there was nothing but silence on the other end of the phone. "Do you know who she was or where she is? She'd be in her early eighties now, I would imagine."

"Leticia Cardoza," her grandmother said slowly. "I haven't heard that name in many, many years. She was a second or third cousin, and she did have your eyes. She died a long time ago; I don't think she was out of her twenties at the time."

A chill ran down Isabella's spine. Instinctively, she'd known that Leticia was dead, but she felt an odd wave of pain. Maybe because she was treading in Leticia's footsteps, doing her job, wearing her necklace, talking to people who'd once loved her.

"What else can you tell me about her?" Isabella asked.

Her grandmother seemed hesitant, which made her more uneasy.

"Grandmother?"

"There was a rumor that she killed herself."

The words took her breath away. Finally, she managed to get out, "Why?"

"Perhaps that's for you to find out. She had your gift, Isabella. And you have her necklace. Maybe it's her spirit that drew you there."

Isabella put her hand to the necklace. "If she killed herself, she didn't care much for our gift, either."

"You're not her, Isabella. You're strong."

Was she? Sometimes her dreams made her feel as if she was going crazy. Isabella drew in a breath. "When I showed you the pendant, did you know it was hers?"

"No. I'd forgotten that Carlos had moved into the house of a cousin. I thought it was tied to him or to your brother."

"I wish I knew what I was supposed to do."

"You'll know what to do when it's time. When you embrace what God gave you, when you believe in yourself."

"I hope you're right." Isabella said good-bye.

Had Leticia killed herself? Harrison had told her that Leticia had left town. Was he lying? Or didn't he know?

EIGHT

The week had flown by, Charlotte thought as she left the house late Friday afternoon. Taking care of the baby day and night, she'd lost all sense of time. Now she understood why all of the new moms who came for their six-week checkups were so excited to be out. It was amazing how much attention one tiny baby could need. She was gaining more appreciation for her own mother by the minute.

Her mom was now in charge of the baby, and she was free. She'd called Joe, hoping for an update, but he wasn't answering his phone, so she headed over to the church. Andrew wasn't in his office, but his secretary directed Charlotte to his house next door, saying he'd gone home for a late lunch.

Seeing the large two-story house with the big front porch and wide green lawn brought a knot to Charlotte's throat. This was the house she'd grown up in when her father had been the minister. She'd spent all of her childhood here, and there were a lot of memories, both good and bad.

She smiled as she climbed the porch stairs, remembering when she'd made out with Andrew on this very porch. They'd had a passionate teenage romance, and she'd thought their feelings were mutual—until he'd cheated on her. Things had fallen apart very quickly. After graduation, they'd gone in different directions, and they hadn't seen each other in more than a decade until they'd both ended up back here in Angel's Bay several months ago.

It was odd how Andrew had stepped into her father's life. She'd never imagined that he would become a minister. She had never thought of Andrew as a particularly spiritual person, but something had happened to send him in that direction. He was still finding his way, but he had a natural talent for counseling and ministering to the community. Some of the older members of the congregation weren't quite ready to accept him as their leader, but he was slowly winning them over with his charm, something he had in abundance. There was a line of single women hoping to become the new minister's girlfriend and possibly his wife.

Although Andrew had been flirting with her since he'd come back, she'd been hesitant to get involved with him again. But she'd been equally reluctant to cut him completely out of her life. It was silly, but deep down inside, when he turned his golden boy smile on her, she felt like that insecure teenager who couldn't quite believe the most popular kid in school wanted her.

The door opened before she had a chance to knock. "Charlie," Andrew said in surprise. "I was just about to head over to your place and see how things were going."

"I'd like to say it's quiet, but Annie's baby is rocking the house."

He smiled. "How do you like your taste of motherhood?"

"It's a lot harder than it looks."

"Come on in. Can I get you something to drink?"

"No, thanks, I'm good." As she stepped into the entryway, she was struck by an unexpected wave of emotion. She could almost smell dinner cooking in the kitchen, hear her mother and father chatting with friends at the dining-room table, see her brother racing his trucks down the hallway, and listen to her sister gabbing on the phone to her boyfriend.

"You okay?" Andrew asked, his gaze sharpening. "It bothers you to see my stuff in your house, doesn't it?"

She took a deep breath. "It's your house now."

"I could still use some decorating help." He led her into the living room which didn't boast much beyond a sofa and two armchairs that didn't look at all like Andrew's taste. "My aunt sent over some furniture," he said in answer to her unspoken question. "I've been so busy with the church that I haven't thought about replacing it."

"Well, it works," she said, taking a seat. "Have you heard any more about Annie?"

"The chief isn't keeping you updated?"

"He is, but I haven't heard anything since he showed me the cross they found near the bag from the market. I can't believe anyone in this town would want to take Annie away from her baby."

"It could have been random."

"That's almost harder to believe, given the circumstances." The doorbell rang, three sharp peals of impatience. "You're popular."

"Looks that way."

She waited in the living room as Andrew went to get the door, but as soon as she heard Joe's angry voice, she jumped to her feet and walked into the entryway.

Joe had his hands on his hips, fury in his eyes, and when he saw her, he looked even more pissed off.

"What's going on?" she asked.

"Your boyfriend here just made things a lot worse," Joe said.

"What are you talking about?"

"Andrew shared Annie's secret with several of the men in question—against my express wishes," he added, sending Andrew a killing look.

"Why does it matter?" Andrew challenged. "We need to get to the truth, and I have a relationship with those couples. I'm the one who set up the meetings between them and Annie. I thought I had a better chance of getting whoever the father is to confess."

"Well, it didn't work that way, did it?"

Andrew frowned. "There's still time."

"Time is what we *don't* have. Dan McCarthy and Steve Baker have hired an attorney. They're refusing to answer any more questions or give their DNA. I can get a court order, but that's going to take a little time. Whatever chance we had of getting someone to give something up without realizing it just went out the window."

Charlotte couldn't believe what she was hearing. "Why would they get an attorney, Joe?"

"To avoid being dragged into a kidnapping charge or having their reputations smeared across town. Because the rumors are all over Angel's Bay."

"I didn't realize. I've been in the house all day," she murmured. "Andrew was only trying to help."

Joe's frown deepened. "This is a police investigation. You both need to stay out of it."

"What are you going to do now?" she asked.

"Keep looking for Annie while I try to set up some DNA tests. Not that paternity will necessarily lead us to Annie, but it will tell us who's legally responsible for the baby. That will get you and your mother off the hook."

Her heart skipped a beat. She'd bonded with the baby, and she felt a responsibility to Annie to keep him safe until she came back. Whoever the father was, he hadn't acted honorably or responsibly so far. "Why would two of the men hire attorneys? They both can't be guilty. I don't think Annie slept with more than one guy."

"They're friends. They could be protecting each other," Joe said.

She glanced at Andrew. "What do you think?"

"That would be my guess," he said tightly, a glint of anger in his eyes.

Joe and Andrew didn't care much for each other, which she found a little surprising since they were both community-minded men. A tiny, vain part of her wondered if their animosity toward each other was in part because of their interest in her, although until very recently, Joe had been married. And Andrew had been out of her life for a long, long time.

"Did Dan or Steve say anything to you, Andrew?" she asked.

"No, not really," Andrew answered. "They both acted surprised. Erin and Tory weren't present when I told them about the paternity issue. I spoke to all of the men privately."

"Someone is lying." Joe fixed Andrew with a pointed gaze. "I'd appreciate it if you wouldn't have any more contact with the parties involved."

"I won't go out of my way, but if someone wants to speak to me, I will listen."

"I'll walk you out, Joe," Charlotte suggested quickly, sensing that Joe didn't like Andrew's answer. "We'll talk later, Andrew."

"Definitely."

She stepped onto the porch, pulled the front door shut, then followed Joe out to the sidewalk. "I've never seen you so mad," she said, stopping by his car.

"Andrew screwed things up."

"I'm sure that wasn't his intent. While I understand that you don't want him in the middle of your investigation, it is possible these men would talk more freely to him, because they've shared some very personal things already. You and Andrew should find a way to work together."

"That's going to be tough to do, with you in the middle."

She drew in a quick breath. They'd both been tiptoeing around their relationship ever since he'd signed the divorce papers. "I'm not in the middle."

"Sure you are."

"Look, Joe, we can't do this now."

"Agreed," he said. "But someday . . . soon."

The promise in his eyes sent a shiver down her spine. She almost called him on it, but she couldn't. Not yet. She needed to find Annie, and Joe's divorce needed to be finalized.

She changed the subject. "I've been thinking about who could possibly want to take Annie, and I wonder if we should try to talk to her father again." The last time they'd attempted that, the man had run them off his property with a shotgun.

"I went up there earlier today. Annie's father is no longer living at that shack. It's been abandoned for at least a few weeks. And he picked up his last disability check at a post office box more than two weeks ago and hasn't been back since."

She'd never thought about the fact that Annie's father had probably been to Angel's Bay in the past few months. "Do you think he ever came by the house and saw Annie?"

"What do you think?"

She thought for a moment. "I can't imagine Annie wouldn't have told us. She was afraid of him."

"Annie might not have wanted to spook you," Joe suggested. "She was happy with you and your mom. She wouldn't have wanted to risk getting kicked out."

"But Annie's father washed his hands of her when she got pregnant. He was adamant several months ago that she was dead to him. But if not him, then who? A random stranger? Or one of the potential fathers? Hiring an attorney seems to imply some sort of guilt. I can't imagine what Tory and Erin must think. And the guys are only postponing the inevitable. It won't be difficult to prove DNA; then the lie is over. I don't get it."

"People do funny things when they're running scared. Actions aren't always logical."

"But what does taking Annie *get* anyone?"

"Maybe she knew more about this guy than that he was just unfaithful."

Goose bumps tickled her nerves. "You have to find her, Joe."

"I intend to."

She liked his confidence, but Annie had been gone several days already. The trail had to be growing cold. "When you find the father, will he automatically get the baby?"

"Barring any reason he shouldn't, I would think yes."

"If he wanted his son, he would have come forward already," she protested.

"But claiming his son might end his marriage."

Charlotte sighed. "I know several of the wives. Not one of them deserves what's coming."

"People rarely get what they deserve," Joe said heavily. "I learned that a long time ago." The flash of hurt in his eyes was gone as quickly as it came. "I'll be in touch."

She nodded. "If there's anything I can do, please let me. I know you don't want amateurs getting in the middle of things. But I care a lot about Annie and her baby. If she wants to give her child away, I want it to be her decision, not someone else's. I just hope it's not too late."

"Let's go, we're going to be late," Megan declared.

Nick was surprised that his daughter cared about the time. But when she jangled the car keys in her hand, he realized why. "I take it you're driving."

"I need to practice. And you said you'd let me," she reminded him.

"All right." He grabbed his jacket as Megan opened the back door. She had announced that she'd agreed to babysit for his cousin Colleen's younger daughter, and while he appreciated Megan's desire to work, he'd hoped to spend some time with her.

Apparently, the only time she wanted with him was while she was behind the wheel of his car. He supposed he should be grateful for that.

"What time will Colleen be back?" he asked as he got into the passenger seat. "And why isn't Cord watching his younger sister?"

"Cord is going to some party. And Colleen said they'd be back around midnight. I can't imagine anything in this town goes later than that."

"I'll pick you up."

"I wasn't planning on walking."

He sighed. Megan was so afraid to let him in, even just a little bit.

"How did it go at the theater today?"

"Fine," she said as she buckled her seatbelt.

"Where did you work?"

"Mostly in the costume shop." Megan shot him a quick look. "Isabella thinks you're a superhero because you saved her life. I told her she didn't know you at all."

That stung, as he was sure she'd intended it to.

She started the engine and adjusted her mirrors.

"Megan, wait. Before we both have to concentrate on the road, I've been wanting to ask you something."

She sighed. "What?"

"Do you remember anything about your life with me before your mom took you to London?"

She stared straight ahead and was quiet so long he thought either she didn't remember or she had no intention of answering him. Finally, she said, "I remember a place with stripes on the window and round tables and ice cream."

"Sweet Treats. It was an ice cream parlor down the street from our apartment. I used to pick you up at preschool, and we'd get an ice cream. You were a vanilla girl, just like me."

She turned to look at him. "How come you picked me up from school? Didn't you have a job?"

"I had a couple of jobs—bartender, courier, bus-boy, whatever I could find. I wasn't qualified for much, with just a high school diploma and a lot of theater experience."

"Why didn't you get a job in the theater, like Mom?"

"I never wanted to act." He paused. "Whatever I thought about your mom, I never doubted her talent. Kendra was really good."

"Yeah, she could make you believe anything," Megan said. A small sniff ended her sentence.

He gave her a quick look and saw tears in her eyes before she looked away. "She loved you. She still does."

"She loves herself the most," Megan said. His daughter might pretend not to notice much, but she saw everything.

"She always wanted you with her, Megan."

"I was a good prop until I got too old."

He hated the cold cynicism in her voice.

"You were lucky she took me with her to London," Megan added. "You got to go to school and become an architect."

"Yes. But most of what drove me to find a career that I was good at and that I could be successful in was you." Expressing his emotions had never come easily for him—one reason he'd never been a good actor. "I wanted to be someone you could look up to, Megan."

"Me? Or my mother?" she challenged. "Did you do it so you could get her back? Isn't that why you came to London and left without seeing me, because she was getting married to someone else, and you realized you were too late?"

"That wasn't it at all."

"You're seriously telling me you don't still have a thing for her? She's beautiful. Every man wants her."

"I don't feel anything for her except extreme disappointment and anger. I messed up, but she did, too. And you were the one to pay for our mistakes. I'll regret that till the day I die."

Megan stared at him for a long moment. "Can I drive now?"

He couldn't read her reaction, but for once, it wasn't a sarcastic comeback. "Sure, let's drive."

Megan was actually a better driver than he'd anticipated, and it was obvious she loved it. It probably had something to do with finally being in control of one part of her life. A few minutes later, Megan pulled up in front of Colleen's house and turned off the engine. "Colleen said she could give me a ride home."

"All right, but if something changes, call me, and I'll come and get you. Doesn't matter what time it is."

He got out and walked around to the driver's side as Megan hurried up the walk. Colleen opened the door and gave Megan a hug. Her eight-year-old daughter squealed with delight and followed up with another hug. He was happy to see their affection; Megan needed love. He hadn't realized how much she needed until now.

Pulling away from the curb, he headed downtown to get a drink. Murray's Bar was crowded when he walked in. A band was setting up in the corner, and the pool tables in the back room were packed. Nick made his way to the bar and was about to order a beer when Michael Murray, the bartender, shouted that drinks were on the house because his brother Shane was getting married.

Nick grinned as Shane glared at his brother. Shane wasn't one to enjoy a lot of attention, and now he was the center of it. Nick couldn't really blame him for not wanting the spotlight. Shane was the black sheep of the Murray family. He didn't just have dark hair and eyes while the rest of the family was fair, but he was also a moody loner who'd gotten into all kinds of trouble in school—the worst coming when he was accused of killing the sister of his teenage girlfriend.

Nick was happy that dark cloud had recently lifted. He'd been good friends with Shane in high school, and while they'd gotten into a lot of trouble together, Shane had always been a good guy at heart.

As the crowd dispersed, Nick moved down the bar. "Congratulations. I guess hell has frozen over if you're getting married."

Shane grinned. "I was lucky enough to get Lauren back. I've got to seal the deal." As the person next to him slid off the adjacent stool, he added, "Have a seat. I hear you're back in town for good."

"It looks that way." Nick accepted a beer from Michael, nodding his thanks. "I can't believe you and Lauren finally worked things out. I never thought that would happen after everything that went down."

"I didn't, either." Shane gave him a speculative look. "I also didn't think you'd be back or that you'd have a teenage kid with you. How did I miss that?"

"I met Kendra the summer you left Angel's Bay. I was stupid enough to get her pregnant. We tried to make things work; they didn't. She took my daughter to Europe with her, and I just got her back. Megan is fifteen now, and she hates my guts."

"Sounds about right. We weren't big on our parents at that age, either," Shane said, lifting his beer to his lips.

"Megan has a lot more to be pissed off about than the normal teenage shit. But she's a handful, man."

"Sounds like she takes after you."

"I pushed a few boundaries in my time, which makes me a hell of a role model for a teenager. How can I tell her not to do what I did? And how can I expect her to listen to me, when I didn't give a shit what my parents thought?"

Shane shook his head. "I have no idea. Try being honest. At least you won't be bullshitting her. And you're not the punk I hung out with fifteen years ago. You've changed. You wear suits to work and probably have some money in your bank account."

"A little."

"I always thought you'd end up playing in a band," Shane said. "You could play a mean guitar."

"I tried to pursue music when we moved to New York, but it didn't work out." He paused. "What about you? You've come back to work with your father's charter boat business? What happened to sailing the most dangerous seas in the world?"

"Been there, done that. Realized that what I really wanted was here."

As the band began to warm up, Nick turned his gaze toward them and recognized Hank Bremmer. They'd jammed together in high school, and he felt a twinge of regret that he hadn't kept up with his music. He'd been so caught up in trying to make himself into someone else, someone better, that he'd lost track of who he'd once been.

He'd lived his life at two extremes. At one time, he'd been completely reckless and irresponsible, living whatever emotion he was feeling and not thinking beyond the next five minutes. That had gotten him into all kinds of trouble. Now he stayed completely within the lines, never broke the rules, saved for the future, and tried not to care too much about anything or anyone. But that wasn't working for him, either. He'd been feeling restless for a long time, but now he was feeling *reckless*, too.

As he lifted the beer mug to his lips, he saw a flash of dark hair at the other end of the bar, and for a second he thought it was Isabella. When the woman turned and he realized it wasn't her, he was shocked by his disappointment.

Isabella strolled through downtown, surprised to find so many people out and about. For a small town, there was a fair amount of action on a Friday night. Joe had gone back to work after sharing a quick dinner with her. He seemed to be consumed with finding the missing girl. The people of Angel's Bay were lucky to have her brother; he was one dedicated cop.

She, however, was at loose ends. Too much quiet gave her too much time to think, which was always a little dangerous where she was concerned, so a walk seemed in order. Although most of the retail shops were closed, she could hear laughter and music coming from some of the bars and restaurants. There was an infectious lightness in the air, as if something good was about to happen——maybe it was just the prospect of the weekend. Judging by the number of colored flyers posted on shop windows, all kinds of events were taking place.

Joe had told her that the town made an occasion out of every possible holiday. She'd thought he was exaggerating, but apparently not. It was fun to be somewhere with such a strong sense of community. She was beginning to see why her brother liked Angel's Bay so much. She also understood why Rachel had not felt as comfortable.

Her sister-in-law was big-city, from her sophisticated sharp-angled hairstyle to her stiletto heels. Rachel liked movie premieres and designer clothes, and she made a good living selling real estate to the rich and famous. No wonder she and Joe had found themselves at an impasse. The one thing they had in common was stubbornness.

Her pulse quickened as she approached the Angel's Heart Quilt Shop. It was after nine o'clock, but the front door was open, the lights blazing. She'd intended to check out the shop tomorrow, but maybe now was a good time.

As she stepped inside, she could hear laughter coming from the second floor. Three women came down the stairs, engaged in conversation. They gave her friendly smiles as they passed by, but didn't question her presence, so she decided to look around.

She'd spent many hours of her life looking at fabrics, but she'd never made a quilt. She'd always been more interested in clothing herself or the people around her, but as she studied the beautiful designs decorating the walls, she had a distinct urge to try her hand at one.

Behind a large glass case on one wall was the original Angel's Bay Memorial Quilt that Joe had told her about. Each square had a different theme and was made of a different material. A placard underneath the quilt read, "In memory of those lost in the wreck of the *Gabriella,* 1850. She perused the squares, wondering which one of them had belonged to one of her ancestors. Joe had said that Fiona Murray was the one to ask. With that in mind, she headed up to the loft on the second floor.

A couple of women were stacking up chairs along the wall, while several others were gathered around the coffee urn and the dessert table. She was pleased to see two familiar faces; Charlotte Adams and Kara Lynch.

"Isabella, hello," Charlotte said as she joined them. "How are you?"

"I'm very well, thanks."

"Do you know Kara?"

She smiled at Kara. "Yes, we met the other day. And Joe said as soon as he wraps up this case, he'd love to come to dinner."

"Great. I hope that will be soon," Kara said, her smile dimming.

"Let's hope so," Charlotte echoed. She reached for the bottle of red wine on the table. "Would you like a glass, Isabella?"

"Sure. What was going on up here?"

"One of our many quilting parties," Kara said. "Do you quilt?"

"I've never actually tried it, but now that I'm here, I'm getting the itch."

"Don't start scratching it, or it will never go away," Charlotte advised with a laugh.

"Charlotte only enjoys stitching up people," Kara said with a grin.

Isabella shuddered at that thought. "I can't imagine." She took a sip of wine, glancing around at the few remaining women in the loft. "I was wondering if your grandmother is here. Joe told me that one of our ancestors might have been on the ship that went down and that we might have a square on the quilt."

"Yes, you do have a square," Kara said. "I tried to tell Joe about it a long time ago, but he wasn't interested."

"Imagine that," Charlotte murmured dryly.

"The family name was Cardoza," Kara said. "Miguel, his wife, Beatriz, and their sons survived the wreck. They were from Mexico and went to San Francisco for the Gold Rush. He worked in the mines, while Beatriz took in mending to make ends meet. I have all of the survivors and their families pretty much memorized," she said. "My grandmother has been in charge of Founders Day since I was born."

"It's funny that your ancestor also made money sewing," Charlotte commented.

Just like Leticia, Isabella thought. The desire to sew seemed to be in her genes. "Do you know anything about Leticia Cardoza? She lived here fifty years ago, and she worked at the theater."

"The name doesn't ring a bell, but I'm sure my grandmother can help. Come by the shop tomorrow. There's nothing she likes to talk about more than family and Angel's Bay history." Kara paused as a slender brunette with sparkling blue eyes joined them.

"Hey, where's my wine?" the woman complained, gesturing at the empty bottle.

"You got here too late," Charlotte told her. "This is Isabella Silveira—Lauren Jamison."

"Silveira, as in Chief Silveira?" Lauren quizzed.

"He's my older brother," Isabella replied.

"Great! Now we can get some gossip on the chief."

Isabella smiled. Her brother had always had his share of female admirers.

"Your brother is a man of mystery," Kara said. "He's friendly, but no one gets too close."

"He has to keep a professional distance," Charlotte put in.

"Is that what you call the distance you two have been keeping?" Kara teased.

Charlotte blushed. "I don't know what you're talking about. And you're going to give Isabella the wrong idea. Your brother and I are just friends. He's married—well, he was married, and I always respected that," she said firmly.

Isabella had seen the way the two of them had looked at each other the night of her accident. Maybe there had been nothing going on in the past, but she wondered if it would stay that way.

"Okay, are we done talking about you and your nonexistent relationship with the chief?" Lauren asked. "Because we need to discuss my bachelorette party."

Charlotte's and Kara's jaws dropped in unison.

"What?

"Are you serious?"

"When?"

"How?"

The questions shot out from Charlotte and Kara while Lauren stood with a giddy smile on her face.

"Shane officially proposed," she said finally, her eyes tearing up. "In the tree house."

"That's the best my brother could do?" Kara asked in disbelief. "And you actually said yes?"

"It was romantic," Lauren defended. "And sexy, too."

Kara immediately put up a hand. "Please, I don't want to know what happened after you said yes. My nephews play up there."

"When's the date?" Charlotte asked. "And by the way, I am so happy for you."

"Thank you," Lauren said. "We want to get married around Christmas or New Year's. It won't be a long engagement, because I need my dad to walk me down the aisle. I want him to know who he is and who I am when he does it." Lauren glanced at Isabella. "My father has Alzheimer's, so time is of the essence."

"I'm happy for you," Isabella said.

"This calls for a celebration," Kara declared. "Let's go to Murray's. I have a babysitter until ten, so I have another half hour, and we're out of wine here."

"I'm in," Lauren said. "Shane went to the bar to tell Michael and whoever else was there; we can join them."

"I wish I could come, but I have to get home," Charlotte said with regret. "My mother is watching Annie's baby, and my time is up."

"Isabella?" Kara asked.

"Oh," she said with a start as their gazes turned to her. "Are you sure you don't want to celebrate on your own?"

"Don't be silly," Lauren said. "It's Friday night. You don't have anything better to do, do you? Besides, you still haven't told us any good gossip about your brother."

"I'm afraid I don't have any. Joe isn't big on sharing."

"Come with us anyway," Kara said. "We'll introduce you around. Lauren and I know a lot of people—even a few attractive single men, if you're interested."

"I'm always interested," she said. "But I'm not planning to stay in Angel's Bay."

"That's what they all say." Kara exchanged a warm grin with Lauren. "But sometimes love gets in the way."

NINE

Kara and Lauren talked all the way to the bar. It was clear they'd known each other for a long time and had a deep friendship that was now going to be tied by blood when Lauren married Kara's brother. Their closeness reminded Isabella that she'd let a lot of her friends go—or they'd let her go.

Before she'd realized that telling people she had visions would freak them out, she'd tried sharing her secret, but it had always backfired. Her friends grew nervous or became guarded in her presence, the relationship turning awkward, then eventually ending. As she got older, she'd learned to hide that part of herself. With Kara and Lauren, there didn't appear to be any secrets, and she felt a wistful yearning for an unconditional relationship like theirs.

Murray's Bar was crowded. They made their way through the standing-room-only bar to see the band that was rocking the joint. Isabella felt a tingle of anticipation that seemed inexplicable until her gaze came to rest on one of the band members. It was Nick. And he was jamming on the guitar like a rock star.

Her jaw dropped in amazement. Gone was the controlled suited-up architect. In his place was a hot guy in faded jeans and an open button-down shirt over a black T-shirt. He looked younger, wilder, sexier, and she couldn't take her eyes off him.

"Is that Nick Hartley?" Lauren asked with surprise in her voice. "I haven't seen him in years."

"He's been in and out of town for the last decade, but he just came back with his teenage daughter a few weeks ago," Kara said, raising her voice so she could be heard over the music. "He's still really good, isn't he?"

He was very good, Isabella thought, watching the way his fingers moved on the strings. A shiver ran through her as she remembered his hands on her earlier, his tongue sweeping through her mouth, his fingers running through her hair, his body so beautifully strong and hard. A rush of heat swept through her. She'd gotten a taste of the fire burning behind his cool exterior, but now she could see it a lot closer to the surface. Nick was feeling the music with his heart and his soul. He never let down his guard when he spoke, but when he played, it was all there.

He looked out at the crowd, his eyes meeting hers. She clung to his gaze for a long moment, everyone else fading into the background. She was so caught up in him that it took her a second to realize that the music had stopped, and the rush of noise was applause. The crowd shifted as the band took a break, and Nick was lost to her view. She let out a breath of relief, feeling shaken by the intense connection she felt to him and the rampant desire to get naked with him and lose herself in his arms, his eyes, and his touch.

Her cheeks warmed, and she fanned her face with her hand.

Kara gave her a smile. "It's pretty hot in here, isn't it?"

She nodded, hoping that Kara hadn't picked up on the look between her and Nick, but judging by the gleam in her eyes, she had. Fortunately, Lauren drew Kara's attention away from her.

"There's Shane," Lauren said with excitement, grabbing Kara's hand. "Let's go see my fiancé. God, I love saying that!"

Isabella followed Kara and Lauren to the bar, where she was introduced to Shane Murray. He was a dark, attractive man with a rough edge to him. He looked like someone who worked with his hands and spent a lot of time outdoors. He was quite different from Kara, who had dark red hair and fair skin.

But whatever rough edges Shane had, they immediately softened when he saw Lauren. He stood up, put his arm around her waist, and pulled her close to him, giving her a smile that was pure love.

"Shane, I can't believe you proposed in the tree house," Kara scolded him. "That's not romantic."

"It's our place," he said with an unrepentant smile.

"And it was very romantic," Lauren added. "Shane, I want you to meet Isabella Silveira, Joe's sister. She's new in town."

Shane extended his hand. "Nice to meet you. What are you all drinking? Michael is buying."

"That was the first round, big brother," the bartender said. "Hey, Kara. I saw Colin in here earlier. Since when aren't you two attached at the hip?"

"Since I had an event at the quilt shop and Colin decided to play cards with Jason and some other guys. I'll take a red wine. Isabella?"

"Same," she replied.

"Michael is my youngest brother," Kara explained as her brother went to get their drinks. "Patrick is the oldest; he doesn't live in Angel's Bay. And I have a younger sister, Dee, making me the middle child."

"Poor baby," Shane teased. "It makes no difference where you landed in the lineup. You run the family, and you know it."

"Well, someone has to," she retorted.

As Kara quizzed Shane on his wedding plans, the band began to play again. A female singer stepped up to the microphone with a poignant melody of love and loss. She had a good voice, but Isabella barely heard her. She was completely tuned in to Nick. She loved the intensity with which he played, the total surrender of control to the emotion in the music. Was there anyplace else where he felt as free to let go? She doubted it.

Kara handed her a glass of wine. "Nick was a

heartbreaker in high school," she said. "What girl can resist a guy who plays the guitar?"

Isabella smiled. "It is quite appealing."

"And Nick is very attractive. He's changed a lot, though. Not in a bad way," Kara quickly added. "He used to ride motorcycles with Shane, cut school, drink, and God knows what else. I guess he finally grew up. Having a kid tends to do that to you."

"Yes," Isabella murmured, only half listening to Kara. Nick's gaze had found hers again, and she had the crazy feeling he was playing just for her.

When the song ended, Nick handed the guitar to another guy and slowly made his way toward the bar, stopped frequently by people complimenting him on his performance.

Eventually, he ended up in front of her. Kara and Lauren greeted him with hugs and rave reviews of his performance, which he brushed off with a disarming smile. She hadn't seen him look so relaxed, so happy. As the conversation flowed easily, Nick's gaze occasionally caught hers and every single time she felt her heart skip.

Finally, Kara announced that her babysitting time was up and she was heading home. Shane and Lauren were engaged in conversation with other friends, so Isabella decided to make her exit, as well.

"I'll walk you both out," Nick said.

She nodded, feeling a tingle of anticipation. She was glad for Kara's presence. The way she was feeling tonight, being alone with Nick was probably a bad idea.

"I'm parked just around the corner," Kara said as they left the bar. "I'm fine on my own."

"What about you, Isabella?" Nick asked.

"Over on Elm Street," she replied. "I didn't know where I'd be going when I came into town, so I just parked at the bottom of the hill."

"We'll walk Kara to her car, and then I'll walk you to yours."

"That isn't necessary—" Isabella stopped as she and Kara said the same thing at the same time.

"Relax, ladies, I've got it covered."

"It was good to see you playing again," Kara said as they started to walk. "I'd forgotten how good you were, Nick."

"I'd forgotten how rusty I was," he said. "I hit some bad notes."

"No one could tell. Where's your daughter tonight?"

"Babysitting for my cousin Colleen."

"Sounds very responsible."

"She has her moments."

As they turned the corner, Kara paused by a mini-van. "This is me. Thanks for the escort, Nick. Isabella, I hope I'll see you soon."

"Good night," Isabella said.

They waited until Kara drove off before continuing down the street. Nick paused as they approached the Java Hut. "Coffee smells good. Want to stop?"

She really should say no, but instead she said, "That sounds great."

Nick held open the door for her, and she walked

into a small, warm café that smelled like coffee beans and vanilla. They ordered lattes from the teenage clerk and sat down to wait for their order. The quiet was nice after the raucous atmosphere in the bar.

"You were really good back there," she said. "I had no idea you were so talented. When did you learn to play?"

"I was six or seven when I picked up my dad's guitar. It was love at first sight."

"Did you ever think about playing professionally?"

"Oh, yeah. I was going to be a rock star, but that didn't work out."

She smiled, tilting her head to study him. "You're different tonight—less tense."

"Music always relaxed me. It was fun to let loose and escape into that world. I'd forgotten what it was like."

"Tell me more about your guitar-playing days."

"I played in a band in high school. We performed at the school dances, town festivals, whatever gig was going on. We planned to tour and make an album after we graduated. But in my senior year, my parents moved us to Chicago for four months to do a play. By the time I got back, the band had another guitar player, and I was out."

"You couldn't find another band?"

"Other things got in the way not too long after that."

"Megan."

He nodded. "Kendra's pregnancy was a big detour." He got up to retrieve their coffees, then sat back down, sliding her cup across the table. "So, enough about me—what's your story, Isabella? What are the Silveiras all about?"

She took a sip of coffee. "Well, I'm the youngest of five kids. My mother is Irish; my father is Hispanic. They fight and love with energy and passion. There's never a dull moment."

"Joe is the oldest?"

"Yes, and I have three sisters, as well. According to my parents, I was a happy accident, but I wasn't ever sure they were all that happy about my arrival. As soon as I hit kindergarten, my mom was off. She didn't want to volunteer on the playground or help out in the classroom or be the troop leader, like she did with my older siblings. She'd put her time in, and she was done. I couldn't really blame her."

"Couldn't you?" he asked thoughtfully.

She tipped her head. "I can't say I was never angry or that I didn't occasionally feel shortchanged, but maybe that's true for every youngest kid. There's always less excitement when you come along. You should see how many photo albums there are of Joe and my older sisters. They must have taken a thousand pictures of them doing practically nothing. But of me, not so many," she said with a small sigh. "Yet I feel bad for even implying that I didn't have a good childhood, because I did. And my parents are great people, well respected, very loved in the community. I have nothing to complain about."

"You can love them and still not think they did

everything right. God knows, my parents screwed up all the time. And the mistakes I've made with Megan—way too many to count." He took a sip of his coffee. "What else?"

"What else?" she echoed, wondering how deep she wanted to take this conversation. "You're awfully curious all of a sudden."

"I want to know what makes Isabella Silveira tick," he said with a smile.

"Let's see. I love to sew and make costumes. I doodle whenever I have spare time on my hands, so some of my designs had their initial sketches done on napkins and the backs of envelopes."

"I do that, too, sometimes."

"Because you can't let a good idea go without putting it down, right?"

He nodded. "That's right."

"I had an idea when I was watching you play earlier." She took a pen out of her purse and sketched quickly on her napkin. "What do you think?" She pushed it over to him.

"Is that supposed to be me or Mick Jagger?"

She laughed. "It's not supposed to be either of you—just a smoking rock-star look. The movie I'm going to work on in January has some musicians in it, so I've been thinking along those lines."

"I like it," he said. "I don't know much about clothes; I tend to stick with the same old look. It's either a business suit or jeans."

"I could give you some other ideas," she said.

He smiled. "I'm sure you could. But let's get back to you. What do you do when you're not working or doodling?"

"I'm a big fan of exercise—everything from kickboxing to spinning to tai chi. Besides organized classes, I run, hike, bike, and dance. It's the only way I know to get rid of my energy. My family nickname is Dizzy Izzy. My father used to tell me I made his head spin, and not in a good way."

"How so?"

"I was always changing my mind, my plans, my address," she said with a grin. "My siblings all knew exactly what they wanted to do from a very early age. They made decisions and stuck with them. Joe married the girl he fell in love with when he was fifteen."

"Isn't he getting a divorce?" Nick pointed out.

"True."

"Some choices don't last a lifetime," he said.

"I guess not."

He sipped his coffee. "I was the odd man out in my family, too. They were disappointed I didn't want to follow in their footsteps."

"Maybe they were at one time, but they're proud of you, Nick. I've heard a lot of raves about you since I started working at the theater."

He gave her a dry smile. "They're trying to get on my good side so I'll handle the renovations for them."

"They love you."

"I know they do," he said more seriously. "They didn't always put me first, and their career decisions were not always in my best interest, but I never doubted their love. I wish that I'd given Megan that kind of grounding."

"It's not too late."

"I hope not, but she's fighting me."

"You have to fight back. If you don't, you really *will* let her down."

"I don't know how to be a good father. When I was a kid, I didn't listen to anyone. How can I expect Megan to listen to me?"

"You're not that wild guy now. Although I liked seeing you play the guitar tonight, because I felt like I was seeing the real you." She paused, sure she was about to get too personal, but she'd come this far . . . "Why do you have so many walls up, Nick? What are you trying so hard to protect?"

He stiffened at her question, a frown returning to his face. "If I wanted an analysis, I'd see a shrink."

"That's a copout."

"Why should I tell you?"

"Because I'm the one asking," she returned.

"I don't even know you."

"Isn't that what we're doing now, getting to know each other?" she challenged.

He blew out a breath, a battle going on in his eyes. "There's something about you that makes me want to talk, and I haven't wanted to talk in a long time."

"Why not?" Even as she asked, she wondered if she had the right to pry into his life when she had secrets of her own. But it was too late to take it back.

He stared at her for a long moment. "Because I wasted too much time talking instead of doing. But I've got my life together now. I have a successful business. I own a house. It's good. It's solid. It's enough."

Despite his forceful words, she heard the uncertainty in his voice. "It is all that. But deep down, you're still the guy who wanted to be a rock star."

"That guy grew up, and I'm not going back."

"Then why did you jump in with the band tonight?"

He sighed. "Temporary insanity."

"Well, you were insanely good. Does it really have to be one or the other?"

"I've never been able to find a middle ground. That's what worries me about Megan; I see a lot of myself in her. And right now, she's all defiance and rebellion. Look at the way she dresses."

"Her hair, clothes, and makeup are the only things under her control right now."

"I know that. But I see a dangerous recklessness in her, which is what I felt after Kendra left. When she took off with Megan, I went on a nine-month bender. I drank and hung out in clubs until dawn. It took me a long time to realize that I wasn't going to get my family back unless I changed my life."

"So you dried out, went back to school, and made a career for yourself. You should be proud of all that."

"I am."

"And you locked that reckless, rebellious guy

away—until tonight. Why tonight? What changed?"

He frowned. "I don't know. I was happy enough with my life, but then Megan arrived, and I rescued you off that hillside, and suddenly, I find myself wanting things I thought I'd forgotten about. You make my head spin, too," he added, his gaze drifting to her mouth. "Why did you have to show up now, Isabella?"

She could have told him that it was destiny, but he wouldn't believe her. Nick was under the mistaken impression that he could control his life if he just wore a tie and followed a few rules. She finished her coffee and stood up. "Let's walk."

After they left the Java Hut, they strolled along the harbor. The boats bobbed lazily in their slips. Just beyond the breakwater, the waves crashed, but the bay was protected and calm. And overhead were a million stars in a clear night sky.

"You don't get this kind of view in L.A.," she said. "It must have been fun growing up here."

"It was a haven from the madness of the rest of my life. When it was off season here in Angel's Bay, my parents would pack me and Tory up and take us on the road. Buses, motels, backstage dressing rooms—that was our world."

"Were you and Tory close?"

"Always. We looked out for each other. I tried to be a big brother when I could, but in truth, Tory had her life together long before me, and she stepped between me and my parents when we were at odds. Which was often." He paused. "After Kendra left, I asked my parents for money so I could go to London and get Megan back."

Isabella stopped walking, hearing the tension in his voice. "What did they say?"

"They didn't have any extra cash," Nick replied, a grimness to his expression. "But it wasn't really about the money. They didn't like the life I was leading. My father said it was time for me to grow up." He gave a short, hard laugh. "Funny coming from him, because he's always been Peter Pan, living in a world where no one ever grows up or has to face reality. Even with these theater renovations, they're burying their heads in the sand." He drew in a breath and started walking again. "Maybe it was good they didn't help me out. It forced me to stand on my own two feet. But a part of me wonders if I would have gotten Megan back sooner if I'd had their support."

"They seem to care a great deal about Megan now," she put in, having witnessed several exchanges between the Hartleys and Megan.

"They always cared. They used to write her and send her gifts, but for a long time, they thought Megan was better off with Kendra. They understood Kendra; she was one of them. It took all of us a while to see her for who she really was. She's a very good actress."

"It must have been strange to grow up with people who could so easily transform themselves into someone else. I'd have had a difficult time figuring out who was being real and who was playing a role," Isabella said.

"You learn not to trust too easily."

"So that explains some of your walls."

"Are we back to that?"

She shrugged. "Just saying."

For a few moments, they walked in easy silence, then Nick asked, "How long will you be staying in Angel's Bay?"

"I don't know. Outside of work, I rarely make plans. I just see where the wind blows."

He cast her a quick sideways look. "Really? What if the wind blows you somewhere you don't want to go?"

"There's always another breeze."

He shook his head. "I used to leave things to chance, but that didn't get me anywhere. You have to go after what you want, or there's a good chance you'll never get it. Despite what you say, I don't believe you're as casual as all that. You must have things you want."

She gave him a long look. "What if I said I wanted you, Nick? What if I went after you?"

He sucked in a quick breath. "You'd be disappointed."

"Why?"

"Because I'm a terrible boyfriend and a worse husband."

"Who said I wanted you to be either one? Not every relationship has to have a label."

He stopped walking, his gaze holding hers. "Would a short-term fling really be enough for you, Isabella? Most women want more."

She'd been testing him a little; now he was doing the same to her.

"What I want," she began, choosing her words carefully, "is to live my life and get to the end without regrets."

He stared back at her. "That's a nice dream, but no one gets to the end without regrets."

"You certainly won't if you keep pretending that who you are now has nothing to do with who you used to be. You're afraid, Nick."

"You're calling me a coward?" he asked in amazement. "I saved your life."

"You're not afraid to be a hero. You're afraid to be who you really *are*."

His eyes glittered with a mix of anger and desire. "You like to live dangerously, don't you?"

"Sometimes."

"Sometimes so do I." He put his hands on her waist and yanked her up against him. "You know where this is going, don't you?"

"I hope so," she whispered, just before his mouth closed over hers.

His kiss deepened, his tongue sliding between her lips. He tasted like coffee and lust and so much more. Nick's hands threaded through her hair, holding her in place, but stopping the delicious onslaught was the farthest thing from her mind. She wanted to touch him all over, to rip off his clothes, break through his walls, and get to the core of the real Nick Hartley. The way he kissed her made her want to take a lifetime exploring his mouth and his body, his heart and his soul.

She shook from the force of her emotions and felt an echoing tremor run through him. Nick tore himself away from her mouth, his ragged breath steaming up the cold night air. His eyes burned with wild, reckless desire, and her heart skipped a beat. But then she saw his battle for control, his withdrawal in the stiffening of his shoulders.

"Damn," he muttered. "What am I going to do about you?"

"Why are you fighting so hard to stay away from me?"

"Because I don't want someone like you."

She drew in a quick, painful breath. He had no idea she'd heard those words before. Not exactly in this context, but they still stung. Turning quickly, she walked down the street to Joe's truck. As Nick followed her down the sidewalk, she dug into her purse for her keys.

"I'm sorry, Isabella. That didn't come out the right way."

She turned, and looked directly into his eyes. "The reason you stopped tonight, Nick, is that you want someone *exactly* like me. Someone who shakes that cage you've locked yourself up in, someone who reminds you of who you really are."

"And who are you, Isabella? A woman who changes jobs and men and addresses every other week? You think that's living life? That's called running away."

She swallowed hard, his words hitting a little too close to home.

"You're afraid of being left behind, so you leave first," he added.

"Exactly." She got into the truck and slammed the door. She turned the key in the ignition and drove off, her stomach churning, her body shaking, her emotions boiling over.

Nick didn't have her pegged exactly right, but he was damn close. And it was sheer hypocrisy to call him out for pretending to be someone he wasn't. Hadn't she done the same thing for most of her life? Hadn't she hidden away the part of herself that she didn't like? But it was so much easier to analyze someone else than to analyze herself.

She let out a breath. Their relationship was getting too intense, breaking all the rules she'd set for herself after Tony. She'd wanted to get close enough to Nick so that she could help him but not so close that she could get hurt. But the lines were blurring. And she was afraid that by coming to Angel's Bay, she'd put something in motion that couldn't be stopped.

What the hell was wrong with him? Nick fumed as he walked briskly down the street. The second he'd seen Isabella in the bar, he'd known that he wouldn't be able to leave her alone. Since he'd rescued her from her car, he'd felt an incredible pull toward her, as if saving her life had tied them together in some powerful and elemental way. He didn't like it. And he didn't want to like her.

She was challenging his decisions, the way he led his life, making him think that he'd gone too far in his goal to be an adult. Yet she was just like Kendra, ready to jump at the best offer.

No, that wasn't true. Isabella was softer, kinder, warmer, with a smile that lit up her eyes. A man could drown in her gaze, die a long, slow death in her arms. *Shit!* He hadn't felt so consumed by desire in a very long time.

He blew out a breath and picked up his pace, breaking into a jog. He ran for a mile before his cell phone rang.

Breathless, he answered, "Hello?"

"It's Colleen. I just dropped Megan off at your house. I didn't see your car, so I wanted to let you know that she was there."

"I'm on my way," Nick said, grateful for the distraction. "How did the babysitting go?"

"Great. Alina was fast asleep when we got home, and the house was still in one piece. I consider that a successful night."

"I'm happy to hear it."

"Megan isn't as bad she makes herself out to be. She even did some dishes for me."

He was surprised. His daughter hadn't shown any tendency toward neatness at his house. When he'd suggested that she pick up her things, she'd retorted that she was used to having housekeepers do that. He wasn't poor, but Kendra got ten million plus a movie. Megan must feel as if she was living in a shack.

"So I'll see you on Sunday, right?" Colleen asked, bringing his attention back to the conversation.

"What's Sunday?"

"The annual sand-castle-building contest. I told Megan about it. You should enter it with her."

"They still have that contest?" he asked in amazement.

"Yes, and I remember when you and your father won it. Maybe that's a family tradition you can share with Megan."

"Do you seriously think my punked-out daughter is going to build a sand castle with me?"

"You won't know until you ask. See you later, Nick."

He didn't have to ask to know Megan's answer; she'd laugh in his face. But he supposed he could put himself out there. Maybe he'd at least get points for trying.

When he got back home, he heard the television on in the living room. As he entered the room, Megan switched it off.

"You didn't have to do that," he said. "It's not a school night. What were you watching?"

"Nothing," she said, guilt flashing through her eyes. She stood up. "I'm going to bed."

"Wait. How was your night?"

"Fine." As she walked by him, she gave him a curious look. "Why are you sweating? Where were you?"

"I took a run down by the harbor."

"At midnight? In those clothes? You don't have to lie. You can tell me you were having sex. It's not like Mom wasn't doing it whenever she could."

"I *wasn't* doing it," he said, uncomfortable being quizzed about sex by his teenage daughter. "I went to the bar and saw some friends, then I took a run to clear my head."

"Whatever," she said, leaving the room.

He sighed, wondering if he'd ever say the right thing to her. He sat on the couch and turned on the television, wondering what Megan had been watching to make her look so guilty, and he was shocked when Kendra's face lit up the screen.

It had been a long time since he'd seen her. He'd buried his memories as deeply as he could, but here she was with her luminous eyes and perfect skin and sensual, catlike smile. Kendra oozed sex appeal, from her long legs to her big breasts—breasts he was sure she'd enhanced after he'd been with her. Her lips looked fuller, too. She was a good actress; the emotions flowed effortlessly. She'd always been able to be whoever she was supposed to be and do it convincingly. She'd played the part of his wife for a few years and the part of a mother for a few years longer, but she'd moved past both of those roles.

He turned off the television and walked down the hall. Stopping at Megan's open door, he found her still awake. She was in bed with the headphones on, but her eyes were open. He moved some clothes off the chair next to her bed and sat down.

She pulled her earphones out. "What?"

"Do you want to build a sand castle with me on Sunday? There's a contest."

She scowled at him. "Are you fucking kidding me?"

He just smiled. "How about an answer?"

"I'm not a baby."

"It's not for babies, it's for families. That's you and me. And don't say whatever," he added as she opened her mouth. "I'd like you to participate." It was risky to let her know how much he wanted something; it usually had the opposite effect on her.

She stared at him for a long moment and then sighed. "Fine, I'll do it. Can I go to sleep now?"

He met her gaze. "It's okay to miss your mom, you know."

"I don't miss her. I hate her."

"You only hate those you love. And I know you love her, even though you're angry at her. Whatever she's done, she's always going to be your mother."

"Don't you get it? She doesn't want to be my mother," Megan said with a sniffle. "That's why she sent me away. She couldn't put me in a puffy pink dress anymore and show me off as her adorable little girl."

"Is that why you dyed your hair and pierced your nose?"

"I wanted to look like myself and not her dress-up doll."

"You accomplished that." He got to his feet. "And for the record, Megan, I don't care what you wear or what color your hair is. You'll always be my daughter. And I will always be your dad."

"How am I supposed to believe you? You were just fine not being my father when there was an ocean between us."

"I was young and stupid, but that's not an excuse. I need a second chance, Megan." A knot of emotion choked his throat. "I don't deserve it, but I really want it."

His words hung in the air for a long moment.

Then she said, "Whatever," her mouth curving into a mischievous grin.

"Whatever?" he growled. "I'll show you whatever." He grabbed a pillow. "War," he declared.

Her eyes lit up, and she scrambled into a sitting position, picking up the pillow she'd been lying on. "War!"

As they pummeled each other with pillows, Megan squealed with delight like the little girl who'd once shared this game with him. He didn't know if she remembered, but he didn't care. For one moment, this wasn't about anything but pure fun.

Finally, they collapsed from exhaustion.

"I beat you," Megan declared proudly.

"No way, *I* won," he teased.

Her silence made him turn his head.

"You used to let me win," she said, a faraway look in her eyes.

His breath caught. "Yes, I did."

"You used to sit on the end of my bed until I fell asleep."

"That's because I was too tired to move." He grinned.

She smiled back as she slid under the covers and put a pillow under her head. "You used to tell me that stupid story."

"About Princess Dandelion," he remembered. "God, I forgot about that."

"And Prince Phillipe," she added. "They hated each other at first. But then they lived happily ever after . . ." Megan's voice drifted away, her eyes closing, her fist tucked under her chin the way she'd done as a little girl.

Nick stayed on the end of her bed until she was fast asleep, holding on to the moment for as long as possible. Tomorrow she'd be back to her trash-talking, rebellious self. But tonight—tonight she was his little angel again.

TEN

"What have you done?" Nick shouted. *"I didn't want this. I didn't want you. You've messed up everything. Why didn't you go?"*

"Nick." She put out a hand to him, but he was storming into the darkness, into the shadows.

There was a beckoning light, voices in the night.

He didn't want her with him, but she couldn't let him go alone. He needed her. He didn't know how much.

Isabella sat up with a gasp, her heart racing, sweat dampening her cheeks. She glanced at the sun streaming through the part in the curtains and was relieved to see it was morning.

As she got up and showered, remnants of her dream floated through her mind. Was it really a vision of something to come, or was she turning Nick's rejection from the night before into something more? Was she trying to convince herself that he needed her, because she wanted a reason to stay, because she wasn't ready to walk away from him?

She hadn't felt such physical attraction to a man in a long time. And aside from that, she liked him. She admired the way he'd pulled his life together after his divorce, his desire to become a good father, his loyalty to a family who hadn't always been there for him. He'd made his mistakes, but he was trying to do better, and who couldn't appreciate that?

Wishing she had answers instead of questions, she stepped out of the shower, dried off, and got dressed.

When she entered the kitchen, she found hot coffee and a note from Joe saying that he was at work if she needed anything. He was really pushing hard to find Annie. The girl's disappearance had affected a lot of people who were becoming her friends, such as Tory and Erin and Charlotte. It was amazing how much she already felt a part of the community; no wonder Joe hadn't been able to leave. She could see how his bruised spirit had healed in Angel's Bay. He'd grown cynical and hard during his years working for the LAPD, and there'd been a dangerous edge to him that now seemed softened. She was surprised that Rachel hadn't seen it and welcomed it. Instead, she'd turned away from Joe. Or maybe it was Joe who had turned away from her. Either way, Isabella didn't see anything changing unless one of them took a step to breach the distance between them.

She downed some coffee, then grabbed her bag and headed into town. She wanted to stop by the quilt shop before going to the theater. Maybe Fiona

Murray could tell her something about Leticia and her family history that would give her some clue to how the past and the present were connected.

Fiona Murray was an older, more fiery version of Kara, with red hair, blue eyes, and freckled, weathered skin. She was in her eighties, but her eyes were sharp, her voice was brisk, and she shook Isabella's hand with a firm grip, then waved her to the couch in her office at the back of the quilt shop.

"I was expecting you," Fiona said. "Kara told me you're interested in your family history. Now that I've seen you, I can understand why. You have the look of Beatriz."

"I do?"

"Oh, yes." Fiona set a photo album on the coffee table in front of them. "I have some photographs of Beatriz taken in her later years, but let me tell you a little about her story first."

"I'd love to hear it."

"Beatriz and her husband, Miguel, made it to shore with their two sons, Isaac and Nathaniel, who were toddlers at the time. The Cardozas were one of the few families to survive the wreck intact. Beatriz and one of my ancestors, Rosalyn Murray, were the creators of the memorial quilt that you might have seen downstairs."

"I did. But I couldn't figure out which square belonged to Beatriz."

"Beatriz didn't make a square."

Isabella was surprised and confused. "I thought all of the survivors had a square."

"Beatriz didn't lose anyone, but she wanted to honor those who were gone, so she sewed the squares of the families who had no survivors to memorialize them. Unfortunately, the ship's manifest was also gone, so she had to rely on the other survivors to determine who had been onboard. She spent many decades trying to find the names of everyone. She traveled back and forth to San Francisco, not wanting to miss anyone. Those names are sewn along the sides of the quilt, mixed in with the pattern of the stitching."

Fiona opened the album. The first photograph was an eight-by-ten of the quilt, and Isabella scooted forward so she could see better.

Fiona moved her finger along the stitching design that ran around squares on all four sides. "If you look closely, you can see the names."

"I can," Isabella replied. In fact, as she stared at the picture, her eyes blurred, and she felt as if she were going back in time.

Despair and guilt filled her heart as she pulled the needle in and out of the fabric. So many names. So many lives lost. She could hear the screams in her head when she went to sleep at night. She could see the fear in the eyes of everyone around her as the ocean threatened to swallow them whole.

"She really cared about them," Isabella murmured, lifting her gaze to meet Fiona's. "Beatriz felt tied to those who didn't make it."

Fiona was watching her closely. "Yes. There was a reason for that." She paused. "Beatriz had your eyes, Isabella."

Her pulse leaped. "How do you know?"

Fiona turned several pages until she found the one she wanted. "This photo is in black and white, but even so, her gaze jumps out at you."

Isabella put a shaky hand to her heart as she stared at Beatriz's image. She could see herself clearly in the eyes and the face of a woman who'd lived a hundred and fifty years ago. It seemed surreal.

"Beatriz told my great-grandmother that she'd seen the wreck coming," Fiona continued, "that she'd tried to tell the captain, but he thought she was hysterical. She was able to convince her husband and a few others, including my great-grandmother, and they got to the first lifeboat while everyone else was trying to ride out the storm. She saved my family and hers, but she felt guilty for those who didn't make it."

Isabella knew exactly how Beatriz had felt, the frustration and anguish at not being able to prevent something horrible from happening.

But at least Beatriz's family had believed in her, and she had saved their lives. That was something.

"Beatriz wasn't the only one who had your eyes." Fiona turned the page again.

This photo was in color and taken in front of the theater in what was probably the early 1950s, judging by the clothing, the hair, and the nearby cars. The scenery faded into the background as Isabella stared at the young woman with long black hair and unusually blue eyes who gazed straight into the lens, straight into Isabella's eyes. There was a sadness there, or maybe it was weariness.

"Leticia," Isabella murmured. "It has to be her. He said I looked just like her." She raised her gaze to Fiona. "Harrison Hartley almost fainted when he saw me. I think he loved her."

"I always thought he did," Fiona said with a nod. "But Harrison married Alice shortly after Leticia left town. No one spoke of her again."

"You actually knew Leticia?" Isabella asked, eager to hear more about the woman whose pendant had called her to Angel's Bay. "What was she like?"

"She was quiet, almost like a shadow." Fiona's gaze perused her face. "Like you, and yet not. Your features are similar, but you have a life, a strength, an energy in your eyes that she lacked. It was almost as if she was afraid of herself." Fiona drew in a breath. "Leticia left town after a fire at the theater in which Harrison's younger sister, Caitlyn, died. She was in the costume shop, I believe, or somewhere close by. The Hartleys were devastated, and I'm sure Leticia was, too. Caitlyn was a beautiful girl, so full of life— a wonderful actress and a bit of a wild child."

"My grandmother said that Leticia killed herself. Do you know how she died?"

"Her car went off the road around Big Sur. There were no other vehicles involved, but it could have been an accident."

A tingle ran down Isabella's spine. Leticia had

died in the same kind of accident that she'd had a few days ago. And she'd been rescued by Nick—the grandson of the man Leticia had loved. There were far too many coincidences to ignore.

"You don't think it was an accident?" she queried.

Fiona shrugged. "I honestly don't know. Leticia seemed to carry the weight of the world on her shoulders."

Isabella knew that feeling all too well. "Thanks for your time," she said, getting to her feet.

"Are you all right?" Fiona asked quietly, concern in her eyes as she stood up. "All of this happened a very long time ago."

"Yes, but I'm afraid that something else is coming," she said, the words slipping past her lips before she could stop them.

"Because you've taken Leticia's place in the costume shop? Erin told me that you're a designer."

"Just like Leticia. And you might have guessed that sometimes I see things in my head, the way she did. The way Beatriz apparently did, as well. But it doesn't appear that any of us has been very good at stopping the bad from happening."

"Beatriz saved her family."

"And Leticia? What did she do?"

"I don't think we know her whole story. Maybe that's why you're here now."

Isabella thought about Fiona's words as she drove to the theater. Knowing now that both Beatriz and

Leticia had shared her eye color and her gift made it seem that coming here had been inevitable. But what was she supposed to do? Her vague dreams about Nick being in danger weren't like seeing a ship go down or a theater go up in flames. She had no specific enemy to fight, no warnings to give—not yet, anyway. And even if she did have details, who would believe her? What was the point in seeing the future if she couldn't do anything about it?

Frustrated, she stopped at a red light and pounded her hands against the steering wheel. She'd tried to give up her gift more than once, after her high school boyfriend had died and after she'd lost her best girlfriend. She'd deliberately chosen to lead a life without the intense emotions that always seemed to trigger the visions, and it had worked for a while—until a damn necklace had changed everything.

Reaching back under her hair, she tried to open the clasp. She wanted the pendant off—but like the other two times she'd tried to release the catch, it wouldn't open. She yanked on the chain, but it didn't break. Jeez, did she need wire cutters to get it off?

The car behind her honked impatiently. The light was green, with a line of cars behind her. She hit the gas.

She was tempted to leave Angel's Bay. Maybe the dreams would go away if she wasn't so close to the connections of the past.

But could she live with herself if she left and something bad happened to Nick or to Joe? At least if she stayed in town, she'd know she'd done everything she could. And she'd be there to pick up the pieces, to try to fix things . . . which was all she ever did.

Nick was in the courtyard talking to his father and another man when Isabella arrived at the theater. He spoke in animated tones, enthusiastically waving his hands as he discussed options for renovating the face of the theater. Despite his reservations about getting involved in the job, it seemed to be perfectly suited to him. Like Nick, the building was a study in contrasts, the solid foundation and the strong pillars versus the creative and imaginative whimsy of the architectural details. Maybe he could use both sides of his brain on this job.

As the conversation ended, Nick's gaze swung to hers. He said something to the men about catching up with them inside and then walked over to her.

Her nerves tingled at his approach. She'd been thinking about what she wanted to say to him when she saw him again, but she hadn't come up with anything.

"Isabella."

There was a hint of wariness in his tone, as if he wasn't sure of his reception. She felt a bit the same way. Their last encounter hadn't ended well.

"Nick. How's it going?"

"Fine. Just discussing some initial plans with my father and one of the local contractors."

"You're going to do a great job, Nick."

Surprise flashed in his eyes. "I haven't fully committed."

"You will." She fidgeted, then said, "Well, I should get inside. There are a lot of fittings scheduled today."

He put a hand on her arm. "Wait." His fingers tightened as he gazed down at her. "I didn't like the way things ended last night."

"How did you want the night to end?"

"I don't know, but not like that. I like you, Isabella."

"I know," she said softly. "That's the problem, isn't it?"

"It's a bad time."

"I don't think it's about time. It's about fear. I get it, Nick, because I'm afraid, too. You and me together—we're intense. It's too much. So you were smart to call a halt. But if you want to keep some space between us, you're going to have to let go of my arm."

He pulled his hand away.

"It's all good," she said, forcing a smile. "I'm only going to be in town a short while. No sense in starting something we can't finish."

"Yeah," he said. "No sense in doing that."

"I'll see you around." She felt his gaze on her as she made her way into the theater, but he didn't call her back, because she'd just given him exactly what he wanted—or at least, what he thought he wanted.

*   *   *

The costume shop was crowded when Isabella arrived, and Mariah introduced her to the women who had volunteered to do fittings and make alterations. Everyone welcomed her with open arms. No one was an outsider in Angel's Bay. Once you crossed the town line, you were in. That was true of theater life, too, where everyone shared the same passion, the same quest for perfection. It didn't matter where you came from or who you were, as long as you did your job. That's all anyone cared about. And Isabella was happy with the chaos. She didn't want time to think about Nick or Leticia or anyone else; she just wanted to work.

Just after noon, Kara Lynch came in for her costume fitting. "My grandmother said she spoke to you this morning," Kara said as Isabella helped her into her costume.

"Yes, I found out quite a bit about Beatriz. I didn't realize she was so closely tied to your family."

"The quilt was really Beatriz's idea, although Rosalyn Murray usually gets credit for it." Kara gave Isabella a smile. "I guess this means you're one of us."

She smiled back. "I guess it does." She got down on her knees to check the length on Kara's dress. "This needs to come up about an inch." She put in a pin to mark the spot, then stood up to take a look at the fit.

"Last night was fun," Kara said. "I can't believe

my brother is finally getting married. He's been in love with Lauren since he was seventeen years old, and I'm so happy they finally found their way back to each other. He was always the roamer in the family, the one who couldn't settle anywhere. But now he's putting down roots here in Angel's Bay, the one place he never wanted to stay. It's funny how things work out."

"What do you think about the bust?" Isabella asked. "Shall I let it out a bit?"

"Probably. Breastfeeding has made me much bigger than I used to be. Colin is ecstatic," she added with a laugh. "I don't know what he'll do when I finally put Faith on a bottle full-time."

Isabella liked Kara's warm humor and her lack of pretense. With Kara, what you saw was what you got. She wished she could be that transparent.

"By the way, I'm going to have an engagement party for Shane and Lauren next Saturday night," Kara added. "You have to come. I'm hoping Nick will come, too. He and Shane were good friends at one time." Kara gave Isabella a speculative look. "You and Nick seemed to be getting along well last night."

She cleared her throat. "Well, he did save my life."

"Is that all that's going on? Because I picked up on a definite vibe between you two. I almost got the feeling that Nick was playing just for you."

She'd had that feeling, too, but had chalked it up to her mad attraction to him.

"Nick could use someone like you," Kara said.

Her words were in direct contrast to what Nick had said the night before. "Why do you think that?" Isabella asked curiously.

"Because you're creative and passionate about what you do, and despite Nick's transformation into a suited-up businessman, he's got a soul. All you have to do is listen to his music to know that."

"He's not looking to get into a relationship right now. He's busy with his daughter and his business."

"That's usually when love happens," Kara said with a grin.

"Well, I'm not looking for love."

"Why not? Is there someone in L.A.?"

"It's not that."

"Then what?" Kara prodded.

She shrugged. "Love usually leads to pain, and I'm not interested in heartbreak. I want to have fun. That's it."

"I imagine Nick is pretty fun. He certainly had that reputation in high school."

Isabella laughed. "Stop trying to matchmake."

"I can't help it. I want all of my single friends to get married and be as happy as I am."

Isabella was touched that Kara already felt they were friends; the woman clearly had a big heart. She finished taking measurements and then said, "That's it. I'll have it ready for your final fitting next week."

"Great."

As Isabella helped Kara out of her costume, Tory entered the room, announcing that there were sandwiches and drinks in the rehearsal room for anyone who was hungry. A mass exodus followed her words.

"You certainly know how to clear out a room," Kara said as she threw a sweater over her leggings and tank top.

"I guess," Tory said vaguely.

"Are you all right?" Isabella asked, noting the tense lines around Tory's eyes. "You don't look like you got much sleep last night."

"I didn't."

"What's going on?" Kara asked, compassion in her eyes. "Were you worrying about Annie?"

"Not just that." Tory drew in a big breath and then let it out. "I'm sure you'll hear this soon if you haven't already. I asked Steve to stay at his mother's house last night." She bit down on her bottom lip. "He's hired a lawyer, and he won't answer questions about his relationship with Annie. How can I assume anything but the worst?"

"Dan McCarthy got a lawyer, too," Kara said. "Colin told me last night. Maybe they're just trying to protect their reputations."

"Or each other," Tory said harshly. "They've been good friends for a long time. If only one of them got a lawyer, it would be obvious who was guilty. I never thought a time would come when I wouldn't trust my husband." She tucked a loose piece of hair behind her ear. "I can't believe I said that out loud. What if I'm wrong? But what if I'm right? God, what if I'm *right*?"

"Don't go with the worst-case scenario," Kara advised. "Wait until you have more facts."

"Facts are exactly what Steve is trying to avoid," Tory said bitterly. "And if he cheated on me, he should really tell me, because, lawyer or not, he'll have to eventually give his DNA. If he won't, I will. I have his toothbrush, his hairbrush. The truth is going to come out. I just don't know if I'm ready for it." She shook her head. "Anyway, I don't have time to do this now. I'm sorry I dumped on you two."

As Tory left, Kara turned to Isabella. "Well, that doesn't sound good. I hope Joe can find Annie so we can put all these rumors to rest."

"Me, too."

After Kara left, Isabella took advantage of the quiet to get some sewing done. An hour later, she decided to take a break. She headed into the main theater, curious to see how far along the sets were and how the auditions were going.

She sat down in the last row, watching two women play a scene. Despite the construction going on around them, the women seemed fully invested in their characters. Nick's parents sat at a nearby table, taking notes and offering an occasional suggestion to improve the delivery of the dialogue.

As a man slid into the seat next to Isabella, she looked up and was surprised to see Harrison Hartley.

"I was hoping you'd gone home," he said.

"What are you afraid I'm going to find out?" she asked directly. "I already know you were in love with Leticia. But what I don't know is why Leticia left town. Or why her car went off the road." She looked into his eyes and saw no shock, just pain. "You told me she left—not that she died. And you asked me if I was her granddaughter. How could I be, if she died a week after she left here?"

"I wasn't sure she really died," he said quickly. "After her car went into the ocean, they never found her body. I told myself that a miracle had happened, that she'd survived and gone on to live her life the way she was meant to."

Isabella stared at him, shaken by the reminder that if not for Nick, she might have ended up like Leticia, in a watery grave. But Nick had saved her. Harrison had let Leticia go.

"Why are you here?" Harrison asked again.

"The pendant," she said simply. "My brother found it in my uncle's house and sent it to me. That night I dreamed of Angel's Bay."

"That's crazy."

"Is that what you told Leticia when she shared her visions with you—that she was crazy?"

He didn't answer for a long moment, his jaw tight with emotion. His gaze was fixed on the stage, but his mind was far, far away. "Leticia tried to warn me that trouble was coming. I thought her imagination was just a beautiful, quirky part of her personality. She wanted me to listen, to believe in her, but I didn't. I'll never forgive myself for that. If I had listened to Leticia, my sister Caitlyn would be alive today."

"What did Leticia see?" Isabella asked.

"She said Caitlyn was in trouble. That she was dating a boy who would cause her harm. The night

I gave her the pendant, Leticia was particularly agitated. She'd had a vision while she'd dressed Caitlyn for her performance. But I didn't want to hear it. It was Leticia's birthday, and I only had a short time to spend with her."

Isabella put her hand to the necklace, emotions swirling around inside her, whispers from the past urging her to listen.

"Leticia kept telling me that we needed to go back to the theater. But I knew it was going to be the last chance for us to see each other; I was getting pressure from Alice to set a wedding date."

"Why didn't you break it off with Alice if you were in love with Leticia?"

"Alice was the woman I was supposed to want. She fit into my life; Leticia didn't. I had big ambitions. I didn't want to be held back."

At least he was honest enough to admit the truth, Isabella thought, although that didn't make her like him any more. She was beginning to think Leticia had been a fool to love him.

"I told Leticia that I didn't want to waste our time together worrying about something she couldn't even define."

An immense sadness flowed through Isabella. She could feel Leticia's disappointment, her pain at his unwillingness to see her as she really was.

"Later that night, we saw the flames from the hillside," he said.

"You were at the falls," she said, another piece of the puzzle snapping into place.

"How did you know that?"

"Just go on."

"Yes, we were at the falls. It was a beautiful place, dark, romantic, private. By the time we got back to the theater, the firemen were pulling Caitlyn's body out of the building. She was dead." He turned to look at her. "Leticia was stricken with guilt. And so was I."

"Neither of you started the fire," Isabella pointed out.

"But maybe we could have stopped it." He gazed into her eyes. "You see things like Leticia did, don't you?"

"I thought you didn't believe in her visions."

"But I should have." He paused. "Is something going to happen? Because if it is, I won't ignore it this time."

"I don't know."

"When you do know, don't let anyone stop you from talking about it. Leticia said her biggest mistake was not believing in herself enough to make *me* believe. Don't make the same mistake. Don't let anyone else get hurt."

"I don't know if I can stop anything," she said helplessly. "Seeing the future doesn't give me power."

"Doesn't it?" he challenged.

Just then, Tory came toward them. "Grandpa, I need your help. Can I borrow you for a minute?"

"Yes, of course," he said, rising to his feet. He gave Isabella a quick nod.

She watched them walk down the aisle. Nick's

grandmother had joined his parents by the stage. When Harrison reached the group, he slid his arm around his wife, who gave him a soft smile.

Maybe Harrison had been infatuated with Leticia fifty years ago, but he'd made a life with Alice and created a family that had spawned several generations. Isabella didn't want to mess with any of that.

And while she was intrigued by the history, deep down, she still felt certain that her dreams were not about the past but about the future—because Nick wasn't in the past.

Speaking of Nick . . . Her breath caught as she saw him walk out of the wings with his uncle. He had a roll of blueprints in his hands, and as she watched, he paused, pointing up to the private box closest to the stage. His uncle nodded, saying something Isabella couldn't hear.

She got to her feet with a gnawing feeling in her gut. Was she just feeling unsettled by her conversation with Harrison, or was it something more? The restless feeling drew her toward the stage. Nick hadn't seen her, caught up in his conversation with his uncle. But as their discussion ended, Nick turned and their gazes met—again.

A familiar blast of heat swept through her. Whenever they were in the same room, it was just him and her. Everyone else faded into the background. She didn't know if the others were paying attention, but it didn't matter. She couldn't look away.

He beckoned to her, and she walked up the steps.

He moved across the stage to meet her. "I was just going over some ideas to renovate the balcony area."

She looked out at the auditorium. The view was different from the stage, one that most people didn't get to see. "It must be strange to be up here under the lights." She still couldn't shake the uneasy feeling, which was even more powerful now.

"I never liked it," Nick said. "Are you all right, Isabella?"

"I'm fine." But even as she said so, she felt a wave of dizziness. She put her hand on his arm to steady herself.

Lights flashed in her head, exploding in shards amid a cacophony of screams. On instinct, she dragged Nick across the stage, barely registering his protest—a protest quickly silenced as a heavy light came crashing down onto the stage, exactly where they'd been standing.

And just like in her head, the glass shattered into a thousand pieces, and screams rocketed through the theater.

ELEVEN

Nick's heart pounded against his chest, his breath coming fast as he looked back to where he was standing seconds before.

Everyone was frozen in place, including him. All he could feel was Isabella's body close to his. She'd wrapped her arms around him, and he was holding on to her, too.

She'd saved his life. But how had she known? Had she heard something? Seen something snap above their heads?

Suddenly, his uncle started shouting, someone called down from the catwalk, and the stage crew sprang into action.

Tory and his mother hurried up to the stage, both breaking into speech at once. "Are you all right?"

"How did that happen?"

"Thank God you moved just in time."

"Just in time," Nick echoed, looking at Isabella. "Thanks to you. You have great reflexes."

She nodded, then stepped away. "I got lucky."

It was the same thing he'd said when he'd pulled her out of the car wreck, and a chill washed over him. Was it luck that kept throwing them together? His body still hummed from the adrenaline rush of the near miss and Isabella's body wrapped around his. Her instinct had been to protect him before she'd thought about protecting herself.

"Thank you, Isabella," Tory said, giving her a hug. "He's a pain in the ass sometimes, but he's the only brother I have."

"I should get back to work," Isabella said quietly. "I'll see you all later."

"That was way too close," Tory said as Isabella left.

"Are you sure you're all right?" his mother asked, a worried look in her eyes. "I can't believe that light came down. We haven't had an accident like that in years; everyone is always so careful."

"I'm fine," Nick replied. "We should find out what happened, though."

"Uncle Richard is on it," Tory said.

"I hope this isn't a sign," his mother said worriedly.

"The curse?" Tory quizzed.

"What curse?" he asked.

"This production is the same play that never finished its run because of the fire," Tory explained.

"We tried to put it on again fifteen years ago, but we ran into a string of problems and eventually decided to do something else," his mother added, concern lingering in her eyes.

"I'm sure the light falling had more to do with poor workmanship than with a curse," he said, unwilling to buy into the idea. "You both have too much imagination. I'm going to take off. I need to find Megan." He glanced down at his watch. "She said she'd come by here after the football game, which had to have ended by now."

"It's good that she's making friends," Tory commented.

"I'm just not sure they're the right friends."

He picked up the blueprints from where he'd dropped them, his gaze catching on the slivers of glass littering the stage. He hadn't seen or heard a thing—not a crackle or a pop or anything. How had Isabella reacted so quickly?

Shaking his head in bemusement, he headed down the steps. As he entered the lobby, he ran into Isabella again. She was obviously on her way out, her keys in her hand.

"You're leaving," he said, a little surprised.

"I'm having trouble concentrating today," she said, walking quickly through the front doors.

He followed her into the courtyard. "The light falling shook you up."

"Yes, it did."

"Isabella, wait," he said as her pace increased.

She paused, obviously eager to be gone. "What?"

"How did you know that the light was going to come crashing down?"

She stared back at him uncertainly, something in her eyes that he couldn't decipher. "I sensed it. It's not a big deal."

"You saved my life."

"I don't think the light would have killed you. I probably just saved you from a few stitches."

"You were close enough to get hurt, too."

"Well, we're both fine," she said shortly.

"You're suddenly in a hurry."

"And you're suddenly not," she said in exasperation. "Aren't you the one who's always saying we need to keep our distance?"

"That sounds like me," he said with a smile that softened her expression ever so slightly. "What are your plans for the day?"

She hesitated. "I'm not sure. When I stopped in town earlier, someone left a flyer on my windshield for something called a Wild Turkey Shoot. I thought I might check it out."

"Wild Turkey Shoot? What will this town come up with next?"

Her lips curved into a smile. "It seems there's a new event every other day." She started walking again. "I like the festive atmosphere, the feeling of celebration. You don't get that in the big city."

"True, Angel's Bay has never seen a holiday it didn't want to celebrate. I've spent most of the last decade in L.A., and I'd forgotten. I'm still getting used to—" He stopped in shock as he saw two teen-agers making out by a motorcycle close by. "What the *hell* is she doing?"

"Take a breath, Nick," Isabella advised.

All he saw was a haze of red fury. That junior thug had his tongue down his daughter's throat. "Megan!" he shouted, striding forward.

His daughter jumped away from the boy, her face flooding with red as she looked from him to the boy and then back again.

"What are you doing?" he demanded.

"What does it look like we're doing?" the punk had the nerve to ask, a smirk on his face.

Nick took another step forward. The kid must have sensed his anger, because he quickly hopped onto his bike, said, "See you, babe," and took off down the street.

"Was that the same kid who got you suspended from school?" Nick asked Megan. "The one who was drinking?"

"Will isn't bad," Megan defended. "We weren't doing anything. He just gave me a ride."

"You weren't *doing* anything?" he echoed. "Are you kidding me?"

"We were kissing. I'm fifteen. What's the big fucking deal?" she demanded, going into offense mode. "I'm sure you were doing more than kissing when you were my age."

"That was different," he spluttered, knowing it wasn't different at all. But he couldn't think of something better to say, nor did he know what to do.

"I'm going inside," Megan declared, and walked by him as if his opinion meant nothing to her. And it probably didn't.

He blew out a breath and looked over at Isabella, who gave him a sympathetic look. "I am a terrible father."

"You haven't had much experience. You'll get better."

"When? She's almost grown-up as it is." He frowned. "I don't like that kid she's hanging around with. Did you see that look on his face? I know that look. I used to *give* that look. What am I going to do? Should I give her space or go after her?"

"I don't know, Nick. I'm not a mother."

"But you were a teenage girl."

"Well, my teenage self would have been horrified if my father had caught me kissing one of my boyfriends, and I would have wanted a little time for him to get past that image. In fact, I probably would have hoped we'd never talk about it."

"I *am* going to talk about it—but not right now." He sighed. "I'm overreacting, aren't I? It wasn't that bad, was it?"

"It reminded me of what we were doing last night."

"But we're adults."

"Yes, we were acting really grown-up at the time," she said dryly.

As she turned toward her truck, he found himself unwilling to let her go. "Since Megan needs time to cool down, maybe I should check out the Wild Turkey Shoot with you. I could use a drink."

"Do you think that's a wise idea, the two of us together?"

"We've already escaped death once today. What's the worst that could happen?"

"I don't remember any bars out here," Nick said as he directed Isabella toward the outskirts of town. The flyer just listed the event, address, date, time, and charity contribution. He grew increasingly more doubtful as they took a side road leading past small farms and stables.

As Isabella took a right on the next dirt road, he saw colorful flags waving in the distance and a parking lot filled with cars. He hadn't taken two steps out of the truck before he realized that they weren't going to be doing shots of Wild Turkey.

"I don't think this is about drinking," Isabella said.

"You tricked me." He gazed at the pen filled with squawking turkeys.

"I didn't know. I'm an outsider, remember." She slammed the door of the truck, giving him an unrepentant grin.

"Yeah, right," he said, unable to resist smiling back at her. Isabella's cheeks were rosy, her hair blowing in the wind, not a speck of makeup on her face, but she was gorgeous. Every time he looked at her, he couldn't seem to look away.

"So what do you think the deal is?" she asked.

He read off the nearby banner, "Catch a wild turkey and win a free Thanksgiving dinner. Donations go to the Good Samaritan Family Shelter. It looks like ten dollars buys you five minutes to catch a turkey. If you don't get one, you're out. But your money goes to a good cause."

"Sounds like fun and it's for charity. We should do it, Nick."

He could think of a lot of other things he'd rather do with her than chase a turkey, but, as usual, he was having trouble getting the word *no* past his lips.

"Nick?" Isabella prodded. "I just asked you if you wanted to catch a turkey."

"What if I said I wanted to catch you?"

"I'm not running," she countered.

"Not yet, but you will. You said you never stay in one place. Has there ever been anyone you wish you'd stuck around for?" When she was silent, he persisted, "Have you ever been in love, Isabella?"

She took a quick breath. "That's a very personal question."

"Like you haven't asked me any?"

She was quiet again, then said, "Once. A long time ago. And I didn't leave him—he left me."

"That's difficult to believe."

"It's the truth. Now, I'm going to go catch a turkey." She walked over to buy a ticket.

Nick watched the current contestant in the pen. The teenage boy wasn't having much success corraling a turkey, but he was impressing the teenage girl perched on the edge of the fence yelling encouragement. And Nick wanted to do the same.

He walked up and told the ticket taker to make it two. "We'll do it together," he told Isabella.

She smiled. "Sounds like a plan."

They watched their predecessor make one last attempt before the clock ended his time. The kid was dirty and sweaty and supremely pissed off at having failed in front of his girlfriend.

Nick had a feeling that if a sixteen-year-old, agile boy couldn't trap a turkey, he and Isabella were going to have their work cut out for them. "Any idea how we're going to do this?"

"Not a clue."

"Ready?" the starter asked them.

Nick grabbed his net with both hands, took a look at the turkeys, and picked out a likely victim. "Let's go."

The starter blew his whistle, and they were off. He charged his turkey—the less time the turkey had to react, the better. But the bird was quicker than he expected. Nick swiftly tossed the net, but his foot slipped, and he did a belly flop into the mud.

He sputtered, spitting dirt out of his mouth as he got back up to face the laughter. Not only was Isabella chuckling, but the rest of the crowd gathered along the fence was also enjoying the show.

"Let's see you do it," Nick challenged.

Isabella tried a softer approach, wheedling like a turkey whisperer. But in the end just as she closed in with the net, the turkey batted her away with madly fluttering wings that sent her falling back on her butt.

Her expression of dismay was hysterical.

"Why don't you chase them toward me, and I'll toss the net," Nick suggested. "We might have better luck."

"Okay." She pushed her hair out of her face, leaving a streak of dirt across her forehead, then waved her arms gently, moving the birds toward him.

He crept up quietly behind one, holding the net wide to toss it over the unsuspecting turkey's head.

"One minute," the timer shouted, his voice scaring the birds.

Isabella laughed as they took off.

"Thanks, pal," Nick told the timer.

The guy shrugged. "Better hurry. You're almost done."

Isabella was moving another couple of birds in his direction, and he stepped forward quietly, hoping not to startle them.

He was close, so close.

So was Isabella. She had her net ready in case one of the birds came back at her.

A glance passed between them, and she mouthed softly, "One, two, three."

They charged the birds, hurling their nets. In doing so, they both slipped in the mud as the birds squawked in protest.

The next thing he knew, he was sprawled on the ground with a net over his head, the turkey long gone.

Nick peeled the mesh net away from his face.

Isabella was doubled over laughing, pure joy on her face. He loved the way she laughed, with her whole heart and soul, even though her amusement was directed at him.

"What do I get for catching you?" she asked, wiping away a tear of laughter.

He got to his feet. "Did you do that on purpose?"

"Of course not," she protested as they walked back to the gate. "You just got in my way."

As they left the pen, Nick saw one of his long-time friends, Jason Marlow. A local cop now, Jason had recently started dating, Brianna Kane, the widow of another former friend.

"Nice job, Nick," Jason said, slapping him on the back with a laugh.

"See how you do, before you start gloating," Nick retorted.

"Have you met Brianna?" Jason asked.

"Hello again," he said, smiling at her. When he'd last met her years ago, she'd been engaged to Derek Kane. "I'd shake your hand, but as you can see, I'm a little dirty. This is Isabella Silveira. Isabella, this is Jason Marlow. He works with your brother."

"The famous Isabella," Jason said, his smile broadening. "I heard about your dramatic arrival in our town. Joe has had me hounding every business along that stretch of highway in search of the car that ran you off the road."

"I told him to forget about it," Isabella said. "There's nothing to be done now, and I want to move on."

"Your brother doesn't let things go."

"He's stubborn," Isabella agreed.

"It must be a family trait," Nick put in.

Isabella made a face at him, then turned to Brianna. "I wouldn't go there in nice clothes," she said. "It's pretty slippery."

"Jason is on his own." Brianna smiled.

"And I will succeed," Jason added. "I've got a four-year-old to impress."

"My son, Lucas," Brianna explained. "But he already thinks Jason is a superhero, so this really isn't necessary."

Lucas came running over with the tickets. Jason swung him up into his arms, and it was easy to see the love between the two of them. The longtime bachelor had turned into a family man.

So many things were changing, Nick thought. Shane getting married to Lauren. Jason dating a woman who had a kid. And he was living with his fifteen-year-old daughter and trying to ignore the hottest woman he'd ever met.

"You two going to stick around?" Jason asked.

"And enjoy your eventual humiliation?" Nick asked. "As much fun as that would be, I think we'll be going."

Jason laughed. "Nice to meet you, Isabella."

"You, too. I'm sure I'll see you around."

As Jason, Brianna, and Lucas headed toward the pen to await their turn, Nick walked Isabella back to the truck. "How come almost every time I'm with you, I end up in the mud?" he asked.

"We must stop meeting this way," she agreed. "But you have to admit, that was fun."

"I don't know about that. But *this* is fun." He pulled her against his muddy chest and planted a kiss on her lips. As soon as his mouth touched hers, he pulled her closer, deepening the kiss because he wanted it so much. Her immediate response set him on fire.

When he finally let her go, his gaze dropped to her sweet, hot mouth. Her breasts heaved as she breathed hard, drawing his eyes lower. He burned to see her naked, to put his hands on her breasts, on her ass, on every beautiful inch of her body. Seeing the same flare of desire in her eyes, he swallowed hard.

"We should go," she said quickly.

"Yes. Right. Go where?" he added, his brain muddled.

"Your car. Is it at the theater?"

He had to think. "Yes."

As she got into the truck, Nick adjusted his jeans, then got into the passenger side. He rolled down the window as they pulled out of the lot, needing the cold, crisp ocean air to cool the fever that was Isabella.

They didn't talk on the way back to the theater. When she pulled up next to his car, she didn't look at him, either. Why?

"It's getting harder to say good-bye to you," he told her.

"You've been wanting to say good-bye since the second we met," she reminded him.

"I didn't know you then."

Her eyes filled with shadows as she turned toward him. "You don't know me now, Nick."

"You're beautiful, funny, free-spirited, creative, kind . . . What don't I know?"

"A lot."

"Why don't you tell me?"

"Why should I? You want me one minute, and the next you don't. You ask me to stay, then you tell me to go. So I'm going—as soon as you get out of the truck."

As he watched her drive away, he knew the last thing he wanted was for her to go. He just wasn't ready to ask her to stay.

TWELVE

Isabella had just stripped out of her muddy clothes when the doorbell rang. She threw on Joe's robe and went to the front door. She was shocked to see Nick on the porch.

"What do you want?" she asked.

"I tried to go home."

"It doesn't look that way."

"I even tried to get Megan to go home with me, so I'd have a good reason not to come over here. But she was busy with my mother and she didn't want to leave."

"If you're bored, I'm sure you could find something to do that doesn't involve me."

"I'm not bored." He gazed into her eyes. "Tell me to go, Isabella. Tell me you don't want me. Tell me this is a crazy idea."

She swallowed hard. "This can't just be on me, Nick. It has to be your choice, too."

"My choice is you," he said.

The simple directness of his words took her breath away.

She extended her hand, and his fingers wrapped tightly around hers as if he didn't intend ever to let her go. He stepped inside and shut the door. "Your brother isn't here, is he?"

She shook her head. "I just talked to him. He won't be back until late tonight."

He pulled her up against him, mouth to mouth, hip to hip, toe to toe. His mouth descended on hers, rough, hungry, and demanding, his tongue sweeping past her lips. His hands yanked impatiently at the tie of her robe, then slid inside to cup her breasts.

She moaned. "Let's get you out of those muddy clothes." She pulled him down the hall to the bathroom and turned on the shower. Then she turned to him, her hands teasing with the edge of her robe.

Nick stared at her with passion-filled eyes.

She made him wait, letting the anticipation build, then let the robe fall to the floor.

Nick sucked in a breath. "You're gorgeous." He put his hands on her hips as he leaned in to kiss her. His mouth trailed down her jaw, tracing a line along her collarbone, then dipping down to taste one nipple, then the other, sending a wave of delicious pleasure through her.

She reached for his shirt, unbuttoning it as quickly as she could, then moved below his belt. He already had an impressive bulge going, and she lingered there while he shrugged out of his shirt. Then his jeans and boxers were off in record time. His ruggedly sculpted body made her mouth water. He was amazing. And he was hers.

She stepped into the shower as the steam fogged up the room around them. Nick moved behind her and grabbed the bar of soap off the shelf.

"Let's get you clean," he said with a wicked smile as he soaped up his hands and placed them on her breasts, his thumbs swirling around her nipples.

She drew in a breath as he played her with his sensual hands and his sexy mouth. The water streamed over her head as she slid her hands down his muscled back, her fingers molding his buttocks, pulling him closer, his mouth sliding down the side of her neck.

He dropped to one knee, his mouth trailing down her abdomen, his hands parting her thighs, and then he gave her the most intimate kiss of all, teasing and tasting in delicious torture that left her shaking with need.

When the water began to cool, Nick shut it off and pulled her out of the shower, wrapped her up in a big terry-cloth towel, and kissed her long and deep, filled with promise. They stumbled across the hall to her bedroom, the wet towel coming off as the backs of her knees hit the edge of the bed.

He came down on top of her, and his dark gaze met hers. Cupping her head with his hands, he kissed her again and again and again. It wasn't nearly enough. She pushed him onto his back, then straddled him. "My turn to play," she said with a smile.

His eyes blazed with desire. "Whatever you want. Just don't stop."

"I don't plan on stopping until we're both . . ." Her voice drifted away as she sank onto his erection. "Really, really satisfied." And as she moved against him, she had a feeling that was going to take a long, long time.

God, she was beautiful, with her exotic eyes, dark hair, and beautiful skin. Nick loved watching her ride him so freely and with so much joy. There was nothing tame or boring about Isabella; she didn't hold back. She wouldn't let him hold back, either. She wanted everything from him, and he wanted to give it to her.

The tension built to an unbearable point where he was torn between wanting it to go on forever and needing blessed release. His hands gripped her ass; his blood roared through his veins.

She leaned forward, pressing her lips to his. "Let go, Nick," she whispered.

Her soft voice was all he needed to jump. He pulled her hard against him as he thrust hard and hungrily, stroking her body until she cried out and he shuddered with a powerful climax.

He couldn't catch his breath, his heart beating in triple time as Isabella nestled next to him, her head on his chest. He closed his eyes, tightening his arm around her, wanting to stay like this forever.

Her breathing softened, and her lids drifted

closed. He drew in a slow breath and let it out. His mind was threatening to jump into instant analysis, but his body wasn't ready to join in. For the first time ever, he felt completely satisfied, as if he'd found the one person in the world who really meant something.

The thought scared him. He didn't believe in soul mates. He wasn't even sure he believed in endless love.

But Isabella made him want to believe.

He drew in a breath and let it out. He didn't have to make any decisions now. She certainly wasn't asking him to.

She was asleep, her cheek against his heart, her hand spread across his abdomen in a sweet caress. For now, it was just about this moment. This really good moment.

The trees were thick, the branches scratching her face as she followed him deeper into the woods. Nick charged ahead, and she saw the danger before he did.

"No, stop, Nick!" she screamed.

"Isabella, wake up!"

Nick's voice dragged her out of the terrifying darkness, and she opened her eyes to see him staring at her with concern. Her fingers were digging into his biceps, and she forced herself to let go. "I'm—I'm sorry."

"That was some bad dream. You're still shaking."

She scooted into a sitting position, pulling the

sheet up over her breasts. "I didn't realize I'd fallen asleep." She was amazed that she'd drifted off with Nick in her bed. Sex was one thing, but actually sleeping with a man wasn't something she did very often.

"I must have worn you out," he said huskily.

"You did." She smiled. "You were amazing."

"So were you. What were you dreaming about?"

"I—I don't know."

"You yelled my name." He sat up against the headboard. "What's going on, Isabella?"

"Nothing, it was just a nightmare."

He stared at her for a moment. "When we first met that night on the cliff, you said you'd dreamed about me."

She'd hoped he'd forgotten that. "I had a head injury. I didn't know what I was saying."

"How could you dream about someone you'd never met?"

"Well, I couldn't, so there's your answer. I'm thirsty. Do you want something to drink?"

"Hang on," he said, grabbing her arm. "Why are you suddenly being evasive?"

"Why are you suddenly being persistent? What does it matter what I dreamed? I'm awake now. Just let it go, Nick."

"Why should I?"

"Because you don't want to get involved with me, and you're not going to like my answer, and it's going to ruin a perfectly wonderful afternoon!" She knew that as sure as she knew anything.

"Now I'm even more curious. Just tell me, Isabella. Please."

He was asking her to trust him, and she wanted to. Because she liked him. She cared about him. She wanted nothing but truth between them. Could she take that risk?

"You're scared," Nick said in wonder. "I can see the fear in your eyes. What is it, Isabella?" He tucked her hair behind her ear. "Talk to me."

She drew in a breath for strength. "I told you that my grandmother believes I have a special gift, that I sometimes see things before they happen."

"Like today, at the theater. You saw the light falling."

"When I grabbed your arm, I saw the glass exploding."

"Is that what you were dreaming about now?"

She shook her head. "No. It started weeks ago, when Joe sent me this necklace. He found it in my uncle's house."

"It's pretty," Nick said, his gaze dropping for a moment to the pendant.

"It was given to a relative of mine; her name was Leticia. She had eyes the same color as mine. And the person who gave it to her was your grandfather."

Surprise flashed in his eyes. "No kidding. When was that?"

"About fifty years ago. After I got the pendant, I started dreaming about Angel's Bay. I saw a man who was always in the shadows, and I began to worry that Joe was in trouble. I barely slept for two weeks. I finally decided to come here and see if I could figure out what was happening. That night, when you pulled me from the car, I knew the man I'd seen in my dreams was you. There's trouble coming your way, Nick. And I don't know how to stop it."

He ran a hand through his hair. "What kind of trouble?"

"I don't know."

"That's not very helpful."

"That's why I didn't want to tell you. I kept hoping I'd see something more clearly."

"Maybe it was just the light falling on the stage."

She shook her head. "My dreams always stop after whatever is going to happen happens."

"You said you're not always right, though."

She could see the doubt in his eyes. She *had* to make him believe her. "I'm right enough of the time."

"Like when?" he asked.

"Does it matter?"

"You want me to believe you. I need some proof."

She sighed, then said, "Okay. When I was sixteen, I was in love with a boy named Tony Gallardi. He was everything to me. I had never felt such intense feelings for anyone, and it scared me, because getting emotionally connected to someone usually made my dreams worse. But I couldn't stop myself; I fell head over heels.

One day, we got caught in the rain, and Tony lent me his jacket. I wore it to bed, because it felt like his arms were around me." She paused for a breath, the memory still vivid. "I dreamed that he was going to be in a car crash. I called him up in the middle of the night to warn him, but he laughed and said I was being silly, that it was just a bad dream. I had the same dream the next two nights. I didn't tell him again, since I knew he wouldn't believe me, and he'd start thinking I was crazy. I'd already lost too many friends by talking about my visions."

Nick's jaw tightened. "He was in an accident, wasn't he?"

Isabella nodded. "That weekend, he and two friends were driving home from a party and were hit head-on. He died on impact." She blinked back tears. "I couldn't forgive myself for not trying harder to make him believe me."

Nick put his arms around her. "It wasn't your fault, Isabella."

"I know that logically, but I *saw* it, Nick. I saw it, and I didn't stop it."

"What were you supposed to do? Prevent him from getting into a car for the rest of his life? Besides, not all of your dreams come true," he reminded her. "How could you know that one would?"

"But enough of them *do* come true. I've tried to talk myself out of this more times that I can count, Nick. I don't want these visions! *No one* wants to know the future, especially when they can't stop it. When I do try to stop it, things go haywire. A few years ago, I told a friend that I couldn't meet her for dinner because I had a bad feeling. So she went home unexpectedly and found her fiancé in bed with another man. They broke up."

"You did her a favor, then."

"But she blamed me for ruining her life. Like I said, no one really wants to know the future. Sometimes ignorance is bliss." She searched his eyes, wondering what he was thinking, but he wasn't giving much away. "Now you know why I don't get close to people—why I move around a lot, why I don't make plans. I know better than anyone that sometimes you can't change fate."

"You can't hold yourself responsible for anyone else's life, Isabella," Nick said gently.

"It's hard not to, when you see something bad about to happen to someone you care about. You couldn't stand by and do nothing, either. You ran down a slippery hillside in the pouring rain to save a stranger."

"That was different. I could do something tangible to help you. I could get you out of the car. But there was nothing you could do to change what happened to Tony."

"Maybe if I had been more open to my visions, I would have seen more. I would have known when it was going to happen, or how. But I was afraid to look. I still am. I exercise like a fiend so that I won't dream when I sleep. I don't have deep relationships, because love makes things worse."

"It doesn't sound like living your life on the surface has changed anything for you, not when a necklace can send you halfway up the state," he pointed out.

"I tried to resist, but the pull was too strong. You and I were connected before we even met. I think it's because the necklace is tied to Harrison and Leticia, and we're connected to them."

"What was going on between my grandfather and this woman?"

"He was in love with her, even though he was engaged to your grandmother."

"Okay, but that was a long time ago. What does that matter now?"

"I think it just connects us. It's not related to the danger in my dreams."

"If I'm going to be in danger, then I'll deal with it. Although I can't imagine what that would entail. I'm not exactly living on the wild side anymore."

"I wish I knew, Nick. I thought if we got closer, maybe the dreams would become more specific, and I would know what to do."

"So you were using sex with me to clear your head?" he asked.

"I didn't mean it like that." She saw the teasing light in his eyes, and her tension eased. "Do you think I'm crazy?" she asked, not sure she wanted to hear his answer.

"Aren't we all a little crazy?" he countered, a warm look in his eyes.

"Whether you believe me or not, Nick, I'm not leaving until the dreams stop and I know you're safe. You saved my life. I owe you that much."

"You don't owe me anything, Isabella. If you want to stay, stay. If you want to go . . ."

"Go?" she finished when his voice trailed away.

"Not yet," he said. "Don't go yet."

"Are you sure that's what you want?"

He pushed her down on the bed. "All I want right now is you, all of you. And, if you want to shout out my name, feel free."

She smiled. "Give me something to shout about, and I'll see what I can do."

Isabella gave a satisfied sigh as she got out of the shower for the third time that day. She felt almost scarily happy, because nothing this good could possibly last. She returned to her bedroom and quickly dressed, then picked up Nick's T-shirt off the floor and tossed it onto her bed. He must have forgotten it when he'd reluctantly put on his muddy clothes and gone home to his daughter.

The front door opened and shut, and Joe called her name. She pulled a sweatshirt over her head as he appeared in the doorway.

"Hey," he said. "I picked up a pizza. I didn't know if you'd eaten."

"I haven't, thanks. You look tired," she commented, noting the dark circles under his eyes.

"Long day of nothing," he said with a sigh. "I went up into the hills, trying to find Annie's father, but there was no sign of him. I have no leads to go on. I have no idea where Annie is."

"You're doing your best."

"Effort doesn't matter. It's results that count." His gaze fell on Nick's T-shirt and the rumpled bed, and Isabella could see him adding it all up in his head, his investigative mind not missing a detail.

"Who does this belong to?" he asked, picking up the shirt.

"Nick," she said unapologetically.

"You seem to be ending up with a lot of his clothes," he said. "What's going on with you and him?"

"We're . . . friends."

"Looks like more than that."

"It's not a big deal, Joe."

He gave her a thoughtful look. "Nick has a kid, and from what I understand, he's planning to live here permanently. You're not going to stay. Your life is in Los Angeles."

"Are you done pointing out the obvious?" she asked, not at all happy with the direction of the conversation.

"I don't want you to get hurt."

"I know what I'm doing," she said, although deep down, she wasn't at all certain of that.

"I hope you do. I'm going to take a shower."

As he left the room, she blew out a breath, feeling a little disturbed by his pragmatic questions. She didn't want to think about the future—not when the moment was so nice. Maybe this afternoon was all they'd have, or maybe not. But she wasn't going to regret what had happened between them.

Still, part of her wanted today to be the start of something, not the end. And as for him having a kid, she liked Megan. She liked the idea of helping Nick and Megan find their way back to each other. Stitching broken threads together was what she did best.

But what about *her* thread? When was she going to take a chance and put herself in the picture? She had no idea; she never had visions about her own future. Those remained completely out of reach. Why?

Her grandmother's words echoed through her mind. *Because you're not connected to yourself, Isabella. You only look out, you don't look in. You don't take care of what means the most: your own soul.*

Maybe her grandmother was right, but she didn't know how to accept this part of herself. To date, all it had ever brought her was pain. Shrugging the dismal thought out of her mind, she headed to the kitchen.

She was just putting some pizza on a plate when the buzz of Joe's cell phone drew her attention. The shower was still running, but she knew how eager he was to get information on Annie, so she picked up the phone. It was an L.A. number that she recognized. For a split second, she thought about letting it go to voice-mail, but curiosity got the best of her.

"Hello," she said. "Is that you, Rachel? It's Isabella."

"Oh, it's you," Rachel said with some relief. "Teresa told me you'd gone to visit Joe. Is he there?"

"He's taking a shower. Do you want me to have him call you?"

"Yes. Tell him it's important. I really want to talk to him."

There was an urgency in Rachel's voice that made Isabella worry. "Is there anything I can do? You sound upset."

"I need to talk to Joe. I think—I think I might have made a mistake."

Isabella's stomach flipped over.

"Make him call me, Isabella. I know he won't want to, but he needs to. We have a lot of history together."

"I'll do what I can." She put the cell phone down. Did Rachel want to get back together with Joe?

Joe walked into the kitchen, saw her with her hand on his phone, and shot her an inquiring look.

"Your phone was ringing. I thought it might be the station, but it wasn't."

"Who was it?"

"Rachel. She wants you to call her back. She was very emphatic about it." Isabella saw the stiffening of his jaw. "Rachel said she thought she made a mistake."

He drew in a breath and let it out, then opened the fridge and grabbed a beer.

"Are you going to call her?" she couldn't help asking.

"I don't know. Right now, I'm going to have some pizza."

"Joe—"

"This isn't your business, Izzy," he warned.

"Rachel wants you to remember how much time you have invested in your relationship with her."

"And you think I've forgotten?" he challenged. "Believe me when I say I remember everything. Every last thing."

THIRTEEN

Charlotte couldn't remember what she used to do at night before she'd stepped into Annie's motherhood shoes. Now her life was all about the baby. She propped her feet up on the living-room coffee table as she fed him and flipped through the television channels. As usual, there was nothing worth watching on Saturday night, so she settled on a reality show about housewives who looked nothing like any housewives she knew.

Her mother was out with her friend Peter again. Charlotte had no idea where that friendship was going, but she was trying not to think about her mother being with a man. It was too weird.

She smiled as the baby waved his tiny hands while he drank his bottle. He'd been happier today, and she had a feeling that her growing confidence was having a positive effect on him. They were starting to get comfortable with each other. And now that he wasn't crying so much, she was beginning to enjoy him. He was beautiful, with his perfect skin, so smooth and new. His little toes and fingers were works of art, and the fine hair on his head was adorably wispy. She'd fallen in love, she realized, she was head over heels for this little guy. She could spend hours just looking at him. And he wasn't even hers.

She sighed, feeling a yearning that she'd managed to push aside for most of her life.

The baby stopped sucking, his eyelids drooping. She set the bottle down and put him on her shoulder, gently patting his back until she got a burp. Then she wiped his face and settled him on her lap again as he drifted off to sleep. Even though the last week had been difficult, she didn't regret the experience. In fact, it was difficult to imagine *not* taking care of him; he had become a big part of her life.

Not that she wouldn't jump for joy at Annie's return, because he needed his mother far more than he needed her. But there was no denying that this little boy had stolen her heart. He was so innocent, so deserving of all the best in the world. She wanted that for him with a fierceness that surprised her and scared her a little.

She had to remind herself that he wasn't her baby, and if Annie didn't come back, other things would have to happen. The DNA tests would reveal who was the biological father, which would bring him into the picture, and there was no doubt that Social Services would also get further involved. They'd already had one visit from a social worker to make sure the baby was in a safe environment.

Fortunately, her mother had an excellent reputation as a foster parent, so for the moment, they'd been okayed to keep him.

The fact that the biological father hadn't come forward since Annie's disappearance really bothered Charlotte. If he was local, he had to know his son had neither of his parents with him. And if the man wasn't completely stupid, he had to know that within days, his identity would be revealed. So what the hell was he waiting for?

Her tension made her arms tighten, and the baby squirmed a little. "Sorry, baby," she whispered. She rocked him gently until he fell back asleep, then leaned forward and put him into the car seat on the coffee table, where he liked to nap. Her mother had cautioned her against holding the baby all the time while he was asleep, for fear that he wouldn't learn to sleep anywhere but in someone's arms. Since her mother had raised three kids, Charlotte figured she knew what she was talking about. But she would have been happy to hold him while he slept. There was something about that warm weight in her arms that made her feel more content than she had in a long time.

A sudden crash at the back of the house made her jump to her feet, her pulse racing. "Who's there?" she yelled.

She went down the hall, feeling a breeze, as if something was open. She quickly reached into the closet and grabbed an umbrella as a makeshift weapon. She peeked into her mother's bedroom. It was neat as a pin. Next was Annie's room, and she was shocked to see shattered glass on the floor under a broken window.

She ran into the living room, grabbed the baby's car seat and the phone, and raced into the bathroom. Heart pounding, she locked the door in case someone was in the house, then dialed 911. The house seemed quiet, but she could barely hear anything above the rush of blood in her veins and the dispatcher's cool, calm voice telling her an officer was on the way.

A few moments later, she heard a siren, and the dispatcher told her that an officer was at her door. At the peal of the doorbell, she picked the baby up in her arms and went out to answer it. She was relieved to see Jason Marlow on the porch. "Thank God!"

"What happened, Charlotte?"

"I heard a crash, and the window in Annie's room is broken."

"Stay here," he ordered as he moved down the hall. She remained in the doorway, prepared to make a quick exit if she had to. The baby had settled in against her breasts, oblivious to anything going on around him.

Another car came down the street, the headlights blinding her for a moment. It stopped behind Jason's patrol car, and then Joe got out and jogged up the steps, his eyes filled with concern.

"Are you all right?" he asked.

"Yes. Jason is checking Annie's room. The

window is broken. I don't know if someone was trying to get in."

"I'll check the yard."

She waited by the front door. A moment later, she heard Joe and Jason talking to each other. Certain that whoever had broken the window was now gone, she went down the hall to Annie's room. Jason was standing next to the window, and Joe was outside it, flashing a light around the ground beneath.

"Someone threw a rock," Jason told her, pointing toward a heavy, jagged rock lying next to the dresser. "It's going to be difficult to get any prints off it, unfortunately."

She was shocked. "Why would someone throw a rock through the window?"

"Vandalism could be one explanation," Jason said.

"And another?"

"Burglary."

"It seems awfully coincidental that someone would choose our house to break into, and Annie's room in particular," she said.

"I agree," Joe said, entering the room. "There's no one outside now. Jason, why don't you check with the neighbors, see if anyone saw anything?"

"All right." Jason gave Charlotte a reassuring smile. "We'll catch whoever did this, Charlie. Don't worry."

"Let's go into the other room," Joe said, motioning her toward the hall.

She returned to the living room and sat down

on the couch. Now that Joe was there, she felt a lot more secure.

Concern showed in his dark eyes. "Where's your mother?"

"She's out with a friend. What do you think this is about, Joe?"

"Probably Annie." He paused. "Your car wasn't in the driveway or in front of the house."

"I had it serviced today, and my mother took her car to dinner. Why does that matter?"

"It's possible someone thought the house was empty. Did you react to the sound of the glass breaking?"

"Yes, I yelled, 'Who's there?' Kind of stupid, huh? As if a burglar would yell back."

"Not at all stupid. You probably scared them off."

"They sure scared me. I hid in the bathroom," she admitted.

"Good idea," he said with approval.

"I didn't know what to do. I didn't want to run outside, and I had the baby, and it all happened so fast. This kind of thing doesn't happen in Angel's Bay."

Joe sat down next to her and put a comforting hand on her thigh, which shook her even more. In protective mode, he was even more sexy.

"I'll find out who did it," he promised. "But you're safe now."

"Why would the break-in be tied to Annie? Unless . . . someone is going after her baby?"

"I don't think so," he said with a shake of his

head. "Maybe she left something behind, something that's important in some way."

"We already know who the possible fathers are. What else could she have had?"

"Any number of things. Besides the father's identity, she might know something else about him. Perhaps something he doesn't want anyone else to know. The guy can't run from his DNA, but if there's something else he wants to keep hidden . . ." Joe shrugged. "I can't help thinking that this baby is the tip of some iceberg."

"I know a couple of the guys and their wives. I can't imagine any of them doing this."

"You never know what goes on behind closed doors."

"I guess not."

"How are you and this little guy getting along now?" he asked, his gaze dropping to the baby.

She stroked the baby's back. "Much better. We seem to have a truce going."

Joe smiled, lifting his gaze back to hers. "That's good." When the look between them went on too long, he cleared his throat. "I'll get some plywood to cover that window until you can get it replaced."

"That would be great." As they stood up, the doorbell rang again.

It was Andrew. He gave her a worried smile and sent a tense nod in Joe's direction. "I saw Jason next door. He told me what's going on. Are you all right, Charlie?"

"I'm fine."

"What can I do to help?" he asked.

"Stay out of it," Joe said sharply.

"I was talking to Charlotte," Andrew returned calmly.

"Why don't you come in?" she said, not wanting to continue this conversation on the porch. It wouldn't be long before the neighbors descended, once they heard about the break-in.

"I'll check with Jason," Joe said shortly. "And I'll get some plywood for you."

"I'd appreciate it. And thanks for coming so quickly."

Andrew stepped into the house as Joe left. "Are you really all right?"

"I'm a little unsettled. I just wish I knew who threw the rock and why—whether it was random vandalism or something more deliberate. My mother is going to freak when she gets home."

"Where is she?"

"Out with her boyfriend."

Andrew raised an eyebrow. "Boyfriend? Is that new?"

"She calls him a friend, but they're spending a lot of time together. His name is Peter Lawson."

"Oh, right. She brought him by the church the other day."

"She did?" Charlotte was surprised. The church had been her father's sanctuary. For her mother to take another man there was unthinkable.

"He seemed like a nice guy," Andrew added as they returned to the living room. "Do you like him?"

"I don't know him. They've taken their friendship out of the house, and since Annie disappeared, I'm aware of little else going on outside these walls."

Andrew moved forward to take a closer look at the sleeping baby. "He looks like an angel."

"Sometimes he does," she said with a smile. "Not always. So, were you coming over here anyway, or did you just run into Jason and decide to check up on me?"

"I was on my way over. I spoke to Dan McCarthy and Steve Baker today."

"I thought you were staying out of it."

"I appreciate the chief's desire to run a clean investigation, but I know these guys. Dan went to school with us, Charlie."

"I know. I can't imagine that he would be the father. Or Steve, for that matter. Both Tory and Erin are sweethearts. It's crazy. But Andrew, Joe had a right to be upset with you for sharing that information. I'm annoyed, as well. It was Annie's secret, and I gave the information to the police to be used in their investigation not for you to share around town."

Andrew frowned. "I apologize if I overstepped, but I thought someone might open up to me. At any rate, I asked Steve and Dan to reconsider their positions and remember the big picture. This child needs a father. And if that's one of them, he should step up, because the truth will come out in the DNA."

"How could they not know that? Are they complete idiots?" she couldn't help asking.

"They're scared. And they've been friends a long

time—a friendship that's been solidified by their struggles with fertility."

"You think it's one of them, don't you?" she asked, a sinking feeling in the pit of her stomach.

"I wish I didn't. I thought I was a better judge of character. But I would never have suspected either of them of trying to perpetrate such a big lie." He paused. "So, what about Annie? Is there anything new?"

"No." As the bell rang again, she got up to answer the door. Joe and Jason were together.

Something had happened. She could see it in their eyes. "What?" she asked worriedly.

"Just before you reported the break-in, Delia Simmons saw a man in army fatigues driving a beat-up truck down the street," Jason said.

There was only one man who fit that description. "Annie's father?"

"Possibly," Joe put in. "Mrs. Simmons didn't recognize him, but her description sounds a lot like Carl Dupont."

Charlotte's heart began to race. "Why would Annie's father try to break into the house? He hasn't had anything to do with her in months. Do you think he wanted to see the baby? Or . . ." A half-dozen other scenarios leaped into her mind, none of which made her feel any better. The man had mental problems, and she wanted nothing to do with him.

"It's impossible to say," Joe replied. "I'll put a patrol on your house, but I don't think he'll be back tonight, Charlotte. He took off when you yelled earlier, and that's a good sign. Whatever he wanted, he didn't want to get caught or to use force.

"Mr. Hooper, your next-door neighbor, has some plywood. He's putting it up for you right now," Joe added as they heard the sound of hammering. "When will your mother be home?"

"Not till later," Charlotte said.

"I'll stay," Andrew quickly offered. "I can sleep on the couch."

She wanted to say that wasn't necessary, but she was still a little shaken, especially by the idea that Annie's father might be involved.

"You might want to consider staying with friends," Joe suggested.

Did his suggestion come from a desire to get her out of the house or away from Andrew? "That would be difficult with the baby and my mother," she said. "It would be easier to stay here. And my mother will be home later, so we'll be okay."

"Don't worry, Charlotte," Jason said reassuringly. "I'm on duty tonight, and I'll keep a lookout. We're not going to let anything happen to you."

She felt absolute confidence in the three men surrounding her. "Thank you all. I really appreciate it."

"I'm going to dig deeper into Annie's father's past," Joe said. "Call me if you have any concerns, Charlotte." He shot Andrew a dark look, then followed Jason out to their cars.

As Charlotte closed the front door, she turned back to Andrew. "I'd love your company until my mother gets home, but you don't have to spend the night. You have to get ready for church tomorrow."

"You can help me work on my sermon," he said with a smile. "That was my plan for tonight."

"On a Saturday night? All work and no play, Andrew?"

"The person I want to play with keeps telling me she's busy," he said pointedly.

"Then I can't imagine why you keep asking."

"I have nothing but faith. She's so beautiful and amazing in so many ways that it's impossible for me to walk away."

She shook her head. "You knew just what to say to a girl when you were seventeen, and you still do."

"I got better results back then," he said dryly.

She smiled. "What do you say to ordering in some food? It's late, but I'm starving. I was waiting for the baby to go to sleep."

"I'm in. Whatever you want."

"I was thinking Antonio's. I love their spaghetti bolognese."

"Get a couple of orders of garlic bread and salad," he suggested. "I'm hungry, too."

Before she could move, the baby began to squirm and cry, a distinct odor coming from his diaper. "I think someone needs a change." She gave Andrew a mischievous look. "What do you think?"

"About what?" he asked warily.

"Diaper duty."

His expression showed absolute horror. "I don't know how to change a diaper."

"It's not hard, and it would be good training for you. You're going to be a family man one of these days."

"I'll wait until one of those days," he retorted.

"I thought you wanted to help me," she teased.

"I have my limits."

She laughed. "Finally. The guy I used to know is back again."

"What are you talking about?" he asked in confusion.

"It's been difficult correlating your new perfect, holy self with the kid I used to hang out with—the one who wasn't always good and trying so hard all the time."

"It's part of my job to be an example."

"I'm not part of your job," she reminded him. "You don't have to be the minister with me."

"That's exactly why I want to be with you," he said seriously. "Everyone else puts me on a pedestal."

Charlotte decided to get back to the subject at hand. "I'll change the baby. You can order the food."

"Now you're talking," he said. "Charlie, I can promise you this: if you marry me and have my kids, I'll change diapers."

His words took her to a place she didn't want to go. "Promises, promises," she said lightly as she headed down the hall.

Annie's room was cold. Although the window had been boarded up, glass remained on the floor.

She laid the baby on the changing table on the opposite wall and quickly changed his diaper. She was getting better at the task and not so bothered by his squirming as she had been. She changed his onesie, too, and then picked him up. "Okay, little guy," she said as he blinked his eyes at her. "You need to stay awake for a while, because I might need a chaperone."

An hour later, they'd finished dinner and moved the crib out of Annie's room and into Charlotte's bedroom. Her room was up a few stairs, over the garage, and the windows couldn't be reached from the street. She laid the baby down, watching as he settled into sleep.

Andrew leaned against the doorjamb, smiling. "You look very natural doing that," he said.

"I'm getting a lot of practice."

He moved into the room and sat down on her bed, making himself a little too comfortable for her taste. He tilted his head and patted the bed next to him. "Sit down, Charlie."

She took a wary seat on the edge of the bed. "If my mother comes home and sees us in here together, she'll be very unhappy."

His gaze turned serious. "Charlotte, I want something serious with you. Something that could lead to marriage."

She drew in a breath at his blunt words. "We haven't even gone on a date in more than ten years."

"Because you keep avoiding me. What are you so scared of? Do you really think I'll hurt you again?"

"Maybe. I don't know if it's wise or even possible to rekindle a flame that burned out a long time ago."

"Lauren and Shane did," he pointed out.

"They're the exception. Most people grow up and apart."

"We have a lot in common. We want the same things."

She picked at the edge of the bedspread. "I'm not sure that we do." She glanced up at him. "I'm not sure I want children."

His jaw dropped in surprise. "Really? But you're so good with Annie's baby. And you love kids."

"I can love kids and still not want to be a parent. That would be a deal breaker for you, wouldn't it?"

He didn't answer right away. "I don't know. I'd have to think about it. I've always wanted a family. A kid to throw a ball with. A little girl who looks like you. How could that be bad?"

His words pierced a deep pain, and her eyes welled up.

"What's wrong?" he asked, his gaze searching hers. "You can tell me, Charlie. I've seen something in your eyes before, but you always try to hide it. I hurt you when I cheated on you in high school, but I hope you know now that you can trust me."

"I—I can't . . ." She shook her head, biting down on her lip as words that should never be spoken swelled to the surface.

"You can't trust me?"

"I can't talk to you," she said tightly.

"Something is eating you up inside. What is it?"

She stared at him for a long moment. Maybe she should tell him. It would forever change their relationship, but it was information that was long overdue. "I got pregnant in high school." Her words came out in a rush.

Andrew blinked. "What are you talking about?"

"Just what I said." She felt immediately lighter. She hadn't realized how tired she'd been of carrying around that secret. "I got pregnant senior year of high school."

His face paled. "No, you didn't."

She looked him straight in the eye. "Yes, I did."

"I don't understand. You didn't look pregnant. I never heard anything about a baby. How could you hide it?"

"I lost the baby. I miscarried at three months."

"Three months," he echoed. "You were pregnant for three months? Why didn't you tell me?" He jumped to his feet, anger emanating from him in waves. "How could you keep that a secret?"

"What would you have done? You were already with someone else."

"I would have . . . I don't know what I would have done, but you should have told me, Charlie. Did you hate me that much?"

He didn't understand at all. "I *loved* you that much, Andrew. You broke my heart. I gave you my virginity, and two days later, you had sex with someone else. And not just that night, and not just with her. You made a point of showing me that I didn't mean anything to you."

"I couldn't handle what I felt for you," he said. "I had big dreams, Charlie. I was going to be a pro baseball player. I didn't want to be tied down to someone. I didn't want to change my plans."

"Then you shouldn't have had sex with me in the first place," she said, still pained by the rejection after so many years.

"I didn't know what to do. I was scared. I acted like an ass."

"Yes, you did."

"But you should have told me you were pregnant," he said with more fire in his voice. "How did that even happen? We used a condom."

"Maybe it didn't work. Or maybe . . . you weren't the father." She'd never said those words out loud before, not even to herself.

Shock spread across his face. "There was someone else?"

"Do you think I should have stayed faithful to you, after what you did to me?"

"Who was it? When did it happen?"

"It was at the beach party. You and Pamela stripped down naked and ran into the ocean. Remember that?"

He didn't have to answer. She could see it on his face.

"I was drunk and feeling sorry for myself and I just wanted to leave," she continued. "I went through the woods toward the parking lot to see if I could find a ride home. Someone was there." She took a quick breath. "Things happened."

Andrew sank down on the bed. "What are you saying? Were you assaulted? Did you just have sex with whoever was there? What?"

"He told me the best way to get back at you was to show you that I didn't need you—that I didn't care what you were doing. In my drunken, depressed state, it sounded like a good plan. He kissed me, and I kissed him back. And then . . ." Her voice faltered. "The whole thing took about three minutes. I was so ashamed of what I'd let happen. And I was angry, too. There were so many emotions going through my head. Shane found me crying, and he took me home. I made him promise not to tell anyone, and I never said a word, either. Not until now."

Andrew stared at her with angry eyes. "Who was it? Who was the other guy?"

"That doesn't matter."

"The hell it doesn't."

"It doesn't," she snapped back. "It was a long time ago. You wanted to know my secret—there it is. That's all I'm willing to say."

He got up again, pacing around the room as if desperate to find a way to burn off the adrenaline racing through him. Finally, he stopped. "Okay. You're right. It all happened more than a decade ago. We made mistakes, but we learned from them. I'm glad you told me. Maybe now we can finally move on." He paused, giving her another questioning look. "But I don't understand why you don't want kids in the future."

"Because losing that baby was the worst thing

that's ever happened to me, Andrew. I don't think I could live with that pain again. And as a doctor, I know there's no way to prevent it. Sometimes it just happens. Maybe God has a hand in it."

He shook his head, compassion filling his eyes. "No, Charlie. God wasn't punishing you."

"You don't know that."

"I do," he said with quiet conviction. He sat back down on the bed and put his hands on her shoulders. "You didn't do anything wrong."

"I didn't go to the doctor, Andrew. I didn't tell my mother until a couple of months went by, and then she wanted to wait even longer. My dad never even knew."

"So the only people who know about this are you, your mother, and me?"

Andrew would hate knowing that she'd told Joe about her pregnancy before him. "A few other people know."

"The other guy?"

She shook her head. "No."

"I really wish that you'd told me about it. I could have helped you get through it. I don't think I was that much of a bastard."

"I'm not convinced you would have helped me, Andrew. We weren't even talking by the time I missed my period. And like you said, you had big dreams that didn't include me. If I'd told you I was pregnant, you would have flipped out. The man you are now is not the guy you were then."

"I'm very aware of that," he said. "And you might

be right; I might have let you down. I wasn't thinking straight back then."

"When did you start thinking straight?" she
asked curiously. "There's a big gap between us at seventeen and us today. There's been a lot of years in
between."

"Those years don't matter."

She shook her head. "That's like saying a big part
of your life doesn't matter. I don't even know why
you decided to become a minister, Andrew." She
paused as she heard a car pull into the driveway. "My
mother is home. We can't talk about this in front of
her."

"She must have thought I was the father. I don't
understand why she's never . . ."

"Treated you badly?" she finished. "I've wondered
that myself. Maybe she disliked you at the time,
but since you came back as the minister, you seem
to have a halo over your head. There's nothing she
would like more than to see me marry a minister and
live the life she led."

"There's nothing I'd like more, either," he said.
"And now that we've cleared the air and you've let
me back into your life, I'm not going anywhere. I
screwed up with you before. I want a second chance.
Will you give me that?"

"I don't know."

"Then I'll just keep asking until you do know."

FOURTEEN

Nick went for a run early Sunday morning. The beautiful, sunny day didn't fit his restless mood. He'd spent most of the night thinking about Isabella, remembering how incredible she'd felt in his arms, and wondering what the hell he was going to do now. She might be the right woman, but it was the wrong time.

Rebuilding his relationship with Megan was his first priority. He didn't have many years left before she grew up and moved on in her life. He'd lost so much time already; he couldn't lose any more.

But Megan wasn't as eager to spend time with him. She'd spent the evening with her cousins, coming home as late as possible. Then she'd gone straight to bed. He didn't know if she was just embarrassed at being caught making out yesterday or angry at the way he'd responded.

He should have handled it better, but seeing her with that punk had sent his blood pressure skyrocketing. He'd had to fight not to take a swing at that smirking, cocky face. He had to get a grip. Megan was going to have boyfriends, and he had to figure out how to deal with them.

When he reached the empty summit, he stopped to catch his breath, feeling disappointed. He'd had the crazy thought that Isabella might be there again. They'd ended up so many times at the same place at the same time.

He stretched his legs as he thought about her. She'd shaken him up on a lot of levels. He didn't know if he could buy into visions, yet she'd shoved him out from under a falling light that could have severely injured him. If nothing else, she had incredible instincts.

But what about the idea that he was in some sort of danger? He didn't know of any enemies. He didn't think he'd even pissed anyone off lately, except his daughter.

It was odd, though, that the dreams had started after Isabella had received a necklace that his grandfather gave her ancestor. And his grandfather had tried to warn him away from her. Maybe the dreams had more to do with his grandfather than with him, with whatever trouble had split Harrison and Leticia up fifty years ago.

Or maybe Isabella's visions were another reason he should stay away from her. He'd grown up with people who thrived on drama. He'd married an actress and paid a heavy price for not being able to tell when she was sincere or when she was acting. Now he was getting involved with an imaginative costume designer who enjoyed working in the fantasy world that he'd rejected. And she claimed she was psychic.

She didn't need her head examined; *he* did.

Isabella might be beautiful and interesting, with a smile that made his gut clench every time she turned it on him, but she was also trouble. Yet as he thought about never seeing her again, it was almost unimaginable. Even now, he was missing her. How could that be? She'd only been in his life a short time, but it felt as if she'd always been there.

And she felt it, too. The only thing that made him feel marginally better was that she was worried about falling for him as much as he was about falling for her. Isabella had been rejected before by people she cared about. She'd also lost someone she loved. There was a vulnerability in her that made him want to put his arms around her and tell her that she didn't have to keep running, that she didn't have to keep pretending that nothing bothered her.

She'd said he had guard walls, but so did she. Hers were just masked by smiles and laughter. But, like him, she kept people at a distance, even though they didn't realize it.

With a sigh, he headed back down the trail, making quick time getting home. When he entered the kitchen, Megan was sitting at the table eating cereal and reading a magazine, earphones in her ears.

He motioned for her to remove them, which she did with a reluctant frown.

"What?" she asked impatiently.

His daughter was very good at going on the offensive, but he was getting used to it. "I'm glad you're up. The sand-castle contest starts in an hour."

Dismay ran across her face. "I thought you were joking about that."

"Not a chance. I'm very good at building things. We have a good shot at winning." He lifted the canvas bag he'd picked up from his parents earlier and pulled out a red shovel and a matching pail. "I have supplies."

"For a five-year-old, maybe," she said with disdain.

"They'll work."

"I can't do it. I have other plans."

"Yeah? What?"

"Hanging with my friends."

"Like the friend on the motorcycle? Was that Will Harlan?"

She flushed a little at the reminder. "He's nice, and he likes me. I don't know why you had to be such a jerk yesterday."

"I didn't know you had a boyfriend."

"He's not my boyfriend. We're just . . . talking."

"You weren't exactly talking."

She flushed angrily. "What's it to you?"

"I'm your father." He saw her roll her eyes, but he wasn't backing down. "We should maybe discuss . . . stuff."

"You mean sex?" she asked bluntly.

"Have you had sex?" he asked, appalled at the thought.

"No—not exactly." Despite her bold conversation, her cheeks turned red. "I'm not going to talk about this with you."

He wondered what *not exactly* meant, but he didn't have the guts to ask. "You should speak to someone. You need to be safe."

"I know how to be safe. I'm not stupid." She got up from the table, took her bowl to the sink, and dumped it out. Then she turned to him, hands on her hips, stubborn determination in her eyes. "Stop trying to be my father. It's too late."

"I'm not trying to be your father. I *am* your father," he said forcefully. "I am going to ask you questions and expect answers. And I will do everything I can to protect you and keep you out of trouble. I want you to have a good life. Late or not, I'm here, and I'm not going anywhere." He saw the doubt in her eyes. "You have to believe that, Megan. I didn't give you reason to trust me in the past, but I mean what I say. You're my first priority."

"You say that now, but—"

"But nothing. I mean what I say," he repeated. "I'm not your mother." It was the first time he'd said something openly critical of Kendra, but there it was.

Megan looked a little surprised, as if she couldn't believe anyone else saw her mother the way she did. "How would I know that you're not like her?"

"You'll have to give me some time to show you. I'm not lying. I would do anything for you."

She shrugged. "Whatever."

She put her earphones back in and went down

the hall to her room. Two steps forward, one step back. But he was making progress.

"Finally, I get my big brother for a meal," Isabella said as the waitress at Dina's Café set down two large breakfast orders. They'd gone all out, ordering pancakes, eggs, bacon, and hash browns.

"Sorry," Joe said, giving her an apologetic smile. "I haven't been around much since you got here."

"You've been busy. How did the search party go?" Joe had told her about the rock being thrown through Charlotte's window the night before and the quick search party he'd organized to go up into the hills to look for Annie. He had a hunch that Annie's father, a recluse, might be involved in her disappearance.

"We didn't find anything, but we only covered a small area. I'm hoping to get a bigger search group organized for tomorrow. Once we hit the work week, fewer people will be available."

"I'd be happy to come."

"Then you're on." He paused, discomfort flitting through his eyes. "I was wondering about something."

"What's that?" she asked.

"Your sixth sense—does it work for finding missing persons?"

"You don't believe in a sixth sense," she said, hoping he'd refute it. "And I know that over the years you've worked with psychics you thought were scam artists."

"That's true, but you're my sister, and I know you're sincere."

"What are you asking me, Joe?"

"Do you have any idea where Annie is?"

"No. But . . ." She hesitated, not sure she wanted to put herself out there.

"But what?" he prodded.

"If you gave me something that belonged to her, that she wore or touched, maybe I'd see something. I can't say for sure. I usually only have insight into people I'm emotionally connected to." She was touched that he would even consider asking for her help, but she had her doubts. "Most of what I see isn't even decipherable."

"I know it's a long shot, but I'll ask Charlotte for something of Annie's—just in case."

"How is Charlotte?"

"I spoke to her briefly this morning. No more trouble at her house, so that's good."

"I'm glad." She sipped her coffee. "I know you've been busy, but have you thought any more about calling Rachel back?"

His gaze was steady and cool. "Don't push, Izzy. Some things are beyond repair."

"You like Charlotte, don't you?"

He signed. "How many ways do I have to say it's not your business?"

"Come on, Joe, I'm your sister. If you can't talk to me, who can you talk to?"

"I don't need to talk to anyone. And if you don't get your nose out of my business, I'm going to start poking into yours. Maybe I'll have a little chat with Nick Hartley."

She held up a quick hand. "Okay, I'll back off."

They ate quietly for a few moments, then she said, "I meant to tell you that I spoke to Fiona about the shipwreck and our ancestors. It turns out Beatriz, who co-created the original quilt, is related to us. She and her husband, Miguel, and their two boys survived the wreck—the only family that was intact getting to shore."

He scooped up a forkful of eggs. "You've got that look in your eye."

"What look?"

"You're getting hooked on this town. I've seen it happen more than once, especially when people find out they're related to one of the founders."

"The town has a fascinating history," she said. "I wonder if anyone will ever find the shipwreck."

"Who knows? But in the last couple of months, a few things have washed ashore, including the ship's bell. It's at the museum if you want to check it out."

"Why hasn't anyone been able to locate the ship, with all the advances in electronics and technology?"

He shrugged. "I have no idea, but I'm hoping Angel's Bay doesn't suddenly become the site of a salvage operation. There have been some queries since the bell came to light. And then there's the damn angels," he grumbled, taking another sip of his coffee.

"What angels?" she asked, intrigued.

"The ones people like to pretend they see flying around the north point of the cliff, allegedly carving out some map to the hidden treasure or some other cryptic message. To me, it looks like just cracks and crevices created by the wind and waves and saltwater spray."

"Now, there's the pragmatic brother I know and love. I'd like to see an angel! How cool would that be?"

He laughed. "Very cool and completely impossible."

"I don't believe that anything is completely impossible. I'll have to take a look at that cliff. Maybe I can figure it out."

"Maybe you can," he said with a grin.

"You love all this stuff, too, Joe—that's why you don't want to come home."

"Angel's Bay is my home now," he agreed.

She slowly nodded. "Yes, I can see that. You're connected. All those loose threads from the past are tying you here."

"Not everything is a metaphor for sewing. But I'm sure you'll be working on the Angel's Bay quilt in no time."

"I'd love to work on that quilt," she said eagerly. "Do they remake it?"

"Every chance they get," he said dryly. "So what are your plans for the day?"

"I hear there's something happening at the beach. I thought I'd check it out. Do you want to come with me?"

"I wish I could, but I want to get down to the station."

"You do have people who work for you," she reminded him.

"I know, but the longer Annie is gone, the less chance we have of finding her."

"Any more leads on the biological father?"

"I've set up DNA tests for tomorrow, but we won't have the results for a while."

"Nick's sister, Tory, seems pretty concerned about her husband."

"She probably should be," Joe said heavily. "He's not acting like an innocent man."

Isabella sighed. "I really like her. She's been so welcoming to me. I hope it doesn't turn out to be her husband who cheated."

After leaving Dina's Café, Isabella walked toward the beach. It was a gorgeous Sunday, and there was a festive air, as if everyone realized that the sunny days of fall would soon be giving way to winter, so it was time to enjoy the great weather while they had it.

At the far end of downtown, she joined a throng of people walking down a hilly trail that led from the bluffs to a wide spread of sandy beach. A judging table stacked with trophies and ribbons was on a temporary riser. Speakers had been set up, and a young teenage band was warming up. Sand-castle-building stations were marked by thin sticks with colored flags.

As the warm sun beat down on her shoulders, she took her sweater off and tied it around her waist.

"Hey, Isabella," Tory called.

She turned, shading her eyes, to see Tory approaching. The other woman was dressed in jeans and a T-shirt and carrying a bucket and a shovel. She looked more relaxed than the last time Isabella had seen her. "Hi. How are you?"

"Great. Are you building or spectating?"

"Definitely spectating. Looks like you're going to be digging."

"No just bringing in some extra equipment," she said with a smile. "Nick and Megan have entered the contest."

"Really? Where are they?"

"Over there." Tory pointed toward a spot near the water. "Come with me?"

Isabella didn't even think of refusing. She wanted to see Nick again. She hadn't dreamed about him last night, or if she had, she'd forgotten, because for the first time in a while, she'd woken up feeling refreshed, eager to face the day, excited to see him again.

Not that she anticipated a warm welcome. Nick had no doubt put his walls back up. He'd started withdrawing the minute he'd put on his clothes the day before, and she couldn't blame him. The intensity between them had blown both of them away, and she wasn't any more certain of what to do about it than he was.

So she would play things light and easy, the way she knew how . . .

But as soon as Nick looked up and saw her, she realized it wasn't going to be easy at all. She sucked in a quick breath as his dark gaze settled on her mouth, and memories of their afternoon together flashed through her mind, lighting up all of her senses. She cleared her throat, hoping she wasn't giving anything away, but she hadn't expected to feel so much with one simple look.

Fortunately, Tory distracted Nick by handing him her bucket and shovel. "Here you go," she said.

"Thanks," Nick replied, barely giving his sister a glance. "How are you, Isabella?"

"Good. I'm good," she added, feeling a little awkward despite her best intentions.

A slow smile crossed his lips. "Me, too."

She quickly glanced away. She needed to look at someone who wouldn't make her blood pressure shoot up. "Hey, Megan."

"Hey," Megan replied with her usual sulky, bored expression. She sat cross-legged on the beach, her gaze toward the ocean, as if she couldn't care less what was going on behind her.

"You were lucky to get a spot so close to the water," Tory put in. "It's important to build the foundation with wet sand."

Nick gave his sister a disgusted look. "I know what to do. I'm an architect."

"Of sand?" she challenged, a grin on her face.

"It's not that different. And if you want to build a castle, pay your own entry fee and get a spot."

"I can't help?" Tory asked. "It looks like fun."

"She can help," Megan said, glancing over her shoulder.

"Nope, not a chance. This is a father-daughter project," he said firmly. "No sisters allowed."

"It's a stupid project," Megan threw in as she got up and ambled across the sand toward them.

Despite her attitude, Isabella had a feeling that the teenager wasn't completely unaffected by her father's attempt to win her over. She just didn't want to show that she cared. In Megan's world, loving someone usually meant losing them.

As Isabella's gaze moved to Tory, she saw a flash of pain cross her face. Nick's casual reference to his father-daughter project had obviously hurt her in some way.

"I'll be back," Tory muttered, walking away.

"Now you pissed her off," Megan told him.

Nick frowned, looking from his daughter to Isabella. "Why would she care that I want to do this with Megan?"

"I think it reminded her of the baby she doesn't have. I'm sure she'd like nothing more than a mother-daughter moment."

"Shit!" He cast a quick look at Megan. "I'd better go talk to her. Do you want to get started?"

"I'll wait," Megan said unenthusiastically, flopping down onto the sand again.

Isabella sat next to Megan as Nick went off to find Tory. For a minute, they just watched the waves gathering offshore.

"This is so lame," Megan said with a sigh. "I have better things to do today."

"You're making your dad happy."

"I don't know why," she said with complete bemusement.

Isabella smiled to herself. "Maybe because he's your dad. He is trying, Megan."

Megan shrugged. "Did you do any father-daughter stuff with your dad?"

"Not much," she admitted. "At least, nothing that was just the two of us. Some other sibling of mine was always involved—usually Teresa. She had our dad wrapped around her little finger, knew just what to say or do to get her way. I was in awe of her manipulative power. Now she works it on her husband," she added with a laugh. "And he seems to love it."

Megan scooped up a handful of sand and let it drift through her fingers.

"Is everything okay?" Isabella asked, a little concerned by Megan's quiet.

Megan didn't answer right away, then turned her head and said, "I don't know what he wants from me."

"Are we talking about your father or the kid you were with yesterday?"

"I know what Will wants from me—sex," she said bluntly. "But him . . ." She tipped her head toward Nick, who was talking to Tory. "I don't get him. He wants nothing to do with me for most of my life, and then he suddenly wants to be my best friend."

"And you can't trust that he's sincere. I understand."

Megan turned her gaze back toward the ocean. "He'll disappear like he did before. It's only a matter of time."

Despite Megan's fatalistic statement, Isabella sensed that was the last thing she wanted to happen. "I don't think Nick is going anywhere, no matter how much you test him. You're his first priority. He might not deserve a second chance, but what do you have to lose? You might be surprised."

"I'd be shocked," Megan said cynically. "You're really an optimist, aren't you?"

"Not always, but in this case, I think there's a good chance that you and your father are going to find a way to make things work. Because you both want that to happen."

"We'll see."

Isabella looked up as Nick returned, kicking up sand with his bare feet. "Is Tory all right?" she asked.

"She's just stressed out with everything going on in her life." He grabbed a shovel. "Megan, look alive." When she glanced up, he tossed it to her.

She reluctantly caught it with a roll of her eyes. "Couldn't you at least get shovels that weren't fucking pink?"

He laughed. "Hey, you look better with it than I do. So what do you think—should we go for the classic castle with the moat? Turrets, drawbridges, that kind of thing?"

Megan gave him an amazed look. "Yeah, right. Like you can do that."

"Oh, I can do it," he said confidently. "We're going to win that trophy. No one here will be able to touch us."

"I don't care about a stupid trophy."

"How about if we win, I let you drive me down to Montgomery next weekend?"

Megan's eyes lit up. "Now you're talking."

The mayor got on a bullhorn, announcing the start of the competition, which would last for sixty minutes. At the end of that time, a winner would be chosen by a panel of judges.

Megan got to her feet. "What do you want me to do?"

"Take the bucket and fill it with wet sand," Nick instructed. "I'll start digging," he said, falling to his knees.

"Looks like more mud in your future," Isabella told him as Megan rolled up the legs of her jeans and ran down to the water's edge.

He grinned back at her. "I might need another shower later. You interested?"

Her cheeks warmed. "Hush, your daughter is nearby."

"I doubt I could shock her. You wouldn't believe the things that come out of her mouth. I don't think her mother was giving her much supervision the last few years."

"I don't think she was getting much of anything the last few years. This was a good idea. Maybe building a sand castle will be the first step in rebuilding your family," she suggested.

"I'd be happy if it just turned out to be a sand castle. I'm trying to make realistic goals so I can meet them. I can't let myself get derailed."

"That must be my cue to leave."

His eyes darkened. "The last thing I want, but—"

"But this is your time with Megan. I get it."

Megan returned, but instead of dumping the bucket full of wet sand into the hole Nick had created, she let it fly on his head, a smile of pure wicked pleasure on her face.

Nick sputtered as Isabella burst out laughing.

"Oops," Megan said. "Missed. I'd better get some more." She dashed away as Nick wiped the mud from his eyes.

"Have fun," Isabella said with a grin, jumping back quickly as he tossed a handful of mud in her direction. "I'll see you later."

As she walked down the beach, she caught up with Tory again, who had paused to talk to another friend. "You didn't get far."

"Mr. Walker wants to try out for the play," Tory said, tipping her head toward the fat, balding, middle-aged man walking away. "He tries out every single year, and he's terrible, but he's convinced he's a star waiting to be born."

"It must be difficult, turning away your friends."

"We try to find small parts or backstage jobs whenever we can for the locals," Tory said, falling into step with her. "It truly makes it a community production, and then everyone tells their friends to come, and we sell more tickets." She paused. "I'm going to get some coffee. Do you want to join me?"

"I'd love to."

"Great." Tory cast Isabella a sly look. "And on the

way, you can tell me what's going on between you and my brother."

"I don't know what you're talking about," Isabella said with as much innocence as she could muster.

Tory laughed. "You're going to have to do better than that."

"Who's the most special baby in the world?" Charlotte asked the little boy who was kicking his legs at her as she finished changing his diaper. "You are, in case you didn't know. You are the cutest little boy ever." The baby almost seemed to smile. "So not as much crying today, okay? We have to work as a team." The baby's eyes drifted closed. "Why do I get the feeling you aren't paying any attention to me?"

She felt a little silly having a conversation with a newborn, but there was no one else around, and she was feeling restless. In her pre-babysitting life, she'd kept a busy schedule with work, and jogging, and keeping up with friends, but since this little boy's arrival, she'd spent a lot of time in the house. The beautiful sunny day was beckoning to her, but her mother had gone to church and also had lunch plans, so she was on her own for a while. Getting outside would have to wait.

"You need a name," she told him, "but I'm afraid to give you one. I wouldn't want to confuse you if your mom comes back and wants to change it."

She hated that she'd thought in terms of *if* Annie came back rather than *when*.

The sound of her doorbell brought relief. Someone she could talk to who might actually talk back. She picked up the baby and went to answer the door.

Her heart skipped a beat when she saw Joe on the porch. He was dressed in jeans and a T-shirt, looking even sexier than usual, and a little jolt of electricity ran down her spine.

"Hello, Charlotte," he said. "I wanted to update you on our search this morning."

Judging by his tone, it wasn't particularly good news.

"It's not bad," he said quickly, obviously reading the worry in her eyes. "It's nothing. We found no trace of Annie or her father. We're going to widen the search area tomorrow."

She let out a sigh. "I guess no news is better than bad. Do you want to come in?"

"Is Andrew still here?"

"No, he's at the church," she said, leading him into the living room.

"But he slept here, right?"

"On the couch," she said, meeting his gaze.

"Your mother likes him, doesn't she?"

"She's over the moon about him. He's a minister, and she'd love to see me follow in her footsteps. You should have seen the sparkle in her eyes when she first came in last night and saw him." She put the baby in his car seat on the coffee table and sat on the couch. "I know Andrew has gotten in your way on this case, but his heart is in the right place. He's not a bad guy."

"Sounds like you're back on Team Andrew," he said, sitting down across from her.

"What team should I be on?" she asked, feeling a little reckless. Joe flirted with her, but he always pulled back.

Joe drew in a deep breath, then let it out. "We should drop this."

"You started it," she reminded him.

"It was a bad idea. You and Andrew have a history."

"We do," she agreed. She hesitated for a moment. "I told Andrew about my teenage pregnancy last night. We were talking about Annie's baby and my stepping into this instant but temporary motherhood, and it just came out. I'd been thinking about telling him ever since he got back, but I wasn't sure it was worth getting into after all this time."

"How did he take it?" Joe asked.

"He was shocked and angry that I didn't tell him when it happened. Not that it mattered in the long run."

"Does Andrew know you told me?"

She shook her head.

"Why did you tell me before him?" Joe asked curiously.

"You're easy to talk to. You don't judge me—and I'm not used to that. My parents had such high expectations, and with Andrew a minister, I can't help but feel I'm going to fall short with him, too. Yet I don't want to pretend to be someone I'm not."

She paused. "What I didn't tell you before is that

I was never sure if it was Andrew's baby. I also had a one-night stand, or better described as a five-minute stand, when I was really drunk and depressed. So that's all of it—though I'm sure you're not at all interested."

"You know I'm interested, Charlotte."

She shifted uncomfortably at the intensity in his eyes and tried to lighten the mood. "These sleepless nights are making me really talkative. I was chatting to the baby earlier, and he dozed off in the middle of my sparkling wit."

Joe smiled. "I can't imagine how he could do that."

She smiled back. "Shocking, I know."

Silence fell between them, and it wasn't as comfortable as she would have liked. She wasn't very good at reading Joe. He'd had a lot of practice not revealing his emotions, which she imagined made him a good cop, but it also made him difficult to get to know.

"So you and Andrew are good?" he asked.

"I think so. I gave him a lot to think about, but ultimately, my keeping it a secret didn't really affect him. If anything, I saved him from three months of worrying about what to do."

"Why did you save him from that?" Joe asked.

"Because of the other guy. I was ashamed, hurt, angry." She let out a sigh. "I was so messed up. Part of me just wanted the pregnancy to go away. But then, when it did, I felt guilty, as if wishing it had made it happen."

"You know that's not true."

"Logically, yes. But my heart has never been as convinced."

"From what you've told me, Andrew didn't treat you very well in high school. Is that what's holding you back with him now?"

"Partially." The other part was her interest in Joe. He gave her a thoughtful look.

"What?" she prodded. "What are you thinking?"

"I was wondering how well you know Andrew. You didn't see him for more than ten years, right? What was he doing all that time?"

"He was going to school for quite a bit of the time. I don't really know. We haven't talked about those years much."

He nodded. "That's what I thought."

"What? You think he's hiding something?"

"Andrew tries a little too hard."

"It's difficult to take on the role of spiritual leader for a community that watched you grow up. He's trying to earn respect. Why do you sound suspicious of him?"

"Sometimes he seems too good to be true," Joe said simply.

Had Joe picked up on something that she hadn't? "Are you aware of something specific that you want to share?"

"No, forget I said anything."

"So, back to Annie," she said. "I'd like to get out and search for her myself."

"You're doing the most important thing, taking care of her baby."

"I know that's true, but it doesn't feel like enough—and I have a case of cabin fever. Do you think it would be all right if I took the baby for a walk in the stroller? I don't want to put him in any danger."

"I'm sure you'd be fine, but why don't I go with you?" he suggested. "It's a nice day, and I could use a walk, too."

"You're on," she said, getting to her feet. "I'm craving a soy latte with a hazelnut sprinkle. I hope you don't mind a stop."

"Not at all," he said.

She grabbed her bag and snapped the baby seat into the stroller. Then they were ready to go. "I've never felt so excited to get out of the house," she said with a laugh as Joe opened the front door. "This is the baby's first trip, too, since he came home from the hospital."

"I hope he doesn't sleep through it."

"I'm fine with his sleeping. When he's awake he can get loud."

"Isabella used to be like that when she was a baby," Joe said, following her out onto the porch. "I remember going to sleep with earphones after she was born."

"How is Isabella liking Angel's Bay?"

"She's fitting right in, working at the theater, making friends."

"Maybe she'll stay. It would be nice for you to have some family around."

"It would, but I doubt it will happen. Izzy doesn't stay anywhere for too long."

"Why is that?"

A thoughtful look entered his eyes. "You know, I'm not really sure. Her constantly changing plans have always been kind of a family joke, but the more time I spend with her, the more I realize that I don't know her as well as I thought I did. I was twelve when she was born and out of the house long before she hit high school. I always thought of her as a free spirit with a quirky personality, but there's a serious side to her, a vulnerability, that I never noticed before."

"Maybe she hid it," Charlotte said as they walked down the street.

"Why would she do that?"

"Because we all try to live up to who people think we are. In my family, I was the screw-up. Sometimes I screwed up on purpose, just to be who they thought I was."

"Maybe you could have changed their minds by not screwing up," Joe suggested.

"That thought was far too logical for me," she said with a grin. "Now, you, as the oldest and the only son, were probably spoiled rotten. Your parents no doubt adored you. Your sisters looked up to you. I'm betting it was pretty fun to be you."

He laughed. "I had it all right."

"I hope I'll meet your parents sometime. Do you think they'll ever come to Angel's Bay?"

"They might, if I ever invite them."

"Why wouldn't you?"

"They're disappointed in my decision to divorce. They're very religious."

As much as Charlotte wanted to know more about his divorce, she was reluctant to go there. She certainly wasn't an objective observer, because on the few occasions when she'd had contact with Rachel, she hadn't been all that impressed. Whether that was because Rachel wasn't all that nice or because she wanted Joe for herself was debatable.

"Anyway," Joe said, "they'll get over it."

"Do you think you will?" she asked.

He gazed down at her for a moment. "Yeah, I think I will."

FIFTEEN

"You're very popular, Tory," Isabella commented as she opened the door to the Java Hut. Nick's sister had been stopped several times on their way into town from the beach.

"Small-town life," Tory answered with a smile. She gave her order to the cashier, then told Isabella, "This one's on me."

"Thanks," she said as they sat down at a small table to wait. "You seemed a little upset earlier. Everything all right?"

"Yes. Watching Nick and Megan just reminded me of the fact that I don't have the family I've always wanted. Not that I begrudge Nick. He and Megan should have always been together. I was angry with him for a long time for not trying harder to make that happen, and I'm so glad she's here now. I just want those silly, small family moments with a child of my own."

"I hope you get them."

"Me, too." Tory got up to retrieve their coffees. "I'm also worried about Steve. Hiring a lawyer makes no sense to me, and while I want to believe him, I'm having trouble doing that." She took a breath and looked around to make sure no one was in earshot. "I think Steve might have cheated on me with Annie."

Isabella chose her words carefully. "It's one thing to think it and another to know it for a fact."

"Which is why I think Steve doesn't want to give his DNA. Because until he does, it's speculation."

"Or he's just concerned about his privacy," Isabella said, playing devil's advocate.

"It would be unimaginably difficult to find out that Steve cheated on me. But even worse would be knowing that he turned his back on his baby. The biological father should be stepping up. Why has he left his son with Charlotte? Not that she's not capable and wonderful, but this man has a responsibility to his child."

"I agree. Is it possible that Annie lied? I don't know her, so I could be off base, but it seems strange that so much time has passed since she disappeared, and no one has come forward to claim the baby."

"I guess it's possible, but . . ." Tory's voice drifted away.

Isabella looked over her shoulder to see what had caught Tory's attention, and was surprised to see Joe and Charlotte through the café window. Charlotte was pushing a baby stroller, and Joe had his hand on the small of her back. He was smiling at Charlotte, and Isabella hadn't seen that kind of tender look on her brother's face in a very long time.

As they stepped into the café, Charlotte offered a big, warm smile.

"Isabella, Tory, hello," she said.

Tory paled as Charlotte pushed the stroller next to the table.

The baby was adorable, Isabella thought. He was fast asleep, with his little hands at his side, his fingers so tiny, his expression so sweet.

"His first public appearance," Charlotte said. "We both needed to get out of the house."

"I'll get your coffee, Charlotte," Joe said, "Soy latte with hazelnut sprinkle, right? You don't want decaf, do you?"

"God, no," Charlotte said with a laugh. "I need something to keep me awake."

"He's perfect," Tory said, staring in fascination at the baby. "Just beautiful." Her voice caught. "How could anyone not want him?"

Charlotte's gaze softened, and she put a hand on Tory's shoulder. "I'm sorry, honey. I didn't think when I brought him out that—"

"Don't be silly. Of course you should be out. You should do whatever you want to do. I have to go." Tory jumped to her feet and ran toward the door, almost knocking over a woman in her haste to escape.

"What's going on?" Joe asked, returning to the table.

"Tory just saw the baby she thought she was

going to get," Charlotte said quietly. "I didn't think. I was worried about running into Annie's father, but I forgot about the adoptive parents."

"I'll go after her." Isabella got to her feet. "It's not your fault, Charlotte. She had to see the baby sometime."

"Tell her I'm sorry," Charlotte said.

"I will."

Isabella caught up with Tory at the corner, just as she was about to step into traffic. She grabbed Tory's arm as a driver laid on his horn. "Hold on there. We need a green light."

"The baby—he was going to be mine," Tory said, her eyes dazed. "I really thought I was going to be a mother. I was going to push him in the stroller around town, and people would stop and say how cute he was. And some people wouldn't know that he was adopted, and they'd say, 'He looks just like you.'" Tears rolled down her cheeks.

"Let me take you home." Isabella led Tory to Joe's truck, parked a couple of blocks away. Tory didn't say anything along the way, and her silence was even more unnerving. It was as if she wasn't even aware of reality. When they arrived at Tory's house, Isabella followed her inside.

Tory disappeared down the hall. Isabella hesitated, not wanting to be intrusive, but she couldn't imagine leaving Tory alone in the state she was in.

She moved through the house, stopping at an open door. The room was sparsely furnished with a rocking chair and a twin bed. The walls were light blue, and there was a wallpaper strip of colorful alphabet blocks running along the top.

Tory sat in the rocking chair, her arms wrapped around a stuffed white teddy bear. "A friend of mine gave me this bear the first time I got pregnant. She didn't know it was a good idea to wait three months before sending any presents. Neither did I."

"Do you want me to call your mom or Nick?"

Tory shook her head. "No." Her mouth trembled, more tears slipping out of her eyes. She brushed them away as she rocked in the chair. "When we bought the house six years ago, Steve said this would make a perfect baby's room. We could plant a garden and put in one of those rock waterfalls in the yard. Then we would sit in here and look out the window and rock our baby to sleep. It was the most beautiful image, and I've carried it around in my head all these years. We got this chair the second time I got pregnant. When I made it one week past three months, we thought we were out of the woods. But we weren't." She took a breath. "It's never going to happen for me. I won't be a mother. I have to find a way to accept it."

Isabella had no idea what to say in the face of such raw pain, but she had to try. "Even though this adoption didn't work out, you'll have another chance. You're young, Tory. There's still time to have a family."

"Is there? I don't even know if I still have a husband. The past few years, I became obsessed with having a child. After the first two miscarriages, nothing happened for almost three years. So we tried in-vitro. I gave myself injections, spent a lot of money, and it didn't work. When Steve brought up Annie's baby and her situation, it was the first time I'd ever considered giving up on having my own child and adopting." She took a minute and then continued.

"After we talked to Annie, I became really hopeful. She's a sweet girl, and we hit it off. When I put my hand on her stomach and I felt the baby move, I thought it was the best decision I could make. I knew there were other couples who wanted the baby, too, and that the father was unknown, but once I felt that little kick, I was hooked. He was going to be my baby. How stupid was that?"

Isabella felt helpless. The woman was breaking apart in front of her; she needed to get someone to help.

"I'll be right back," she said.

Tory didn't reply, just kept rocking back and forth, her gaze on the window, probably focused on that beautiful image she had in her head.

Isabella rifled through Tory's purse, found her cell phone, and punched in Nick's number. Glancing down at her watch, she wondered if he was still on the beach. The phone rang so many times she was about to give up hope, when Nick answered in a breathless voice.

"Tory?" he asked.

"No, it's Isabella. I'm at her house, and she's

really upset, Nick. I know you're busy at the beach, but we ran into Charlotte with the baby, and I think Tory is having some kind of breakdown."

"I'll be right there," he said immediately.

Nick never paused when someone was in trouble, she thought as she set Tory's phone down. He just acted. It made her wonder why she was so hesitant to get involved with her own visions. Maybe she needed some of his courage.

Returning to the bedroom, she found Tory still rocking, still clutching the teddy bear to her breasts as if it were the baby she wanted so badly.

"Can I get you something?" she asked.

Tory shook her head.

At least she'd responded to the question; that was something. Isabella left the room and went outside to wait for Nick. He pulled up in front of the house five minutes later. As he stepped out of the car, a flurry of sand flew off him. He must have just left the beach.

He ran up the driveway toward her, his expression concerned. "Where is she?"

"Sitting in the baby's room, rocking and crying and staring out the window."

Nick moved into the house and down the hall. "Tory?" He entered the room and went down on one knee in front of her. "Are you okay?"

She shook her head. "It's really over, Nick. The dream—it's done. You were right. Love is nothing but pain. I hurt all over." Her voice broke. "I'm not going to be a mother. I'm just not." Her face crumpled, and her shoulders shook, and she collapsed against Nick in a torrent of sobs.

Isabella left them alone and went into the kitchen. She filled the teapot with water and turned on the stove. Digging through Tory's cupboards, she chose a soothing chamomile tea. The pot had just begun to steam when Nick walked into the room, looking as if he'd been through the wringer.

He sighed and sat on a stool by the counter. "I got her into her bed. She fell asleep in about one minute."

"She wore herself out," Isabella said. "She needed that cry."

"I hate seeing her suffer."

"Do you want some tea?"

"I'm not much of a tea drinker. Is there anything in the fridge?"

She opened the door. "Orange juice, milk, and fruit punch."

"I'll take some orange juice. The glasses are in the cupboard on the left."

She poured him some juice and set the glass on the counter. "I'm sorry I had to interrupt the sandcastle building. I know you wanted to spend time with Megan."

"You didn't interrupt; we were done. We came in second." He shook his head in disgust. "The mayor's cousin won—talk about rigged. Our castle was far superior."

"Where's Megan now?"

"She bailed on me as soon as they handed out

the trophies. She went off with two girls, but I'm not convinced that's who she'll stay with. She was very vague about her plans."

"Megan is fifteen. She's going to like boys."

"Don't remind me." He drank the rest of his juice. "So tell me what happened with my sister. Tory saw Annie's baby and flipped out?"

"Pretty much. We were getting coffee, and Charlotte and Joe came in with the baby. Tory couldn't take her eyes off that little boy. It was as if she was seeing the life she was supposed to have flash in front of her eyes. I could see that she was shaken, so I drove her here. I think she finally faced the fact that she wasn't going to get that child. Somewhere in her head, she still had hope."

Nick's mouth drew into a grim line. "Tory deserves to be a mother. It's all she ever wanted to be. When we were kids, it was always her and her dolls, making up pretend families, acting out the parts. That was her dream. She likes working at the theater, but I've always thought it was just what she did while she was waiting to be a mother."

"She could still have kids. There are children who need homes and babies who have yet to be born." Isabella paused. "But Tory also seems to be confused about her husband."

"I heard he hired a lawyer, which is ridiculous. If it's his kid, he should just say so and do the right thing. I didn't plan on getting Kendra pregnant, but I never thought about walking away. Hell, I married her, and I was a teenager. Steve is a grown man. He's got a dental practice and money in the bank."

"But to acknowledge the baby, he would have to admit he cheated. And he obviously doesn't want to do that."

"He's not going to be able to run away from his DNA."

Isabella rested her arms on the counter. "What's ironic is that if Steve *is* the father, then there's a chance he and Tory will end up with the baby if Annie doesn't come back. But I don't think that connection has sunk into Tory's head."

Nick stared back at her. "You're right. I don't know if Tory could take Steve back if he cheated on her and lied about it for all these months."

"If he comes with that baby, I don't know how she'll turn him away."

"Good point." He ran a hand through his hair. "Love sucks."

"Sometimes," she agreed, meeting his gaze.

He gave her a long look, then slid his hand across the counter and covered her fingers. She drew in a quick breath at the heat of his touch.

"It doesn't go away," he murmured in bemusement. "The first time you took my hand that night on the cliff, I felt as if I'd been branded. The heat was incredible, like something electric flowing between us." His fingers tightened around hers. "But it's not just the way you touch me."

"It's not?"

He shook his head. "It would be easier if it was. Every time we say good-bye, I tell myself that's it. That I'm going to play it cool the next time I see you. That I'm not going to touch you again or kiss you or . . ." His voice trailed away as his gaze settled on her mouth.

She drew in a quick breath. "Nick, if you really want to keep it cool, you can't look at me like that."

"I can't help myself." He raised his gaze to hers. "My grandfather told me the first time he saw you that you would cast a spell on me, and he was right."

"I'm not a witch."

He smiled. "Then how come I'm feeling bewitched?"

She smiled back.

"If you can see into the future, tell me how this is going to end," he continued.

"I never have visions about myself," she reminded him.

"Did you dream about me last night?"

"No."

"Maybe the dreams will stop now that you warned me that I was in danger. Maybe that's all you were meant to do."

"It's possible, but I don't think so."

"If the dreams started with the necklace, why do you still wear it? Wouldn't you have more peace of mind if you took it off?"

"It doesn't come off. The clasp won't open. I could cut it off, but I'm afraid to go that far."

"Let me try," he said, getting up and moving around behind her.

She lifted her hair so he could see the clasp.

He fiddled with it for several minutes, then said, "It does seem to be stuck." His hands dropped to her waist, and he nuzzled her neck with his lips. "But this is nice. God, you smell good."

She turned in his embrace. "What happened to keeping your hands off me?"

"I can't help myself." He lowered his head and gave her a long, tender kiss filled with the promise of so much more.

Her heart sped up as she leaned into him, putting her hands on his shoulders, pressing her breasts against his hard chest, moving her legs between his, the intimate memories of the night before flashing through her with nerve-tingling sensations. She wanted nothing more than to strip him out of his clothes and have him do the same to her. Already his hands were stroking upward, his thumbs caressing her breasts, making her ache with need.

But this wasn't her house or his. It took all of her strength to push him away. "Nick, we can't. Not here," she said with a breathless gasp.

"We should go somewhere."

"You said you wanted this to end."

"And you said we should live in the moment. I like your philosophy better."

When his mouth closed over hers again, it felt as if she'd found home. Their bodies, their minds, their hearts—everything was in sync, everything was right with the world.

And then the front door slammed.

They jumped apart.

Isabella was still catching her breath when Steve strode into the kitchen, calling Tory's name. When he saw them, he froze.

"What's going on? Where's Tory?" His gaze moved to Isabella. "Who are you?"

"I'm Isabella. We met at the theater the other day," she reminded him. "Tory is asleep."

"In the middle of the day?"

"She wasn't feeling well."

"Because of you," Nick interrupted. "Tory is messed up because of this adoption and the rumors about your fidelity. Did you screw that girl, Steve? Did you lie about the baby?"

With each bullet-shot question, Steve tensed, and Isabella could see the guilt in his eyes. Nick could see it, too.

"You son of a bitch!" Nick launched himself forward, and his fist connected with the side of Steve's jaw. He stumbled and fell against the wall, knocking off a picture.

Nick moved forward again with vengeance in his eyes, and Isabella knew that the stunned, soft-in-the-middle dentist was no match for Nick. She grabbed his arm as he pulled it back for another blow.

"Don't," she said.

He sent her an angry glare. "He deserves it."

"Not from you," she replied. "This isn't your fight. It's Tory's. He's her husband; she has to deal with this."

"And she's my sister. It's my job to protect her."

"I think you broke my nose!" Steve took his hand away from his face and stared down at the blood on his fingers and his shirt.

"What's going on?" Tory asked as she stepped into the kitchen. Her eyes were still sleepy, but her voice was stronger now.

"Your brother hit me," Steve said, fury in his eyes.

Isabella grabbed a towel off the kitchen counter and handed it to Steve to stop the flow of blood from his nose.

Tory looked from her husband to Nick. "Why? What happened?"

Nick's jaw tightened. "Ask your husband, Tory."

Tory swallowed hard, looking as if that was the last thing she wanted to do.

She knew, Isabella realized. Deep down, Tory knew, but hearing it would make it more real.

"This is between Tory and me," Steve said. "Would the two of you go?"

"No, I want them here," Tory said quickly.

Steve put out a hand to his wife, a silent plea for forgiveness for what he was about to say, but Tory backed up next to Nick and stood with her arms folded across her chest. She looked as if she was gearing up to take a bullet.

Steve drew in a long, deep breath, then released it. "Okay, if this is how we have to do it, then here it is. I had a brief affair with Annie last year."

His words stole the air from the room, leaving a

thick, tense silence. When Tory didn't speak, Steve continued, "I'm sorry, Tory. I never meant to hurt you. It didn't mean anything. I was lonely. I was tired of planning sex around ovulation and injections. I just wanted it to be mindless and no big deal. It was a stupid, thoughtless mistake."

"A mistake?" Tory echoed in amazement. "*That's* what you think it was? You got a girl pregnant— a very young girl. And you left her on her own for nine months."

"It was wrong. I love you, Tory. I don't love her."

"What about the baby?"

"I didn't know there was one until Annie jumped off that pier. She hadn't told me."

"That was several months ago. Once you did know, how could you not stand up and declare that he was your son?"

He gave her an incredulous look. "How could I claim him when you were so desperate to have a child? It would kill you to know I'd conceived a baby with another woman. I thought Annie would give the kid to someone far away from here, but then Andrew kept getting the locals involved, and I had to do something. I thought we could adopt him, and then we'd all win."

"We'd all *win*?" Tory echoed in astonishment.

"Yes. Annie would be free to live her life without the responsibility of being a mother, you would get the child you always wanted, and I'd be fulfilling my responsibilities. It was a good solution all the way around."

Isabella could see that he'd rationalized it all in his head. But Tory obviously wasn't buying it. Neither was Nick, who still looked as if he wanted to kick Steve's ass.

"No, it was *not* a good solution. We all would have been living a lie," Tory said. "How many nights did you and I talk about Annie and speculate about who was the father? You threw out other names. You lied to me over and over again." She stared at her husband as if she'd never seen him before.

"I got caught up in it," he admitted. "I had to go all in. I didn't know what else to do."

"You should have told me the truth as soon as you knew Annie was pregnant. Hell, you should have told me that you had an affair when you had the affair."

"I couldn't tell you that. I loved you. I still do," Steve repeated. "You're the only woman I want to spend my life with."

Tory started shaking her head even before he was done speaking. "How could I ever trust you again?"

"Just give me a second chance," he pleaded. "I'll do whatever you want. I swear, it will never happen again. And just think, we can raise that little boy together. We can have the family you've always wanted."

"Do you know where Annie is?" Tory asked, anger burning in her eyes. "Did you have something to do with her disappearance?"

Steve gave her an incredulous look. "God, no! I have no idea what happened to her. I think she ran away."

"The cops don't believe that."

"Well, I didn't have anything to do with her disappearance."

"You've lied before. You could be lying now," Tory said with a sad shrug. "I don't know you anymore."

"Yes, you do. I'm the man you married," he said, desperation in his voice.

She gave a definitive shake of her head. "That man wouldn't have hurt me like this."

Steve swallowed hard as he saw the resignation on Tory's face. "Don't give up on me—on us."

"You're the one who did that. How many times was it? How many times did you have sex with her?"

"You don't want to do this, Tory."

"Yes, I do. How many times?"

"Three, four, maybe."

Tory nodded, her jaw tight and unforgiving. "I knew it wasn't just once."

"This can still work out," Steve coaxed. "When Annie comes back, she'll give us the baby. She was reluctant to do so without you knowing the truth. Now that you do, there won't be any decision to make. You can be a mother, Tory. We can raise that little boy together."

Isabella's stomach turned over as she watched Steve dangle the ultimate prize. If Tory ignored his infidelity, she could have what she always wanted. But at what emotional cost?

Isabella glanced at Nick, seeing the same fear in his eyes, that Tory might look the other way to get that baby she needed to feel complete. But what kind of life would they be bringing that child into?

"Tory, please. Don't make any snap decisions," Steve pleaded.

"Don't pressure her," Nick cut in. "She can decide any damn thing she wants."

"I don't know," Tory said slowly. "When Annie comes back, she might not want to give up her child at all."

"Her hesitation was because of me," Steve said. "She didn't like the lie, either."

"Why did you get a lawyer? Why did you act so outraged when the rumors started?" Tory asked. "You've had so many opportunities to come clean, Steve. But every time, you chose to lie. I don't understand that. Were you stupid or so arrogant that you didn't think you'd ever get caught?"

"I'll apologize to you until the day I die," he swore.

"That doesn't change what happened." The fight seemed to go out of Tory, and she sat on the stool. "You need to go now."

"You heard her," Nick said. He put his arm around his sister's shoulders, providing a united front.

"I'll give you time to think, but I'm not giving up on us, Tory," Steve replied. "We love each other. I want to raise the baby with you. I want us to be a family. And no one will ever be able to take him away from us. Even if Annie doesn't want to let us adopt, we'll get shared custody. Annie doesn't have any money. She can't compete with what we have to offer."

"Get out," Nick said forcefully, as more tears gathered in Tory's eyes. "She'll call you if she wants to talk to you."

"I'm leaving. But I'll be back."

Isabella followed Steve out of the kitchen.

He gave her a look of confusion as he reached the front door. "She's going to forgive me, right?"

"I don't know. Some decisions are very hard to forgive."

Steve walked out to his car, looking beaten. The house of lies he'd been building had come crashing down.

Tory had been dealt a devastating blow, and Isabella couldn't imagine how long it would take for her to recover. Nick would have to help her pick up the pieces, and they both needed time to figure out what to do.

She lifted her purse off the hall table and left, shutting the front door behind her.

SIXTEEN

Late Sunday night, Nick peeked into Megan's room and saw his daughter curled fast asleep in her bed. Despite her disdain for the sand-castle-building contest, their second-place trophy was displayed proudly on her dresser. He smiled and quietly left.

Back in his own room, he kicked off his shoes and stretched out on the bed. It was after ten, too late to make a phone call . . . When he closed his eyes, all he could see was Isabella. She seemed to inhabit every breath that he took, and with each passing day, she became more entangled in his life.

He thought about the necklace that she claimed had brought her to the bay. How it had been given by his grandfather to one of her ancestors and how he and Isabella were now involved. Just another strange, spine-tingling coincidence. Isabella would say that none of it was coincidental, that fate was playing a hand. And it was hard not to agree with her. Yet believing that they had been destined to meet wasn't easy, either.

Opening his eyes, he stared up at the ceiling considering his options. His heart jumped as his phone rang, and he didn't know if he was getting as intuitive as Isabella or just being hopeful, but somehow he knew it was her.

"Sorry to call so late," she said. "I've been thinking all night about Tory, and I just wondered how she was after I left."

"She actually pulled herself together. Facing Steve and the truth wasn't as hard as all the uncertainty. But she's going to need time to digest everything that's happened and figure out what to do next."

"Will you tell your parents?"

"I'll leave that to her. She's not looking forward to being the next hot topic of gossip in this town."

"From what I've seen, the people in Angel's Bay really love your sister. They'll have her back."

"She'll still have to go through it. I wish I could fix this for her," he said with a sigh.

"I know you do. We're kind of alike that way," Isabella said. "I want to fix Joe's relationship, too."

"Does he want it fixed?"

"I think his soon-to-be-ex-wife does. Rachel keeps calling him, but Joe won't call her back. Rachel has been with Joe so long I feel like she's one of my sisters. They got married when I was in middle school and I grew up with her. But I can see how Joe's life has changed, and he's happy. So maybe I should leave it alone."

"I doubt you could change your brother's mind, no matter how hard you tried."

"Probably not," she agreed.

Nick settled in more comfortably on the bed. "What did you do tonight?"

"Had dinner with Joe, took Rufus for a walk, then looked through the boxes in my uncle's basement for more ties to Leticia, but I didn't find anything." She drew in a breath, then said, "I've spent most of the last hour trying not to call you. Then I gave in."

His pulse leaped. "I would have called you, but you don't have a cell phone, and I thought it was too late to call your house."

"Joe isn't here. He went back to the station. He's obsessed with organizing search parties and trying to track down Annie's father. I did tell him about Steve's confession regarding paternity. Maybe it wasn't my place . . ." Her voice trailed away in worry.

"Hey, protecting Steve's ass isn't high on my list."

"You were a good brother today."

"And you were a good friend." She didn't answer, and the silence made him wonder what he'd said wrong. "Are you still there?"

"Yes. It's just that friendships have always been a little tricky for me. I either scare people off, or I keep so much distance that the friendship isn't worth much."

"If they scare that easily, they're not worth having as friends. You can't keep running, Isabella. You can't keep waiting for the wind to blow you where you need to go."

"I don't know where I need to go. That's why I let the wind decide."

"I think you know what you want." He paused, reflecting for a moment on his own choices. "I always knew what I needed to do, even when I wasn't doing it. I just pretended not to. Maybe you're doing the same."

"I wish I was normal," she said with a heartfelt sigh.

"Then you'd be boring as hell. Besides, we all have our quirks. Here in Angel's Bay, a lot of people have claimed to see angels."

"Did you ever see one?"

"Can't say that I have."

"You don't believe in angels or visions, do you, Nick?" Isabella asked.

"I'm more comfortable with things that are real."

"Like buildings."

He could hear the smile in her voice. "Yeah. Designing buildings that can survive centuries and stand through earthquakes and other natural disasters makes me feel like I've accomplished something. You can see it, touch it, and it's not going anywhere."

"It's so great that you found something else that you loved besides music, Nick. You're an awesome guitar player, but you're also a really good architect. You have vision and imagination—even though you're building something solid, there's whimsy to it. I saw it in your sketches for the theater, the arches of the windows, the curves along the private boxes. You might have turned your back on your parents' world, but some of what they love about the theater rubbed off on you. You think beyond the obvious. Isn't that what plays are all about, involving the imagination, evoking emotion, transporting someone to another place?"

He'd never thought about it like that, never wanted to admit that he'd taken anything from his past into the present.

"I think I've put you to sleep," Isabella said, breaking the lengthening silence.

"No, you just gave me something to think about. But I don't want to think anymore."

"You want to sleep."

"Actually, I want to make love to you. I want to hear that little catch of your breath when I hit just the right spot." Her breathing quickened, and his pulse began to race. "What are you wearing right now?" he asked.

"Pajamas bottoms and a camisole. Very sexy," she said with a low, throaty laugh.

"I'll bet. Are you sure you're not too hot?"

"It *is* getting a little warm in here. I might have to take my top off."

He heard a rustle of clothing that tightened his groin.

"That's better," she added with a sigh.

He pictured her lying in bed, her long hair draping over her beautiful breasts. "You're killing me, you know that?"

"Maybe you should take something off, too."

"My pants are getting tight," he said.

"Then what *are* you waiting for?"

"Are we really doing this?" he asked, half amazed.

"I don't know what you're doing. I'm just getting more comfortable," she teased.

"Me, too," he said, kicking off his jeans. "Okay, my pants are off. It's your turn."

"Now I'm turning off the light." She let out a sigh. "I wish you were really here, touching me."

He flipped off the light next to his bed, letting the dark take away the last bit of reality. "Me, too. In the meantime . . . here's what I want you to do." He told her in exact and loving detail.

She laughed. "Wow. You really do have an imagination."

"Are you with me?" he asked, his nerves tensing as he waited for her answer. Not just because he wanted to have a little fun but because he wanted her to be with him. Even though he'd pushed her away and told her he didn't have time for a relationship, even though she'd declared herself to be a free spirit with no intention of lighting anywhere soon.

"I'm with you, Nick," she said. "At least for tonight."

It wasn't nearly enough, but for the moment, he'd take it.

Monday morning, Isabella woke up feeling more refreshed than she had in a long time. She'd never had phone sex before, and while it was nowhere close to the real thing, sharing the experience with Nick had made her feel even closer to him. And afterward she'd slept all night without any troubling dreams.

Maybe he was right. Maybe all she was supposed to do was warn him to be alert. But the pragmatic part of her wondered what good that would do.

In the meantime, she was going to work. The theater was busy when she arrived, and she jumped into her sewing along with the other volunteers. She soon lost herself in the beauty of the costumes and didn't realize how much time had passed until Tory stopped in just after lunch and motioned for her to join her in the hallway.

Tory gave her an apologetic smile. "I'm sorry you had to take care of me yesterday. I feel like a fool."

"Please don't. You have enough on your plate to worry about."

"I've never fallen apart like that before. I'm the one in the family who holds things together."

"You were due."

She nodded. "Perhaps. Anyway, I just wanted to say thank you. It was really sweet of you to watch over me. And I'm glad you called Nick."

"I wasn't sure if I should have called your parents."

"Heavens, no," Tory said. "Not that they wouldn't have wanted to help, but they're so distracted with the show. They don't need to deal with my problems."

"I thought you might take some time for yourself today."

Tory shook her head. "There's too much to do.

I've got to set up for the barbecue on Wednesday and go over a million other details. My parents would have flipped out if I hadn't shown up today because I was feeling sorry for myself. The show must go on, you know," she added with a brave smile. "If I learned anything from them, I learned that. I'll see you later."

After Tory left, the rest of the day passed in a blur. Sewers came and went. Every time Isabella ventured out of the costume shop, she found herself looking for Nick, wondering if he might stop by to work on his plans, but she never caught a glimpse of him.

By seven o'clock, everyone else had gone home. Isabella had stayed behind to finish one particularly tricky seam, but after the long day, her eyes were beginning to blur, and her neck ached. She set the material aside and stood up, stretching her arms high over her head. Then she picked up the dress and hung it on the rack. It was time to call it a day.

But when the door opened and her stomach flipped over, she knew that she'd been waiting for just this moment.

Nick stepped into the room, looking gorgeously sexy in jeans and a maroon sweater, the sleeves pushed up to his elbows. He walked across the room and slid his arms around her waist, pulled her up against his chest, and took his time kissing her, long and deep, until she was trembling.

He lifted his head. "Hi," he said huskily.

She drew in a shaky breath. No man had ever set

her on fire so easily. Every moment that they weren't together, she missed him, almost ached for him. It was terrifying to wonder how she would ever get through life without him. *Stay in the moment, and stop worrying about tomorrow.*

"Hi, yourself. I thought you were going to keep your distance," she reminded him.

His hands tightened on her waist. "I'm addicted to you. I'm going to need a twelve-step program."

"Is the first step letting go of me?"

"That would probably be a good idea," he said, but his hands tightened on her waist.

"Or you could start the program another day?" she suggested.

"Are you my enabler?" he asked with a smile.

"Yes, and you're mine. I was hoping I'd see you today. Every time I left this room, I was looking for you."

"I had to stop myself from heading over here a couple of times. You're hell on my work ethic." He grinned. "Did you dream of me last night?"

"No. You wore me out."

"That was fun. But next time, let's do it together."

"You've got a deal." As she saw him glance at his watch, she had a feeling next time wasn't going to be very soon. "Are you on your way somewhere?"

"I need to pick up Megan. She wants to see that boyfriend of hers tonight. I tried to tell her it's a school night, and she laughed in my face. So I thought I'd stall as long as possible."

"So I'm just part of your stall, huh?"

"The best part," he said, stealing a kiss.

"Good answer. Megan is in the auditorium, I think. She was helping with the rehearsal earlier, and she seemed to be into it. I might have even seen her smile a few times. Oh, and she asked me about dresses, as in what to wear to the homecoming dance. I told her I'd help her shop for one—if you don't mind."

"Not at all." He slipped his hand through her hair, cupping the back of her neck for another kiss.

"You should get Megan," she told him, but his lips covering hers made it difficult to speak.

"I will in a second, but first, let me show you how much I want you—"

A loud bang broke them apart, and Isabella looked over to see a furious Megan in the doorway. She'd dropped a box of accessories on the floor.

"So this is what you've been doing while I've been waiting upstairs for you," Megan said, clearly angry.

"I'm sorry," Nick said. "I didn't realize you were waiting."

"For more than an hour."

"I'm not that late."

"Yes, you are, and you would have been later if I hadn't come down here." Her accusing gaze swung to Isabella. "You were after him all along. That's why you were being nice to me. You wanted my dad, and I was your ticket in."

"That's not true," Isabella said, appalled that Megan had jumped to that conclusion.

"I was so stupid," Megan said, ignoring her. "It's not like a million other people haven't done the exact same thing with my mother. I just made the mistake of thinking you were my friend."

"I *am* your friend." She hated the way Megan was misreading the situation, but the young girl was so worked up she couldn't see anything but her own pain.

"And you," Megan said, firing at Nick now. "All that bullshit about how I'm your first priority. You don't want me. You want *her.*"

"You're my daughter, Megan," Nick said firmly. "Our relationship has nothing to do with Isabella."

"Not until you decide to marry her or live with her and dump me out on my ass."

"That won't ever happen," he assured her.

"Well, I don't care if it does. You two can go ahead and screw each other, because I'm done with both of you."

"Dammit," he swore as Megan ran out of the costume shop.

"Go after her," Isabella said. "Fight for her. That's what she needs you to do."

As Nick left the room, she put out a hand on the worktable to steady herself. She felt horrible for upsetting Megan and ripping apart the fragile relationship between father and daughter. Would either one of them ever forgive her for it?

SEVENTEEN

Nick reached the sidewalk in front of the theater just in time to see Megan flying down the street on the back of her boyfriend's motorcycle. She must have called Will earlier, when she'd gotten tired of waiting for him. *Damn.*

He ran to his car in the nearby lot and jumped in, but by the time he pulled out on to the street, there was no sign of the motorcycle. Well, he'd find them. And when he did, he'd take Megan home and make her understand that he loved her and that she was his first priority.

As for Isabella, he'd make it clear that that was over, too. It had to be, he told himself firmly. He had to prove to Megan that he could put her first.

Finding Megan wasn't as easy as he'd thought it would be. He tried all of the local hangouts, then stopped by Colleen's and quizzed her son Cord about where Megan might have gone. Colleen agreed to go to his house to wait in case Megan came back while he was out looking for her. He stopped by the pizza parlor, the arcade, and the movie theater. He even went to Will Harlan's house, but his mother was out, and his father was drunk and had no idea where his kid was.

Two hours later, frantic and frustrated, he pulled up in front of Isabella's house.

She opened the door, concern in her eyes.

"I can't find her," he said. "She went off with that kid on the motorcycle, and I've been all over town. You've got to help me."

"Come in."

He walked into the house. "Is your brother here?"

"No, I haven't seen him since I got back from the theater. Have you talked to Megan's friends?"

"She doesn't have any, besides that kid. I spoke to her cousin Cord. He gave me some ideas, but none of them panned out." He paced around her living room. "I've screwed this up, Isabella. I've lost her."

"You haven't lost her. She's just mad and licking her wounds. She'll come home."

"I can't just go home and wait. I did that before." Memories of those first horrifying moments from a dozen years ago ran through his mind. He'd returned home from work to find half the closet cleaned out, Megan's favorite dolls gone, and a note on the refrigerator. He hadn't known what to do then, so he'd gone out and gotten drunk. That wasn't going to work this time.

"Nick, this isn't before." Isabella's voice brought him back to the present. "Angel's Bay isn't that big.

We can find her. Let's think." She paused. "You were a teenager in this town. Where did you go when you were looking for trouble?"

He ran a hand through his hair. "There are a couple of beaches south of town where we used to do bonfires, but that was more in the summer. I've been to the other places, even the old haunted Ramsay house, where we used to drink in the basement. But they finally boarded that place up so no one can get in." He paced around the room, then stopped abruptly. "The falls. We used to go to Hidden Falls."

"So did your grandfather and Leticia," Isabella said, an odd look in her eyes.

He didn't like the coincidence. "I don't think their fifty-year-old love affair has anything to do with Megan."

"We should still check it out."

He hesitated. "I don't know if you should come. She ran away because we were together."

"I know that, but I want to help. It's driving me crazy to sit here and do nothing. I never wanted to hurt Megan. I'll just help you find her, and then I'll disappear. I promise."

He didn't want her to disappear, but he couldn't think about that right now. Megan was somewhere out there, angry, hurt, and reckless, a dangerous combination.

"I'll get a flashlight," Isabella said, moving toward the desk. She grabbed the light and her coat and headed toward the door. "Don't worry, Nick.

We're going to find her, and you'll make everything right."

He wasn't sure he could make everything right— but he would kill himself trying.

"Did you ever bring a girl up here?" Isabella asked Nick as they parked at the bottom of the trail and got out of the car.

"Too much of a hike for me. I was a lazy partyer."

They headed swiftly up the trail. "In L.A., we used to park off Mulholland Drive up in the Hollywood Hills," she said. "There were a couple of turnouts where you could sneak some alcohol and have a great view. Not that we were looking at the view."

"Sounds like you had a little wildness in your past."

"The flip side of my parents' lack of attention was that I had a lot fewer rules than my siblings did. My sister Teresa used to complain that they never let her do half of what I did. She was always keeping score of who got what. It used to drive Joe nuts."

"I can't imagine having four sisters. One is enough for me."

"Yeah, but being the only son, Joe was like the king of the family. When it was time for dinner, all the girls were expected to help cook, set the table, and clean up, but somehow Joe always got out of it." She stumbled over an exposed root, and Nick grabbed her hand.

"This might be a wasted trip," he said. "Kids used to come up here, but I'd forgotten how dark it was, and it's quite a hike."

"It might be easier to do on a motorcycle. There's enough room."

"True," he said grimly.

"Don't get ahead of yourself, Nick. Megan isn't a pushover."

"She's a girl. She's vulnerable."

"But she is used to taking care of herself."

"She grew up rich, Isabella. She had servants and chauffeurs and went to private schools. What does she know of the real world?"

"She knows that people can't always be trusted."

"Yeah, she knows that," he agreed with a heavy sigh.

As they neared the falls, they could hear the sound of music and laughter. Nick began to walk more quickly, and she had to jog to keep up with him. He was a man on a mission, hell bent on getting his daughter back. She just hoped he was prepared for possible fallout. "Wait, Nick," she said breathlessly, putting a hand on his arm, bringing him to a stop.

"What?" he asked impatiently.

"Most teenage girls don't want to be dragged away from their friends by their irate fathers. There's a difference between letting her know you care and embarrassing her. Just think for a minute. Nothing horrible has happened. She's spending time with her friends. It sounds like they're having fun," she added as laughter rang through the woods. "You have to keep things in perspective."

"Okay, you're right. But I need to talk to her."

Nick pushed his way through the thick trees. He wasn't being quiet, but she doubted that anyone could hear them over the music and the rush of water coming from the falls.

When they reached the clearing, they saw three kids sprawled on a blanket next to two motorcycles. Beer bottles were strewn on the ground, and the smell of weed permeated the damp air. Megan wasn't there, but her boyfriend was.

The girl in the group jumped to her feet as they approached. The two boys got up more slowly, especially Will.

"Where's Megan?" Nick demanded.

"She left," Will said sullenly.

"What do you mean?" Nick asked. "Where did she go?"

"She didn't like the party, so she took off."

"You let her walk away from here by herself? Are you out of your fucking mind?" Nick shouted.

"Dude, she ran away into the woods," Will said, taking a step back. "We looked for her, but we couldn't find her. She'll come back when she's tired of being mad."

"Which way did she go?" Isabella interrupted, sensing a fight about to erupt that wouldn't bring them closer to finding Megan. She turned to the girl, who seemed very nervous. "Did you see where she went?"

"She went over there through the trees." The girl pointed across the clearing. "She said she was going home."

"That's not the way home," Nick bit out.

"I tried to tell her that," Will said. "She wouldn't listen. She was pissed off before we even got here."

Isabella saw Nick's fists clench, and she jumped between him and the kid. "We need to find Megan. You can deal with him later."

"I *will* deal with you later," he promised.

As they headed into the woods, Isabella heard the motorcycles take off. It grew quieter as they got farther away from the falls. It was also darker; the thick woods didn't allow much moonlight to squeeze through. Thankfully, the flashlight gave them some illumination.

"Megan!" They took turns shouting.

There was no answer. The woods were thick and dark, and Isabella couldn't imagine how scared Megan must be. Where was she? Had she found her way back to the trail and gone home? She was a smart girl. It seemed unlikely that she'd keep wandering aimlessly in the woods, even if she was upset.

"Where *is* she?" Nick echoed, dragging a hand through his hair as he stopped to get their bearings, then took out his cell phone. "Dammit, I can't get any reception. What if she's not here in the woods? What if she found the trail and made it into town? She would still be several miles from home."

"She could have found a ride in town. A lot of people know her from the theater. Anyone could have helped her out." Isabella fell silent for a moment, the faint sound of rushing water breaking the quiet. "I think we should go back to the falls. Megan will try to find her way back there. Whatever happened with those kids, they're her friends."

"Then why did she run away from them? Do you think that punk tried something with her?"

Isabella could see how crazy Nick was making himself. "I don't believe he hurt her. Come on, let's go back." She put out her hand, and after a moment's hesitation, Nick took it. When they returned to the clearing, the area was empty.

"I'm going to see if I can get hold of Joe," she said, taking out her own phone. "We might get better reception here." She got Joe's voice-mail and quickly explained the situation. "I'm with Nick, and we're looking for Megan. She got upset and ran off into the woods. We're up by Hidden Falls. I'll call you later, but don't worry about me."

When she got off her phone, she saw Nick on his. He ended the call a moment later. "Colleen said Megan hasn't come back, but she'll stay at my place tonight until we get back," he said tersely. "What now? I can't go home knowing she's out here somewhere."

"Then let's wait here for a while. Maybe Colleen will call you soon and tell you that Megan is home."

Isabella sat down on the blanket the teenagers had left behind while Nick walked around in circles until he tired himself out enough to sit.

"I hate this," he said.

"I know."

For a few moments, they sat in silence, the only sound coming from the water splashing down the rocks. While it had been her idea to wait, now she was beginning to rethink that. It was going to get colder and darker, and memories of the past were teasing at her brain. The longer she stayed in Angel's Bay, the more she realized that she wasn't connected just to Nick but to the town.

"I should take you home," Nick said half-heartedly.

She shook her head. "Not a chance. We're in this together."

"You and me together is what started all this." He stretched out on his side. "You know that Kendra sent Megan to me because she was getting married again. A few days ago, Megan asked me how long she'd be my first priority. What would happen when I met someone? Wouldn't I just toss her aside like her mother did? When she saw us together tonight, she must have seen it happening all over again."

"And instead of waiting for you to dump her, she dumped you." Isabella understood perfectly, and she couldn't blame Megan for reacting so strongly after what she'd gone through. "You'll get another chance, Nick. I'm sure of it. She'll calm down. It was just a kiss. You have to keep things in perspective." She lay down on her side, facing him. "Did you ever run away from home?"

"I ran away from a road trip and came home. Does that count?"

"What happened?"

"We were in San Francisco. It was the end of summer; I was fourteen. My best friend was going to have a kick-ass party at the beach, and I wanted to go. My parents said we weren't going to leave for another week, so I hopped on a bus and came back on my own. They were pissed. But by the time they caught up with me, I'd already been to the party, so I didn't really care. Their punishments never lasted; they'd ground me for a month and forget after two days. Follow-through wasn't their thing."

She nodded. "So you got away with a lot."

"Too much, probably. I started to think I could do anything without consequences. Turned out I couldn't."

"Tell me about the years in between, when you had finished school and gotten your life together but didn't have Megan yet. Were you involved with anyone?"

"Nothing serious. I went to school in L.A., got a job there afterward, and rented an apartment in Santa Monica. I made some friends who weren't musicians or theater people, and I had a life. Most of it involved working."

"Do you miss your L.A. life?"

"I thought I would. I came back because I had a house here and Megan would have extended family around. I thought it would be a better environment than L.A., and it is starting to feel like home again," he said. "I'd lost touch with all of my friends. But seeing Shane the other night, Kara, Charlotte,

Lauren, Jason . . . even though most of us left, we all came back. Fortunately, my firm in L.A. is happy to let me telecommute, so I'm able to keep some business going with them, as well as operating my own small firm here." He gave her a curious look. "What about you? What's your work like?"

"I freelance, working solo or in collaboration with other designers on film projects mostly. I grew up in the backyard of the major studios, and my grandmother had some connections in the business that got me get started."

"Were you always in costumes, versus contemporary fashion?"

"I've done both, but I do love creating clothes that are part of a story. The period pieces are really fun, because some of the gowns are layers and layers of material with beading and embroidery. No one makes clothes like that anymore. But I also like designing for contemporary films, where the subtle clothing choices emphasize part of the plot or the character's background." She paused, seeing the smile on his face. "What's so funny?"

"You light up when you talk about your work."

"So do you. We both like to leave our mark on the world in a tangible way."

"I never thought about it like that."

"Didn't you? Come on. You're too competitive not to imagine people talking about your buildings."

"All right. Guilty," he admitted. "What about you? There must be someone in L.A. waiting for you to come back."

"I was seeing someone for a few months, but that ended a while ago."

"Why did it end?"

She drew little circles on the blanket with her finger. "Because I didn't want to tell him who I really was. And he made it easy, because he didn't ask."

"Why did you tell me?"

She lifted her gaze to his. "You're different."

"How?"

"For one thing, the dreams I've been having are about you, so I thought you would need to know."

"And the other thing?"

"I knew I could trust you," she said, gazing into his eyes. "Maybe because you saved my life, because we met in a moment that was honest and real."

Nick stared back at her. "When you dreamed about me being in trouble, did you see any of this?" He waved his hand toward the falls.

"I'm not sure. I've had visions of this place that didn't involve you. When I touched some of Leticia's things, I had a flash of her and your grandfather meeting behind the falls. Your grandfather later told me it was their trysting place. They were here the night the theater burned down. They saw the flames from the hillside when they went back down the trail. By the time they got to the theater, your grandfather's sister, Caitlyn, was dead."

"My grandfather told you all that?" Nick asked in surprise.

"The other day at the theater. Leticia felt guilty. She'd had visions that Caitlyn was in trouble, that she was keeping company with some boy who wasn't good for her. But that night your grandfather didn't want to talk about Caitlyn, or Leticia's imagination, as he called it. He wanted to give her the necklace for her birthday and spend one more night with her before he had to marry your grandmother. After Caitlyn died, he felt guilty for putting his selfish affair first. Leticia left town. She ran her car into the ocean off the road just north of Big Sur. No one knows if she did it on purpose or if another car was involved."

"That's quite a story," he said slowly.

A chill ran down her spine as she thought of all the similarities between Leticia's story and her own. "You saved me, but Harrison didn't save Leticia. And neither of them saved Caitlyn."

Nick sat up, a new energy in his body. "Caitlyn was sixteen, close to Megan's age."

"It's not going to end the same way," she said quickly.

"Do you know that?" he asked, jumping to his feet.

"If you mean, have I seen something about Megan, I haven't."

He paced around the clearing. "I don't know what to do."

"There's nothing to do right now, Nick. We just have to wait until dawn so we can keep searching."

"She could be in town. We could be in the wrong place."

Isabella didn't think so. Her nerves were tingling, and this place was familiar to her. Because of Leticia? Or because of Nick? She'd sensed that trouble was heading his way; was this it? "What do you want to do?"

"What do *you* think?"

She didn't want to be wrong. Not this time, not with this man. "Let's wait."

Nick sat back down on the blanket. "It's killing me to think of how scared she must be right now. She talks tough, but she's still a little girl on the inside. She's my child, and I'd cut off my right arm for her."

"I know you would."

He stretched out on his back, and she curled up next to him, resting her head on his chest. She could hear the rapid beat of his heart. Eventually, it began to slow to a steadier pace.

With a sigh, Isabella tried to relax. She didn't know when she fell asleep, but soon she was dreaming.

The branches from the trees scratched her arms. Nick was running faster and faster, his fear and his hope driving him forward. She could smell smoke. Food cooking. Through the trees—there was a tent, a barbecue next to a cooler. Her heart stopped.

Megan was crying, tears streaming down her dirty face, twigs in her hair, terror in her eyes. She was sitting on the ground in front of the tent. She jumped up at their approach and cried out. Was it a shout of welcome or of warning?

Something glinted in the sunshine, then a long shadow fell.

Nick didn't see the danger coming. She had to stop him. Oh, God, what if she was too late—again?

"Nick!" she screamed. "Nick!"

"Isabella, wake up," Nick said. "Isabella."

His hands held her shoulders as he shook her awake. She blinked her eyes open in a daze.

"You were dreaming—about me."

She nodded, her throat too tight to speak.

"What did you see?" he demanded.

She swallowed, her throat sore from her screams. Early-morning sunlight slanted through the trees.

"Isabella," he repeated.

"I'm not sure," she said slowly, the details already blurring in her mind.

"You're just afraid. You don't want to be wrong."

"I've been wrong before."

"That was before. That was with other people," he said forcefully. "This is me and you, Isabella. We're connected. You came here because of me. You came here for this moment. It's here." He let his words sink in. "I believe in you."

Her heart turned over, and tears filled her eyes. Did he truly mean it?

"I do," he said softly, reading the doubt in her eyes. "There have been very few people in my life I can honestly say I have faith in, but you're one of them. Now you have to believe in yourself. Whatever you got right or wrong before doesn't matter. It's all about now."

"I saw Megan sitting on the ground in front of a tent. She was crying, and you rushed over to her. But someone came out of the shadows. I think . . . I think he had a gun."

Nick paled. "Where was the tent?"

"It was in the woods. We ran through the trees." She strained to remember. "The hill rose behind her. I feel like there was a stream nearby." The splash of water echoed through her head, but was it from her dream or the nearby falls?

"Let's go," he said. "We'll follow the water."

She realized that he was talking about the creek runoff from the falls. Getting to her feet, she said, "It's not much to go on."

"It's better than nothing. Was there anything else?" he asked as they walked toward the far end of the falls.

"There was a barbecue and a cooler. It was a campsite. Megan must have stumbled across it."

"But she was crying," Nick said tensely. "So whoever set up that camp scared her or hurt her."

Isabella's stomach turned over at the thought of how many hours had passed and what might have happened to Megan. Why hadn't her dreams been more specific? Why hadn't she tried harder to force the visions to come?

Nick grabbed her hand. "Don't go backward. Stay with me."

"Are you reading my mind now?"

"Blaming yourself is only going to get in the way." His grip tightened. "You and me, Isabella. Feel me. Feel my link to Megan. We're all connected. You came here to Angel's Bay to save me. Now I need you to help me save my daughter. Which way?"

She gazed at the trees ahead. "To the left," she said, going with her instincts and praying she'd be right.

Nick charged forward, and they ran through the trees, the creek water their constant companion. The sun moved higher in the sky, making it easier to see. A few minutes later, Isabella smelled smoke.

"We're getting close," she said. "I can smell the fire." Her nerves tightened. She felt as if she was back in her dream, the branches scratching her arms, a break in the woods coming closer and closer.

Finally, they broke into a clearing. It was all there: the tent, the barbecue, the cooler, and Megan sitting by the tent.

"Megan!" Nick shouted.

His daughter jumped up in relief, tears streaming down her face.

Isabella looked around. Shadows fell from the trees, none of them moving. Yet danger was coming. She could feel it, but she couldn't see it.

Megan took a step toward her father, then froze. "Daddy, look out!" she screamed as a man came around a tree, a rifle in his hands.

Nick ran toward Megan, putting his body in front of her like a shield.

Isabella saw the man lift his gun, and her heart stopped as he took aim. His gaze was focused on Nick and Megan. He hadn't seen her. He didn't know she was there, and this time, she was not going to let the worst happen.

She rushed the gunman from the side, taking him by surprise. She tackled his midsection, hearing the gun go off as they fell to the ground. His weight crushed her. She tried to shove him away, but he slammed his fist into her face, and her head bounced off the dirt. Dazed, she thought for a terrifying moment that this might be it for all of them. She couldn't see Nick and had no idea if he'd been shot, but she could hear Megan crying.

As her attacker scrambled toward his gun, Nick came up behind him and threw him down. Fists flying, Nick went after the man with the unrelenting fury of a man fighting for his child's life. The man collapsed on the ground, but Nick hit him again and again.

"Stop! He's unconscious," Isabella said as she got to her feet. "Stop, Nick." Even if the other man deserved to die, she didn't want Nick to kill him. "Megan needs you," she said.

Her words finally got through. Nick ran back to his daughter, who launched herself into his arms.

Isabella picked up the rifle and moved a few feet away from the man, keeping an eye on him in case he woke up.

"Are you all right?" Nick asked, searching Megan's face as his hands ran up and down her arms.

Megan gave a sob as she nodded her head.

Nick pulled her back into his embrace. "You're safe now, honey. No one will hurt you. I'm going to take care you."

Tears gathered in Isabella's eyes. She hoped Megan could believe him, because the way the two of them clung together was proof of how much they needed each other.

A sudden movement in the tent made Isabella stiffen. "Nick!" she said urgently as the flap of the tent began to move.

He looked up, then pulled Megan behind him. "Who's there?" he demanded.

"It's okay, Dad," Megan said. "It's just a girl. She was nice to me."

A face appeared through the open flap, then the other girl slowly crawled out of the tent. Her thick blond hair was down to her waist, her face pale, her blue eyes shocked. She looked from them to the man on the ground. "Is he—is he dead?" she asked, stumbling to her feet.

"No, he's just unconscious," Nick said. "Who are you?"

"Annie."

Isabella gasped. "You're the girl everyone has been looking for?"

Annie tipped her head toward the man who'd attacked them. "That's my father. He kidnapped me, and he wouldn't let me leave."

"Are you all right?" Isabella asked, moving quickly to the girl's side. "Did he hurt you?"

Annie shook her head. "He just slapped me a few times."

"Everyone is so worried about you. My brother,

the chief of police, sent search parties out scouring these hills."

"He did? My dad said no one would care that I was gone. All they wanted was my baby. Oh, God, how is he? Is he okay?" she asked, her voice breaking.

Isabella set the rifle down and put her arm around Annie's shoulder. "He's fine. Charlotte has been taking care of him. But I know everyone will be happy to see you. We need to call nine-one-one," she added, turning back to Nick.

"There's no service out here," Annie said.

"We're going to take you home." She glanced at Nick. "Any idea where we are?"

"I know the way," Annie said. "My father's car is through the trees, but he has the keys in his pocket."

"I'll get 'em." Nick strode forward and knelt next to Annie's father. The man groaned as Nick pulled out his keys, but he didn't open his eyes or make any attempt to fight back.

"Is he going to be all right?" Annie asked, worry in her eyes. "The war made him crazy, you know? He wasn't always like this."

"As soon as we get service, we'll call for an ambulance," Nick said. "Let's get out of here."

As they approached the beat-up old car, Isabella felt her nerves tighten once again. Carl Dupont was still lying motionless on the ground, so why was she feeling on edge? As she walked around the front of the car, an image flashed through her mind.

The car was headed straight for her, two people

struggling in the front seat. It turned at the last second, and she hit the brakes . . .

"Isabella?" Nick questioned as he opened the back door for Annie. "What's wrong?"

"This was the car that ran me off the road on the coast highway," she said in amazement. She looked at Annie. "Your father was driving. You were headed straight toward me, and then he made a quick turn. That was the night he took you, wasn't it?"

"I saw a car skid across the road on our way out of town, but I didn't know what happened after that. That was you?"

"Yes." Isabella should have been used to the unexpected connections by now, yet this one shook her.

"I was trying to get him to turn around," Annie said. "I made him angry, and he drove faster. I thought for a while he was going to kill me."

"But he didn't," Nick said. "And he's not going to hurt anyone ever again. Now, let's get going."

"Megan, you sit in the front with your father," Isabella said.

"Are you sure?" Megan asked uncertainly.

She gave her a smile. "Absolutely. I don't think your dad will be able to drive if he can't see you. He's been so worried about you." She got into the backseat alongside Annie, while Megan and Nick settled in the front.

"I'm really sorry I ran away," Megan said.

"I'm sorry you felt the need to run away," Nick replied, giving her a tender look. "I don't want that to ever happen again."

"How did you find me?" Megan asked.

"We went to Hidden Falls," Nick replied. "We ran into your boyfriend. He's not good for you, Megan."

"I know," she said quietly.

"Did he hurt you?" Nick asked, an edge in his voice.

Megan quickly shook her head. "No, he was just being stupid. And I was so mad I didn't want to hang out with him. I didn't think I was going to get lost, but I got confused in the woods. I tried to get back to the falls, but I couldn't find them.

"When I saw the tent, I thought it was a family camping, but then her dad came at me with a gun and told me that I wasn't going to be able to leave, because then the enemy would know where they were." Megan's voice broke. "I was scared, but Annie told me he wouldn't hurt me." Megan flung a look of gratitude in Annie's direction. "I'm sorry he took you, but I'm glad you were there."

Annie nodded, fatigue etched in deep lines around eyes that shouldn't look as old as they did. Isabella couldn't imagine the ordeal she'd gone through.

Despite Annie's exhaustion, she had enough wits about her to direct them down some narrow dirt roads that eventually led them to the outskirts of town.

When they got out of the hills, Isabella took out her phone and called her brother. "Joe, I've got some good news. We found Annie."

"How the hell did you do that?" he asked in amazement.

She could have told him that for once in her life, her gift of insight had been a true gift, but she just said, "It's a long story, but we're headed into town. We're taking Annie back to Charlotte's house. Her father's in the woods and needs an ambulance. I'm going to give Annie the phone. She can tell you where he is." She handed the phone to Annie, who in a halting but clear voice directed Joe to the campsite.

Then Annie handed the phone back to Isabella. "He said he'd meet us at Charlotte's house. You're his sister, huh?"

"Yes. I was on my way into town the night your father ran me off the road. Fortunately, Nick saved my life." She smiled as Nick's glance met hers in the rearview mirror. "Everything worked out the way it was supposed to."

"You were crazy, tackling Annie's father," Nick said. "He could have shot you."

"I thought he'd shot you for a minute."

"He missed when you knocked him down."

"You were really brave, Isabella," Megan said. "You saved us all."

She smiled. "Joe taught me how to tackle a long time ago. He'll be happy to know it finally came in handy."

EIGHTEEN

Charlotte hung up the phone, thrilled with the news Joe had just delivered. Annie was fine and was on her way home—thank God! The nightmare was over. She walked down the hall and opened the door to the baby's room. He was fast asleep in his crib. "She's coming back, sweetie," she whispered. "Your mother is coming home." As she said the words, she felt a little pang at the knowledge that things would change, that she would no longer be his primary caregiver. But that was silly. She had a career to get back to, and he needed Annie, not her.

The doorbell rang, and she ran down the hall to answer it. Expecting Annie or Joe, she was surprised to see Steve and Tory Baker. She knew in that instant what they were going to say, and she felt a jolt of disappointment that Steve had cheated on Tory. She'd thought he was a good man, but the way he'd treated Tory, Annie, and the baby was shameful. She noted his black eye and suspected that someone else had taken him to task for his behavior.

"I need to talk to you, Charlotte," Steve said. "About the baby. Can we come in?"

"Of course. You have great timing. Joe just called and said that Annie is on her way home, and she's fine."

"Thank heavens," Tory said with genuine relief. "What happened to her?"

"I don't know any details, just that it had something to do with her father. Sit down." She gestured toward the living-room couch.

"Where is the baby?" Tory asked, her gaze flying around the room.

"He's asleep in the other room."

"I'm sorry I got so upset the other day," Tory said. "It was a shock to see the baby and realize . . ." Her voice trailed away. "Anyway, that's not why we came here."

Charlotte took a seat in the chair across from them. "Do you want to wait until Annie gets here?"

"It doesn't matter," Steve said heavily. "You might as well know now. I'm the father of the child." He drew in a deep breath, as if he couldn't believe he'd finally said it. "Annie was working for Myra's cleaning service. She used to clean my office late at night after everyone went home. I ran into her one day, and we started talking. She was a sweet young girl who looked up to me. One night, things went farther than they should have."

"You don't have to tell me this," Charlotte

interrupted, seeing the pain in Tory's eyes. "This is between you and Tory and Annie."

"You've been taking care of the baby, and you have a right to know," he said. "I should have confessed a long time ago, but Annie getting pregnant when Tory couldn't seemed like the worst possible irony. I couldn't bear the thought of telling Tory, so I didn't. Annie said she would give the baby up. I thought it would be to someone who didn't live in Angel's Bay, but then Andrew started talking to everyone, and I knew that the adoption couldn't go through without my signature."

"So you cooked up a clever plan," Charlotte said, unable to hide the snark in her voice. Steve Baker had taken advantage of a young, innocent girl; he didn't deserve forgiveness. And he didn't deserve Tory.

"I thought it was a win for everyone," he explained. "Tory would get her baby. Annie could have her life back, and I could fulfill my fatherly responsibilities."

"Don't you want to see him?" Tory interrupted her husband. "We've been sitting here for several minutes, and you haven't even asked how your son is or if you could see him."

A pulse beat rapidly in his jaw. "I—I don't know the right thing to do. What's going to hurt you more, if I want to see my son or if I don't?"

"Do you want to see him?" Charlotte asked. "He's a beautiful little boy. I know, because I've been holding him and feeding him and comforting him while his mother was missing and his father wasn't interested."

Steve stared back at her. "I've wanted a kid as much as Tory has. But I wanted my son to be with her." He turned his pleading gaze on his wife.

"Well, we don't always get what we want," Tory said sharply.

A clatter of voices and footsteps on the porch interrupted their conversation. Charlotte got up to open the door, Steve and Tory on her heels.

The first person she saw was an exhausted, weepy Annie. "Oh, honey," she said, pulling her into her arms. "Thank God you're all right."

Annie hugged her back, so tightly Charlotte could feel every bone in her body. She didn't see any signs of physical injury, but she suspected there were many emotional scars.

"My father took me off the street," Annie said. "He told me that since the baby was born, he needed me to come home. I didn't want to go, Charlotte, but he didn't give me a choice. I was scared, and there was no one around."

"You're safe now," Charlotte said, hugging her again. Over Annie's shoulder, she could see Joe approaching the porch. Nick, Isabella, and a teenager she thought was Nick's daughter were also there. She let Annie go and said, "I don't know why you're all here, but come in, please."

As she stepped back to let the group enter, Annie's gaze fell on Steve. Her jaw dropped, and she looked from Steve to Tory in panic.

"He told us he's the father," Charlotte cut in.

"You all know?" Annie asked in bemusement.

"Let's all sit down," Charlotte suggested.

As the others moved into the living room, Annie hesitated. "Can I see him?"

"Of course you can, honey," Charlotte said immediately. "He's been missing you like crazy."

"I don't know if he'll recognize me now. I've been gone so long," Annie said uncertainly. "I don't want to scare him."

"You couldn't possibly do that. You're his mother."

"We were only together a couple of days."

"You were together for nine months. He knows your scent, your voice, your touch. It's going to be fine." When Annie didn't look convinced, she added, "Tell you what. You sit down in the living room, and I'll bring him to you."

Charlotte hurried down the hall. The baby was just waking up. He blinked at her, and his mouth moved into what she was sure was a smile. Her heart split in two. She was really going to miss mothering him. Even though they might continue living in the same house, depending on what decisions Annie made, it would be different now. But that's the way it should be.

"Your mommy is back, little guy," she said as she picked him up. His warm weight in her arms made her heart ache. "But you and I are going to be friends forever. Deal?" She pressed her lips to his forehead and inhaled the sweet scent of baby as she sniffed back a tear. This moment wasn't about her.

She quickly changed his diaper and took him down the hall. The group was amazingly silent, considering all of the unanswered questions that had to be ringing through everyone's mind. They were all waiting for her, for the baby, because he was what it was all about.

Annie was sitting in the armchair, and Charlotte put the baby in her arms. "I took really good care of him for you. But he's been wanting you since the day you left."

Tears ran down Annie's cheeks as she stared at her son in wonder. "He's so big now," she murmured. The baby reached out and grabbed a strand of Annie's long blond hair, twisting it with his tiny fingers. "Do you think he knows who I am?"

Charlotte met her questioning gaze. "Absolutely. He cried for hours after you disappeared. He was looking for you."

Annie's mouth trembled. "I should have fought harder to get away. I didn't know what to do. My dad is so strong and so crazy, and I didn't know what would happen if I didn't go with him. I thought he might try to hurt the baby—but if he had me, then he'd leave the baby alone."

Charlotte squatted down in front of her. "You protected him. That's what mothers do."

Annie looked past Charlotte to Steve and Tory. "I have to say I'm sorry," she said, focusing on Tory. "For being with your husband," she added courageously.

Tory gave a tight nod, as if she couldn't trust herself to speak.

Annie looked at Steve. "Do you and your wife still want to adopt him?"

Shock turned to wariness on Steve's face. "I—I don't know. Tory?"

Tory stiffened, and Charlotte couldn't imagine the pressure she was feeling. She might finally have the opportunity to raise a baby, but the child would always represent her husband's infidelity.

Charlotte wasn't sure she wanted Tory to say yes. Was it fair to put this innocent child in the middle of their embattled marriage? "Annie, you don't have to do this now," she said. "You're exhausted. And everyone has a lot to think about."

"Charlotte is right," Tory said, her eyes filled with pain. "You need to think about what you want to do. And you need to talk to Steve about it." She drew in a shaky but determined breath. "I would love to be a part of your child's life, Annie, but you love him, and I think you want to be his mother."

"I don't know if I'll be any good."

"You will be," Tory assured her. "Because you're his mom. And I'm not."

"You're being so nice to me. I don't deserve it," Annie said.

Tory got to her feet. "Whatever happened in the past shouldn't affect your son. Do what's best for him, Annie. That's all I ask of you. Because being a mother is a precious, precious gift. It doesn't happen for everyone. Don't throw it away unless you're really sure that's what you want."

Charlotte fought back tears as Tory's words reminded her of the baby she'd lost so long ago.

Tory walked over to the baby, touched his forehead with the tip of her fingers, and gazed down at his face for a long moment. Then she turned back to her husband and said, "You don't deserve him. But you'd better do right by him now."

The pulse in Steve's jaw was beating in triple time as he stood up. "I will do what's right," he said, looking from his wife to Annie. "I'll support you, Annie, and the baby. I should have stepped up a long time ago. But I'll do better."

Neither Annie nor Tory looked that inclined to believe him.

"You should go," Tory told her husband. "I'll get a ride home from Nick."

"All right. If that's what you want."

After Steve left, Tory turned back to the group. "Now I want to hear what happened, Nick. I got your message last night that Megan had disappeared, and I spoke to Colleen, who said you were out looking for her. But how did you all come to be together? How did you find Annie?"

"Megan went up to Hidden Falls with some friends and ended up getting lost in the woods," Nick said. "Isabella and I went searching for her, and we found her this morning. Megan had stumbled into the encampment that Annie's father had set up. There was a bit of a struggle, but we took him down."

"Isabella tackled him," Megan put in.

"What?" Joe asked in anger and surprise. "What were you thinking, Izzy?"

"Nick and Megan needed my help. He pulled a gun on them," Isabella said, "so I had to act. I hit him the way you taught me, Joe. Then Nick did the rest."

"We were going to search that area later today," Joe said. "I wish we'd gotten to you sooner, Annie."

"Joe has been working nonstop on finding you," Charlotte said. "We were all so worried about you. So what happened while you were with your dad?"

"Not much. We moved a couple of times. He said the enemy would be coming. I cried a lot, and he got mad and hit me a couple of times. He said it was for my own good. I told him I missed my baby." Annie held the baby in her arms a little bit tighter. "He said I didn't deserve a child, because of my sins. That the baby would be better off without me and that everyone here just wanted the baby, not me. I was so tired I got confused. I thought he might be right for a while. But deep down, I knew he wasn't. He's just a sick person who needs help."

"We're going to make sure he gets it," Joe said quietly. "He served his country. It's time his country served him. He's at the hospital now. We need to make sure he's not a danger to you or anyone else or even to himself."

"I think your father tried to break into the house a couple of nights ago," Charlotte said. "Did he tell you that?"

Annie nodded. "He said he would get my things so I'd understand that I was never going back. But he didn't return with anything."

"I scared him off," Charlotte said. "I'm just so happy this is over and that you're back."

"We should get going," Nick said. "Megan's had a long night. Tory, are you ready?"

Tory started, her gaze still lingering on the baby. "Yes, I'm ready."

"I am sorry," Annie said again to Tory. "I didn't want you to ever find out. You were really nice to me when we met, and I felt so guilty."

"We all make mistakes," Tory said with a generosity that Charlotte admired. "The important thing is to do the right thing now."

"I'll catch a ride with Joe," Isabella said, exchanging a quick look with Nick.

Charlotte walked the others to the door. As Nick, Megan, and Tory left, she saw Andrew coming up the walkway. She instinctively pulled the front door shut behind her and met him on the porch.

"What's going on?" he asked. "Has something happened?"

"Annie's back. Nick and Isabella found her in the woods."

"Praise the Lord. Is she all right?"

"She will be. Her father wanted her back with him once the baby was born. Nick and Isabella had to wrestle a gun away from him. Joe is going to make sure that he gets help and doesn't get near Annie again."

Andrew nodded. "That's good. I'm really happy everything has worked out."

He didn't look all that happy, Charlotte thought, wondering if he was put out that he hadn't had more to do with the resolution. But maybe she was reading him wrong.

"What about the adoption?" he asked.

"Steve Baker admitted to being the father. Annie obviously hasn't had time to make any decisions, but I suspect she's going to keep the baby. And Steve has promised to provide child support. I'm not sure his marriage to Tory will last, but maybe she'll find a way to forgive him. She's a very generous person."

"As are you." Andrew gave her a smile. "You went above and beyond the call of duty taking Annie in and mothering her child. You were good at it, too. I wonder if the experience will make you reconsider having your own children."

She wasn't quite ready to admit that. "We'll see."

"Do you mind if I come in and say hello to Annie?"

She hesitated. "Joe and Isabella are inside. Annie is exhausted. Maybe later would be better."

"All right." He paused. "Now that Annie is back, I'm going to hold you to that dinner date you promised me. I've had a chance to think about what you told me the other night, and I wondered if that secret was what was holding you back from seeing me again."

She wasn't sure how to answer that. "It was part of it but not all of it."

"Well, let's put it to rest and move on. I want to start over, clean slate. What do you think?"

"I'm not sure it's possible to do that."

"At least, promise me one thing."

"What's that?"

"Give me a chance to compete with the chief."

She stiffened. "Joe and I aren't seeing each other."

"Not yet," Andrew said. "I want an opportunity to show you who I am now. Just think about it. We already know the worst of each other. Maybe now we can find the best."

Joe paced around the living room. Through the window, he could see Charlotte talking to Andrew, and as usual, his blood pressure began to rise. It figured that Andrew would show up when all of the work was done and try to cash in on the celebration. He didn't like Andrew and didn't particularly trust him, although he seemed to be alone in that opinion. Andrew was quickly growing in popularity as his charismatic sermons brought more and more people back to church.

"Who's out there?" Isabella asked curiously, walking over to him as Annie took the baby into the kitchen for a feeding.

"Reverend Schilling. Charlotte's high-school boyfriend," he said shortly.

Isabella raised a curious eyebrow at his tone, and he could have kicked himself for revealing so much. He decided to change the subject. "When you left me that message yesterday, I had no idea you were out in the woods all night. Why didn't you call me back and ask for help?"

"We didn't need help. We were just going to wait by the falls until Megan came back, and I didn't think there was anything you could do in the dark. I was going to call you this morning, but we lost service."

"I can't believe you went after crazy Carl Dupont," he said with a bemused shake of his head. "I hope Nick realizes how amazing you are."

"He seems to be happy enough with me at the moment," she said with a smile.

He grinned. "You like him?"

"Yes." She sighed. "Way too much."

"Why too much?"

"Because I don't know if we can be together. Megan ran away because she saw Nick and me kissing. Her mother dumped her on Nick so she could get married, and all Megan saw was Nick doing the same thing to her. She needs her father's attention."

"Don't you think Nick is capable of giving you both what you need?"

"He's got a lot of guilt to work off. I'm not sure he could justify taking any happiness that might come at Megan's expense. And I can't blame him; they need each other. But I think after seeing her father throw himself in front of a gun for her, Megan will begin to accept that he really does love her. So no matter what happens, a lot of good came out of this."

"It's amazing that Megan ran into Annie and that somehow you and Nick were able to find her." He gave her a pointed look. "Want to tell me how that happened?"

She nodded. "I had a vision. It was vague and hazy as always, but Nick pushed me to look at it, embrace it. He told me that if I couldn't believe in myself, he'd believe in me."

Joe saw emotion well up in her eyes and knew that had meant a lot to her. "He's in love with you."

"I think he might be," she said softly. "And he knows that I'm a little bit crazy, which makes it even more remarkable."

"You have a lot to give any man. I hope he's worthy."

"He saved my life."

"And you saved his and quite possibly his daughter's. Maybe you should come work for me. You've solved more crimes than I have this week."

She smiled. "Thanks, but I'll stick to my sewing."

"Are you going to stay in Angel's Bay?"

"I don't know yet."

Joe paused, his gaze catching once again on the couple on the porch.

"Joe," Isabella said, "is Charlotte the reason you don't want to call Rachel back?"

He cleared his throat. "Charlotte has a line of men who'd like to take her out, including the one at the door."

"You never used to be afraid of a little competition."

"It's been a long time since I had to fight for a

girl. But I thought you wanted me to reunite with Rachel."

"I want you to be happy, Joe."

"I want you to be happy, too. Maybe you should stay here and see what happens."

Nick tucked Megan into bed as if she was a little girl. After dropping Tory off at her house, he'd made Megan a big breakfast, encouraged her to take a hot shower, and now she was settling in for a nap. She hadn't slept a wink the night before, and she was so exhausted she'd almost fallen asleep over her pancakes.

"I'm sorry, Dad." She gazed up at him now. "I messed things up for you and Isabella."

He sat down on the bed next to her. "Isabella is special to me, but you have a huge place in my heart that belongs only to you, Megan. I was there when you were born, when you first opened your eyes. I held you when you were a baby. In the middle of the night, it was always me and you." He took a breath for strength. "When your mom took you away from me, I was destroyed."

"I'm still kind of mad at you for letting me go." she said, "but I don't want you to send me away. I want to live with you, not Mom."

He'd never thought he would hear those words. "I want you to live with me, too."

"I'll piss you off," she warned him.

"And I'll make you angry, as well. But I will

never send you away—no matter what you do. I love you, Megan. I've never been as scared as I was last night, when I realized you were out in the woods all alone."

"You jumped in front of me when that guy was going to shoot us," she said.

"What else would I do? You're my child. I'd die for you." It was the absolute and utter truth.

"Well, I'd rather you didn't die. I need you to teach me how to drive. And maybe play the guitar."

His breath caught in his chest at the love shining out of her eyes. For the first time, she wasn't afraid to show it. "It's a deal."

"I'm going to sleep now for a long time," she said with a sigh. "You should go talk to Isabella."

He shifted uncomfortably. "I'm sorry that you saw us kissing."

"It wasn't that big a deal."

He raised an eyebrow. "You ran away."

"I know, but I had a lot of time to think last night. You're going to be with someone, so why not her? She's nice. And she did save both of our lives today." She gave him a funny look. "It's weird how you guys keep doing that for each other. If you two don't belong together, I don't know who does. You should go talk to her."

"I'm staying here with you."

She shot him a disgusted look. "Dad, don't be stupid."

"Megan, I'm happy for it to be just the two of us for a while."

She smiled sleepily. "We're going to be fine." And with that, she drifted off to sleep.

Isabella walked onto Joe's back deck and gazed out at the sea. She saw whitecaps on the horizon and thought about the shipwreck that had tossed so many people into the sea, some of whom had made it to the bay and found a new start in a new place. The image resonated with her, and she felt sad at the thought of leaving.

But to stay here and not be with Nick was unthinkable. They could hardly keep their hands off each other, but he needed to be with Megan. And she loved him more because of his determination to do right by his daughter.

"I'm headed back to the station," Joe said, stepping onto the deck. "Are you going to be all right, Izzy?"

She glanced back at him. "I'll be fine. Thanks, Joe." She turned back to the view, wondering if it would take more courage to leave or to stay.

A few moments later, she heard a sound behind her and turned, thinking that Joe had forgotten something, but it was Nick.

"Your brother let me in," he said.

"How's Megan?"

"She's taking a nap." He walked over to her. "And she told me that letting you go was a stupid idea."

Isabella swallowed hard. "I saw her face when we kissed in the costume shop. She looked betrayed."

"Her perspective changed overnight, especially after she saw you rush a man with a gun to save my life. Her life, too."

"I'm getting a lot of credit for making an impulsive and risky decision."

Their gazes connected for a long, intense moment.

"Joe said you're thinking of leaving. I don't want that to happen."

Her heart flip-flopped.

"I want you in my life, Isabella. Last night, you stayed by my side through the dark and the cold. You fought with me and for me. You're strong and brave and someone I can count on. You showed me what it's like to have a partner. I don't want to lose you."

She shook her head, her eyes blurring with tears. "Oh, Nick, whatever I did for you, you did ten times more for me. You believed in me when I couldn't believe in myself. You gave me the courage to accept a part of myself I've been running away from my whole life. I'm the one who's grateful."

He stepped forward, sliding his arms around her. "We need each other, Isabella. We're both better together than apart."

She looked into his eyes, seeing the promise of a future that she yearned to explore. "It's been pretty fast and intense."

"And I don't see it ever slowing down, because we connect on an incredibly deep level. I'm not asking you to give up your life for me. I can build us a house in L.A. or here or anywhere. You and Megan and I can be a family. We can make it work."

"I love you, Nick. So much I don't know what to do with it all."

"Then stop fighting me. The universe wants us to be together. Don't you know that by now?"

"You told me you didn't believe in destiny."

"I've changed my mind. Besides, I saved your life. That means you belong to me."

"And I saved yours. So you belong to me," she said with a smile.

"Exactly." His lips touched hers, setting off a fiery heat that burned to the tips of her toes.

"Do you need to get back to Megan soon?" she asked.

"No. She told me that she was going to sleep for a long, long time," he said with a wicked smile.

"Funny, I was thinking of taking a nap, too," Isabella said with a grin. "Want to join me?"

"I thought you'd never ask."

Here is
a sneak peek at
the next heart-tugging Angel's Bay romance
from bestselling author

Barbara Freethy

Coming soon from Pocket Books

It was a night for dreaming. New possibilities, new goals, new resolutions. But would the dreams last past the stroke of midnight?

They never had before.

With a sip of champagne, Charlotte Adams tried to force the negative thoughts out of her head. She was normally an optimist. She didn't spend time worrying about the future or thinking about the past. Living in the present had been her mantra for more than a decade, but the past few weeks of hectic holidays, family changes, and now the flipping of the calendar were making her feel . . . restless. She glanced around the crowded living room, wondering if she could possibly make an escape, but there was a mass of people between her and the nearest exit.

The mayor, Robert Monroe, and his wife, Theresa, had invited half the town to their New Year's Eve party so they could show off their newly renovated home, the stately Sandstone Manor. Sitting at the edge of a bluff on the north end of Angel's Bay, the manor was an old and very grand estate that had fallen into disrepair over the past thirty years at the hands of a wealthy and eccentric recluse. The seven-bedroom, five-bathroom house with the castlelike turrets, dramatic bay windows, and alleged ghosts had always been a fascination for the town and when it had suddenly come up for sale two months earlier, the Monroes had snapped it up. Tonight, everyone who'd been lucky enough to get an invitation to the party had accepted, dying to get an inside look at the magnificent home.

Well, Charlotte had had a look; now she just wanted to get some air. She made her way through the dining room, past the buffet tables laden with shrimp and crab, and into the kitchen, where a busy catering staff didn't give her a second look. She slipped out a side door onto a patio overlooking the sea and reveled in the blessed quiet.

It was a dark night, the moon and stars hidden behind a fog bank that had rolled in just after dusk. The cold, misty breeze felt good against her face. Maybe she could stay out here until the party died down and then leave without raising questions. Because there would be questions if she tried to ditch before midnight. Almost all of her friends were inside. And they wanted her to be as happy as they were.

Sighing, she rested her arms on the wood railing, thinking about how many changes they'd all gone through in the last year. Colin had recovered from his shooting. He and Kara were not just a couple but a family now, with their baby getting bigger each day. Jason and Brianna were about to start the new year no longer enemies but lovers. And then there was Lauren and Shane, who were getting married in two weeks.

Lauren had asked her to be a bridesmaid and while she wasn't looking forward to adding another bridesmaid dress to her closet, she was excited to stand up for them. Lauren and Shane had been her friends since childhood. And they'd been through a lot before finding their way back to each other.

Everyone was settling down, and this damn New Year's Eve party was making her wonder what the hell she was doing with her own life. She had a good career and loved being an OB/GYN, but her personal life was nowhere near as settled. What else was new? She'd always had great friendships with men, but relationships were another story. It was her fault. She had trouble with trust, with commitment, with letting anyone get too close. She didn't want to be vulnerable and she did not want to get hurt. In other words, she was a coward when it came to love.

The door opened behind her, followed by Kara's cheerful voice. "Charlotte, I've been looking all over for you. It's almost midnight. What are you doing out here?"

"Getting some air." She tossed Kara a light smile, hoping her friend wouldn't see past it.

"It's freezing," Kara said with a shiver as she wrapped her hands around her waist. Her dark red hair blew in the breeze, goose bumps traveling down her pale arms.

"It feels good," Charlotte replied, even though her short black party dress was no match for the winter wind. Nor was Kara's equally skimpy turquoise mini. Neither one of them had dressed for the night with winter weather in mind.

"Okay, what's wrong?" Kara asked, giving her a speculative look.

"I just don't like New Year's Eve. Everyone makes such a big deal about it, and the night never lives up to its hype. I'd just as soon skip the whole thing, flip the calendar and be done with it."

"Would your cynical mood have something to do with a man?"

"No."

Kara raised an eyebrow. "Really? Because I thought you were coming with Andrew, and he doesn't seem to be anywhere in sight."

"Something came up. He said he'd try to get here before midnight."

"Then he will, because Andrew will not miss a chance to kiss you. He's been after you since he got back to town." Kara paused. "I hope no one is in trouble and that's why he's not here."

"He didn't give me any details when he called." And she hadn't asked for any. In fact, she'd been a little relieved. Attending the New Year's Eve party together in front of the entire town was quite a statement and she wasn't sure she wanted to make that statement yet. Andrew Schilling was a big part of her past and they'd been getting to know each other again since he'd returned to town to take over as minister at what had once been her father's church, but as for the future, that was still to be decided.

"Ready to go inside?" Kara asked with another shiver.

"Actually, I was wondering if I could find a way to grab my coat and bag and leave without anyone noticing."

"That seems doubtful. And just because you don't ring in the New Year doesn't mean the future isn't still coming. You have decisions to make, Charlotte. You came back to Angel's Bay to take care of your mom after your dad's death, but she's doing better now. She even has a new man in her life."

"Don't remind me."

"And then you had to stick around because you took in Annie and she was about to have a baby, but the baby has been born, and Annie is handling motherhood much better than anyone expected."

"Are you about to point out how completely unneeded I am around here?"

Kara smiled, meeting her gaze. "We all need you, Charlotte. We all want you to stay. But what do you want? You're the first one to volunteer, to jump in when someone needs a hand. You're an incredible friend. You don't think twice when it comes to someone else's happiness, but what about you? What will make you happy?"

"I don't know. I never thought I'd be here as long as I have been. I didn't make a long-term plan. I was just going to wing it. But—"

"Angel's Bay got into your soul."

"The people sure did. I'd forgotten what it was like to have friends who've known me my entire life. And I'm enjoying practicing medicine in a small community where I have time to get to know my patients."

"So, maybe you should stay, have your things shipped here, unpack, settle in—if not with your mother, then in your own home. There are some lovely new townhouses up for sale, or if you want something older, I could help you find one."

"And earn yourself a nice commission," she said with a smile.

Kara grinned back. "That, too. But you don't have to decide tonight. In the meantime, if you really want to escape, I'll make an excuse for you. That's what friends are for, right?"

"Thanks, Kara, and you don't have to worry about me. I'll be fine tomorrow."

"Will you be? Or will you just have your guard back up?"

Kara was a little too smart, Charlotte decided. "Let's go in before your husband sends out a search party."

"He'd need one in this place," Kara said, moving toward the patio door. "It's more spectacular than I imagined. Theresa certainly got everything she ever wanted. Did you see her diamond necklace? That thing must be worth a fortune."

"I saw. I knew they were well off, but I didn't think they had that much money." Robert Monroe had been an accomplished defense attorney in San Francisco before moving to Angel's Bay several years earlier to not only practice law but serve as mayor. They'd always made a point of showing off their wealth but never to this extent.

"I heard one of Robert's uncles died recently, and they inherited a hefty chunk of change, which was how they could buy this house."

"It is an amazing place."

"I would feel happier for Theresa's good fortune if she'd been a little nicer to us in high school."

Charlotte nodded in agreement. Theresa and her beautiful band of cheerleaders had been a year older than Charlotte, but they'd ruled the school with their own special brand of meanness. And Theresa's younger sister, Pamela, had been Charlotte's personal nemesis.

"I'm sure if Theresa hadn't wanted to impress us with this house, we'd have been left off the guest list," Kara said. "Frankly, it's a little too old and cold for me. And then there's the ghosts."

"I haven't seen any," Charlotte said with a smile.

"Well, they lay low when there's a crowd. I know you're not a believer, but I am," Kara said, her gaze turning serious. "When Colin was in a coma, right after Faith was born, I saw his spirit in my hospital room. He told me it would be all right, and it was. I got a miracle."

"You did," Charlotte agreed. But she thought Kara's

visit from Colin had probably been the result of painkillers, a traumatic birth, and no sleep.

"You don't believe me, do you?"

"I've been hearing about angels in this town since I was a little girl. So far they've stayed far away from me."

"Maybe you need to open your mind to the possibilities. And I'm not just talking about ghosts or angels," she added pointedly. "There are a couple of men who'd like to get a little closer to you. Perhaps you should let them. You're not getting any younger."

"Now you sound like my mother."

Kara laughed. "I just want you to be as happy as I am."

"Then let me have Colin, he's perfect," she said with a laugh.

"Not a chance." Kara paused, her hand on the door. "Don't forget you're coming over to our house tomorrow for chili and football. While the guys watch the game, we can help Lauren make her wedding favors."

"I'll be there. Now stop stalling. I want to get out of here before midnight."

Kara sighed. "I wish you would wait. You could miss out on an awesome kiss."

"I'll take my chances."

"Fine."

They'd barely returned to the party when Kara was quickly swept into conversation with Colin and another couple, so Charlotte slipped through the crowd, heading toward the hallway. As she turned the corner, the front door opened, and Andrew walked in. Tall, lean, with golden blond hair, bright blue eyes, and an irresistible smile, Andrew looked more like a male model than a minister. She wasn't the only one who thought so. The Kelleher sisters rushed forward, offering him hugs and kisses. The sisters were in their late thirties and known to frequent the local bars on Saturday nights trolling for eligible men. Apparently, they had Andrew in their sights. She could rescue him . . .

Before she could make a move, the front door opened again, and Joe Silveira entered the house. The sexy chief of police was night to Andrew's day. Joe had thick, dark brown hair, olive skin, intense eyes, and a rough edge that had been sharpened by his career as a cop. He was more rugged than Andrew, more physical, but where Andrew was talkative and outgoing, Joe kept most of his thoughts to himself.

It had been weeks since she'd seen Joe. He'd gone to L.A. just after Thanksgiving when his father suffered a stroke, and he hadn't been back since. She'd almost forgotten how attractive he was, how her stomach flipped every time she saw him. Joe had heart-breaking potential, too.

She really should have left the party when she had the chance. Because both men's gazes were swinging in her direction.

Someone shouted, "*One minute to midnight.*"

She felt an overwhelming desire to run for her life.

"*Thirty seconds.*"

Andrew and Joe were moving toward her, their efforts hampered by the crowd. What was she going to do—kiss Andrew, then kiss Joe, or vice versa?

Way too much pressure.

She turned and fled in the opposite direction. The grand staircase was the only open path. She ran up the stairs, ignoring the surprised look of a passing maid. She hoped to find refuge in some out of the way bathroom.

"*Ten, nine, eight . . .*" The chant from the crowd grew louder.

She turned one corner, then another. The house was

huge and easy to get lost in and perfect for hiding out. She moved further down the hall, stopping abruptly as the lights went out.

Surprised cries, nervous screams echoed through the house along with shouts of "Happy New Year." What the hell had happened to the lights?

Someone's arm brushed against her shoulder, knocking her slightly off balance. And then the shadowy figure was gone. How could they make their way so quickly through the darkness?

Turning around, she took a few tentative steps forward, putting her hand along the wall for guidance. She needed to find her way back to the staircase. A chorus of "Auld Lang Syne" rang out from below. Apparently, the blackout hadn't dimmed the party's champagne-fueled spirits. She followed the noise, happy when some specks of flickering light appeared. Someone had obviously lighted some candles. She reached the staircase with relief, her hand hitting the banister as the lights came back on. She blinked at the sudden onslaught of light, then moved quickly down the stairs.

She had just reached the bottom step when shrill screams lit up the air. It took a moment for them to register over the party chatter. But as the screams continued, the crowd hushed. She looked up as a maid appeared at the stop of the staircase.

"Mrs. Monroe," she cried with a wild wave of her hand. "Please, someone help. I think she's dead."

Joe Silveira pushed his way through the crowded hallway. Charlotte gave him a shocked look as he passed her on the stairs. He'd had a bad feeling when the lights went out, and now he knew why. One of his officers, Jason Marlow, was right on his heels. Another officer, Colin Lynch, told everyone else to stay where they were.

As he reached the landing, the middle-age maid burst into a flurry of agitated words, a mix of Spanish and English. "Show me," he said firmly.

The woman moved down the hallway, stopping at the last door on the left. She pointed and said, "In there."

"Wait here," he told her.

The master bedroom was the picture of luxury, a huge king-size bed, heavy ornate furniture, and a sitting area complete with fireplace and big-screen television. The mayor certainly lived well, he thought, his mind registering the details with an efficiency gained from visiting too many crime scenes to count. He noted the open drawers in the dresser, the scent of perfume in the air, and the beautiful, skinny woman sprawled on the floor of the bathroom. Theresa was on her back, her skin pale against her bright red cocktail dress. Her short blonde hair was streaked with blood, a pool appearing under the back of her head, which rested on a marble floor.

He squatted down next to her and put a hand to her neck. Her pulse was faint but present. "She's alive." While Jason called for an ambulance, he checked to make sure Theresa was breathing, then took off his coat and covered her with it as Jason went downstairs to find a doctor.

The mayor rushed into the room a moment later. Robert Monroe gasped at the sight of his wife, his eyes widening in shock. His mouth opened, but no words came. It was the first time Joe had ever seen the mayor speechless.

"Oh my God," he finally got out, dropping to his

knees. "Theresa." His gaze ran down his wife's body, then flew to Joe. "What happened?"

"I don't know yet. Your housekeeper found her like this a few minutes ago."

Robert's gaze returned to his wife. He picked up her hand. "She's so cold, but she's alive, right?"

"She's breathing," Joe said shortly. "Paramedics are on their way."

"She can't die. We're going to Paris in the spring. Theresa has always wanted to go to Paris."

"What happened to the lights?" Joe asked, cutting off his ramble.

"I don't know. My contractor went out to check and the next thing I knew the lights were on."

"Who's your contractor?"

"Gary Hoff. Why are you asking me about the lights?" Robert asked, confusion in his eyes. "Do you think Theresa slipped in the dark?"

"It's possible," he replied, his mind racing through a dozen other scenarios. Had someone wanted the cover of darkness for another reason? He glanced down at Theresa, noting the red scratch marks on her neck. "Was your wife wearing a necklace?"

Robert followed his gaze, his jaw dropping. "Her diamond necklace is missing." He lifted up his wife's hand. "And her wedding ring. Someone robbed her. Right here—in our home," he added in disbelief. "Who would do that?"

Before Joe could answer, Jason returned with Charlotte and Ray Bennington, an ER doctor at the clinic. Joe stood up, allowing Dr. Bennington to take a look at Theresa.

"Colin is posted at the front door, Davidson at the

back," Jason reported. "We're not letting anyone leave until we have a handle on what's going on."

"Good, because it looks like Mrs. Monroe's diamonds are missing."

Charlotte gave him a startled look. "Are you serious?"

"Unfortunately, I am." He turned to Jason. "Start talking to the guests. See if anyone saw anything."

"I'm on it." Jason passed the paramedics on his way out of the room.

Joe pulled Charlotte to the side as the paramedics moved into the bathroom. He'd come to the party for one reason; he'd been hoping to see her, maybe even steal a kiss at midnight. He'd been thinking about her for weeks, missing her warm smile, her beautiful blue eyes, her silky blonde hair. Seeing her now in a skimpy black dress that showed off her slender legs and sexy body, he wondered what the hell he'd been thinking, staying away so long. Not that he'd had a choice. His family had needed him. But damn if she wasn't more beautiful than he remembered. He just wished their reunion wasn't in the middle of a crime scene.

"This is crazy," Charlotte muttered, hugging her arms around her waist. "At least Theresa is still alive."

"Let's hope she stays that way."

Charlotte gave him a worried look. "What do you think happened?"

"I think someone wanted her jewelry and she got in the way."

"But to steal a necklace off someone's neck? That's pretty bold."

"And personal," he said, thinking about what kind of thief he was dealing with.

"Like a friend?"

"Obviously not a very good one." He paused, tilting

his head to the side. "Did you see anything? I saw you come down the stairs just before the maid screamed."

"Oh. No, I didn't see a thing," she said, stumbling a bit. "The lights went off, and it was pitch black."

"Did you hear a scream? An argument? Anyone call for help?"

"I heard a lot of screams when everything went dark. But nothing that sounded like someone was in trouble."

"What were you doing up here, Charlotte?"

"I was looking for a bathroom. I was at the other end of the hall," she said, not quite meeting his gaze.

He didn't know what to make of her nervousness, her evasiveness. Charlotte wouldn't hurt anyone. She was a kind, generous person who went out of her way to help people, but there was something she wasn't telling him.

Before he could probe further, he saw the maid hovering in the doorway.

"Mrs. Monroe is still alive?" she asked.

"Yes," he said. "They're going to take her to the hospital."

"Thank God." She made the sign of the cross on her chest. "I was so worried. She was so still. And there was so much blood."

"You found her, Constance?" the mayor interrupted, stepping into the bedroom as the paramedics put Theresa onto a stretcher.

"Yes," the woman answered.

"Did you see anyone else near this room?" Joe asked. "Maybe in the hallway, on the stairs?"

The maid hesitated, then glanced at Charlotte. "I saw her."

Charlotte paled. Before Joe could say anything, the mayor jumped in.

"Charlotte?" Robert questioned sharply. "What were you doing up here?"

"I was in the hallway when the lights went out. I didn't see Theresa."

"You never liked her," Robert said, suspicion entering his voice. "She didn't want to invite you, but she felt she had to because of her mother's relationship with your mother. She said you'd been horrible to her sister. That you'd always been jealous of them." His voice rose as he took a step forward.

Joe jumped between the mayor and Charlotte. "You need to go to the hospital with your wife," he said firmly. "Let me take care of the investigation."

Robert looked like he wanted to argue, but finally he stepped back. "You find out who did this, Silveira. You find out who almost killed my wife."

"I will."

Charlotte let out a breath as the room cleared. Her eyes were more worried now. "Joe, you don't think I had anything to do with this, do you? I'm not a thief, and I would never attack someone."

"Is there bad blood between you and Theresa?"

"Her sister and I didn't get along in high school, but that was a dozen years ago. Theresa and I aren't best friends, but we're civil to each other. She did invite me to the party, although I think she just wanted to show off her house and her diamonds, but that's just who she is. I doubt half the people here are really her friends."

He knew Theresa well enough to agree with Charlotte's assessment. While he'd managed to maintain a good working relationship with the mayor, he was very aware that while the Monroes thought they ran the town, there were more than a few people who thought they should be run out of town. Unfortunately, the only person in the vicinity of the attack, according to the maid's recollection, was Charlotte. The fact that she had a bad history with Theresa was another strike against her.

"Why did you come upstairs?" he asked.

"I already told you. I was looking for a bathroom."

"And the three on the main floor wouldn't do?" Something flickered in her eyes. "You're lying, Charlotte. And you're not very good at it."

She hesitated. "Fine, I was going to leave before midnight, but there were too many people between me and the front door, so I came up the stairs, thinking I'd just wait for a few minutes and then go."

"It's a New Year's Eve party. Why would you leave before midnight?"

Her cheeks grew warmer. "I had my reasons. You can't believe I had anything to do with this."

"I'm still going to need a better answer." He saw tension and conflict in her eyes, but he didn't think her turmoil had anything to do with Theresa. "Who were you running away from, Charlotte?"

She gave him a long look. "Do you really want to know?"

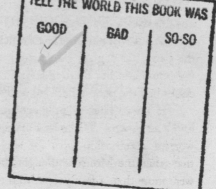

TELL THE WORLD THIS BOOK WAS

GOOD	BAD	SO-SO
✓